ON THE HUNT

BOOK 8 IN THE RYAN KAINE SERIES

KERRY J DONOVAN

To healthcare workers, emergency first responders, and everyone who risks their lives for others, I salute you!

CHAPTER ONE

Wednesday 3rd May – Danny Pinkerton
Amber Valley, Derbyshire, UK

Danny had only seen the woman for a few seconds. At the time, he didn't know her name or anything about her, but her bruised and bloodshot eyes and the fear expressed in them drew his attention.

She'd been in the front passenger seat of a white Range Rover stuck in traffic, two miles from the Aspire Hospital, Nottingham—a traffic jam caused by the failed attempt on Melanie Archer's life.

In those few brief moments, the injured woman's plight had touched Danny's heart.

He'd been trudging along the side of the road, dressed like a vagrant in ripped jeans and a grubby polo shirt, covered in someone else's blood, but when she'd looked at him through those bruised and swollen eyes, he couldn't let it go. The metal splint taped to her nose confirmed her as a woman in discomfort.

At first, he assumed she'd just left the Aspire following a nose job, but the way she reacted to her driver's aggressive proximity fired off warning bells in Danny's head. Then, after a brief exchange of words, the driver had raced away in the Range Rover, ignoring Danny's request for a lift and leaving him standing in the driving rain. But as the driver made the turn, he showed Danny the SUV's tailgate and the cherished licence number it carried, *RNP III.*

During his sodden jog to the hospital, Danny contacted Corky, and it had taken the talented hacker mere seconds to identify the SUV's registered owner, one Robert Neil Prentiss. Corky also provided the man's home address and the name of his wife—Marian Jennifer Prentiss.

––––––––

Deep in the Amber Valley, twenty miles northwest of Derby, Chequer Way stood pretty much in the middle of nowhere, but Danny's slow, overnight drive-by had shown him plenty.

The security wall running along the front of the pretentiously named "Prentiss House" stretched out for a little over one hundred and fifty metres. The only gap in the brickwork allowed for a grand entrance, flanked by stone pillars that were crowned with prancing horses carved from white marble. Recessed from the road by a short gravel driveway, a pair of electrically operated wrought iron gates protected the opening, defending the floodlit home from whatever rampaging hordes the owners most feared.

Behind the gates, Prentiss House—more a mansion than a working farmhouse—stood in all its glory. Sandstone walls shone bright under the orange floodlights. Imposing and expensive.

Pompous or what?

Danny didn't need to be hit over the head with a lump of sandstone to recognise valuable real estate when he saw it. No doubt about it, Robert Prentiss was loaded.

Didn't give him the right to beat his wife, though.

No bloody way.

So, now he'd made the trip, what was he going to do?

He couldn't exactly breach the fortress, knock on the front door, and ask the householder how long he'd been beating his wife. No way. There could only be one response to such a question.

Prentiss would refute the charge and dismiss Danny from the grounds. The bugger might even call the police and try to have Danny arrested. And where would that leave the possible victim? No, such a bumbling, half-arsed approach might even make the situation worse for Marian Prentiss.

Danny needed proof.

Not the same level of proof required by the UK's stodgy legal system. Oh no. He just needed enough to convince himself of the rich man's guilt. Then, and only then, would Prentiss receive his lesson.

Only then would the bastard learn what it felt like to be on the receiving end of a thumping.

Danny parked his leased, mid-range BMW 3-Series in a layby two miles to the north, returned on foot under the cover of darkness, and completed a surreptitious circuit of the defensive wall. He found another opening at the rear barred by a pair of solid wooden gates, which he scaled with ease. Keeping to the deep shadow, Danny skirted around to the front of the house and found a row of rhododendron bushes where the wall formed a corner, then dropped to his haunches.

Inside the wall, landscaped gardens to the front, rear, and sides showed the intensive work of someone with green fingers. Mainly set to lawns and with well-stocked herbaceous borders, the grounds at the rear contained numerous outbuildings, including a detached triple garage, a large greenhouse, and two small wooden sheds.

Danny's hiding spot gave him a good view of the house's frontage and most of the rear. He settled in for the long haul, his back propped against the cold brickwork. He grew colder by the minute, but the memory of Marian Prentiss' bruised and battered face warmed him and drove him on. What was a little discomfort compared to her injuries?

He rolled his shoulders, stretched his neck, and pointed the Zeiss Victory SF 8x42 binoculars—the one piece of surveillance equipment he hadn't forgotten—at the front of the house, making the most of the floodlights' illumination.

The entrance portico—two white-painted columns supporting a triangular canopy—aimed for impressive but only hit excessive and ostentatious. Two steps led up to a semi-circular floor covered in black and white tiles laid out in a chessboard pattern. Double doors, panelled and painted black in a high-gloss finish, wore wrought iron furniture. Two huge lionheads with thick metal rings in their mouths acted as knockers. Two more formed the handles. Raised iron rivets fastened enormous wrought iron hinges into the woodwork, trying to give the impression of a drawbridge.

Fuck's sake, what a mess.

Danny raked the binoculars across the façade, looking for security cameras or motion-activated spots, but found none. He returned the binoculars to his small rucksack and settled back to wait.

At 01:30, the floodlights powered off, plunging his world into blackness. It left Danny blind and immobile until his natural night vision took over. While waiting for the house to sleep and before venturing out of his obbo point to take a closer look, Danny replayed his most recent conversation with Corky.

————

Behind the wheel of the BMW on his way towards Amber Valley, Danny cleared his throat before tapping the comms unit in his ear.

"Hi Corky, what you got for me, over."

"Plenty, Danny-boy. Plenty. Whatcha need first?"

Danny grinned. If he hung around for Corky to comply with correct comms protocol, he'd be waiting forever.

"Names and bios will do for a start, over."

"Corky sent them to your mobile half an hour ago."

"I'm driving. Can you give me the bullet points, please? Over."

"Yeah, okay. Sure. Like, why not. After all, it ain't like Corky's not got a million other things to do, is it?"

"Sorry Corky," Danny said, slapping some life into his cheeks. "I appreciate all your efforts, mate. I really do. Hoped you'd save me a little time, is all—"

"*Nah, just joshing, Danny-boy. Corky's happy to oblige. Just a sec.*"

To Danny's surprise, the active map on the dashboard's GPS screen shrank into a corner, and Corky's round and bearded face took its place.

Jesus!

He nearly lost control of the BMW.

How the tech genius achieved the trick, Danny would never know. Corky was able to do things beyond the scope of even the most gifted military techies.

Apart from the small-scale map, the screen behind Corky showed nothing but a white wall, which made a change from the usual panoramic view of sea and sky he preferred.

"Whatcha, Danny," Corky said, his cheeks fattening into a grin. "Much better speaking face to face, yeah?"

Danny returned the grin. "Sure is."

"This way, we don't need none of that 'over and out' bullshit, neither."

"If you say so, Corky."

The GPS map indicated a left turn in eight hundred metres, and Danny slowed to make the manoeuvre.

"Didn't know these consoles had built-in cameras."

Without bothering to indicate—no cars about to make it necessary—Danny turned left, straightened the wheel, and fed more fuel into the engine. The big BMW surged ahead.

"You'd be surprised what the manufacturers hide inside their 'infotainment systems', Danny-boy. These days, Big Brother is always watching you."

Big Brother and Corky!

But at least Corky was benign.

"Okay," Danny said, moving things along, "so who exactly is our target?"

"Robert Neil Prentiss, aged thirty-six. Owns *Prentiss Haulage Limited*, and operates from a distribution centre on the outskirts of

Derby. Likes to call himself, 'Robbie P'. That's the geezer on the screen right now."

Corky pointed over his shoulder and a colour headshot of a man emerged on the white background. Strong face, square jaw, light brown eyes. Some might say good-looking. Danny tried to match the image with the driver of the Range Rover from the previous afternoon, but it didn't really work.

In the headshot, Robbie P had short hair, was clean shaven, and the smile reached his eyes. The headshot made him seem warm and friendly, but looks could be deceptive.

"How old's that picture?"

Corky shrugged. "Dunno when it were taken, but that pic were uploaded to the company's website three months back. Why?"

Danny sniffed. "Bloke I saw driving the Range Rover had long dark hair and a beard. Didn't get a clear sight of him through the tinted windows, though. Might be the same guy, I guess. You couldn't find anything more recent?"

Corky pinched his lips together and shook his head. "Nah, not really. Corky found a few publicity shots of Robbie P when he opened a distribution centre in Hungary eighteen months back, but the quality's poor and there aren't none any newer than that online. By the way, his hair were short in them pics, too. And he didn't have no beard."

"Find anything interesting on the wife?"

"Nothing much. Marian Jennifer Prentiss. Maiden name, Turvey. Aged twenty-eight. They've been married five years. No kids yet. She's got herself a degree in Fine Arts from Nottingham Trent University."

"Anything worrying in her medical history?"

"Didn't find nothing in her NHS records."

"No emergency admissions for unexplained injuries? Broken bones? Facial trauma?"

"Er, nope." Another headshake.

"What about the damage I saw to her face yesterday? No record of that on the Aspire's records?"

Corky scrunched his mobile face into a wince. He almost seemed embarrassed. "Yeah, now that's where Corky's had a little bother. As you know, for some reason, the Aspire's computer systems fell over last night."

"You don't say." Danny couldn't prevent the irony invading his voice.

Danny knew all about the Aspire's computer troubles. He knew, because he'd asked Corky to disable their IT infrastructure long enough for him to break into its dental clinic and "liberate" Melanie Archer's replacement ceramic crown. The same ceramic crown she'd been paroled from prison for the day to have fitted.

"What happened, Corky? You didn't break their IT system, did you?"

"Nah, 'course not. It ain't nothing to do with Corky, and it ain't permanent, neither. The hospital's IT service provider is running a system-wide diagnostic sweep on account of the unplanned shut-down. Just means that Corky can't interrogate the system right now. At least, not safely."

Danny relaxed into his seat.

"How long are you going to be locked out?"

Corky's wince transformed into a deep scowl. "Now listen here, Danny-boy. What part of that explanation said Corky were locked out? Corky ain't never been locked out of a computer system in his life! Bloody insulting, that is."

Keeping a straight face and concentrating on the road ahead, Danny raised a hand in apology. "Sorry Corky. Didn't mean to upset you."

"Locked out! Ain't no way Corky's locked out. He's keeping his distance for security purposes, that's all. Get it? Any outside interference on the Aspire's systems at this stage will lead to questions Corky don't want no one asking. Is that clear?"

"Yes, Corky. It's clear. I get it. And again, I'm sorry. Any idea how long the systems are likely to be inaccessible?"

"The idiots are taking their time over the security scan. They say it'll be down 'til at least midday. Typical. If Corky were running the systems check, it would already be done."

Danny nodded. "I understand. Can't be helped. Until then we're blind, yes?"

The chubby hacker's cheeky grin returned. "On the other hand, Corky did discover who provides Mr and Mrs Prentiss with their medical insurance. It's a company called *Notts Private Health Services*. Seems they agreed to cover the costs of 'emergency treatment' at the Aspire Hospital under Robbie P's account. Apparently, two nights ago, she tripped and fell down the stairs. Broke her nose and right cheekbone."

Yeah, right.

Danny clenched his fists and tried not to grind his teeth. "The bastard hit her."

Corky tilted his head to one side in agreement. "Looks that way. What you gonna do?"

Good question.

"Corky hates wifebeaters. You gonna give the guy a good thumping?" the hacker asked, excitement shining bright in his eyes.

"Probably, but I need to do some obbo first. I want to be certain of my facts."

"The facts seem clear enough to someone with perfect vision."

"Maybe, but I'm not in the habit of turning people over without proof. Before doing anything serious, I'll try to get Marian on her own. It would be good to hear her side of the story. You never know, her injuries might well have been accidental." Danny tried to sound convincing, but failed miserably. He happened to be as certain as Corky of Robbie P's guilt.

"So, anything else you need from old Corky?"

"A layout of the house would be useful?"

"More 'bullet points'?"

"Please."

Corky coughed into his hand. "Okay, here you go." His gaze slid to the left and he started reading, probably from another monitor. "The architect's plans are online and Corky's been taking a shufti. Robbie P started renovating the house six years ago, right after they moved in and renamed the place. The house has two storeys and an attic.

Ground floor's got three receptions, a home office, a sun room, and a kitchen with utility room. First floor has four bedrooms, two with en suites, and a family bathroom. The attic has planning permission for a granny annex, but the work stopped three years ago. Dunno why. Maybe the bugger ran out of money."

"Can you find out?"

Corky winked. "Next thing on the to-do list, Danny-boy. Corky reckons *Prentiss Haulage Limited* might have stretched their finances a bit thin when they opened that satellite hub in Hungary. Seems to be something fishy going on there. Like, who chooses chuffing Hungary for their base of operations? Hardly the epicentre of the European haulage trade. Ain't that many routes to and from the major agriculture or manufacturing centres, you know."

"You'll keep searching, I imagine?"

"If there's anything iffy going on, Corky's gonna find it."

The BMW's headlights dipped automatically as its sensors registered the dazzling full-beams of an approaching vehicle. Danny squinted and waited for the ignorant prick to pass before speaking again.

"Don't suppose Prentiss House has a burglar alarm or surveillance system you can hack into?"

Corky shook his head and his expression turned glum. "Nah, 'fraid not. They got an alarm and a CCTV setup, but it ain't hooked up to the web, at least not yet. Corky can't give you ears or eyes inside the house without splicing directly into the system. And there ain't no way that's happening any time soon."

"Okay, mate. I'll have to do it the old-fashioned way. Thanks for everything. I'll find a spot inside the grounds and lie doggo for a while. If and when Robbie P heads out to work in the morning, it'll give me a chance to ask Marian about his behaviour. Assuming he leaves her home alone."

"Good luck with that, Danny-boy. Corky's off now." He chuckled, faded away, and the GPS map expanded to fill the screen again.

Slowly, one by one, the stars blinked out and a pale dawn washed away the darkness of night.

Danny shivered, the morning dew had long since soaked through his clothes, and the chill had worked its way into every joint of his body. Should have come better prepared. A groundsheet would have helped, but no point crying about that now. Wasn't as though he could call on anyone for help, either. For the first time in years, he was operating solo, which felt both good and bad. Good, to have no one questioning his actions or monitoring his performance. Bad, to have no one to bounce ideas off, not even the captain.

What had originally seemed like the most obvious thing in the world—save the girl, punish the arsehole—had turned into hours of waiting in the perishing cold. Hours of double-guessing and doubt.

Earlier, his post-floodlight searches hadn't added to his small pool of knowledge. Peering through windows and pressing his ear to the glass achieved nothing. Heavy curtains hid the view inside, and double-glazed windows on the ground level prevented all sounds filtering through into the night. A complete bust.

He'd been deaf and blind to whatever was going on inside Prentiss House and had failed to add to Corky's intel.

A thermal imaging camera might have told him how many people were in the house and where they slept, but he'd forgotten to pack one in his haste to "save the damsel in distress". Another bloody mistake. One of many. No groundsheet, no parabolic microphone, no infrared or night vision glasses, no nothing. Damn it, he wasn't even armed.

What did Rollo used to say? "Fail to prepare and you might as well prepare to fail, laddie." Yep, the team's quartermaster wasn't averse to spouting the odd platitude or three.

And anyway, why the hell would he need a weapon?

Danny faced nothing but a wifebeater. A bully and a coward, not a Taliban insurgent, and Danny knew how to handle bullies.

Around him, the dawn chorus welcomed the onset of day and the temperature rose with the sun. With the minimum of movement,

Danny loosened his joints and warmed his muscles in preparation for whatever the morning would bring.

Before him, Prentiss House remained silent. The curtains hid what went on behind the ground floor windows, and shutters covered those on the upper two floors.

Once again, Danny waited.

————

The middle of the three high-security garage doors rolled up to expose the gleaming white and ludicrously expensive Range Rover 5.0 V8. Brand new, the top-of-the-range beastie would have set Robbie P back more than £130,000. The powerful monster's engine growled in smooth anger. White exhaust fumes spewed from the tailpipe, and the SUV pulled slowly out of the garage and into the daylight, some thirty-five metres from where Danny hid amongst the rhododendrons.

Finally, after damn near seven hours freezing his nuts off, Danny had movement.

He allowed himself a little fist pump.

Here we go!

The Range Rover rolled forwards and stopped outside the grand front entrance, purring, waiting for release. Behind it, the garage door rolled down and clunked into place. The driver's door popped open and a swarthy man with long wavy hair and a trimmed beard climbed out. Slightly below average height but powerfully built, the man wore a dark business suit, white shirt, muted brown tie, and polished leather shoes. He bore a striking resemblance to the driver from the previous afternoon.

Yep, the same guy he saw driving the Range Rover yesterday afternoon.

Robbie P?

Danny raised the binoculars, focused them on the man. Pale blue eyes shone out of a weather-beaten face.

Blue eyes?

Can't be right.

Danny tweaked the knurled nut of the binoculars' focus adjuster to sharpen the image further. Yep, the driver's eyes were definitely blue.

Shit!

Definitely not Prentiss.

The headshot Corky had thrown up on the BMW's infotainment screen showed Robbie P with light brown eyes, not blue, and Corky's bio confirmed it. The bio also stated that Robbie P stood at nearly six foot two, but the driver was no more than five nine.

What the hell was going on?

The swarthy man, Driver, glowered at the closed front doors and peeled back the sleeve of his jacket to reveal a heavy gold watch. He all but tapped his foot on the gravel in his impatience.

Driver waited another thirty seconds before shouting something guttural in a language Danny didn't understand. Moments later, one of the front doors opened and a second man in a business suit stumbled out, propelled by the stiff-armed punch of a third man.

The man in the suit bunted into one of the columns supporting the portico's canopy and fell to his hands and knees.

The third man stayed in the open doorway. He wore blue jeans and a white T-shirt under a sleeveless denim vest. Squat with a shaved head, his muscular arms and thick neck were covered in black ink—prison tats.

Tats shouted, "*Idióta*," and coughed out a harsh laugh.

With his back to Danny, the fallen man scrambled to his feet. He raised his hands to Tats, shouted, "Don't hurt her. Please don't hurt her again!" and spun towards Driver, finally showing his face to Danny.

Robbie P!

Fuck.

In that instant, Danny realised his mistake. Robbie P was no more a wifebeater than Ryan Kaine was a terrorist.

What the flaming hell had he stumbled into?

CHAPTER TWO

Wednesday 3rd May – Danny Pinkerton
Amber Valley, Derbyshire, UK

From his hiding place in the shrubbery, Danny watched an evil grin split Driver's face. "Follow my instructions and no more violence will be necessary," he said, his accent thick.

Robbie P wiped his mouth with the back of his hand. "Y-Yes. I promise. But, please don't hurt my wife again."

Driver beckoned with a flick of his fingers. "Come!"

Robbie P rushed from the shade of the portico into the sunlight and hurried towards the Range Rover, dusting himself off and smoothing out the creases in his suit along the way.

Danny knelt, silent and helpless, as Robbie P dived into the Range Rover's rear passenger compartment. Driver pushed the door, which closed with an expensive-sounding clunk, and swaggered, still smiling, to his position behind the steering wheel.

Seconds later, the SUV pulled away. It rolled sedately along the gravel driveway to the open security gates and turned right, heading towards Derby.

In the doorway, Tats waited, arms folded and biceps bulging, until the Range Rover moved out of sight behind the wall and the gates started closing. Then, laughing, he turned and headed back inside the house.

The moment the front door closed behind Tats, Danny took off. Crouching low, he used the bushes and mature trees for cover and hugged the wall.

Tats' laugh had carried no mirth. Danny didn't need to be a mind reader to know what was going on inside the tattooed thug's shaven head.

Still on the move, Danny dug into the breast pocket of his boiler suit, took the special glasses from their protective case, flipped the "activate" switch, and slipped them on.

"Danny to Corky," he panted, keeping his voice low. "Are you there? Over?"

Three seconds of silence ensued.

"*Hey there, Danny-boy. Corky's listening. What's up?*"

"Hang on a minute. Be right with you. Over."

Breathing hard, Danny reached the place where the wall arced inwards to form the gated entrance and knelt in the shade of the column. On the other side of the wall's arm, the wrought iron gates met with a metallic clang, and the hum of electric motors fell silent.

Breathing heavily and keeping to the shadows, Danny stood, lowered the zip of his boiler suit, and struggled out of the grubby workwear. He rolled it up tight, hid it at the base of the wall, and faced the house again.

"*With you moving about like that, Corky's getting seasick,*" the hacker said, as caustic as ever. "*Why was you running?*"

"Shit's hit the fan here. Over."

"*How come?*"

"Tell you later. I'm about to make the approach. How's the picture?"

"*It'd be clear and sharp, if you could learn to stop moving your head so much.*"

"Sorry, mate. Needs must. I'll try my best, but things have to look natural. Okay, here I go. Please keep your eyes and ears open. I'm going in blind. No idea what I'll find in there. Out."

"*Yes you do. Corky sent you the plans.*"

"Not what I meant. Heading in now. Danny, out."

Danny took a settling breath, stepped around the wall into the middle of the gravel driveway, and started walking. He glanced down at his freshly revealed clothes. Work boots, chinos, polo shirt, leather jacket. All dark, all chosen to look reasonable even when heavily creased. Hopefully, he'd be acceptable enough to pass muster.

Time to dial up the charm, Danny-boy.

Not that he expected charm to get him far with someone like Tats. He plastered a pleasant smile to his face and stepped up his pace, aiming straight for the entrance portico.

Danny had been staring at the entrance for most of the night. From his hideout in the grounds some sixty metres away, the portico looked ridiculously overblown. Up close his impression didn't change. This was a large house trying its best to be imposing. Trying and failing. Mutton dressed as lamb.

Here goes.

Still smiling, Danny bounded up the steps, marched across the chessboard surface, and grabbed one of the iron rings. It was heavier than he expected. Might have even been real antique.

That's a surprise.

He smashed the ring against its raised strike plate twice—the thuds echoed loudly through the interior—and stepped back.

C'mon, Tats. Where are you?

When nothing happened for thirty seconds, Danny repeated the knocking. This time, he used even more force.

Behind the door, footsteps clacked on a hard floor, growing louder. The spyhole on the middle of the left-hand door darkened. Danny looked straight at it, maintaining the smile.

A black handle turned and the same right-hand door opened to reveal a scowling Tats. His shaved head exposed the white spiral-flex cable running from an old-fashioned earpiece into the front pocket of his denim jacket. A suspicious-looking bulge near the jacket's left armpit told Danny two things. Tats carried a gun and was most likely right-handed. He filed the information away in case he needed it later.

As tall and strongly built as Danny, Tats filled the part-open doorway, blocking Danny's view of the interior.

Danny pricked up his ears, but the inside of the house remained ominously silent. No screaming. No crying. No one else's footsteps.

Where was Marian Prentiss? Had Tats finished her off already?

"Corky here. Running facial recognition. Get back to you real soon."

Danny smiled inwardly, but didn't let the reaction show on his face. Corky was a Godsend. The little man certainly knew his stuff.

"How you get here?" Tats asked, his heavily accented voice booming beneath the canopy. He glanced towards the front gates.

While keeping a close eye on the dark man's right hand, Danny gave him the benefit of his most engaging smile. For all the response it generated, he might as well not have bothered.

"Simple enough," Danny said, pointing over his shoulder to the pathway. "I walked."

Tats opened the door a little wider, squeezed through the gap, and pulled it shut behind him. He leaned closer, trying to threaten. Not usually prone to intimidation, Danny was neither impressed nor daunted.

"How you get through gates, asshole?"

Danny let his smile drop, but maintained his position, refusing to back down.

"They were open."

"No. Gates always locked."

"Not this time, my friend. But I have to say, you're much quicker than most," he said.

Tats frowned. "Huh?"

"Didn't take you very long to sum me up."

"What you say?" Tats asked, his frown deepening.

"Normally, it takes even the most discerning of individuals a little time to determine that I am, in fact, an arsehole." Danny nodded and reprised the smile.

"Fucking smartass!"

Tats leaned even closer to Danny. He clenched his fists, cracking his knuckles.

Unfazed, Danny maintained his position.

"Yes, I'm one of those, too. You're very good, you know. Really quick on the uptake. Do you have any other insults, or are you going to ask who I am and who sent me?"

Tats bristled. The flat muscles attaching his neck to his shoulders tensed. His fists tightened, and his forearms rippled. He looked ready to attack, but something stopped him. Some doubt. Tats clearly wasn't used to this sort of response from an unexpected and unannounced visitor. More to the point, he didn't seem accustomed to visitors at all. Tats glanced behind Danny, looking for ... what? Backup? The return of Driver?

"Well?" Danny demanded.

"Huh?"

"Oh dear. You're obviously not as bright as I initially gave you credit for. Ask me who I am, fool!"

Tats took half a pace forwards. "You fuckin—"

"No, no," Danny said, raising his index finger for silence. "Wrong move. The boss won't give you any credit for attacking a visitor whom you've not fully vetted. My God, man. You've not even asked my name or what I'm doing here."

Danny's interruption struck home. Tats stopped advancing and peered hard at him, sticking out his chin in the process.

"What your name?"

Danny shook his head. "Not telling you now. You've been too rude. Let me speak to Mrs Prentiss."

Tats frowned in confusion again.

"*Got him,*" Corky said, finally.

Keeping his hand raised in case Tats attacked, Danny took a backwards step. "About time. I couldn't delay this clown much longer. What do you have?"

"What you say?" Tats demanded. "You go now before I—"

"Will you be quiet for a just one moment? I'm talking to the boss. Please carry on, sir."

Tats blinked, raised a hand to the side of his head, and used his index finger to press the earpiece more firmly in place. He blinked again, then stared hard at Danny.

"*There's an Interpol Red Notice on this bloke,*" Corky said. "*Name's Csaba Nemeth. Hungarian. Real nasty piece of work. Escaped prisoner. Doing twenty-five to life for some real bad stuff. Multiple rape. People trafficking. Worst charge was the extended abuse of a minor. Suspected of murder, too. Take care, Danny-boy.*"

Keeping eye contact with Tats—Csaba Nemeth—Danny held a hand to his ear and nodded. "Okay, sir. I'll tell him."

Nemeth tapped his ear a couple of times and shook his head again. "My radio not work."

"That's okay, Csaba," Danny said, stepping closer and holding out his hand. "The boss told me to introduce myself. I'm Danny, latest member of the team. How you doing?"

"Yes?" Nemeth said. Confusion still raked his face, but he took Danny's hand. "No one told me about new—"

Danny yanked hard, straightening Nemeth's right arm and tugging him off-balance. He shot a vicious left jab into the Hungarian's exposed ribs. At least one bone cracked. Maybe two.

Nemeth grunted. Crumpled. Folded in on himself. His knees buckled.

Danny punched him again. Another rib snapped. He released his grip and shot the webbing between his thumb and forefinger into the Hungarian's throat. Nemeth collapsed to his knees in a gasping, gargling, coughing heap. His hands reached up to his throat, fingers scrabbling, fighting for air.

In Danny's ear, Corky chuckled. "*Nice one, Danny-boy. Them fists is lethal. Mr K couldn't have done it no better. Corky's glad we're on the same side.*"

"Me too."

Slowly, Nemeth toppled to the chessboard tiles, gagging, eyes streaming, floundering. Helpless. He lay on his back, one arm held tight around his chest to protect his damaged ribs, the other bent, its hand clutching at his throat. Danny swung his foot and kicked Nemeth in the bollocks, hard, merciless. Nemeth howled.

Danny repeated the crippling attack, his boot's steel toecap delivering untold, maybe permanent, damage.

Two vicious, pitiless blows, and Danny didn't give a fuck.

"*Ouch. That's a bit nasty.*"

"Multiple rape and the abuse of a minor, you said. Over."

"*Okay. Gotcha. Understandable. Do it again for all Corky cares.*"

"Nemeth won't be messing with kids again in a hurry. Over."

"*Fair enough. Want Corky to call Interpol or the National Crime Agency for you? They've been hunting the arsehole for the past eight months.*"

"Not yet," Danny said, keeping his voice down. "Something's fucked up here, mate. I need to find Marian first. Over."

Keeping an eye on the spyhole in the door and an ear open for noises inside the house, Danny dropped to one knee. He relieved the quivering, rapist-paedophile of his weapon—a Beretta PX4 Storm—and checked the load. Nineteen round magazine, fully loaded. What the hell was all the firepower in aid of?

Danny told Corky what happened between Robbie P and Driver, while patting down the still groaning, spluttering Nemeth. He found a wallet bulging with notes, a smart phone, and loose change. Danny pocketed the wallet, powered down the phone—Corky might find a use for it later—and slipped it into the same pocket.

"We must have missed something, Corky. Over."

"*Whatcha mean, Danny-boy?*"

"I mean, what's Robbie P gotten himself into here? What's a shit-for-brains thug like Csaba Nemeth doing here, and what's the story with Driver? Robbie P *is* just a businessman, yeah?"

"*You know what Corky knows, Danny-boy. Maybe he's pissed off the Magyars somehow. After you've found Mrs P, Corky's gonna dig deeper into Prentiss Haulage. Loads deeper, but that ain't happening 'til later. Okay? Corky can't leave you without backup.*"

"Aw, does that mean you're worried about me? Didn't know you cared. Over."

"*Nah. Just means Corky don't want the blame if you gets hurt. Mr K and the doc will be pissed, and Corky wouldn't want that.*"

Nemeth continuing to twitch and groan. A dark wet stain had spread across the front of his jeans and down the legs, but Danny couldn't tell whether it was blood or urine. Probably a mixture of the two.

Danny ripped out the miserable creature's earpiece. He yanked the Hungarian's right hand away from his groin and the left from his throat, turned him onto his front, and used the spiral-flex cable to tie them behind his back. Nemeth put up no resistance, but turned onto his side and curled into a foetal ball, mouth open and flapping for air. His face had turned a nasty shade of purple.

"There's something serious going on here, Corky. Driver ordered Nemeth around. He sounded like the boss. Must have a hell of a lot of juice to spring Nemeth from a Hungarian prison and transport him all the way to the UK. A hired hand like Nemeth wouldn't be able to manage it on his own. As for how the bugger ended up at Prentiss House ... Anyway, that's for another time. I'm going in. Danny, out."

Danny wiped his feet on a welcome mat that actually said "Welcome" and reached for the lionhead handle on the door Nemeth used. He twisted the handle and leaned against the door. It opened as quietly as before. A wave of warmth wafted into his face. It smelled of lavender air freshener.

Inside, the large entrance hall made Danny's jaw drop. Straight ahead, a wide central staircase with marble treads split in two halfway up to the first floor. The walls were painted a cream colour so deep it might have been clotted Devon, and the flooring matched the one in the portico in both material and pattern.

Oversized chess pieces, hip height, lined the walls. Major pieces only, no pawns. The four rooks—one in each corner—doubled as plant pots and contained what looked like plastic ferns. The knights had been converted into low-level lampstands complete with silk shades.

The décor said something about the owners and about the designers who pandered to the whims of their clients, and nothing it said happened to be complimentary. The entrance hall could have made the set of *Love Island*.

He grabbed Nemeth by the collar of his jacket and quickly dragged him into the house and across the hall. The groaning man's leather shoes squeaked and left black scuffmarks on the chessboard tiles. He also left a thin trail of blood. If Robbie P and his missus employed a housekeeper or a cleaner, they'd have their work cut out to polish the floor back to a shine. Danny hauled Nemeth all the way around to the back of the hall and deposited him behind the staircase, out of sight.

Danny stopped, listened. Heard nothing but the creaking of an old house being warmed by the rising sun. The entrance hall stood empty, all six internal doors were shut tight. Above him, the house remained quiet. No footfalls, no quiet conversations, no TV or radio.

Silence.

Focusing on the ground floor, Danny used the memorised architect's plans to picture what lay behind each closed door. From left to right in a circle: office, downstairs cloakroom, kitchen—the double doors of the entrance—dining room, front room, and, finally, the sun room which overlooked the rear gardens.

He hesitated, trying to decide where to go first.

Fuck's sake, Danny. Move!

The front room would be as good a place as any.

He hurried across the hall, skirted the staircase, and paused outside the door. He pressed an ear to the panel and held his breath. A quiet whimpering.

He knocked gently. The whimpering stopped.

Silence trundled through the house once more. Even Nemeth had stopped his pitiful and evermore feeble whining.

21

CHAPTER THREE

After receiving no answer, Danny knocked again and entered a room large enough to house a basketball court, but without the benches. Every piece of furniture in the room faced a curved TV the size of a multiplex cinema screen. Throw rugs, soft furnishings, upholstery, walls. The overarching colour pallet was green—subtle tones a-plenty. If the entrance hall held all the charm and comfort of a modern railway station, this room was tasteful and felt almost homely by comparison.

Bright sunlight flooded through a triple row of bifold doors, one of which was open, allowing the sage green curtains to billow into the chilly room.

An enormous, six-seater sofa dominated the space in front of the TV. Cowering in the far corner, surrounded by half a dozen throw cushions and hugging a stuffed toy—a brown-and-yellow-spotted giraffe—Marian Prentiss turned towards him.

The dark bruises beneath her bloodshot eyes still looked angry

22

and painful, her nose still protected by a metal splint brace. She looked at Danny with disinterest. Her reaction to a total stranger entering her front room couldn't have been more surprising, or disconcerting.

Rather than shout and scream at his intrusion, she returned her eyes to the TV's muted screen. The programme—a man and a woman sitting on a red sofa, chatting—typified the blandness that was daytime scheduling.

Danny stepped further into the room, but kept a decent separation between them for fear of spooking her.

"Mrs Prentiss?" he asked quietly.

She turned her head to study at him once more. Confusion on her damaged face turned to vague recognition.

"Who ... Do I know you?" The husky and nasal tone to her voice confirmed that her injury still had quite some healing to do.

"No," he said, shaking his head. "At least, we've not actually been formally introduced."

"What ... do you want now?" Although she tried to hide it, the poor woman couldn't mask the fear tainting her voice.

"Nothing, I'm here to help."

"That's what *he* said. At first."

"Who?"

Marian shot a frightened glance at the door before lowering her eyes. She hugged the giraffe tighter as though seeking its comfort and protection. Another gust of chill wind billowed the curtains and raised goosepimples on her bare arms. She didn't seem to notice.

"Vadik."

"The one driving the Range Rover?"

Slowly, suspicion in her eyes, she dipped her head in a nod. "Yes."

"Who is he?"

"Don't you know? You work for him!"

"No, Mrs Prentiss. No, I don't."

She frowned and her lower lip trembled. Tears dripped from the bloodshot eyes and ran down the outside of the splint. She licked them away from her chapped lips.

"Are you okay?"

"As if you care!"

Finally, an appropriate reaction. Anger. Fitting, but misdirected.

"I do care, Mrs Prentiss. That's why I'm here."

She looked past Danny and towards the open door he'd entered through. "Where's ... where's the other one?"

"Csaba Nemeth?"

She frowned and sucked air through her teeth, wincing at the movement. "No one told me his name. Evil man. An animal."

"Big guy. Ugly, covered in tattoos?"

Again, she shot a glance at the open door.

"Y-Yes. Him."

"Did he do that to you?" Danny raised a hand to indicate her injuries.

The breath caught in her throat. She pressed her lips together, nodded.

"You know he did."

I know for definite now.

The wind blew another blast of cold air into the lounge. Danny rushed to the other side of the room and pushed the central hinge on the bifold doors. They swished on pneumatic tracks and closed with a satisfying click. He drew back the curtains and the room brightened even more. All the while, he felt Marian's eyes boring into the back of his head. Yet, still she didn't move. She seemed resigned to his presence.

"That's better," he said, rubbing his hands together. "Bitter in here."

He returned to his original place near the door, giving her a wide berth. No crowding. At any moment, she could start screaming. The last thing Danny needed.

"Nemeth and I had a 'free and frank exchange of views'. He won't hurt you again."

She clamped her jaw closed and grimaced. The injury wasn't confined to her nose and eyes, but extended to the side of her face. The swelling too.

"I don't believe you."

"Nemeth's out of action. I promise."

"Vadik said that, too. He's a liar."

She jumped to her feet and scrambled away, keeping the settee between them, another line of defence to augment the protection offered by the little giraffe.

"Who are you?" she demanded, her voice raised, almost shouting.

Danny lifted his arms, hands open in an attempt to placate. "I'm a friend, Mrs Prentiss. Here to help. Really."

She pointed to the open doorway. "And him?"

"I told you, there's no need to worry about Nemeth. He's not going to hurt you again. Won't be able hurt anyone for a while."

She lowered the giraffe slightly. "Really?"

Danny dipped his head. "He's behind the staircase in the hall, tied up, and in no condition to go anywhere. I promise." He smiled gently, encouragingly. "Go see for yourself if you like."

Her knees buckled. She grabbed the back of the settee, teetering on the edge of collapse for a moment before straightening.

"You're lying! I-I don't believe you. This is some sort of trick. A sick joke."

Still smiling gently, Danny shook his head. "No tricks. No jokes. Stay there a sec. I'll be right back. I need to check on our tattooed 'friend' anyway."

He took the mobile from his pocket and hurried out of the room, which was just as well. Csaba Nemeth had made something of a miraculous recovery. Danny found him sitting upright and leaning against the wall behind the staircase, struggling to push himself to his feet.

On seeing Danny, the Hungarian redoubled his efforts to stand. The soles of his leather shoes squeaked on the tiles and he slid up the wall and onto his feet. A stream of words spewed from his bloodied and battered mouth. Danny didn't need to speak Hungarian to understand their meaning. He raced towards the bound man and kicked him in the nuts again.

Third time's a dream.

Nemeth's rant ended abruptly. The tattooed man doubled up, collapsed to his knees, and bent forwards, forehead connecting with the tiles. Danny's follow-up boot to the temple ended all resistance. It probably ended Nemeth, too. Not that it mattered. Although kicking a man in the head when he was bound and helpless might have offended the Marquess of Queensberry, Danny didn't give a shit. Given the opportunity, he'd have offered every paedophile on the planet the same treatment. Men who beat up women, too.

Without bothering to check the pulse at the downed man's throat —dead or alive, it didn't matter—Danny raised his mobile.

"Say 'cheese', old man." He pressed the button and the image of the pathetic, curled blob of a man saved to the camera roll. "Oh, not to worry. A smile won't improve the picture a whole lot."

He returned to Marian and showed her the photo. She burst into tears—these seemed like tears of relief. Danny again stepped back to his spot by the door and waited for her to recover. It didn't take more than a few seconds before she'd quietened enough to look up at him again.

"Are ... are you from the police?" she asked, a tremble in her voice.

"No, Mrs Prentiss. I'm just here to help."

"One of Robbie's friends?" Again, she frowned. This time, a grimace didn't follow it. Adrenaline must have been masking the discomfort.

"No, Mrs Prentiss. Your husband and I have never met."

"You're not one of them? Really?"

"I swear. Is there anyone else in the house besides the two of us and the cretin with the tattoos?"

"No." She showed him the ghost of a smile.

He took a speculative step forwards, watching for a response. She didn't flinch. He moved closer. Again, she held her place behind the settee.

"Would you mind?" he asked and pointed to the cushion closest to him. "You and I need to talk."

She shuffled to the front of the settee but made no move to sit.

"It'll be more comfortable if we sit," Danny said quietly. "You stay on that side. I'll keep my distance waaaaay over here." He added a cheesy grin.

The woman, who turned out not to be a battered wife, tugged a sweater from the arm of the settee and draped it over her bare shoulders before lowering herself tentatively into the corner of the leather unit. Once surrounded by the comforting cushions, she crossed her long legs.

Questions raced through his head, demanding answers, but she needed time to settle. Pushing her too hard too soon would most likely be counterproductive.

Marian took a deep, stuttering breath and looked him up and down, studying hard.

"I-I've seen you somewhere before. I … know it. If you're not one of Robbie's friends or … one of *them*"—she glanced towards the entrance hallway—"who are you?"

"My name is Danny," he said, starting with an easy one. "Danny Pinkerton, but if you ever call me Pinkie, I'll be most upset." Again, he smiled. "If I look familiar, it's because you saw me … yesterday afternoon. Outside the Aspire Hospital. Remember the accident? The traffic jam?"

He paused to give her time to remember.

"My God!" Her hand reached up to her throat. "The hitchhiker covered in mud and … blood. We barely spoke. What are you doing here?"

Danny took a deep breath before launching into the story. This part could easily become a little sticky.

"I saw your injuries and your reaction when the driver reached across you. You were really scared. I thought the driver was your husband." He shrugged and grimaced in apology. "When you drove away, I memorised your car's number plate. A friend of mind has access to the DVLC database and—"

"You thought Robbie was driving the car?"

"A reasonable assumption at the time. Your husband's the registered owner and the Range Rover is really … Well, I didn't think he'd let anyone borrow such an expensive piece of machinery. I put two and two together and came up with—"

"Five," she said, almost as a sigh. "You assumed I was a battered wife? Well you were wrong. Dead wrong. Robbie wasn't driving, and he didn't hit me. He would never hit me. Not ever."

Danny cast his mind back to the previous day. It had been raining heavily, and the Range Rover's tinted windows made it difficult to see inside to the driver.

He'd so misread the situation.

"An easy mistake," he said. "I'll apologise to your husband when you introduce me, but .... can you tell me what's happening here?"

"You won't believe me. This is a nightmare. It's going to sound like the plot of a gangster movie."

"Try me."

"Robbie and I are being held against our will."

"That," Danny said, feeling the weight of the Beretta in his jacket pocket, "I've already gathered."

"Right, yes, of course. Erm, well ... two nights ago," she began, speaking to the giraffe, "Robbie returned from w-work with two armed men. I'd never seen either of them before. R-Robbie told me they intercepted him on the way from the d-depot." She stopped talking, swallowed, and looked up at Danny. "Robbie runs a haulage company. It's based in Derby."

Danny nodded but didn't tell her that he probably knew as much about her husband's business as she did.

She took another deep breath and continued, her voice growing stronger all the time. "Robbie said they forced him into the back of his car and drove him here. When they arrived we thought they were going to rob and maybe kill us, but they just kept us here ... in this room ... at gunpoint. At first, they said nothing. Wouldn't answer any of our questions. Just stood there"—she pointed to where Danny had stood when he'd entered the room—"aiming their guns at us. Terrifying. I-I ... soiled myself." Her chin trembled and she lowered her eyes to the soft toy again.

"That's natural. Nothing to be ashamed of," he spoke quietly, trying to offer comfort.

Marian nodded. "I know, but ... the one outside ... Nemeth ... he laughed at me. Humiliated me. Robbie wanted to fight them, but they had the guns. It was useless."

She broke off. A tissue appeared in her hand and she dabbed gently at the tears.

"Is that when Nemeth hit you?"

"No. No. I asked ... b-begged the other one, the one who introduced himself as Vadik Pataki. The one who took Robbie away this morning. I-I asked him if I could have a shower and get changed. He said no. Then his mobile phone rang. He left the room to take the call while the other one, Nemeth, guarded us. Five minutes later, he returned and said I could change. Nemeth took me upstairs to my room. The way he l-looked at me ... I-I thought he was going to ... to ..."

She broke down again. This time, wracking sobs accompanied the tears. Danny wanted to reach out in comfort, but it didn't seem appropriate. He waited, giving her more time.

He checked his watch. 08:47. Still early. Wherever Robbie P had gone, wherever Vadik Pataki had forced him to go, they wouldn't be away forever—hopefully. Danny needed to speed things along, but couldn't force the issue.

Slowly the sobs quietened. Eventually, they stopped. Watery eyes found Danny's.

"Sorry," she said, "it's embarrassing. I never cry. Not ever. But this is ... this situation is ...." She took another deep but fragmented breath.

"Are you okay to continue?"

Although she nodded and said, "Y-Yes, I think so," she fell silent again.

"Nemeth took you upstairs?" Danny prompted.

"Yes. Yes, that's right."

"Did he touch you?"

She shook her head, lowered her eyes to the giraffe. "Only to grab

29

my arm and push me into the bathroom. He let me take some fresh clothes from the closet first."

"After that?"

"I showered and changed and we came back downstairs."

"And your injuries?"

Again, she shook her head. "Th-That happened later. When we came back here, the other man, Vadik, was asking Robbie questions, but Robbie was refusing to answer."

"What sort of questions?"

"Work stuff. Dates and schedules. Bank account passwords. I-I don't have anything to do with Robbie's business. That financial stuff goes right over my head." She swallowed, and the accompanying grimace suggested it hurt. "I just take care of the house and the gardens. I'm doing an online course on interior design." Distractedly, she waved her hand around the room. "This is my work."

"Very nice," Danny said, not knowing what else to say. "So, your husband refused to answer the man's questions?"

"Yes, he claimed to have no idea what Vadik was talking about. That's when ... that's when the pig started ... started hitting me."

Danny ground his teeth together and clenched his hands into fists. If he hadn't already done so, he would have returned to the entrance hall and introduced Nemeth to the steel toecaps on his boots.

"I was a mess. Screaming. Blood everywhere. Robbie begged them to stop. Promised to tell them everything. Then I must have passed out."

"You lost consciousness?"

"Y-Yes. Woke up in bed, panicking. Could hardly breathe. Robbie was with me. They'd locked us in our bedroom. He was crying. Telling me how sorry he was for what they'd done. I tried to ... to tell him it wasn't his fault, but I-I couldn't catch my breath. My nose wouldn't stop bleeding. I was gagging. Blinding headache. Never been so scared."

She stopped talking again, breathing deeply through her mouth, panting.

"Do you need a break? Would you like a cuppa?"

She nodded. "Y-Yes. Yes please."

"Kitchen's that way, right?" Danny pointed through the door he'd already used twice. "Through the hall?"

"Yes. H-How did you know that?"

"I'm a good guesser. Come on."

Danny stood, closed the gap between then, and held out his hand. She looked up at him and hesitated a moment before taking it in a firm grip. He helped her up and released her hand only when certain she wouldn't topple over.

"Before we go, can you tell me where the man took your husband?"

"They've gone to the office. Vadik said Robbie needed to be at work on time as normal. Something about ... nothing could interfere with the exchange. Whatever that means. As I said, I don't really have much of an involvement with the business. Don't know what they were talking about, but ..." She sighed and stopped talking.

"But?"

Her eyes locked with Danny's for the longest time since he'd burst in to the house.

"There was something ... I don't know. Something strange about the way Robbie acted."

"Strange? In what way?"

"Well, he kept telling me how sorry he was. How everything was all his fault."

"Because you were attacked?"

"No ... yes. Well, sort of. But it was more than that. The way Robbie and Vadik acted together. It was almost as though they knew each other before we were taken hostage."

Danny nodded but didn't know what to say. The whole situation kept getting stranger, more complicated. He needed to dig deeper, but Marian looked about ready to collapse onto the settee again and he'd promised her a cuppa.

"How long does it normally take your husband to get to work?"

"This time of the day, over an hour. Traffic can be terrible."

"Are you expecting a call when they arrive? I mean, is this Vadik character going to check in with Nemeth?"

She shrugged. "I-I don't know. They didn't mention a call. Vadik just told Nemeth to guard me until they got back this afternoon. Told him to keep his hands off me, too. The pig looked disappointed, but promised to do as he was told." She shuddered, probably at the thought of spending most of the day alone in the house with the bastard who'd done so much damage to her already.

Danny nodded. They had time. Maybe not long, but hopefully enough.

"So, are you ready for that cuppa?"

She nodded.

"Okay, let's go."

He took her hand again and led her through to the kitchen, trying to block her view of the splodge he'd left behind the staircase, but she stopped and took a long look at the man who'd attacked her.

"Sorry for messing up your décor, but I imagine the tiles will scrub clean."

She shook her head. "I haven't started in the hall yet. The house is still a work in progress. The entrance looks like a mausoleum. We've been decorating, room by room, from the top down. My God, you don't think I designed this monstrosity, do you?"

Danny shook his head. "Of course not."

It wasn't the first time he'd been proven wrong that day, and he didn't mind lying to hide yet another mistake.

"If I was wearing shoes and not these slippers," she said, lifting her foot, "I'd go over there and kick his head in some more."

"And I'd do nothing to stop you," Danny said, delighted to be telling the truth once more.

She took over and led the way into a bright, modern kitchen.

"Tea or coffee?" she asked, filling the kettle from a chromed tap that looked as though it might have cost Danny a week's pay. The kitchen was an understated blend of creams and greys, with the occasional burst of sunshine yellow. Minimalist modern. Airy. Nice.

"Coffee please. Did you design the kitchen?"

She smiled beneath the nose splint. "I did. You like it?"

"I do. It's sleek. Elegant."

"Thank you. That's what I was going for."

Danny made his way to the full-length French doors overlooking the manicured gardens. If he'd craned his neck hard enough, he might have been able to spot where he'd spent most of the night.

He watched Marian's reflection as she fussed over the brewing process. In her kitchen, doing normal things, she seemed to draw out of herself. It relaxed her, made her more composed.

After setting aside the coffee pot, she turned and leaned her back against the counter.

"Thanks for giving me time," she said. "Now, where was I?"

Danny grimaced. "Upstairs in bed, struggling to breathe."

CHAPTER FOUR

Wednesday 3rd May – Danny Pinkerton
Amber Valley, Derbyshire, UK

"Y-Yes, that's right," Marian whispered, struggling to maintain control. "I was drowning in my own blood. I-I thought I was going to die."

"Must have been horrible," Danny said, imagining her terror.

As a former member of the Special Boat Service, he'd been close to drowning often enough to sympathise with her. Yes, he'd also suffered injury and battled through to the other side. The difference between the two of them was that Danny had undergone training to help him cope with the physical and mental effects of battlefield stress and trauma. Marian, on the other hand, was a woman whose whole life revolved around personal comfort and interior design. She'd been totally unprepared for the horror. However, here, standing in the kitchen she'd designed, she could begin the recovery. A recovery that could only continue if Danny helped extricate her and Robbie P from the danger they'd fallen into.

Although, how the hell he could accomplish such a feat on his own ... but he wasn't alone. Not entirely.

"It was awful," she said, folding her arms into a hug. "I tried lying down, sitting up, standing. Nothing seemed to help. Robbie was beside himself. Crying, screaming at them for help. I must have lost consciousness again, because I woke in the passenger seat of the car. Vadik was driving. He told me they'd made a deal. Robbie would behave himself if they took me to hospital."

"You were lucky to get into the Aspire."

She shook her head gently. "Not really. We pay a fortune for private health insurance. Our carrier agreed to pay for the emergency surgery. The Aspire is the nearest hospital with a private surgical ward, and they always seem to have spare capacity ... so long as there's enough money to pay for the treatment."

"Usually the way," Danny said, trying for noncommittal.

Marian continued. "The surgeon stopped the bleeding and rebuilt my nose. They wanted to keep me in overnight, but Vadik forced me to discharge myself. The nurses gave me a prescription for pain killers and some fresh dressings. Then they made me sign a disclaimer before letting me go."

She paused long enough to pour out their drinks and handed Danny an elegant cup and saucer. He ignored the saucer and held the cup around the body for fear of breaking the impossibly delicate-looking handle.

"We got back here early yesterday evening and they kept us locked in the bedroom overnight. They took our phones and threatened us with dire consequences if we made a noise or kicked up a fuss."

Danny tasted his coffee. Strong and black. The way he liked it, only in far less volume. Two more tiny sips and he drained it. She added cream and brown sugar to hers and sipped delicately, taking care to avoid jogging the nose splint.

"Do you have any idea what they're after?"

She drank a little more before lowering the cup and setting it, and the saucer, onto a coaster. "None. As I said, I don't have a clue about the business. Robbie and I tend to keep a good work-life separation. I have my studies and my volunteer work, and he has his company and his golf. But ... come to think of it, things have been different lately."

"In what way?"

She paused long enough to refill Danny's cup, but not her own.

"Difficult to say, really. Robbie's been tense for months. Travelling abroad unexpectedly. Missing social engagements. Staying late at the office and leaving for work even earlier than normal. I tried talking to him about it. Told him I was worried, but he just laughed it off. He said I was imagining things. Typical of Robbie." She took a long, faltering breath before continuing. "He tries to protect me from the difficult stuff. Robbie thinks I'm an airhead, incapable of working things out for myself, but ..."

Tears filled her eyes again but she held them back, sniffled, and carried on.

"Even though Robbie doesn't want to admit it, I think the business has been struggling. Trade with Europe has dropped because of that political nonsense with the EU, and the transport industry has always struggled to cope with change. Robbie's been trying to diversify, find new routes, acquire new businesses, but it's been a real struggle. At least, I think it has."

She reached for her drink, but instead of picking it up, she cradled the little cup tightly in both hands as though for warmth.

The reason for *Prentiss Haulage Limited*'s expansion into Hungary suddenly became clear. As did the presence of Csaba Nemeth and Vadik Pataki. It seemed that Robbie P had climbed into bed with the wrong people and the consequences had shown themselves in Marian's injuries.

Danny would have liked to allow the silence to stretch out for a little while but, with Robbie P under the control of a Hungarian hard man, time didn't tick slowly, it fairly galloped along like one of Mike's thoroughbred horses. He cleared his throat to gain her attention.

"These people are taking one hell of a risk. Abduction, false imprisonment, assault and battery. If they're caught, they face serious prison time. Whatever they're doing, must be worth the risk. Big money in it. About that phone call Vadik took. Were there any others?"

"Yes. He took three yesterday and another this morning. And before you ask, he left the room each time. I didn't hear anything. Not that I'd have been able to understand what he was saying."

"Did Vadik have an accent? Was he Hungarian, like Nemeth?"

"Difficult to say. I didn't really notice one. If anything, he spoke too well. Too precisely. It was like he was trying too hard."

"Like he was using a telephone voice?"

The merest hint of a smile made its way to her lips, but it disappeared in an instant. Smiling must have hurt.

"Yes, that's right," she managed through yet another wince. "My mother used to call it 'minding your Ps and Qs'. Does that help?"

Danny shrugged. "Dunno. Might do. Any information you can provide could prove useful. Now don't be worried. I'm not going to be speaking to myself, but I need to call someone."

"Sorry?"

"Despite my rather inelegant appearance, it might surprise you to learn that I actually have friends. I'm not working totally alone."

For the first time since entering the house, Danny tapped the arm of his glasses. "You there, Corky? Over."

"*Yep. Corky's been earwigging everything. Seems like you got the old 'abusive hubby' angle dead wrong, eh?*"

Marian pressed herself harder against the kitchen surface and slid away.

"Who are you talking to?" she asked, clear agitation in the words.

"Don't worry, Mrs Prentiss." He turned his head and pointed to his ear. "I'm wearing an earpiece. On the other end of the line is one of the greatest technical wizards the world has never seen. At least that what he keeps telling us all."

Danny winked and the tension in Marian's shoulders eased. She relaxed enough to return to her earlier spot and pick up her coffee cup even though it rattled in its saucer.

"*Oi! Corky heard that.*"

"I know, Corky. Over."

"And it happens to be true!"

"I know that, too, Corky. Over."

"So, what's it you want from this here great tech wizard, then?"

"I imagine you're running a check on Vadik Pataki, assuming that's his real name. He's the guy who drove Mr Prentiss from the house this morning? Over."

"Oh, so it's 'Mr Prentiss' now, not 'Robbie P'?"

"As you can see, I've got company. Given how wrong we were about this situation—"

"Oi, Corky weren't wrong about nothing. You was the one who got all hot under the collar about him being a wifebeater. Too sensitive by half, you was. Too quick to judge."

"Okay, Corky. Point taken. Definitely my mistake. So, what's the answer? Do you have an ident or not? Over."

"Do you want to include Mrs P in this conversation?"

"It might be easier for her to see and talk to you, but I don't have a spare earpiece. Over."

"That don't matter. Pop back to the TV room and don't forget them coffees."

"Have you found a way to hack into the house's security system? Over."

Corky chuckled. *"Not exactly. When you was talking to Mrs P in the front room, Corky noticed they have a smart TV, linked to the web. Didn't take Corky long to isolate the signal and hook in. There ain't that many satellite receivers in Amber Valley. See you in a tick."*

"Mrs Prentiss, one of the quirkiest men on the planet has just consented to give you an audience. I hope you feel suitably honoured."

Marian raised one darkened eyebrow. "To be absolutely frank, Danny, I have no idea what to think."

At least she'd started to use his first name rather than run away, screaming. Progress indeed.

"Understandable. Shall we go?"

"Go where?"

"Back to the lounge, or TV room, whatever you call it."

"It's the salon."

'Course it is.

Despite Corky's advice, he ignored the miniscule cups and escorted Marian back to the "salon". This time, they didn't spare any thought to the bloody mess behind the staircase, which still hadn't moved.

Danny glanced down at the toecap of his right boot. There were no obvious signs of blood or skin, but the boots were finished. He'd seen enough forensics documentaries to know how difficult removing trace evidence from stitched leather boots could be. Overnight, he'd stuck thin transparent film over his fingerprints for the same reason.

As expected, nothing had changed in the salon but the programme on the TV. Instead of the chatting couple, a single, scruffy-haired man with a round face and scraggy beard stared out from the huge screen. Fortunately, Corky had recently given up his habit of wearing garishly colourful Hawaiian shirts and had swapped them for slightly more sombre polo shirts. This one, in black, could have allowed him to pass unnoticed anywhere. A distinct improvement.

The background showed a plain green wall to match the salon's colour palette rather than Corky's usual palm trees in front of a star-covered night sky. Corky was playing sensible for Marian's benefit, and Danny appreciated his efforts.

They sat, taking more centralised positions on the settee than earlier, and the impish little hacker smiled. He was either manipulating the colour contrast on the screen, or he'd had his teeth whitened recently. Danny guessed the latter, which would explain the improved dress sense. For the past few months, the team had been discussing the idea that Corky had found himself a proper girlfriend. The consensus decided that wonders would never cease.

"Whatcha, Danny," he said and turned to face the host. "Morning Mrs Prentiss. Corky's really sorry to see what that arse—er, ... what happened. Csaba Nemeth were a nasty piece of work, but you don't need to worry about him. He ain't breathing no more."

Marian's hand shot up to her mouth. "He's what? Oh my God." She turned to face Danny, who stared back, unblinking.

"Don't go wasting no sympathy on Csaba Nemeth, Mrs P," Corky continued. "He don't deserve none of your tears. Corky's been digging into the bastard's background. Nemeth was doing hard time for people trafficking, child abduction, and sexual assault. Then the police found evidence of him killing a five-year-old girl and burning her body, after he'd spent three weeks … Well, Corky can leave the details to your imagination. It weren't pretty. The evidence were overwhelming, DNA, witnesses, the lot. The police set up another trial, but it seems like the arsehole—'scuse my French—had powerful friends. During his transfer from the high security prison to the court, they sprung him. Killed a policewoman and shot two others in the process. One of them won't never walk again."

Corky frowned and shook his head. A lock of hair flopped in front of his eyes. He brushed it away but it fell back again.

"A countrywide manhunt couldn't find him. That were months ago. Rumours spread that he'd been freed and murdered in retribution for killing the child, but … The rapidly cooling corpse in your hallway shows up that particular theory as a load of nonsense, yeah?"

During Corky's explanation—the longest single speech he had ever heard the hacker deliver—Danny took a moment to ponder the similarities between Csaba Nemeth's story and that of Melanie Archer. The parallels between them were uncanny. Only the outcomes differed.

Both had been accused of murder, and both were on temporary release from prison. Both prisoners' transports had been attacked, and both had been freed. During each escape, people had died and been injured. But after that, the stories diverged. Significantly.

While Nemeth's friends plotted his escape and killed people in the process, Melanie Archer's enemies intended to kill her, but their plans had fallen foul of the captain and Danny. To save Melanie Archer, Danny and the captain had killed and maimed the would-be murderers, but only because they had to. Definitely not by choice.

The stories needed to keep diverging. The guilty Csaba Nemeth lay dead in a pool of his own blood and faeces, but the innocent Melanie Archer still lived. If the captain and Danny had anything to do with it, she'd stay that way.

"...you listening to this, Danny?"

Corky's words cut into his thoughts.

"Sorry, Corky," he said, glancing at Marian, who was staring at him, her expression unreadable. "What did you say?"

"Corky asked what you wanted him to do next," the little hacker asked, showing disappointment in the way Danny was ignoring him.

"I need time to think."

Marian shifted her position. She'd clasped her hands and pressed them into her lap. "My God, what's Robbie got us into? With a man like that involved ... They intended to kill us, didn't they?"

Danny met her eye. Nodded. "Men like Csaba Nemeth don't leave witnesses behind."

"Robbie ... he's in danger. Vadik's going to ..."

"Let's not get too far ahead of ourselves. They kept you both alive for a reason, and for the same reason, your husband's important to them. They need him to do something for them, and they're using you as leverage. It must be related to his work." He turned to the TV screen. "Agreed?"

Corky shrugged. "Agreed."

"Any idea what that might be?"

Again, Corky shrugged. "Could be anything. Corky's not had much time to dig. Been busy with other stuff. Mr K's been keeping Corky busy lately, you know."

"Mr K?" Marian asked.

"A friend," Danny answered for Corky. "The best you'll ever have. I'll tell you more later. Corky, do you have a location for Mr Prentiss?"

"In his office at the haulage yard in Derby."

"Are you sure?" she asked. "Is he ..."

"Yeah, certain," Corky said, smiling inappropriately. "Corky's been following your hubby's Range Rover on the traffic cams ever since it left your house. They arrived about fifteen minutes ago and went straight up to the fourth floor. Mr P's at his desk and Vadik Pataki's in the room with him. They're sitting in the office in silence. Ain't saying nothing. I can see your hubby right now on his laptop camera. Fancy take a butcher's for yourself?"

Marian shuffled to the edge of her seat and sucked in a deep breath. "Yes please."

A rectangular window appeared in the middle of the TV screen, pushing Corky's window up and across to the top left corner. A haggard, puffy-eyed Robert Prentiss occupied the centre of the window. Forearms on the desk, he hunched forwards, close to the camera, and kept glancing from the top left of his screen to his wrist. He was keeping a close eye on the laptop's clock and his watch as though staring at the time could speed it up. Or slow it down.

Vadik Pataki sat in a leather chair behind him, legs crossed, a smug smile on his dark face. He looked relaxed and comfortable. Unlike Robert Prentiss, Vadik Pataki had all the time in the world.

"Oh God," Marian said, "he looks awful."

"Corky," Danny said, "can Vadik tell we're watching this?"

"Not a chance. Corky's disabled the light on the laptop's camera. To anyone in the room, that there camera's inactive."

Danny grinned. Corky really did think of everything.

"Nice one, Corky."

"It ain't nothing, Danny-boy."

"What's Robbie doing?" Marian cut into the love fest.

"Looks like they're waiting for a bank transfer to go through," Corky piped up. "Mr P's laptop is logged into the company's bank account. He keeps refreshing the screen every couple of minutes."

"Money?" Danny said, trying not to sound underwhelmed. "A kidnapping for ransom. How much are they demanding?"

"Nah," Corky said, scratching his scraggy beard, "that ain't it at all. Mr P's waiting for a transfer *from* OTL Bank in Hungary. He's expecting a one-million-five-hundred-thousand-euro deposit *into* the Prentiss Haulage account."

"He's doing what?" Danny asked, totally gobsmacked.

"That ... that just doesn't make sense," Marian said, slumping back into the settee. "You must be wrong."

"Nah. Corky ain't never wrong with stuff like this. That there laptop is open to the company account and waiting for one and a half million euros, which is really interesting. You know why, Danny?"

Danny sighed.

Here it comes.

Corky loved to play the Quiz Master to show off his skills.

"No, Corky, I don't know why. Care to enlighten us?"

"Happy to, Danny-boy. Happy to. Well, it's like this—"

A bell rang somewhere inside the house.

"Corky, hang on a minute." Danny shot a questioning look at Marian. "What was that?"

Fear showed on her face. "Oh my God! Danny, someone's just opened front gates."

Danny jumped up and raced to one of the windows facing the front of the house. He peeled the heavy curtain a few centimetres away from the wall and peered through the gap. The double gates at the front of the house were swinging slowly open. So far, they'd made it half way. Behind the gates, a dark blue Mercedes waited. Fully tinted windows hid the occupants.

Shit! What now?

CHAPTER FIVE

WEDNESDAY 3RD MAY – Danny Pinkerton
Amber Valley, Derbyshire, UK

Danny stared at Marian. Even though she looked terrified, he had to ask. "Are you expecting visitors?"

She shook her head. "No. No one. We ... the gates shouldn't open on their own. Only Robbie and I have the keycode. W-What's happen—"

Danny raised a hand for silence. He removed the spy glasses and propped them in the window, making sure the camera angled towards the gates.

"Corky, how's that?"

"Tilt them to the left a smidge." Danny nudged the specs and Corky nodded. "Perfect."

A picture of the gates appeared in the window on the TV screen, replacing the one of Robert Prentiss in his office.

Good, that'll work.

Danny returned to the settee and reached out a hand. Marian took it without hesitation—a good sign.

"Is there a panic room?"

"No. Why would we need a—"

"What about a basement? We need a room with solid walls. Somewhere safe."

She rubbed her forehead. "I-I don't. I ..."

"Quickly, Marian."

"The wine cellar!" she shouted, pointing towards the kitchen.

Danny started towards the door, pulling her with him. At the same time, he tugged out Nemeth's Beretta. Nineteen shots should be enough. Although he was nowhere near as accurate over long distance as the captain, at close range Danny usually hit what he aimed at.

On the TV screen, the gates were fully open. The Mercedes nudged forwards.

"Corky," he said, turning back to the door, "I need a running commentary. Over."

He allowed Marian to lead him across the entrance hall, towards the kitchen. The whole time, Corky's description rolled through his earpiece.

The Mercedes crawled along the gravel drive and stopped in front of the portico. The doors opened and three men in dark suits jumped out. Each carried a semi-automatic handgun. Corky couldn't make out the manufacturer. The front passenger, whom Corky described as a *tiny little blond bugger*, had a phone to his ear and was orchestrating the others. He pointed towards the house. While Blondie stayed safe behind the car, protected by metal and glass, the other two approached the house.

Danny shot a glance at the front doors. Unlocked!

"Wait," he whispered, and they made a rushed detour.

He released Marian's hand, turned the key, and slid home the four bolts—all heavy, all solid. The best he could do.

They headed for the kitchen again.

One of the lionhead handles squeaked as it turned. Loud banging rattled the doors, but they held firm.

"Hurry," Danny urged, pushing her onwards.

Marian's frantic whimpering stabbed him through the heart. He was trained for this shit. She wasn't.

The kitchen's brightness brought more worry. How secure were the French windows? When would Blondie send his minions around to the back? Danny checked the locks. All secure. At least, as secure as glass doors would ever be. The rear exit, a solid oak stable door, split in the middle, was locked, too. All its bolts thrown. Those doors would stand firm enough.

"Where's the cellar?"

She headed deeper into the kitchen and stopped beside the massive two-door American fridge. The digital clock on the central panel read 09:19.

He'd been in the house less than an hour when it had seemed like most of the day. She pressed a panel on the wall next to the fridge. A hidden door popped back to reveal a small opening with concrete steps leading down and around to the left—the original part of the house. With solid walls, the bricks painted the same light grey as the kitchen panels, it would do well enough.

He pointed her down into the darkness.

"Go. Find somewhere to hide. Stay there until I call you."

Behind them, the banging continued. The front doors were holding, but for how long?

The banging stopped as quickly as it started.

"Corky, what's happening? Over."

"*The pocket-sized boss-man's screaming. Speaking Hungarian. Corky's software's working on the translation ... Yep. He's telling them to leave it and search the rest of the house. ... Wait. Crap.*"

"What's that? Over."

"*Boss-man's just told them to kill the woman and Nemeth. The murdering rapist bastard has outlived his usefulness and can't be trusted. His words, not Corky's.*"

"What's happening with the other two? Over."

"*One's going left to search around the back, the other's heading to the right. The first one'll be with you in a few seconds. Hurry, Danny. Hide!*"

"Hide? Moi?"

Not happening, Corky!

He was in no mood to hide.

He clicked the earpiece into rest mode.

Marian hesitated until Danny gave her a gentle push. She reached out to throw a switch on the brick wall.

"No!" he whispered. "Keep it dark." He powered up the internal light on his mobile and handed it over. "Turn it off once you've found somewhere safe. And keep quiet."

Fear shone bright in Marian's eyes, but she had enough wits about her to say, "Be careful, Danny."

Brave woman.

"Always," he whispered and gave her a confident smile.

She turned and hurried down the steps and around the corner, the mobile's white light leading the way. Moments later, it disappeared, extinguished.

Danny pressed the panel closed. It blended seamlessly into the run of floor-to-ceiling kitchen units. It could have been made for the job of hiding a panic room. For camouflage, he dragged one of the tall kitchen chairs in front of the panel. It didn't look out of place.

Movement flashed in his peripheral vision.

The first intruder slowed as he reached the French doors. Danny ducked and crouched behind the island.

The man—long, dark hair, drooping Zapata moustache— stopped. Zapata squinted and leaned closer to the window. He shielded his eyes with both hands, straining to see inside. The butt of the Heckler & Koch P30L in his hand clinked against the mirrored glass. In the right hands, the 9mm with its fifteen round mag, was accurate and deadly.

In the right hands.

The words didn't describe Zapata in any way. The moustachioed idiot had no idea about covert searching. Anyone with half-decent military training would have crouched low, stayed out of sight, but not Zapata. The man had no idea who he faced. As far as he was concerned, he'd been sent to kill a terrified woman and her distracted rapist guard.

They probably intended to make the double murder look like a break-in gone wrong. Whatever their actual game, they'd already demonstrated their ruthlessness. Marian's injuries showed that clearly. These men had no mercy.

Danny smiled.

No mercy.

Two could play that game.

Zapata wore a business suit and silk shirt. No body armour.

Danny raised the Beretta, took aim. Centre mass. Although unfamiliar with his stolen weapon, he'd fired a Beretta PX4 Storm before.

Zapata stood tall and still and was less than three metres away. Even though the double-glazed panel would affect the first bullets' trajectory slightly, Danny still couldn't miss. Two shots, rapid fire, would do it. Not a problem.

"Corky," he whispered, "I have the first man. Where's the second one? Over."

The stable door's lever handle dropped, waggled, and a palm slammed against the upper panel, giving Danny his answer. The door rattled in its frame.

Zapata turned towards the noise. He shouted something. The handle stopped moving. Man Two answered, his words muffled by the woodwork. Zapata spoke again and turned his face to the glass once more, looking for movement.

Danny slowed his breathing. His heartrate fell.

Wait, Danny. Wait for it.

Man Two roared.

Something hard slammed against the back door. An upper panel splintered. The door buckled, but held firm. Another louder roar followed. A second blow. The top half of the stable door crashed open and slammed against the wall. The bottom half stayed in place. Under the impetus of his shoulder charge, Man Two folded over the bottom panel, cracking his head against the door jamb. He let out a string of swear words. Danny didn't need a translator to know a cuss when he heard it.

Danny took careful aim at Zapata.

He fired twice.

The first bullet destroyed the toughened glass panel, and the second followed through the cleared opening. It punched through the middle button of Zapata's silk shirt. Eyes widened in surprise, the attacker fell forwards, landing face-first in a pile of glass granules. More glass rained down on top of him.

Danny fired on the turn. Bullet three tore into Man Two's door-opening shoulder. Bullet four drilled a neat, nine millimetre hole into his forehead and exploded out of the back of his head in a spray of bone, blood, and brain matter. In slow motion, Man Two's body sagged and flopped over the bottom door, arms hanging down. A Sig P226 slipped from his lifeless hand and clattered into the floor tiles.

The gunshots rang in Danny's ears. Man Two was dead, no longer a threat. He changed focus.

Zapata still breathed, although the growing pool of blood saturating the pile of shattered glass suggested it wouldn't be for long.

Neither man had fired a shot.

"*Jesus, Danny-boy,*" Corky said, his voice trembling. "*What happened, man?*"

Danny told him.

"*Shit, you okay?*"

Danny couldn't remember a time when Cory had asked after his wellbeing.

"Peachy," he answered.

There would be no revulsion for taking these two lives. Zapata and Man Two would have happily murdered Marian and one of their own. They deserved no one's pity, and no more of Danny's time.

"What's Blondie doing? Over."

"*Nothing much,*" Corky said, stronger, already recovering from the shock. "*He's still on the phone. Corky's trying to break into their signal, but it ain't easy. Taking longer than normal. Their service provider's changed their encryption protocols recently. Tricky little buggers have developed a triple-lock, double-redundan—*"

"No need for the details, Corky. What's he saying?"

"*Idiot thinks them shots were his men taking out Mrs Prentiss and*

Nemeth, and that's what he's telling whoever's on the other end of the line. They're laughing about it." He paused and added, "*Evil fuckers, these.*"

Danny sniffed.

Tell me about it, mate.

The earpiece clicked again. "*Okay, so, while old Corky's keeping his eye on Blondie, what's your plan?*"

Good question.

Danny stood and took in the carnage that used to be a beautiful modern kitchen.

Dealing with the housekeeping—collecting the H&K from the pile of broken glass and the Sig from the floor next to the dripping corpse—gave him time to think.

"What's happening with Robert Prentiss? Can you put that window on the TV screen again?"

"*Sure thing. Launching it now. They're still waiting for the transfer. Vadik's not looking so relaxed now, though. Getting a little antsy about it, if you ask old Corky.*"

"Thanks, mate. Let me know if anything changes on either side. Over."

Danny took another look at the mess he'd made of Marian's kitchen and sighed. Couldn't do anything to fix it now. As best he could, Danny straightened his jacket and polished the toes of his boots on the backs of his trouser legs. No point looking like too much of a tramp. Marian deserved better.

He shifted the stool and tapped on the hidden panel. It opened silently.

"Mrs Prentiss? Marian, it's Danny. You can come up now."

Shuffling and scraping filtered up through the darkness. A moment later, his phone light snapped on, peeling away the blackness. Marian appeared around the corner, her pale and frightened face looked up, searching for him.

"A-Are you okay?"

He smiled and beckoned her up the stairs. "I'm okay, but your kitchen's a bit of a mess, I'm afraid. Close your eyes and I'll take you through to the salon. No need to upset yourself."

Marian rushed up the steps, threw herself into his arms, and buried the less injured side of her face into his chest.

"Oh my God," she said, her words muffled by his jacket, "the gunshots. I was so scared."

Danny patted her back gently before easing her away.

Tears flowed down her swollen cheeks. He tried to block her view and escort her from the room, but she leaned to one side and stared past him. Marian took in the shattered pane of glass, the stable door, and the bodies leaking various fluids onto her beautifully tiled floor. She gagged. A hand flew up to her mouth. She raced to the sink and vomited, violently. Twice.

"*Poor lady,*" Corky mumbled in another rare moment of empathy. "*Er ... you wanted Corky to let you know if anything changed?*"

Marian ran the cold tap and drank water from her cupped hands, careful not to bump her injuries.

"What's happening?" Danny asked.

"*Blondie's finished his call. He's heading to the front door. Must be wondering why his minions ain't opened up yet.*"

Danny turned, said, "Thanks, Corky," and headed for the entrance hall.

"Marian, stay here," he called over his shoulder. "Please don't touch anything."

He left her at the sink. No reason for her to see what happened next.

CHAPTER SIX

WEDNESDAY 3RD MAY – Danny Pinkerton
Amber Valley, Derbyshire, UK

Danny reached the window nearest the front doors. With his nose pressed against the wall, he eased the curtain aside no more than a crack and watched Blondie pace the chessboard tiles of the portico. Corky's description, "tiny little blond bugger", fitted the man to perfection.

Skinny bordering on emaciated, Blondie wouldn't have topped out at more than one-sixty-five centimetres—five feet five inches in old money. Immaculately groomed, his fair hair had been styled by an expert—trimmed short at the back and sides, and tall on top to add a little height. His dark suit screamed "gangster-chic" and fitted him to perfection. Armani? Gucci? Paul Smith? Danny had no idea. The most he'd ever paid for a suit probably wouldn't have covered the cost of Blondie's silk shirt and tie. The man's shoes—black and polished to a mirror shine—sported five centimetre heels. Danny revised his estimation of the man's height down by the corresponding amount, and took off a little more for the fluffed up hair.

Blondie reached into the breast pocket of his jacket and pulled out a sleek grey mobile. He hit a button and raised the mobile to his ear. He turned his back to Danny and carried on pacing from where he'd left off.

Moments later, the dull rumble of a vibrating mobile sounded in the kitchen. Marian yelped. A glass fell into the sink. Smashed. Footsteps clattered on tiles. She stumbled through the doorway and into the hall.

Danny held a finger to his lips and waved her back into the kitchen. Chin trembling, eyes watering, Marian shook her head. Her hand shot out to the side and found the wall. She shuffled sideways and slid down the wall and onto her haunches. Knees bent to her chest, arms wrapped tight around them, her eyes never left Danny.

He couldn't blame her for not wanting to stay in the abattoir he'd made of her kitchen. Even now, the flies would have sniffed out all the nice warm and wet places to lay their eggs. Already, the smell of blood, evacuated bowels, and emptied bladders would have permeated the neighbourhood.

The mobile's rumble stopped. Danny turned back to the window, listening for the other dead man's phone to ring. Blondie growled. Muttered something under his breath and replaced the phone in its pocket. He spun around, marched to the front doors, and started hammering. The wrought iron ring in the lion's mouth did a sterling job, and the metallic booms thundered through the house. Although they tried their damnedest, the knocks weren't, in fact, able to raise the dead.

Blondie leaned closer to the woodwork. "*Bence, Milán, hol a faszban vagy?*"

"Corky? Translate, please. Over."

"*Blondie's asking where his buddies have gone,*" Corky answered through a chuckle. "*Only he didn't use them exact words.*"

Blondie stepped away from the door, looked left and right, and yelled again. "*Válaszolj neked, kibaszott morók!*"

He undid the button of his lovely jacket, reached around to the small of his back, and pulled out a Sig P226—an exact match for the one Danny liberated from Man Two. In Blondie's right fist it looked more like a Desert Eagle carrying .44 Magnum shells than a slim-built 9mm. Either way, they could both be just as deadly.

"More of the same, but now he's calling them morons as well," Corky said, still chuckling. *"Nasty little man ain't a happy bunny."*

Danny glanced at Marian, held up a hand to keep her in place, and stepped around to the front door. He raised his Beretta. Blondie may be small and might have looked comical in his expensive suit and with his fancy haircut, but he'd ordered Marian's death and deserved no compassion.

And being short didn't mean he shouldn't be taken seriously. The captain wasn't exactly a giant and Danny had seen him in action plenty of times. Ryan Kaine was both fearless and fearsome. A man to have at your side in battle.

Blondie hammered on the door again, shouting some more.

Danny worked the bolts top and bottom. They each slid back against their mountings, making a satisfying clunk.

The hammering stopped.

"A kibaszott időről, idióták," Blondie shouted, sounding slightly further away.

Danny didn't need a translation to understand the relief mixed with frustration and anger in the words. He turned the key in the lock, twisted the handle, and stepped back.

He raised his cocked Beretta to Blondie's chest level—somewhere around Danny's midriff—curled his finger around the trigger, took up the slack, waited.

Still shouting, ranting, Blondie burst through the door, his weapon lowered, unprepared. With one foot over the threshold, half inside the house, he stopped mid-rant and stared at Danny, eyes wide, puzzled. His gun hand twitched.

Danny shook his head and smiled. He pushed out the Beretta, trigger finger ready. It only needed a couple of grams more pressure and ...

"Drop the gun."

He spoke quietly, calmly.

"Who the fuck—?"

Blondie's Sig started to rise.

Danny changed his aim, squeezed the trigger. The Beretta bucked in his hand.

Blondie's right elbow exploded, blood spurted. His Sig popped and the bullet buried itself into the tiles, mere centimetres from his right foot. Razor sharp pieces of ceramic flew up around Blondie's right foot, cutting, slicing. Blood flowed from both elbow and ankle.

The short man squealed, spun, staggered backwards through the doorway. The Sig fell from his lifeless hand, skittered across the chessboard into the shadow thrown by the canopy. It rattled to a stop at the foot of a planter, pointing back at the squealing, rolling Hungarian. His fancy suit no longer held its sharp creases, and the blond hair no longer looked so beautifully coiffed.

Blondie stared in horror at the blood flowing from his shattered elbow, apparently unaware of the claret oozing from the torn ankle. His good hand shot across, clamped over the pumping wound, trying to stem the flow. He turned to Danny, eyes pleading.

"*Segíts kérlek!* ... Help me, please!" he called. His legs gave way and he slumped to the tiles.

Blondie spoke decent English.

Good.

It would make things easier.

"Please!" Blondie shrieked.

The bleeding had slowed. Blondie's hand helped to reduce the blood loss. One arm shattered, the other busy, the little man was no longer a threat. Without help to stem the arterial flow, he'd survive another five minutes, maybe ten. There was no need to rush.

Scuffling to Danny's left. Movement. He spun, levelled the Beretta.

Marian. She gasped, raised a hand to her mouth.

Danny lowered his gun, smiled. "Stay there, Marian. Things are cool."

He faced Blondie again.

Panting hard, sweat shone on a face that had lost even more colour. His lips peeled back to expose gritted teeth.

"Help me, *te rohadék*. I'm ... dying."

Corky translated another cuss.

Danny tutted, wagged a finger, and strode out into the morning light. The temperature had risen quite a bit since he'd last been outside. Some might even consider the day balmy. He breathed deeply, enjoying the fragrance wafting across from the flower garden.

So good to be alive.

Danny stood over the writhing Blondie, but kept well outside arm's reach. He'd seen plenty of apparently dying men using their final breaths to take someone with them to hell. Imminent death gave some men superhuman strength and Danny wasn't about to give the little killer any sort of chance.

"Calling me a bastard isn't likely to elicit my sympathy or encourage me to help."

The dying man blinked rapidly. For a moment, he stopped squirming. "Y-You ... you understand Hungarian?"

Danny ignored the question and scratched at the stubble on his chin. He needed a shave.

"So, what am I going to do with you?" He raised the Beretta, aiming at the man's right eye.

Blondie squealed, tried to scramble away. The heels of his expensive shoes scraped the black and white tiles. Still gripping the wound, he propped himself up on his good elbow and wriggled, squirmed, using the elbow as a crutch to force himself away. Danny allowed him to reach the wall, before squeezing the trigger. The bullet shattered the planter next to Blondie's head, missing him by a few centimetres.

"In case you're wondering, that was shot number six," Danny said speaking quietly. "There are still thirteen left."

Blondie swallowed, recovered some poise.

"Bastard. Do you know who I am?"

"Not yet. Give me a moment. Corky?"

"*This is interesting. Facial recognition just matched Blondie to another Interpol Red Notice. Danny, you are looking at a geezer what goes by the name, Lajos Pataki. The little guy is Vadik's half-brother. Way to keep things in the family, yeah? Lajos is wanted on money-laundering charges,*" *but he ain't had his day in court yet. Want old Corky to dig a little deeper into the Pataki family?"*

"Only if you can spare the time, mate. Over."

Another chuckle. *"Corky's got plenty of time for his friends, Danny-boy."*

"Speaking of friends, things are getting a little hairy here, Corky. Would you mind briefing the captain? Think I might need some backup. Over."

"Yeah. Corky did that the moment facial recognition identified Csaba Nemeth."

"What did he say? Over."

"You can ask me yourself, Alpha One. Over."

The captain's voice over the comms system made Danny smile. He pulled in a deep breath and allowed his shoulders to fall. The captain had spoken over wind noise and the steady rumble of a motorbike's engine—Danny's Triumph Tiger. As far as they knew, the captain's own bike, a Honda Africa Twin, was languishing in a police car impound somewhere in Nottingham.

"Alpha One?" Danny asked. "When was I ever Alpha One? Over."

"This is your operation, Sergeant. You get the top designation. I'm Alpha Two, for now. Over."

Danny allowed his smile to grow.

"Good to hear your voice, Alpha Two. Where are you? Over."

"Close. Alpha Two, out."

The comms unit clicked, but the throaty rumble of the Triumph's engine remained. The rumble grew louder, coming from the direction of Derby. Danny followed the noise as it passed along the outside of the garden wall and slowed to approach the entrance to make the turn.

Moments later, the captain rode through the open gates and hammered along the driveway. Rear wheel sliding, gravel-spraying, he pulled the Triumph to a stop within centimetres of the portico steps. He propped the bike on its side stand and removed his gloves to unfasten his helmet's chinstrap. A moment later, he yanked off the skid lid, stuffed the gloves inside, and rested it on his lap. Dressed head-to-toe in black leathers, he took in the scene swiftly, paying particular attention to the man bleeding all over the chessboard tiles.

Fixing his brown eyes on Danny, he dipped his head.

"Morning, Sergeant."

Danny released his pent up breath.

"Morning, sir. Thanks for coming."

No doubt about it, Ryan Kaine knew how to make an entrance.

CHAPTER SEVEN

Kaine tore off the snug-fitting bike helmet and rested it in his lap. Beneath him, the Triumph's crinkling-hot engine smouldered, cooling quickly after the breakneck cross-country journey.

Corky's terse text message, "Danny's in trouble," together with the address and GPS coordinates to Prentiss House, had set Kaine off on his mad dash without a moment's pause for anything but a quick change of clothes.

If Danny needed Kaine's help, breaking the speed limit the whole way from Mike's place to Amber Valley seemed worth the risk.

He left Lara and Melanie Archer at the farm in the capable and protective hands of Mike and Connor Blake. After all they'd faced over the years, Kaine could afford to spare Danny a few hours of close support.

He'd earwigged Corky and Danny's comms traffic the whole way, but kept quiet for fear of breaking Danny's concentration. Although

Danny was more than capable of handling himself, if Corky thought him in trouble, that was good enough for Kaine.

He took in the scene in a flash.

Danny, a smoking, short-barrelled Beretta in hand, stood over Lajos Pataki, a man so pale he tilted the scale towards albinism.

Pataki sat, propped against the mansion's front wall, his left hand clamped over a shattered elbow. Blood oozed from the wound, squeezing between the man's fingers. Without treatment, he wouldn't last long. Even with treatment, his chances of keeping the arm looked slim to non-existent. Still, if Danny Pinkerton had shot Lajos Pataki, the man deserved it. No doubt about that.

"Morning, Sergeant."

"Morning, sir. Thanks for coming."

"Not a problem. Having fun?" he said, aiming for levity when none existed.

"Not really, sir. This arsehole"—he waived the Beretta at Lajos Pataki—"just ordered a couple of thugs to kill an innocent woman and one of his own men. I'm not overly impressed. How much did Corky tell you?"

Kaine hung the skid lid on the handlebar by its strap, dismounted the Tiger, and marched towards the entrance.

He tapped the earpiece. "Only that you might have stuck your finger into an electric socket. Trouble with the Magyar Mafia, I understand."

"Seems like it, sir," Danny said. He de-cocked the Beretta and slipped it into his jacket pocket. "I was going to let this fool die, but figured he might come in handy. Assuming he survives."

Pataki muttered something under his breath, but Kaine couldn't make it out. The pale-skinned man wasn't showing the same commitment or vitriol he did before being shot. Strange how often that happened.

"Sergeant," he said, squatting in front of the bleeding man, who seemed to be fading faster by the minute, "would you mind if I borrowed your belt, please? This unfortunate man seems to require a modicum of assistance."

While Kaine removed the injured man's jacket—without being too careful about it—Danny unfastened his belt, pulled it through the loops on his chinos, and handed it across.

"By the way, sir," he said, dropping to his haunches and lowering his voice to a whisper. "Who are you today?"

Pataki's eyelids drooped. He was in no condition to hear the conversation or care even if he did.

"Bill Griffin," Kaine answered, equally quietly.

Danny nodded. "Ah yes, I've got you."

Kaine had used the ID before and Danny knew the legend well enough to wing it if necessary.

Danny stood and re-entered the house, leaving Kaine to apply the tourniquet. He didn't bother being overly gentle about it. Pataki's eyes snapped open, and the poor man managed to summon up the energy to start screaming. Weak screams, though. Nothing powerful enough to startle the local wildlife.

"Mrs Prentiss," Danny called over Pataki's renewed raving, "Marian, you can come out now. I'd like you to meet a ... friend of mine."

A woman in her late twenties or early thirties emerged from inside the house. She leaned against the closed door, clutching its handle for support. Her gaze flicked between Pataki and Kaine, but finally came to rest on Danny. Judging by the colour of her bruises, she'd suffered a serious beating at some point in the previous two or three days. She had to be the woman Danny spotted when leaving the scene after they'd saved Melanie Archer.

Inside, Kaine smiled. Like him, Danny had a soft spot for people in danger. In the young man, Kaine had always recognised a kindred spirit.

"Wh-Who are you people?" Marian Prentiss asked, her voice cracking.

Bewildered and clearly under stress, she kept her focus on Danny, and spoke only to him.

"Marian," Danny said, standing close enough to offer support but not to intimidate, "this is Bill Griffin, a close friend of mine. He's come to help us."

"Hello," she said, looking at Kaine before turning to Danny and saying, "Robbie. My Robbie's in danger."

Danny quietened her with a touch on the arm and a headshake.

"I know. We're on it."

Kaine secured the belt tight. The bleeding stopped, but Pataki's arm below the injury matched the colour of Marian Prentiss' bruises. The restriction in blood flow would cause so much tissue damage, he'd likely lose the arm, assuming he survived the upcoming interrogation. Still, after ordering Marian Prentiss' death, the tiny Hungarian thug deserved no one's sympathy, and certainly wouldn't receive any from Kaine or Danny.

Kaine ripped the handkerchief from the pocket of Pataki's expensive-looking jacket and tried to clean the blood from his hands.

"Robbie?" he asked, climbing to his feet.

"Robert Prentiss," Danny answered. "Marian's husband. He's in trouble. Come on, we can show you."

Danny touched Mrs Prentiss' arm before leaning down, grabbing Pataki by the scuff of his collar, and dragging him inside the house. The injured thug tried to resist, but his heart wasn't in it and Danny wouldn't have put up with it even if he had been strong enough to kick up a fuss.

Danny headed to the left and dragged his load towards an open door. Pataki squealed, tried to stand, but Danny was having none of it.

Kaine gave up with the handkerchief and held it between finger and thumb. "Do you have anywhere I can clean up properly and dump this?"

Marian Prentiss pointed to her right.

"Through there ... the kitchen ... but it's a real mess."

"Thanks. No need to worry about that for the moment. You go with Danny, but stay well clear of Pataki. No telling what he's still capable of," Kaine said, smiling softly. "I'll be with you in a sec."

He waited for her to follow Danny and his barely struggling captive before heading into the kitchen. Marian Prentiss hadn't exaggerated. As it stood, the kitchen would never make the pages of *Ideal*

Home Magazine. It was, indeed, a real mess. Flies buzzed. They filled the air and crawled over dead meat and pools of claret.

Danny had blown out the glass panel of one of the doors leading to the garden. A man lay face-down and unmoving in a pile of shiny, blood-soaked pellets. No point checking for life or for danger. No one still breathing could survive for long with his face buried in a pile of shattered glass.

At the far end of the kitchen, a body hung over the bottom half of a stable door. The massive head trauma ruled out any chance of survival. No danger there, either.

Nice one, Danny.

The fact that Danny showed no signs of having been hit—or even overly stretched by the conflict—confirmed that he'd been his usual hyper-efficient self.

Kaine ran the sink's mixer tap until steam started to rise. Taking care to avoid the pieces of broken tumbler, he scrubbed his hands clean. The anti-bacterial soft soap in the fancy dispenser removed all traces of Pataki's blood. Nice smell, too. Flowers of some sort. He dried off on a fluffy hand towel and draped it back over its hanger.

He wouldn't want to add to the mess.

Somewhere in the other side of the house a woman screamed, "No!"

Kaine raced from the kitchen, his motorbike boots squeaking on the polished tile floor. The corner of his eye registered a puddle of red behind the stairs—a blood pool he hadn't noticed earlier.

He slammed open the door Danny and Marian Prentiss had walked towards earlier. It opened into a nicely furnished reception room with a large-screen TV, a larger three-piece suite, and a few other pieces of expensive furniture.

The huge leather sofa dominated the centre of the room, facing the enormous TV. Pataki sat on the floor, leaning against the sofa. Knees up close to his chest, head lolling to one side, injured arm cradled in the good one.

Marian Prentiss stood facing the screen, arms down at her sides, fists clenched. Tears streamed down her face, and her shoulders shook. Danny's hand rested on her upper arm trying to comfort the inconsolable.

The image on the screen came from the desk-level camera of a PC or a laptop. Kaine could just make out the keypad at the bottom of the screen. The background showed an office with shelves filled with books and folders. To the left, a window let in the sun's bright light, lending a warm yellow glow to the scene.

In the centre of the picture, dominating the shot, a man's balding head rested on the polished wooden desk. The head turned to the right, away from the bright daylight, and faced his right hand.

Held loosely in the hand, a gun—a Beretta like the one stuck in Danny's waistband—pointed at the laptop's screen. Gunsmoke wafted in a thin cloud around the muzzle.

The wound at the back of the head matched that of the man draped over the stable door in the kitchen. Blood and brain matter oozed from the fissure, still wet, glistening.

The man was dead.

Very dead.

CHAPTER EIGHT

WEDNESDAY 3RD MAY – Morning
Amber Valley, Derbyshire, UK

"Robbie!" Marian Prentiss wailed. "Robbie. Oh my God ... No."

Danny draped an arm around her quaking shoulders and lowered her into the settee. She scooted into the corner and folded in on herself, face in hands, knees curled up to her chest.

On the floor at the foot of the settee, Pataki sneered at the screen. He snorted and added a weak chuckle.

"You die next, assholes!"

"Bastard!" Danny screamed.

He leapt around the front of the rocking Marian Prentiss and stood over the sneering Pataki. The first blow—a left uppercut—snapped the man's jaw shut and might have broken a couple of teeth. The second—a right hook—whipped Pataki's head up and around to the left, slamming it into the settee's wooden arm.

As if on a loose spring, Pataki's head returned to face front, then flopped down. The jaw dropped onto his chest, and his arms hung loose at his sides. The broken fool stopped laughing. Stopped talking. Might even have stopped breathing.

Danny snarled, grasped a handful of Pataki's hair, cocked his right fist in preparation for yet another punishing blow.

Kaine reached out and grabbed Danny's arm.

"Sergeant. He's had enough."

Howling, Danny spun. Rage filled his eyes. He tore his arm free, made to lunge at Kaine, but stopped. Breathing deeply, he pulled back and shook away the rage.

He opened his fingers and released the tuft of white hair. Pataki's head lolled. The added weight took effect and the unconscious man keeled further over, leaning away from the sofa. Once the sagging body reached past the point of balance, it toppled slowly to the side.

Pataki's head hit the tiled floor in a sickening hollow crack, but he didn't seem to mind. Unconscious or dead men don't seem to mind anything much.

"Sir, I'm ..." Danny broke off. He breathed hard, staring at the reddened knuckles on both hands. "Damn it. I'm sorry."

Kaine gazed down at their captive. "Not a problem, Sergeant. I understand completely."

"Not that, sir," Danny whispered. "I meant, you know. Losing it like that. I don't give a flying fuck about this sod."

"As I said, Danny. Not a problem."

Kaine bent to check the pulse at Pataki's throat. Weak, but still present, surprisingly. Despite his emaciated appearance and the significant blood loss, the little Hungarian thug could certainly take some punishment.

"My only slight concern is, this"—Kaine took a breath and chose his next words carefully—"fool's in no position to answer our questions just yet. Shame that."

"Bastard deserves worse," Danny said, glowering at the fallen Hungarian, whose chest expanded and contracted slightly—the only signs of life.

A cough from the TV caught their attention.

"Can Corky do anything to help? Got loads of answers to plenty of questions, has your old buddy, Corky."

Mercifully, the image on the screen had changed. It no longer showed the mutilated head of Robert Prentiss, but it did show the unusually sombre face of their friendly neighbourhood "information acquisition specialist".

Kaine raised a hand for quiet. In a rare show of worldly understanding, Corky snapped his mouth shut and lowered his head a little.

At the far end of the sofa, Marian Prentiss, still in a tight ball, rocked slowly. She sniffled and tears cascaded down her cheeks.

"They killed Robbie," she mumbled. "He's dead. Oh my God. He's dead. What am I going to do?"

Danny turned but made no move towards her.

"Corky," Kaine asked, "is there any way you can put me through to the doc? We could do with her advice here."

Corky scrunched up his face in the approximation of an apology, and shook his head.

"Nah. Sorry Mr ... er, Mr G," he answered, showing how closely he'd been listening to Kaine and Danny's conversation, "but she's what you might call indisposed right now. Right in the middle of a ... er, little chat. Best not to disturb them unless it's absolutely essential, if you ask Corky."

"Okay, Corky. Point taken."

"Yeah, well, you did arrange the interview in the first place."

"Thanks for reminding me."

As if I'm likely to forget.

After he and Danny saved her life, Melanie Archer had turned down Kaine's offer to set her up with a new identity and relocate her to a place of safety. Instead, she wanted them to send her back to prison. Melanie wanted her day in court to clear her name and reputation.

An honourable but suicidal goal. A goal which Kaine flat out refused to allow.

Returning Melanie to prison would have taken her outside his arc of protection and placed her life in imminent danger—again. Kaine wasn't about to let that happen. With no other options available he'd cut a deal. If she could convince DCI David Jones of her innocence, she'd stay under Kaine's protection long enough for Jones to take up her case and, if possible, have the charges dropped. If not, she would take on a new identity and go into permanent hiding.

Reluctantly, she agreed, which led to the next stage in the story.

That morning, Kaine had visited the unimpressed police officer and "invited" him to interview Melanie Archer at Mike's farm. Jones had refused, but accepted a compromise offer. He'd interview Melanie Archer via a highly secure video link that Corky had designed.

Kaine wished Melanie good luck, and she needed it. Jones had been around the investigative block a few times and was no pushover. If Melanie could convince him of her innocence—as she'd convinced Kaine—Jones would move heaven and earth to help her. At least that's what Kaine was banking on.

By the time Kaine received Corky's summons, Jones was already ninety minutes into the interview—an interview that would determine the rest of Melanie Archer's life. With Danny in clear danger, Kaine didn't hesitate to leave Melanie with Lara, Mike, and Connor Blake as her personal bodyguard.

Kaine turned to face the TV screen.

"Corky, did you see what happened to Mr Prentiss?"

"Sure did. Got it all on camera."

The hacker winced and scratched the side of his face where dark whiskers showed clear against the paleness of his round cheek. His discomfort might have come from the beard, or from watching an actual murder in real time. Alternatively, not one to show much in the way of discretion, he might have been suffering from a bout of wind. Kaine could never tell with Corky.

"Want Corky to play the vid, Mr G?"

Question answered. Wind.

Kaine glanced at Danny, whose expression showed a combination of shock and exasperation, and shook his head.

"Just hold off a minute, please."

Kaine stepped over the comatose Lajos Pataki and approached Marian Prentiss. He dropped to his haunches in front of her, touched her shoulder, and let his hand fall away.

Her head jerked up. She stared into the distance through bruised and swollen eyes that registered nothing but hurt and sorrow. Tears flowed down her cheeks and dripped from her chin. She ignored them.

"Mrs Prentiss," Kaine said, keeping his voice low, "I can only imagine what you must be feeling."

She blinked and more tears fell, adding to the damp patch on her blouse.

"You can?" she said, her vacant gaze sliding up towards the TV screen which no longer showed the horror image that would remain with her forever. "Really?"

Yes, he knew exactly how she felt, but it wasn't the time for an extended discussion on their shared relationship with death.

"We're going to find out exactly what happened to your husband, and—"

"We know what happened," she snapped. Her voice strengthened and she focused on Kaine. "They killed him. Robbie would never have shot himself ... not while ... while knowing they were holding me captive."

Danny lowered himself to the seat beside her.

"Marian," Danny said, "is there anything else you can think of that might help us?"

"I already told you what I know. They abducted R-Robbie outside his office and held us here for two, no, three days. Until just now, I had no idea what they w-wanted. I do know that Vadik Pataki wasn't really in charge. He kept receiving phone calls and leaving the room. But Robbie knew. He must have known. H-He kept telling me we'd be safe ... kept saying it would all be over soon."

She broke down again. More tears leaked from the damaged eyes and ran in tiny rivulets down her glistening cheeks.

Danny leaned closer.

"You said you didn't know what they wanted 'until just now'," he said. "What tipped you off? It had something to do with the amount of money they were transferring, didn't it?"

She tried to dry her eyes with her fingers but without success. It only managed to spread the tears across her injured face. Kaine grabbed a couple of tissues from a box on the occasional table beside the sofa and held them out. She plucked them from his hand, scrunched them up, and dried her eyes carefully before continuing.

"The money transfer, the one point five million euros, it's exactly the same amount as we owe the bank. We re-mortgaged the house and took out an extra business loan to help us expand our operations into eastern Europe. It was a risk, but Robbie said it would pay off really quickly. Robbie ... Oh, God. Robbie!"

She worked the tissue again, taking care around the nose splint. Kaine gave her a moment before asking his next question.

"The business loan, it wasn't from a bank in Hungary, by any chance?"

"No," she said, sniffling. "We used *Third Way Enterprise Limited*. Based in Nottingham. The family has banked with them for years, ever since Robbie's father set up the company back in the seventies."

"But you were expanding into Hungary?"

She sniffled and nodded. "We set up a satellite distribution centre in Győr, using a local haulage company we found on the internet."

"Győr?" Danny asked.

Marian Prentiss hesitated.

"Sixth largest city in Hungary," Corky answered for her, reading from a screen somewhere off-camera. "'Bout two hundred kilometres northwest of Budapest. It's on the main through road to Vienna. Real close to the Danube. Apparently, it's been a manufacturing centre for car engines since—"

"Wikipedia?" Danny said. "Is that how you do it?"

Corky pulled in his chin and his eyes popped, clearly affronted by the insult.

"Bugger off, Danny-boy. Corky has his own information data-bases. He don't rely on no public-access, poorly curated bag of sh—"

"Thanks, Corky," Kaine said, interrupting what was probably going to degenerate into a rant followed by a detailed explanation of his information-gathering process. There wasn't the time.

The clouds of confusion started to peel away, and Kaine could see the clear sky of an explanation for the situation.

"Mrs Prentiss, is there anywhere you can go? A relative or a friend? Somewhere we can take you for safety?"

"No, no. I-I can't leave Robbie ... he needs me." She shredded the tissues and clasped her hands together, pressing them firmly into her lap.

Danny covered her hands with one of his and they disappeared beneath his beefy paw.

"Marian," he said, "Robbie's gone. He's beyond anyone's help. We need to take you to a safe place. Those men, the Hungarians, they haven't finished yet. They'll be sending others to find out what happened to their mates. You can't stay here, Marian. It's too dangerous."

"I-I know he's dead, but someone has to ... to make arrangements. There's the funeral to organise. No ... not a funeral, a cremation. Robbie hated the idea of lying in a hole in the ground, rotting away. We spoke about it ... Then I'll have to notify the family. His brother in Australia. Someone has to tell them what's happened. Everyone loved Robbie. They'll want to attend."

She was rambling, finding it difficult to stay focused.

"Mrs Prentiss, Marian," Kaine said, speaking louder to gain her attention, "is there anywhere safe you can go? Somewhere we can take you? A sister or brother?"

Startled, she shook her head, gathering her wits, her attention returning to the room.

"Rainey. Robbie's sister," she said. "She's lives in Grantham. Oh my Lord, she needs to know about Robbie. I'll have to tell her, too."

Her hand reached into the pocket of her jeans and came out empty.

"My phone, they took it. I-I don't know Rainey's number." She started crying again. "Sh-She's just moved house. I-I can't remember

71

her new address. No idea how to contact her. Don't know what to do."
She turned to Danny. "Help me, please."

"We will," he said, without checking with Kaine first.

Kaine didn't mind. No way was he going to let the Hungarians'
crimes go unpunished.

No way.

"Give Corky your sister-in-law's name and any information you
have on her. He'll find Rainey for you. Won't you, Corky?"

The round-faced man on the screen nodded enthusiastically.
"Yeah, 'course. No probs. You can rely on old Corky. Finding people's
part of what he does. Easy-peasy, lemon ... Well, you know."

Kaine stood and signalled for Danny to follow him to the corner
of the room, while Corky coaxed as much information on Rainey
Prentiss as he could from a distraught Marian Prentiss.

They stood close together watching the interaction between the
hacker and recently bereaved woman. Corky's manner and his gentle
encouragement was a revelation. Who knew he had such
compassion?

Danny turned his back to the TV screen and Marian Prentiss.

"Sorry for dragging you into this mess, Captain."

"Happy to help, Danny. You've done the same for me often
enough."

"Thanks, Captain. And about the way I spoke for you just then."
He winced. "I should have checked with you first. Chain of command,
that sort of thing."

Kaine arched an eyebrow. "Danny, it's like I said earlier. This is
your operation. I'm here as your crew. You're in command."

"What?"

"You heard me, Sergeant. Now, what's our next move?"

Danny's wide-eyed stare was a picture. He hesitated, clearly
unprepared for his latest promotion and his new role.

"C'mon, Danny. Pull yourself together. What's next?"

"Um. Right. Secure the site and move the principal to a place of
safety?"

Kaine frowned. "I saw what you did in the kitchen. Smashed

window and door. Might not be easy to secure this place without a team of builders and a whole load of time. Nice work, by the way. You against three armed thugs? Handled the situation well."

In a heap by the sofa, Pataki still hadn't moved and, given the blood loss and the treatment Danny just delivered, Kaine wouldn't have been surprised if he never moved again. At least not of his own volition.

"I had surprise on my side, sir. We probably won't have that next time."

"You're certain there'll be a next time?"

"Aren't you?"

Kaine raised an eyebrow. "Just making sure we're on the same page."

"Danny?" Corky shouted. "Corky's found Rainey Prentiss. She lives in Grantham alright. It's about fifty miles from where you are right now."

"Thanks, Corky," Danny said, closing on the TV screen.

To Kaine's intense relief, Marian Prentiss concentrated on Danny, pretty much ignoring Kaine and Corky. She'd clearly identified Danny as the leader, her saviour. Good. The deeper she fell under Danny's spell, the better it would be for her. Focusing on Danny minimised the chances of her recognising him as Ryan Kaine. It also meant she'd react quickly and unquestioningly to his instructions. It would help them keep her alive.

"Can you email me her address?" Danny asked.

"Already done that. Programmed it into your GPS app, too. You ain't gonna get lost. Not when Corky's got your back."

"Thanks, buddy," Danny said. "By the way, a couple of weekends back, I spent a few hours chewing the fat with Cough and Stinko."

"You did?" Corky asked.

Kaine raised an eyebrow. First he'd heard of it.

"Yep. They kept banging on about how boring life had been for them since Southampton, now they're working a low-paid security gig in Dudley."

"That right?"

"It is, indeed. Would you mind sending them an invite to join us at Rainey Prentiss' place?"

He glanced at Kaine, who nodded his approval at the excellent idea. If Danny hadn't thought of it for himself, Kaine would have asked Corky to find some warm bodies to strengthen their team. No telling the full extent of the enemy forces they faced. A bunch of wild Magyars wandering around the UK fully armed and happy to kill anyone standing in their way were not exactly the most amenable of tourists.

In any military operation, there was no such thing as being over prepared and, as regular members of Kaine's volunteer army, Ashley "Cough" Coughlin and Stefan "Stinko" Stankovic would bolster the defence team really well. And as for the defensive arrangements, Kaine had just thought of something.

"Mind if I make a suggestion, Sergeant?" he asked.

"Go ahead, Griffin," Danny replied, showing more confidence.

Inwardly, Kaine grinned. It hadn't taken long for Danny to grow into his leadership role. His *temporary* leadership role.

"Even if Cough and Stefan are both free and leave right away, it'll take them two or three hours to reach Grantham at this time of day. And, the fastest route to Grantham from Dudley will take them pretty close to us here."

Danny nodded, picking up on Kaine's meaning quickly enough.

"On top of which," Kaine added, "we have no idea how defensible Rainey Prentiss' place might be, or whether the Hungarians already have her address. Truth is, we don't have any idea what intel they have."

Marian Prentiss flinched but Danny raised his hand and gave her an encouraging nod.

"You never know," Kaine said, eyeing the TV, "they may have access to a Hungarian Corky of their very own."

The English Corky barked out a derisive cough.

"Yeah, like that's ever gonna happen. There's only one Corky, Mr ... G. And you know it."

Danny shot a look at the nicely dressed but crumpled heap on the floor. He ran his fingers through his thick, muddy blond hair, raking the wavy locks from his eyes. "Good thinking, Griffin. This place might be easier to defend until backup arrives. You hear that, Corky?"

"Sure did, Danny. Or should Corky be addressing you as Mr P since you're calling the shots now?"

Danny sighed and shook his head in irritation.

Business as usual from the hacking imp.

"Call me whatever you want, Corky. So long as you keep helping, I'm happy. Do you mind directing Cough and Stinko to us here, please? Tell them to drop everything and floor it."

"Yep. Already on it, Mr P." His accompanying chuckle made the situation feel just like old times.

"Thanks, Corky. Tell them I'll see them right. Full pay, normal bonus rates."

Again, Danny glanced across for approval, and again, Kaine gave it. Anyone who worked with them on any sort of operation whether for *The 83* or not, was entitled to proper reward for their efforts and compensation for any lost income.

They were engaged in a war with a Hungarian mob who were prepared to pay one and a half million euros for the "legitimate" ownership of an English haulage company. Holding Marian Prentiss hostage was the only way they could force Robbie Prentiss to sell up. It also showed that the Patakis weren't short of funding. Somewhere along the line, there would probably be an opportunity to reduce the Hungarians' bank account even further and add to his team's retirement fund.

On top of everything else, Marian Prentiss would need a healthy nest egg to see her through the oncoming bad times. Kaine saw no reason why the Hungarians shouldn't dip their bloodstained hands into their pockets to pay for it.

"Sergeant," Kaine said, "want me to secure the house as best I can? No telling when the next wave's going to arrive."

Given the lack of response to any phone calls Vadik Pataki might have made to his half-brother, the next wave might already be rolling on its way to Prentiss House.

"Yes please, Griffin. I'll help Marian pack."

Danny helped her up from the sofa. She gripped his arm tight, unsteady on her feet.

"We'll need to travel light," he continued. "One case. Essentials only. You might need your passport and all your bank cards. Just in case."

Kaine held the door open for them. As they passed, Marian Prentiss stopped and looked at him. They were of similar height and she didn't have to lift her head.

"You're not from the police, are you?"

Kaine tilted his head. "Actually, Mrs Prentiss, I am. In a manner of speaking." He ignored Danny's quizzical frown.

For once, Kaine wasn't lying. He'd spent the early part of the morning with DCI Jones—in a roundabout way, he had indeed just come "from the police".

On the floor, the small blond creature groaned.

Marian Prentiss whimpered and squeezed closer to Danny, and he hurried her from the room.

Left alone, Kaine turned his full attention to the diminutive thug.

"Hello, Lajos, old chap," he said, his delivery mocking. "Enjoy your little nap? Hope you're feeling a little stronger. You and I are long overdue our little chat."

Rubbing his hands together and baring his teeth in a predatory grin, Kaine approached the incapacitated, would-be assassin.

Lajos Pataki tried to scurry away, but his legs refused to work properly, and he flopped back against the side of the sofa. For once, fear reached his blotched, sweaty face, and terror filled his pale blue eyes.

Kaine allowed his smile to grow.

Lajos Pataki whimpered.

CHAPTER NINE

Kaine took two steps towards his terrified prisoner, but paused. It might be better to let him stew for a little longer. Gain some strength, soak up a little more pain. Let the fear work its magic on what was left of Lajos Pataki's resistance.

Still grinning, Kaine held up a finger in a "be with you in a moment" gesture.

"Corky?" he said, half-turning to the screen and keeping one eye on his prisoner.

"Yes, Mr K? ... Er, sorry. I mean, yes, Mr G?"

"That's okay, Corky. No need to keep up the pretence. You can call me Mr K in front of this piece of filth." He kicked Pataki's bloody ankle and the pallid man squealed. "He won't be in a position to tell anyone anything he learns here."

That's it. Build the pressure.

Crunched up against the side of the sofa, Pataki had taken up his earlier position, cradling his injured arm with his good one, injured leg stretched out in front, ankle still oozing the red stuff. Although the nasty-looking elbow wound had stopped bleeding—thanks to the tourniquet—the white-skinned man seemed even paler than before, almost translucent. Although it could have been a trick of the light.

"So, Mr K," Corky said, "you wanted something?"

"Yes please. Do you have time for a little show and tell?"

The chubby hacker frowned for a moment before the message got through. "Ah, right. You want to see Robbie P's ... er, you know, his demise?"

"If you don't mind. Now Mrs Prentiss is out of the room, I'd like to see exactly what happened."

Corky's face scrunched up again.

"It ain't pretty, Mr K." He looked away and started tapping at a keyboard out of shot.

Lajos Pataki's eyelids drooped and his chin fell towards his chest. Kaine kicked his ankle again. The man's head jerked upright, and his bloodless face creased in pain. Lajos blubbered but didn't seem to have enough fight left in him to scream or curse.

"Stay awake, Lajos. I'll have some questions for you in a minute."

"Okay, Mr K. Here we go."

The window containing Corky's face minimised and slipped up to the top left-hand quadrant of the TV screen, to be replaced with another, larger window. A still image of Robert Prentiss' worried, concentrating face filled the screen. He was alive, but not for long. The clock at the top showed 10:37:42.

"This is the film rewound to ninety seconds before the ... event. Want to see what happens next?"

"Please." Kaine nodded.

"Right you are, Mr K."

The clock started clicking forwards at normal speed.

Robert Prentiss blinked, his eyes fixed on the screen of his laptop, completely unaware that his computer's built-in camera was live, watching the watcher. He licked his lips. Sweat shone on his forehead, dripped into his eyes. He blinked again. Wiped his eyes with the back of a trembling hand. The man was terrified. As though he could foretell his immediate future.

Behind him, a shadowy figure moved closer to the screen, became clearer. Dark-skinned with wavy, shoulder-length hair and a closely trimmed beard, he rose from a seat in the corner and appeared at Prentiss' side, standing over him. Predatory.

Lajos Pataki's half-brother peered at the screen, also blissfully unaware of the spy in the box. He grinned, leaned closer to his prey. Prentiss tried to squirm away, but Vadik grabbed him by the scruff of the neck and pulled him close enough for their heads to touch.

"Where are you going to, my friend?" Vadik snarled, his voice deep and guttural. "Relax. It will not be long now."

From his small window at the top of the screen, Corky raised a hand before speaking. "They're watching the funds transfer from Hungary. It's nearly complete. Yep. And that's the final confirmation. Watch what happens next."

Kaine didn't need the commentary, or any encouragement. He focused his full attention on Vadik Pataki's actions, and his blank expression as he carried them out.

"That is it," Vadik said, releasing his hold on Robert Prentiss' neck and pushing him away. "You are now totally debt free, my friend. And my family are the proud new owners of *Prentiss Haulage Limited*. And what is more, everything is legal and above board. Although, pretty soon, I think we will change name of company to *Pataki Haulage Limited*. It is good name, yes?"

Vadik stood tall. He towered over the seated Robert Prentiss, who had to crane his neck to look up.

"Can I go now? You said Marian and I would be safe—"

"Yes, Robert." Vadik nodded and dropped his left hand on Prentiss' right shoulder, patting it like they were old friends about to part ways.

"All is good, my friend. We are finished now. There is only one thing left to do."

He pointed at the screen. Prentiss turned to look, a puzzled frown on his sweaty face.

Vadik removed his hand from Prentiss' shoulder and leaned away. His right hand came into shot, holding a Beretta. He held his free hand up to shield his face from the splatter, pressed the muzzle against Prentiss' temple, and pulled the trigger.

Robert Prentiss' head blew apart, blood and brain matter flew, spraying the screen with glistening droplets of red and solid pieces of grey and white. The corpse slumped forwards onto the desk.

One good thing. Prentiss didn't see it coming.

An unmoved Vadik Pataki took a white handkerchief from the breast pocket of his smart jacket and wiped the Beretta clean of his prints. He sniffed, took Prentiss' lifeless hand, and folded the fingers around the grip, making sure each was in the correct place. Once happy with his work, he dropped the hand to the desk. The lifeless fingers loosened and the Beretta slipped free, the smoking muzzle pointing at Prentiss' damaged head.

Vadik Pataki sniffed again. He stood back to admire his handiwork and nodded.

"Sorry, Robert, my friend," he said, voice flat, emotionless. "Losing control of your business was simply too much for you. A great pity for such a young man with such a beautiful wife, and so much to live for."

Without a backwards glance, Vadik Pataki turned and left the room, his job done.

From the time he raised the gun and took Robert Prentiss' life to leaving the office, Vadik Pataki's expression hadn't changed. He wore the lifeless face of a killer.

"That," Corky said, expanding his window over the top of the other, "is one cold mother."

"Any idea where he is now?"

"Not exactly. Corky's been searching the traffic cams, but not had any luck so far. One thing's for certain, he ain't in the Prentiss' Range Rover. That big beauty's still parked in the same spot they left it. Vadik must have changed motors."

"Thanks for that insight, Corky."

"Maybe that white-faced arsehole knows where his brother is."

Corky pointed to the injured Lajos Pataki who was still bleeding all over the rug. "Whatcha reckon?"

"He might do, Corky. Let's find out, shall we?"

Kaine fixed the predatory smile back on his face and spun to face the cowering man.

"Right then, Lajos. Are you ready for our little chat?"

CHAPTER TEN

WEDNESDAY 3RD MAY – Danny Pinkerton
Amber Valley, Derbyshire, UK

In the doorway to the Prentiss' master bedroom, Danny waited. Marian needed more time than they had to spare, but he didn't have the heart to rush her. She stood at the foot of the bed, staring at the dents in the pillows, head shaking, chin trembling. Close to losing it again.

"R-Robbie and I've only just finished decorating in here. H-He's never coming back, is he? ... Oh God, what am I going to do?"

Marian threw herself on the bed, pulled one of the pillows to her chest, hugged it as tight as she'd held onto Danny's arm while they climbed the stairs. Moments later, she raised the pillow to her face and took in its scent as though it held the essence of her husband.

Much more of this and he'd start choking up, but there was no time to dwell or to offer sympathy. Her life depended on him and the captain.

Danny approached the bed.

"Do you have a favourite bag?"

Lame. Bloody lame.

She lifted her head from the pillow. "Sorry?"

"Your bags. Where are they?"

"Handbags? I ..."

"No, your suitcases. You need to pack one overnight bag so we're ready to leave when my people ... my friends arrive."

My people! What am I, a gang boss?

"We're leaving?"

She couldn't have fully understood his conversation with the captain.

"Yes. It's too dangerous for you to stay here."

"But I don't want to leave. This is our home." Her face crumpled once more. "My home. This is *my* home."

"Sorry Marian, we have to leave soon, but it won't be for long."

I hope.

"As soon as we've sorted this ... situation out, you can come back."

He intended calling it a "mess", but that hardly seemed appropriate.

Her frown eased. "Oh. That's right, we're going to Rainey's, aren't we."

"That's the plan, yes."

Evasion seemed his best option. It would make it easier for her to cope, at least in the short term, but he doubted heading for the sister-in-law's place would be the best destination. Marian needed somewhere safer. Somewhere the Patakis wouldn't find her.

Definitely not the sister-in law's place.

Since seeing Robert Prentiss' shattered skull on the TV screen, Danny'd had time to think things through a little.

Based on the Patakis' meticulously planned operation to date, they were playing a long game, and playing it for keeps.

On his arrival at the house, Lajos Pataki had ordered Zapata and his buddy to kill Marian and set up Nemeth to take the fall. Marian's murder and Robert's apparent suicide would have drawn a coincidental, but neat little line under their operation. But Danny had blown their plans out of the water.

With Marian still alive and a potential witness, the Patakis' operation would remain compromised. From their point of view, she had to die.

With Marian Prentiss dead, no one would be left to argue against the legal validity of their acquisition of *Prentiss Haulage Limited*. And if her death could be made to look like another shock to Robert's precarious mental state, leading him to blow his own head off, so much the better.

Evil bastards.

Danny wouldn't let them win.

"Your bags?" he repeated, holding out his hand.

Marian loosened her death grip on the pillow and pointed to the left door of two let into the wall on the opposite side of the bed. "My dressing room."

"Okay, please pack enough for an overnight stay. Toiletries, makeup, whatever you need. Don't forget your purse and passport, and don't worry if you miss anything. We can always pick up what you need later. Make sure you're ready to leave when we are, okay?"

She nodded and took his offered hand. He helped her up, but she stood still, an automaton awaiting orders.

"Go," he encouraged. "Pack."

A strangled scream rocked up from downstairs and through the open door, almost loud enough to rattle Danny's fillings. Marian stiffened. Her hand shot up to her mouth.

"Don't worry, Marian. That's just Griffin. I imagine Blondie's not inclined to answer his questions. Won't take long, though. Griffin can be rather persuasive when something rattles his cage."

The scream started up again, but soon turned into broken sobs interspersed with rapid words, probably Hungarian.

Danny smiled. "Told you it wouldn't take him long. Now, please pack what you need. I'll check all the windows and doors on this floor are secure."

Lajos Pataki's capitulation seemed to spark her into life. She rushed across the room and tugged open the door to the dressing room.

"Marian?"

She stopped, turned. "Yes?"

"Is there access to the attic?"

"Um, yes. A hatch in the fourth bedroom closet, with a loft ladder."

"Any windows up there? Skylights or dormers?"

She closed her eyes as though trying to remember, then nodded. "Yes. One small skylight which leads to a metal fire escape fixed to the back wall. Halfway down, it's broken. Totally rusted away. We were going to replace it during the renovation, but ... the plans were put on hold. If you go up there, be careful. It's not fully floorboarded."

Danny cast his mind back to his night's obbo of the place. He'd been concentrating on the living areas, not the roof. Another bloody mistake. At the time, he'd been so certain that Robbie P was a coward and a wife beater, he'd skimped on the basics and hadn't run a full and detailed recon. He should have been more thorough.

If he'd asked Corky for more help. If he'd briefed the captain first. If he hadn't been such a gung ho, arrogant bastard, he might have worked it out earlier. If he'd done his job properly, Robert Prentiss might still be alive.

If ... if ... if.

Shit!

No point in beating himself up. He couldn't change the past. The only way he could help Marian Prentiss was to keep her safe and avenge her husband's murder. It would be Danny's apology to the dead man. Not that a posthumous apology would do Robert Prentiss any good, but it might give Marian closure. It might also go some way to easing Danny's guilt.

As usual, he was being a big selfish bastard.

"The fire escape. Is that the only access to the roof from outside?" he asked, pressing home the point.

Marian hesitated, then dipped her head in a nod. "Yes, but ... as I said, it's broken away. Useless."

"You're certain?"

"Positive. Robbie ... went up there the other day to put some boxes away." Her chin dimpled, close to breaking down again. "He ...

he said it would make a wonderful playroom or a granny annex for when the kids arrived." She blinked away the tears, sniffed, and straightened her shoulders.

Unable to watch her cry again, Danny turned away. "Okay, I'll be right back."

Danny left Marian to her make-work task. For the recently bereaved, keeping occupied helped.

He worked his way through the first floor—all four bedrooms, the en suites, the Jack and Jill bathroom linking bedrooms three and four, and a couple of large walk-in closets. All the windows at the front on the first floor were fitted with wooden shutters. They offered good protection from the winter weather before the advent of double glazing, but would be precious little defence against bullets. Still ... slightly better than glass. He closed and barred them, fastened all the windows, and shut the doors. None were lockable from the outside hall.

He found the loft access in the walk-in closet in bedroom four, where Marian had directed him. To Danny's relief, the aluminium loft ladder creaked and groaned in loud complaint as he climbed. Sight unseen, he considered searching for a screwdriver and removing the ladder entirely, but leaving it in place would be better. If any intruders gained access to the house through the loft, the ladder would be as good as a burglar alarm. Trapped inside a closet, the same intruders would be easy meat to his Beretta.

The loft door opened upwards on creaky hinges, and Danny popped his head through the opening. Daylight shone in a narrow beam through a dust-blurred skylight. He climbed up another two treads and leaned further through the narrow opening. Green chip-board flooring stretched out over the rear half of the cobweb-shrouded loft, its surface piled high with boxes, suitcases, and packing crates. The rest of the floorspace was open joists filled with granulated insulation, yellowed with age.

Danny climbed up and into the dusty, gloomy area. He skirted the narrow border of clear floorboard, shuffled along the joists, and made his way to the skylight. Metal framed and pockmarked with rust, the casement refused to budge—a point in its favour. Interlopers would have to smash the glass to gain entry. With the side of his fist he scrubbed some of the decades-old grime from the inside of the glass and tried to catch a view of the fire escape. Not a chance. The steep downward angle of the roof made it impossible. All he could see was a short run of moss-covered tiles, rolling fields stretching out to the horizon, and a grey sky.

Taking care not to slip from the joists and punch a ruddy great big hole through the fourth bedroom's ceiling, Danny retraced his steps to the opening and descended the ladder. The loft was a weak spot, no doubt about it, but he couldn't think of a way to secure it without time and a whole lot of ironmongery.

He slid down the ladder and dragged a chest of drawers in front of the closet door—the best he could manage at short notice. It wouldn't hold off a determined attack force, but it might delay one long enough for a defender to react. Time would tell.

CHAPTER ELEVEN

WEDNESDAY 3RD MAY – Danny Pinkerton
Amber Valley, Derbyshire, UK

By the time Danny made it back to the master bedroom, Marian had returned to the bed. A small, leather suitcase sat on the floor by her feet. Its pale cream matched the colour of the clutch bag in her hands and resting on the leather jacket draped over her lap. She'd removed the nose splint and applied enough makeup to cover much of the bruising. No amount of cosmetics could hide the swelling or mask the puffy eyes, but she looked a damn sight better than earlier and would no longer draw shocked attention in a crowd. She might turn a few heads, though. No right-thinking individual would ever call Marian Prentiss plain.

"Ready?" he asked, surprised at the speed at which she'd gathered her stuff together.

Marian nodded. "You told me to hurry."

"Excellent. Follow me, but prepare yourself for what you might find in the salon."

She sniffed and gently brought a hand up to her nose, which obviously still hurt, and probably would for a few days to come.

"Wouldn't worry me if your Mr Griffin gutted the ugly little bastard and spread his innards over the hearth rug. Fucker deserves everything he gets."

Danny tried not to let surprise show on his face, but doubted he'd managed the trick. Marian's anger was certainly justified, but her change of accent, from Royal Ascot on Lady's Day to EastEnders down-the-pub-at-the-weekend, was a revelation.

"Don't look so shocked, Danny. I wasn't born with a silver spoon shoved up my arse. Neither was Robbie. We worked hard for everything we got, and ... fuck it." She took a deep, slow breath. "There's plenty of time to grieve. Plenty of time."

She shifting the clutch bag into one hand, hooked her arm under the jacket and picked up the suitcase.

"Want me to carry that?"

She shook her head emphatically. "Not a chance. I can manage, and you need your hands free to keep us safe. Now come on, what are we waiting for?"

Danny couldn't help smiling. The new version of Marian Prentiss was even better than the earlier one. He took point and led her down the stairs.

The captain waited for them in the entrance hallway. He nodded at Danny, before turning to Marian.

"Mrs Prentiss, I've cleaned up in the lounge"—he pointed towards the salon—"and shifted the furniture around a little. If anything untoward happens, you can hide behind the sofa. As long as you keep your head down, it'll be as safe as anywhere else in the house. For the time being, I've left a chair in front of the TV."

"I thought you'd want me to hide in the cellar, again," she said, looking at Danny.

"Sorry, Mrs Prentiss," the captain said, adding an apologetic smile, "the kitchen isn't exactly secure anymore. The lounge is the safest place on the ground floor."

"Okay?" she asked Danny.

"Yes."

She headed away, her low-heeled sensible shoes clapping on the tiles. Danny made to follow, but the captain held out a hand.

"Sergeant, we need to talk."

"It's okay," Marian said without altering her stride or turning her head. "You've got work to do. I'll stay out of the way."

Danny waited for her to enter the salon and collapse into the upholstered chair the captain had placed in the middle of the room, in full view of the hall. She left the door wide open.

Through the open doorway, Danny could just about make out where the captain had pushed the sofa into the corner of the room, flipped it onto its front, and leaned the back against the wall. He'd placed the occasional tables on their sides at each end and piled the throw cushions all around. He'd made what looked like a children's play fort.

"Not much," he said, "won't stop many bullets, but it's the best I could manage at short notice. At least she's protected on two sides."

Danny sighed. "It's no better upstairs. I was thinking of having her hide under a mattress thrown over the bath, but if the Hungarians gain entry, we can't really defend the upstairs. It's too open."

"Might be an idea to reinforce it with a mattress or two. Any single beds upstairs?

"Yep. In bedroom three, top of the stairs. We can fetch them in a minute. By the way, we heard Blondie screaming."

"Who? Oh, you mean Lajos Pataki?"

His grin made Danny relax. Ryan Kaine didn't smile often, and almost never during an operation.

"Yep. Did he tell you anything interesting?"

"A few nuggets."

"Where'd you put him?"

He double-hitched his eyebrows. "Follow me."

The captain led Danny to the downstairs cloakroom and opened the door. Blondie sat on the floor, in abject discomfort, with his legs wrapped around the toilet. The ankle still seeped blood. The captain had secured his knees around the bowl with curtain cord.

For fun, he'd knotted the frilly ends into a neat little love bow, tied over a bowline. A second curtain cord secured the small man's arms behind his back, fixed above the elbows in a figure-of-eight double loop. A third cord, tied in a hangman's slip knot and secured to the u-bend, held Blondie's face over the open toilet bowl. If he struggled, or if he passed out, the noose would tighten and strangle the little fucker.

Without help, Blondie was going nowhere.

Danny couldn't help smirking. He leaned down to ruffle the nearly-white hair which wasn't even close to looking nicely combed anymore. Blondie grunted, turned his head slowly—very slowly. Threatening blue eyes glared at Danny, who wanted more than anything else to see what would happen when he flushed the toilet.

Naughty, Danny. Very naughty.

"One hundred thousand ... euros," Blondie croaked, his lips barely moving.

The words struggled to make it out through a restricted throat.

"Each," he added, after struggling to swallow.

The pale skin on his face had turned an unhealthy shade of grey and matched his injured arm—at least the part below the shattered elbow.

"To let you go?" Danny asked, ever so helpfully.

Pataki tried to nod, but the noose wouldn't allow it.

"Y-Yes, each," he managed. "Two hundred thousand euros. Cash."

Speaking was becoming a real challenge for the poor soul. Holding his head up seemed equally difficult. Danny winked and shook his head. Once again, the handle attached to the end of the chain dangling from the cistern looked ever so inviting.

"And how long would Papa Pataki let us live to spend it?" the captain asked from the entrance hall.

With great reluctance, Danny ignored the wicked enticement of the toilet flush and backed out of the cloakroom.

"Papa Pataki?" he asked, after shutting the door on the hapless and helpless mini-thug.

"Viktor Pataki," the captain said, leading Danny towards the kitchen. "According to Lajos there, Viktor Pataki, the Giant of Győr, is one of the three most dangerous men in whole of Hungary."

"Only one of three? Not absolutely *the* most dangerous?"

Had he not seen Robbie Prentiss' corpse, Danny might have been disappointed at only facing the third placed mobster.

"Not for the want of trying. Apparently, Viktor Pataki's working on it. He's hoping the acquisition of *Prentiss Haulage Limited* will help him weaken the opposition enough to climb the ladder. No point telling you what Lajos says is in store for us when Viktor learns how big a spanner we've jammed into his gearbox. I'll leave that to your imagination."

He opened the kitchen door and stepped aside.

The place hadn't changed much since Danny's remodelling, but at least it was now missing two bodies. The captain had cleared away the broken glass and shut the top half of the stable door. In spite of the smashed frame and shattered metalwork, it somehow stayed closed.

"How'd you repair the back door?"

"Found a toolbox in the pantry with a drill and packet of screws. There was enough residual charge in the drill to drive home a few of the screws. A rudimentary fix, but it should hold them back for a while."

"Pity we can't do anything about the broken glass."

Danny made to step through the doorway, but the captain threw out an arm to stop him.

"Wouldn't go in there if I were you, Sergeant,"

Danny withdrew his foot and placed it securely on a black tile.

"Been busy, Captain?"

Ryan Kaine smiled again. It was in danger of becoming a habit.

"Little bit," he said. "I rather wanted to encourage the bad guys to come in that way. A nice easy entry for them."

Danny looked again. The pile of glass granules had gone and only a bloodstain remained. He couldn't see any obvious booby traps, but that was the point. The captain knew what he was doing.

"IED?"

"Not exactly," he said, dropping the smile. "Aiming for low impact deterrents. Didn't want to damage the house any more than absolutely necessary. I don't imagine Marian Prentiss would appreciate us blowing her home to pieces, although she might want to move on after what happened here. Wanted to give her the option, though."

Danny scanned the rest of the kitchen. All the units on the left remained closed and sleek. The front two gas burners on the stove were alight and turned up to full. Two saucepans with lids stood on the unlit burners behind them.

"Are they on mains gas this far out of town?"

"Good question, and the answer's no," the captain said. "There's a propane tank in a shed out back. It's currently a little over half full." He added a stiff nod as though he knew exactly the way Danny's mind operated.

After working together for so long, he probably did.

"What's in the saucepans?"

"Only water. I'll set them to boil if and when our guests arrive, not before. Don't want all the water to evaporate. Nor do I want steam showing, which would be a dead giveaway."

Danny hiked an eyebrow and nodded. "Sounds like a plan. Where'd you put the bodies? In the cellar?"

"Nope. They were already starting to ripen so I thought it would be a good idea to move them outside with the compost. Found a helpful wheelbarrow out back next to the bins. They're resting peacefully. Not that it matters. Their mothers might miss them, but ...." He shrugged.

"No one else will."

"Exactly. Anything upstairs we can use?"

Danny twisted his lips. "'Fraid not. I've battened down as best I can, but this place wasn't exactly designed as a stronghold. Have you set up any other surprises?"

"One or two, but they're pretty basic. Might fool a raw recruit, but no one with any field experience."

"Given the way Nemeth and the two idiots in the compost blundered around, they didn't seem like well-trained military types."

"We can't rely on the next wave being such amateurs. Before I move the Triumph around to the back, what can you tell me about the battleground. I didn't have time to scout the area, but I'm guessing you did?"

Danny breathed deep. At least he hadn't ignored one of the first basic rules of fieldcraft—scout the terrain.

"The area's rural."

"Yep, I noticed that on the way in."

"Nearest village is four miles southeast. Closest neighbour's a farm, half a mile to the west. One road in and out. Fields all around, and a few farm tracks."

"West is downwind, that's good," the captain said through another grim smile.

Was he actually enjoying himself? Looking forward to the battle? Surely not.

"Good?"

"We won't be disturbed. Less likelihood of causing collateral damage, and few people around to call the police. We don't need the local plod stumbling into a battle and getting themselves hurt."

"Yes, okay. On the negative side, we have no idea of the enemy's strength or the firepower they'll bring along."

"Agreed. However many men there are, they're unlikely to have access to serious artillery, they'll be in the open, and they won't know who they're up against. I'd rather be in here than out there in all that open space. All we have to do is hold out until reinforcements arrive. I asked Corky to brief Cough and Stinko on what they're rushing into. They'll come armed and ready for war. Now, what's our position in terms of weaponry?"

Danny pulled out the Beretta, both Sigs, and the H&K he'd lifted from Zapata. The Sigs' mags held ten rounds each. One was fully loaded, but Blondie's held nine. The H&K had its full load of thirteen, and the Beretta still held fourteen shots.

"Forty-six shots in total. Enough firepower for a decent little skirmish."

The captain pulled three spare mags from his pockets, one for the

H&K and two for the Sigs. "I suppose you were a little preoccupied to search the casualties."

Danny grimaced and added a shrug.

"Things have been a little fraught, Captain. Thanks for saving me a job. I imagine you want the Sigs?" he said, offering them up.

Ryan Kaine was rated as an expert in most of the weapons used in the field, but his first choice would likely be a Sig P226. At least that's the make and model he'd used most often recently.

"Sig, H&K, matters not to me. You can keep the Beretta though. Barrel's too short to guarantee accuracy over twenty-five metres."

"Are we likely to shoot over that distance?"

"Not really, but I do like to be prepared." He pointed to one of the chess pieces that doubled as an occasional table. "I found an old reel of fishing line in the potting shed. Looks thick enough to have a decent breaking strain. While I move the motorbike out of sight, do you fancy setting a tripwire on the staircase in case anyone gets past whoever's guarding the upstairs?"

Internally, Danny winced. They both knew that the only way an intruder would make it past the upstairs defender would be if that defender was dead.

"Sounds like another decent plan to me."

"Yep, I'm full of them. Be right back."

The captain headed for the front door but stopped when one of the mobile phones they'd taken from the Hungarians started vibrating. It rattled against the others in the pile they'd made on the floor at the foot of the stairs.

"Should we answer it?" Danny asked.

The captain scratched his beard. "Let's leave it for now. No point tipping our hand just yet. Best to keep them guessing for as long as we can."

The phone vibrated ten times and stopped. Seconds later, another mobile started vibrating. They let it ring.

"They might be able to trace the phones. Shouldn't we turn them off?"

The captain shook his head. "If the men switched off their phones in the middle of a job it would definitely raise alarm bells. You never know, this way it might appear that they're too occupied to answer. We need as much time as we can."

"Okay, makes sense."

The captain left and Danny set to work.

The fishing reel was old and pitted with rust, but the nylon line it held looked in decent condition. The label showed its diameter as 0.20mm. It looked pretty strong but, a city boy born and bred, Danny knew nothing about fishing and had no idea of the actual breaking strain of a 0.20mm line.

Outside, the captain fired up the Triumph. Its engine note thundered and faded as he rode it around to the back of the house and out of sight of the entry gates.

Danny tied one end of the fishing line to the newel post with a slip knot and pulled hard. The line snapped, but only after he'd used most of his bodyweight. Probably strong enough, but to make certain, he doubled the line and anchored the tripwire to the metal spindles twenty-five centimetres above the third tread from the top. He climbed to the top of the stairs. From the first floor landing, the fishing line was pretty well invisible to anyone who didn't know it was there.

That'll do.

Danny returned to the ground floor, taking care to step over the line on the way down. In his time, he'd seen raw recruits come a cropper that way, and didn't fancy doing a header into the chessboard floor. Apart from the utter embarrassment, tile floors were pretty unforgiving.

Running footsteps crunched over gravel. A car door opened and closed. Another engine started and Lajos Pataki's SUV rolled away in the same direction as the Triumph. As usual, Ryan Kaine thought of everything, as he needed to. His ongoing freedom and his life demanded it.

At the foot of the staircase, Danny doublechecked his handiwork. The translucent fishing line reflected almost no light, which was the whole point. Even though Danny knew it was there, the trip wire wasn't easy to spot in the diffused light of the entrance hall.

Good enough for government work.

More running footsteps and the front doors opening announced the captain's return.

"Hope you wore your helmet, Griffin," he said, smiling and using the name for Marian's benefit.

"For that little ride? Didn't bother."

"You old rebel."

"Less of the 'old', Sergeant."

"What's the weather doing."

The bright light that flooded through the windows earlier had faded since the brilliance of the morning.

"There's a weather front moving up from the southeast. We'll have a squall soon. Anyone outside's going to get a tad damp."

A mobile on the floor started up again—the one they'd taken from Lajos.

"Time?" Danny asked.

The captain nodded. "I think so. Have you thought about what you're going to say?"

"Me? You think I should—"

"As I said earlier, Sergeant. This is your gig. I'm just offering a supporting hand."

Fuck.

Danny had no idea what to say. He bent to pick up the vibrating mobile and checked the screen. Unknown.

Helpful.

"Remember, Sergeant. We have Lajos Pataki."

Danny nodded, cleared his throat, and hit the speaker button so the captain didn't have to strain to listen.

"Hello. To whom am I speaking?" he said, using his father's telephone voice and heading towards the kitchen and away from Marian in the salon. The captain followed.

A couple of minutes later, he ended a rather unhelpful conversation with, "Are you, indeed? Better come prepared, Vadik Pataki. See you soon."

"That didn't go particularly well," the captain said, a master of understatement.

"No," Danny agreed, trying to think three steps ahead. "It certainly didn't."

Leading a team into battle wasn't the same as following, and Danny didn't feel up to it.

"So much for Lajos being our ace in the hole."

"Doesn't look like there's much love lost between our two brothers."

"Half-brothers," Kaine said, spreading his hands in a shrug.

"Ah, yes. Makes all the difference, I suppose. How long do you think we have?"

"No idea. Not long, I imagine. Better do what we can while we wait for backup. If you like, I'll take another quick tour of the grounds and the downstairs."

The captain was actually deferring to him. Would Danny ever get used to the captain asking his permission?

Not a chance.

For want of a better idea, he nodded.

"Er, yes please. I'll pop upstairs again. Those mattresses won't move themselves."

"Good idea."

They separated. The captain headed outside, one of the Sigs drawn and primed. Danny climbed the staircase, negotiating the trap. He made straight for the third bedroom, which contained the two single beds. A room for young guests. Both mattresses were heavy and densely sprung. Not brilliant, but they might stop a bullet that had passed its peak velocity. It certainly wouldn't stop a bullet fired point blank. Still, as Marian's protectors, their job was to make sure the opposition didn't get close enough to do any damage.

Danny hefted the mattress nearest to the door, balanced it on his head, and carried it to the balcony—no point in creating work for himself. He tossed it over the handrail, making sure it missed the chess pieces and landed well clear of the blood pool left by Nemeth.

Nemeth!

Christ, that first, short-lived fight seemed like such a long time ago, but it had been less than three hours. So much had happened in the meantime.

"What the hell have you stumbled into, Danny?" he muttered, shaking his head.

He returned to the bedroom, repeated the process with the second mattress, and carefully jogged down the staircase. He retrieved the first mattress and lugged it into the salon.

Marian sat with her feet tucked under her bottom, hands cradling her belly. She glanced at Danny then turned to stare blankly at the TV screen when he passed behind her and stacked the first mattress on top of the settee. He made sure to leave enough room for her to hide beneath it when the time arrived. *If* the time arrived.

Of course, there was always a chance that Vadik's threats were nothing but bluff and bluster. Even now, the murdering savage could be scurrying back to Hungary, tail between his legs.

Yeah, fat chance.

An ice cube's chance in a furnace.

The captain had told him—in concise detail—of the cold, determined expression on Vadik's face when he'd sidled alongside Robert Prentiss, spoke gently for a while, and then shot him in the head. As blood and brain matter flew, Vadik didn't bat an eyelid. According to the captain, Corky's video showed it in crystal clarity.

The video evidence meant one thing, Robert Prentiss' death could never be passed off as a suicide, not when Corky sent the recording to the police and the media.

No doubt about it, the Patakis' plot was dead in the water. Even without Marian to cry foul, their illegal acquisition of *Prentiss Haulage Limited* would be quashed in the courts. Danny knew it, and Vadik Pataki knew it. Soon enough, everyone who mattered would know it, too.

There would be no real point pursuing the matter, but Vadik Pataki would come. He would definitely come.

The man would want to exact a vicious revenge. Given the chance, he would kill Marian and anyone who protected her out of pure spite, and to cement his position at the top of the family tree.

A man in Vadik Pataki's world couldn't let the people who'd foiled his plans live to shout about it. If he did, his position as a leading thug would become untenable. His underlings would start circling, looking for a way to improve their place in the pecking order. They'd look for an opening, a kill. When one man fell, another would rise to take his place. The way of their world.

A shitty world populated by shitty people.

After stacking the second mattress in front of the first, Danny returned to the entrance hall. What had he forgotten? There had to be something.

The captain stepped through the front door and headed for the kitchen. Water needed heating.

Time to check the upstairs again. He left the salon and climbed the stairs one more time. If nothing else, the exercise was keeping him in decent condition.

"Danny!" Marian yelled.

The fear in her voice sent a chill running down his spine. He reversed his direction and sprinted to the salon. The captain burst from the kitchen and followed close behind.

Marian stood, pointing a trembling finger at the TV.

"Danny. The power's gone off!"

CHAPTER TWELVE

Vadik Pataki stared at the screen on his portable phone. No answer. No fucking answer?

"*Hülye kis vándor!*" he snarled, and ended the connection.

Stupid little wanker!

He scrolled through the portable's directory and tried two other numbers in turn. Neither Bence nor Milán answered. It wasn't like them to go dark in the middle of an operation. Both were a damn sight more reliable than Lajos.

Christ, a fucking gerbil was more reliable than Lajos, the moronic dwarf.

What the fuck's going on?

One simple thing was all he had to do. One simple thing. Kill the woman and Nemeth. Make it look like a home invasion gone wrong. Nemeth had plenty of form for such crimes. The British bobbies would lap it up. The only reason Vadik had sprung the paedophile bastard from jail in the first place was to set him up for murdering the Prentiss woman. It had been one of Vadik's many contributions to the overall plan—one that Papa admired so much.

Nemeth, the musclebound imbecile, had been so pathetically grateful for his unexpected release, Vadik and Papa had laughed about it behind his back. Oh, how they laughed. Lajos had joined in and tried to take credit for the idea. The damnable creature. As though he could have come up with such a brilliant concept.

Now, it looked as though something had gone wrong. Such things were bound to happen when one gave idiots like Lajos important tasks to perform.

One simple thing. That was all he asked of Lajos. The dwarf could not be trusted to do anything more complicated. If Vadik had his way, they would have left the runt in Győr, playing with himself or making good use of the girls Papa kept around the compound to service the men and generate some loose change. But no, Papa insisted he bring the runt of the litter along for the ride.

Papa wanted Lajos to learn the ropes, but the buffoon was led by nothing but his dick. The fool did not have a single working brain cell in his primped and styled head.

Why were the fuckers not answering their damned portables?

During his earlier call, Lajos claimed they were about to deal with the woman and Nemeth and would set up the scene as agreed. Yes. It would not be difficult to fool the British bobbies who could not find their pricks with both hands unless they were given a route map and a compass.

It would not surprise Vadik to learn that Lajos and the others had decided to make use of the Prentiss woman before ending her life.

Yes, that was probably the reason they failed to answer his calls. Stupid bastards. All three would pay for ignoring him. And the punishment would extend all the way to Lajos.

Papa might explode, but it would not be for the first time. Vadik could handle Papa these days. Age had dulled the fire in his belly. Papa, the "Giant of Győr", had lost much of his fearsome power. And besides, Vadik was the elder son and the likely heir. Papa would come around soon enough.

Papa knew the value Vadik brought to the family. Intellect, strength, and respect. Lajos, on the other hand, brought nothing but humiliation.

The cretin brought absolutely nothing of value at all. The dwarf was nothing. Never was, never would be. Illegitimate or not, Vadik would be the next in line.

He leaned forwards in his seat and tapped the driver's broad shoulder.

"Farzin, call yourself a driver? A blind man could do better! Faster, idiot. We are not tourists on a sightseeing excursion."

Farzin pressed harder on the accelerator and the big BMW powered ahead, thrusting Vadik into his seat. The hired man in the front passenger's seat whose name Vadik hadn't bothered to ask, threw a hand up to the grab strap, but kept his head facing forwards. Quite right, too. Whoever the shaven-headed fucker was, Vadik didn't want to see his ugly black face. Local mercenaries, English fucks, recommended by Cousin Ido and hired by the day, did not need to know where they were going or why. They were only required to do as they were told.

Farzin threw the BMW around a tight right-hander, fast enough to push Vadik into the side column. This was more like it.

"Faster, Farzin. What is the matter with you?"

"These shit roads, *főnök*," Farzin shouted in deference over the snarl of the high-powered engine. "They are more like the farm tracks back home. I thought England was supposed to be a wealthy country."

He fought the wheel and centred the SUV into the middle of the potholed and gravel-strewn lane.

"How far to the house?"

"Ten kilometres. Maybe fifteen."

"Get a move on. I want to wrap things up this afternoon and be back at the depot this evening, before the corpses are cold."

"Yes, *főnök*."

Although Farzin said yes, he pushed the SUV no faster. Vadik took it to mean the driver was already working the car to its limits for the conditions. No matter what Vadik said or thought, Farzin would take no unnecessary risks with the life of his *főnök*.

Farzin had been with the family since birth. He and Vadik had grown up together, played together, lost their virginity to the same whore. Farzin would give his life for the family—and Vadik would let him do that very thing.

Loyalty to the family was expected of everyone.

Lajos, Bence, and Milán had failed to report in, and they had failed to respond to his calls. Certainly, they might even now be in the process of completing their fun and ending Mrs Prentiss' life, but Vadik was the true son. The family had not become a massive regional power in Hungary by being stupid or careless.

So far, the English project, the project conceived by Vadik himself, had gone perfectly.

When Robert Prentiss made his initial and naïve approach to the family's representative, Vadik recognised the opportunity immediately and initiated the long-term plan. Apart from the fuckup when Nemeth had gone too far in his beating of the Prentiss woman, things were going smoothly. By agreeing to her hospital treatment, Vadik had dealt with the one and only glitch to the process, and they were almost done. Now, after killing Prentiss, they were right on target and precisely on time.

The only thing left to do was tidy up the loose ends and the first stage of the project would be over.

Although the plan had cost nearly four million euros so far—a mere drop in the piss pot—they now had fully legitimate access into the fifth richest country on earth. They also had unrestricted access to all the other countries along the main trading routes. In terms of its infrastructure, the family was now far more powerful than before, and it had good prospects of much more to come. They now had a bridgehead and would build upon it.

However, if Lajos had really fucked things up, he would pay. Not even Papa would be able to save him.

Vadik relaxed into his comfortable seat for another five minutes before trying again. He dialled Lajos' number first. It rang and rang. Vadik was about to give up and ring Bence when the call connected.

About fucking time.

"*Lajos, hol a faszban voltál?*" he shouted, but the dwarf kept mute.

He waited a couple of seconds, letting the ominous silence drag out before speaking again.

"*Lajos, te vagy?*"

"Hello. To whom am I speaking?"

A man's voice, English. Young, softly spoken. A pansy. Definitely not Lajos.

Shit.

Vadik ground his teeth. Something really had gone wrong. He fucking knew it. Damn the useless fucking dwarf.

Wait, no. Maybe Lajos had simply dropped his portable somewhere? It would not stretch the bounds of possibility for the idiot to lose his phone. This English pansy might have just picked it up.

"Hello?" the pansy spoke again. "I don't suppose that's Vadik Pataki by any chance?"

Fuck.

This was not a man who had found a portable phone, and for Lajos to give up his portable voluntarily was unthinkable. This softly spoken Englishman had taken it. By force. More than likely, he'd killed the useless fucker in the process.

Shit!

Not a major loss perhaps, but if anyone was going to kill Lajos it would be Vadik, not some pansy-voiced English queer. No one laid a finger on a family member and lived to laugh about it with their friends.

"Who are you?" Vadik growled, speaking in his best English.

"Does that matter? We don't know each other, you and me."

Pansy spoke lightly, as though he was about to burst out laughing. A madman without fear for his life?

We shall see!

Farzin glanced in the rear-view mirror, sensing trouble. Vadik nodded and rolled his free hand at him. Farzin returned his eyes to the road and coaxed even more speed out of their vehicle.

"Where is Lajos? Where is my brother?"

"Ah, so I *am* speaking with Vadik Pata—"

"Is he dead? Did you kill Lajos?"

"Of course not. Lajos Pataki is still very much alive. For the moment."

Vadik crushed the portable against his ear so hard it creaked in his fist. "Let me speak to him. I want to speak to my half-brother."

"I'm sorry, Lajos can't come to the phone right now. You might say he's a little indisposed."

"'Indisposed'? What is 'indisposed'?"

"He's on the toilet," Pansy answered, laughing.

He laughed long and hard, braying, goading.

The fucker was treating this like it was some sort of a big joke. A fucking joke! Vadik would teach the pansy-assed English queer not to joke with him and the family.

Vadik pulled the portable away from his ear and hit mute. He turned to the man at his side. Wilfred—the family's pet geek—sat, white-faced and travel sick, sliding his fingers over his computer tablet.

"Wilfred," he whispered, not fully trusting the mute button, "this English freak had taken the portable phone from Lajos. Can you give me its location?"

The seventeen-year-old with the perfect face of a choirboy, turned his head and grimaced weakly at Vadik. He looked as though he was about to vomit over his precious computer.

"It is at the Prentiss house, *fönök*," he answered, turning the grimace into a meek smile.

Wilfred had clearly heard Vadik's side of the phone conversation and had anticipated the request.

Good boy. At least one of the men was worth his pay.

Vadik released the mute.

"If you have hurt Lajos—"

"Of course we've hurt him, Vadik, old man," Pansy said, still gloating.

We? There was more than one. That was good to know. Information, after all, was power.

"How else would we have his mobile? And don't bother trying to call the other three idiots again, either. None of them will answer their phones ever again. Oh dear, such a waste of life. If we were sorry for killing them, we would apologise, but we're not, so we won't. After what they were planning to do to Mrs Prentiss, they don't deserve anyone's sympathy."

"So you *did* kill Lajos?"

"No, no. Not so. Only Csaba Nemeth and the other two clowns. Your little brother is still alive. At least for the moment. We thought we might need a bargaining chip."

Nemeth did not matter, he had already been marked for death, but Bence and Milán, dead? No! Vadik crushed the portable again. Pansy and anyone working with him would die. They would die horribly and slowly. Vadik would make it last days, weeks. He would transport them home and do the work in Győr. He always did his best work in Hungary.

"I make no bargains with you, *tündér*. Do as you please."

"That's disappointing. I thought you'd see reason. Thought maybe we could come to some sort of an arrangement."

"That will never happen."

"After all, we've scuppered your plans," Pansy continued, ignoring him.

Ignore Vadik Pataki?

How dare he!

"My plans? What do you know of my plans, Englishman?"

"We know everything Vadik, old chap. You will never own *Prentiss Haulage Limited*. Not legitimately."

The fucking English queer knows. He really does know. Fuck.

"We have a visual recording of you murdering Robert Prentiss. His death was no suicide. There's no way your little scheme is going to work."

Vadik closed his eyes. Everything he had planned was gone. All that time. All that money. Gone. Up in smoke. All that money wasted. But Vadik had invested so much more in the scheme than money. He had invested his reputation.

"Would you like to hear my proposal, Vadik?" Pansy asked, in his weaselly little voice.

Vadik paused.

A proposal?

Did Pansy want a cut of the profit? The queer did say something about using Lajos as a bargaining chip. Yes, he would listen to a proposal from the Pansy, *the dead man talking*.

Vadik smiled to himself.

Never let anyone say Vadik Pataki ever closed his ears to a business proposal. Perhaps there was still a way to come out of this mess with the business plan intact. There would be plenty of opportunity to dispose of Pansy and his people at some time in the future.

"Continue," Vadik said, with caution.

Yes, Vadik could agree to any proposal Pansy might suggest—and turn him and his friends into *steak haché* later. Preferably, when handing over the ransom money.

"Really? You're prepared to listen?"

"I will listen," Vadik growled the answer, could not help himself.

Wilfred held up his tablet, turning it to face Vadik. Four flashing dots on the screen, three close together and moving, the fourth static, showed their position relative to Prentiss House. Wilfred held up eight fingers. Eight minutes to go before Vadik would meet Pansy and his people face to face.

His pulse quickened in the way it always did before battle. Vadik really could not wait to see Pansy and deliver his own particular brand of justice.

He smiled in anticipation.

"Okay, here goes," Pansy said, still chuckling. "I'll hold off sending the video to the police for six hours."

"Six hours? Why so long?"

"Six hours will give you enough time to reach an airport and head for home before the police can put an All Ports Warning on your arses."

"You expect me to run away?"

"Yes, we do."

"What will you do then?"

"Nothing. Our only goal is to protect Mrs Prentiss."

"And Lajos? What of him?"

"We'll leave him for the police and they will make sure he receives proper medical treatment. The alternative is more bloodshed, and no one wants that."

"Medical attention. Lajos is injured?"

"Haven't you been listening, old man? Yes, Lajos is injured. Seriously so. Now, do we have a deal?"

"I accept your terms," Vadik said without hesitation.

He did not need to think about things. He had already made up his mind.

"No you don't. You answered too quickly. I don't believe you."

"Fuck you, asshole. The Prentiss house will run with blood!"

"Tut, tut, Vadik. It already does."

Another laugh rattled across the airwaves. Pansy seemed to be enjoying himself as much as Vadik would be doing when he reached Prentiss House.

"*Your* blood, fool! I am coming to kill you!"

"Are you, indeed? Better come prepared, Vadik Pataki. See you soon."

"*Rohadék!* Bastard! You will die!" he screamed, but the Englishman had already ended the call.

Vadik rammed the phone into his jacket pocket. It was time to kill. Quietly, while the SUV bounced him around and the seatbelt held him firmly into his seat, Vadik Pataki seethed and worked through his options.

If the first plan failed, a second must take its place. Vadik always had an alternative option ready. "Wilfred, where is it?"

The young man worked his tablet and showed him the screen once more.

"Good. Very good."

CHAPTER THIRTEEN

Wednesday 3rd May – Vadik Pataki
Amber Valley, Derbyshire, UK

"Are you ready, Wilfred?" Vadik demanded.

Wilfred's weak smile and nod did not exactly fill Vadik with confidence, but the family geek had never let him down before and today would not be the first time. At least it would not be, if Wilfred wanted to live long enough to see the sun rise in the morning.

"*Igen főnök. Készen állok!*"

"English, Wilfred. We are in England. It is good to practice our English here. We will need to visit many times now we have an operation in this country. It is ripe for plunder."

The baby-faced genius swallowed hard, his prominent Adam's apple bouncing twice before he could answer. "Sorry ... boss. Yes, I am ready."

"Where is the substation?"

Another deep swallow. Wilfred's weak stomach was troubling him more than usual, and the wallowing of the car as Farzin negotiated the narrow country lanes did nothing to help the legendary motion sickness of the poor fellow.

For a third time, Wilfred raised his tablet to show Vadik the screen. "It is just up ahead. On this side of the road. Two kilometres from the farmhouse, *főnök*."

"Farzin, we are close," Vadik called. "It is on the left up ahead."

Farzin eased his foot from the accelerator and the SUV's forward momentum slowed immediately. The black hired man in the front passenger seat released his hold on the grab strap and stretched his wide shoulders, preparing for action.

Good.

Months earlier, during the planning phase, Papa had questioned his insistence on hiring so many men on the first day of the takeover, but Vadik had made the case. And he made it perfectly.

Prentiss Haulage Limited employed thirty-three drivers, all of whom would have to give way to men loyal to the Pataki family. Vadik argued that issuing thirty-three drivers with their marching orders on the same day could prove challenging unless they had the support of an impressive-looking security team. At the time, the family only had a few people in the UK. Men employed by Cousin Ido and busy doing other things. There would not be enough numbers to ensure the family position. They could, of course, have shipped in many more men from Hungary, but such a mass family exodus from the homeland was certain to have aroused the interest of Europol and that would not do at all.

Including the dead Nemeth, Bence, and Milán, Vadik would have had but seven men at his disposal. He did not include Lajos in the number—he refused to see his idiot half-brother as anything but a liability. Vadik argued that such a force would not be sufficient to quell a riot, if one were to occur. As a result, Vadik, with the reluctant agreement of Papa, instructed Cousin Ido to hire extra men for a total of three days. Mercenaries charged less for multiple days.

As things turned out, the black guy and his men would be earning their exorbitant fees after all.

Vadik ran through the probabilities in his head. He was good at probabilities. In fact, he was good at most things.

How likely was it for the English Pansy to have the proof he claimed?

No. Highly unlikely.

The odds were high that Pansy was talking pure bullshit. Vadik doubted there even *was* a film of him whacking Robert Prentiss. Wilfred designed the system they used to monitor the online money transfer. And Wilfred knew what he was doing. He had even swept the Prentiss laptop computer for spyware, or whatever the fuck it was called. And Prentiss had not been away from Vadik for one moment after they left the house that morning. Not even to use the toilet. On top of that, at no stage during the money transfer did the little green light appear on the computer to show that the internal camera had been activated.

No, Pansy was talking bullshit. There *was* no film of the murder. There could not be.

Vadik nodded to himself. Maybe the day was not lost, after all. Maybe he could salvage the situation. Thanks to his brilliant foresight, he had plenty of men at his disposal. A small army.

Vadik allowed his smile to stretch wider.

There was a real chance that the overwhelming force of their presence would enable Vadik to save the day. If so, Vadik and his superior planning skills would prove to be the saving of the family fortunes once again. He would be the hero who snatched victory from the very jaws of disaster, as he had so many times before.

"There!" Wilfred shouted, pointing at the hedge on Vadik's side of the road.

Farzin stamped on the brakes and the BMW stopped alongside a gated fence that spread across a five-metre gap in the hedgerow. The fence encircled a small rectangle of land set back from the road. Vadik wound down his window and peered out through the opening. Inside the fenced-off electricity substation, four grey metal boxes the size of office filing cabinets hummed away with a threatening power. The words on a yellow warning sign attached to the fence said,

"*Danger of Death*". Above the words, a black triangle and a jagged bolt of lightning striking a prone body made the warning clear enough. Even without a good grasp of the words, he did not actually need to read English to understand the meaning of the sign.

Vadik glanced at Wilfred.

"Which one?" he asked.

"That one," Wilfred answered, sticking out a trembling finger.

He still looked pale from the travel sickness.

Bassza meg! Why am I surrounded by weaklings?

Vadik returned his gaze to the substation, lifted the walkie-talkie, and pressed the button on its side. "The one on the far right," he said, and released the button.

He twisted in his seat to study the BMW behind them, the first of two followers. A door opened and the muzzy-haired Eliasz appeared, carrying a giant pair of bolt cutters and a small backpack. He scurried towards the fence and paused long enough to snap the hoop on the padlock, before stepping through the unlocked gate. He carefully placed the backpack on the leaf-strewn gravel at the base of the target cabinet.

Eliasz scanned the immediate area before dropping to one knee in front of the backpack. After fiddling with something, he leaned away and slowly climbed to his feet. He backed away a few paces then turned and raced back through the open gate to his car, shouting, "Thirty seconds," as he passed Vadik.

Eliasz was not one to stop for pleasantries.

Vadik checked his Tag Hauer.

Farzin needed no instructions. He stamped on the accelerator and their BMW lurched forwards, all four wheels squealing. Vadik twisted in his seat once again, arm raised to read the dial on his watch.

Twenty-three seconds.

Again, his heartrate leapt. He loved the tension of the countdown to a fireworks display.

On the road behind, both black BMWs took off in pursuit.

Nineteen ... eighteen ... seventeen.

Farzin took them some two hundred metres before hitting the brakes, but Obasi in the middle car reacted late and nearly ran into the back of them. Fucking idiot could not drive for shit. Vadik bared his teeth at the second-rate wheelman and gave him the finger, but at least Obasi had shunted his car into the middle of the road. He knew better than to obscure the view Vadik would have of the upcoming pyrotechnics. The rear car pulled up tight behind Obasi. Its driver, one of the hired men, yawned and scratched his beard. How could anyone be bored by fireworks?

Eight ... seven ... six.

Vadik focused his full attention on the gap in the hedgerow, salivating in advance of the upcoming destruction.

Such a turn on. Such power!

Time slowed as Vadik's heart raced. He almost drooled. Beside him, Wilfred's breathing increased, too. The baby-faced geek loved this sexy shit almost as much as Vadik.

Two ... one.

Now!

A ball of orange surrounded in black smoke climbed into the air. The thumping, booming roar followed a fraction of a second later.

"*Kiváló.* Excellent." He pressed the button on the walkie-talkie once more and shouted, "Nice work, Eliasz."

A good leader always praised his men for a job well done.

Vadik held his hand up to Wilfred, who slapped it gently, chuckling like the little kid he was.

"You sure that will work?"

Wilfred nodded. "The house is now dark, *főnök.* As are all the farms and houses within two kilometres."

After watching the fireball dissipate into nothing, a contented Vadik faced front and settled back in his seat.

"Good. Prepare the device."

Wilfred slipped the computer tablet between his legs—guarding it along with his family jewels—and hauled his electronic bag of tricks up from the footwell. It must have fallen when Farzin jammed on the brakes. The device better not be damaged or someone would pay with an eye. Not Wilfred or Farzin, of course. No, they were too valuable. Maybe one of the hired men. They were expendable.

Food for cannons.

Wilfred worked the zipper of the bag and peeled back the padded flap. The shiny box with the dials and switches looked the same as it had back at base when Wilfred demonstrated the system in operation. At the time, the baby-faced genius had tried explaining how it functioned, but Vadik did not understand one word of the technobabble. He did not give a shit *how* it worked. Vadik only cared that it *did* work. And it did! Perfectly.

Wilfred pressed some buttons and turned a couple of dials. Finally, with an index finger poised over a red button, he turned to face Vadik.

"Are you sure, *fönök?*"

"Of course. Why ask?"

"While the signal jammer is in operation, we will not be able to use our own mobile phones or the walkie-talkies, either."

"No matter. Do it."

Wilfred shrugged and jabbed down on the piece of red plastic. Nothing happened.

"Is it working?"

"Yes, *fönök.*"

"How can you be certain?"

Wilfred smiled confidently. "It works. I am certain." The kid pointed at the walkie-talkie. "If you like, test it."

"Good idea."

Vadik hit the button and tried raising Obasi and Eliasz, but neither responded. Of course the jammer worked. Wilfred never failed him.

"Excellent, Wilfred. Excellent." He raised his hand and they shared another high-five.

"Farzin," Vadik said, "let us go. Time to finish these English cretins."

CHAPTER FOURTEEN

Wednesday 3rd May – Vadik Pataki
Amber Valley, Derbyshire, UK

Farzin worked the accelerator and the BMW rolled away, this time more sedately, giving Vadik time to take in the scenery of such a green and pleasant land. A land nearly ready for plundering.

The pothole-damaged road ran along the bottom of a verdant valley. Tall and overgrown hedges broken by the occasional stand of mature trees guarded either side of the narrow road, allowing a stippled and watery sunlight to filter through the new leaves. He recognised oaks, silver birch, chestnuts, but none of the others. Breaks in the hedgerows revealed rolling green fields dotted with cows.

The region reminded him of home. Miles and miles of nothing. Rural emptiness, no good for anything but farmers and wildlife. Not enough people to exploit. Perfect for vegetation and retirement villages, but Vadik was not yet ready to retire. Perhaps Papa might like the place, but nothing would drag Papa away from their stronghold outside Győr—the Interpol Red Notice made sure of that.

They rounded yet another corner and Farzin slowed the car even further. On their left, the hedge stopped and gave way to a red brick wall set two metres back from the road. The ancient and crumbling brickwork stretched up a little over two metres tall. It appeared almost imposing.

In Hungary, the walls protecting the family's main compound were topped with electrified razor wire, but the English did not allow such serious defences. Protection such as that broke something called the Occupiers' Liability Act. Complete nonsense. The Nanny State of Britain in action.

Farzin cursed, pulled the car onto the grass verge, and stopped.

"What is wrong?"

"The gates are closed, *főnök*," he said, pointing ahead to where the wall curved back and the black gates stood, locked firmly shut against each other.

The shaven-headed mercenary with the coal black skin and the wide shoulders in the front passenger seat sniffed wetly, like a truffle pig, and wiped his nose with the back of his hand. Filthy animal. Did the English not understand what handkerchiefs were for?

"*Szar!*" Vadik swore. "Lajos should have left them open for us. He knows nothing."

Vadik slid an enquiring look at Wilfred, who scrunched up his girly face.

"I cannot open them, *főnök*. There is no power to engage the motors."

"*Bassza meg!* Fuck! I did not think of that. Can we blow the gates open?"

Wilfred shook his head and shrugged one of his skinny shoulders.

"The plan was to make it look like Nemeth killed the woman in a bungled burglary. What will blowing the gates apart do to that scenario?"

"You make a good point, Wilfred. I always knew you would earn your keep one day."

"Thank you, *főnök*. I hope I earn my keep every day,"

Vadik reached across to ruffle the kid's floppy hair. Wilfred hated being touched. He also hated anyone doing anything that messed with his perfect hair—an affectation he learned from the fop, Lajos. What was it with the fashion conscious? A genius when it came to electronics, Wilfred was also a slave to his looks and to his personal hygiene. Not a problem. The black man, Truffle Pig, could learn from little Wilfred.

"You still have access to satellite photos on your tablet?"

"Of course, *főnök*."

Wilfred retrieved the device from between his legs and his fingers flew over its virtual keyboard.

"I downloaded one to the memory last night. The damping field made this essential."

He angled the screen so Vadik could see, but kept the device close. Wilfred used technology as his safety blanket, always had. This was fine by Vadik, although he had not always seen it this way. When he had first come across the pre-teen Wilfred, Vadik tried to prise a battered laptop from his filthy fingers. The little freak turned into a complete berserker. Vadik had to beat the kid senseless before the stupid fucker would calm down.

When Wilfred had finally regained consciousness and discovered that Vadik had not only returned the original laptop, but provided him with an expensive, state-of-the-art replacement as well, a grudging friendship was born. Vadik would never take a piece of electronic equipment from Wilfred again, and would kill anyone else who tried to do the same thing. Vadik offered Wilfred protection and, what was to Wilfred, vast sums of money. In return, Wilfred gave Vadik almost unlimited control over the virtual universe.

A fair exchange is no robbery.

Vadik studied the image afresh. The house and its outbuildings dominated the centre of the picture, and was surrounded by the brick wall—the wall they were now stopped alongside. The wall had two openings, one at the front which housed the automatic gates, and another at the rear for access to farm vehicles, Vadik assumed.

The place was trying hard to be a fortress.

Why Prentiss thought he needed to live in a house with such a wall was a mystery. It had done him no good. On top of which, no one had ever built a wall tall enough or strong enough to keep out Vadik Pataki. Especially since Vadik now had such a well-armed military force under his command.

Vadik rubbed his hands together. He had been sitting still for long enough. It was long past time for action. Time to see what the English Pansy had left of his half-brother. Time for people to die.

He pushed open the SUV's door and jumped into a cool English day. Farzin and Truffle Pig followed him out and around the back of the car to join all the others.

Wilfred stayed put inside the car. He would be of no use when things turned angry and was better off sitting in the warm and keeping out of the way.

Four men exited the second car. Three more climbed out of the third. They gathered around their boss, their *főnök*.

Vadik puffed out his chest. He was born for moments such as these. Born for leadership.

He started with the second driver. "Obasi, there is another gate at the rear of the property. Take Eliasz and the rest of the men and make entry there. Spread out around the grounds. Choose your individual targets as you see fit. Farzin and I, together with this one"—he pointed to Truffle Pig—"will enter here. I will lead the frontal assault. Obasi, you and your men will attack from the rear and the sides. Do nothing until you hear my signal."

To avoid confusion, he spoke to Obasi and Farzin in Hungarian, and repeated himself in English for the benefit of the hired men. No one would have any excuses.

Violence stirred the blood. Strong men were forged in battle, and Vadik Pataki was such a man.

He drew the Sig from its holster under his armpit and pointed it at the darkening sky. "Three rapid shots and we all go in shooting. Kill anyone you do not know. Understand?"

Obasi, Eliasz, and Farzin nodded and added their usual feral smiles. All three loved the battle as much as Vadik. Working for the family had bred it into them. Without their love of war and their lust for spilling blood, none would have survived so long.

"Remember," Vadik added, almost as an afterthought, and speaking directly to Obasi, "Lajos is in there. Save him if you can. According to the Englishman, Bence, Milán, and Nemeth are already gone. Of that, we cannot be certain, but if it is the case, we will avenge their deaths with bullets and in blood. Nobody in that house must survive."

Obasi and Eliasz grunted their agreement and raced away. The rest of their team filed into place behind them. They hugged tight to the brickwork until reaching the corner, where they turned right and disappeared into the bushes.

Vadik glanced up. The wall was not high enough to cause too much of a problem, but the occupants of any passing car would be interested to see someone scaling a wall such as this and in broad daylight. Not that another car had passed since their arrival.

Still, caution often paid dividends.

"Farzin," he said, reverting to Hungarian, "pull the car up to the driveway and park in front of the gates." He turned to Truffle Pig. "You, Englishman. Move the other cars alongside this one. Make sure they block the view from the road."

Farzin and Truffle Pig followed his instructions. The boot of each car stuck out into the road a little, but not enough to risk a sideswipe from a passing vehicle, who would see them as visitors waiting to be granted access. At least, that was the way Vadik hoped it looked.

"Wilfred," he called and signalled him to wind down his window. "Listen for my instructions. I will tell you when it is safe to cancel the signal damper."

"What are you going to do?" Wilfred asked, still pale from sitting in the back of a fast-moving car, but recovered enough to form a question.

"Me, Wilfred?" he said, baring his teeth in a snarl. "I am going to kill me some filthy English fuckers."

This was going to be a good day for the Pataki family, and a great day for Vadik. He racked a slug into the chamber of the Sig and turned towards the gates.

. . .

121

Wednesday 3rd May – Vadik Pataki
Amber Valley, Derbyshire, UK

Farzin and Truffle Pig joined him at the closed gates. Not much had changed since he had dragged Prentiss away in the Range Rover that morning. Not that he expected to see many changes, but he was almost disappointed. After the unexpected loss of power, Vadik half-expected to see Pansy and a couple of his friends running around in a panic, trying to escape their inevitable demise, but no.

All was silent and serene.

The gravelled drive stretched out in a left-hand curve towards the front of the imposing two-storey house. Someone, perhaps Pansy himself, had closed the wooden shutters on the upper floor. Not that it mattered. A few wooden panels would not protect those inside from the upcoming heavy assault. It might delay the inevitable for a moment or two, but no longer.

He paused for a moment. Something was missing. What?

There were no cars parked on the drive in front of the house. Lajos would have left his car there. Interesting. Maybe Pansy and his spineless friends had scurried away after all.

Smiling, he turned to face Wilfred, who had raised the window half way. "Can you locate the portable phone from Lajos?"

Wilfred shook his head. "Not without deactivating the damping field."

"Do it, but only for as long as absolutely necessary. We do not want to give the English time to telephone the police."

"One moment."

Wilfred lowered his head in concentration. A minute later, no more, he raised his head again. "Sorry, *főnök*. All the mobiles have been powered off. I cannot locate any of them."

"Is the damping field back in operation?"

"Yes, *főnök*."

"Good. Keep it that way until we are finished here."

Vadik nodded to Farzin. "We need to find an easy way in. I do not wish to climb walls in this suit."

Truffle Pig sniffled again, stretched out a powerful arm, and heaved against the left-hand gate. It opened, squeaking loud enough to wake the dead. Poor Bence and Milán came to mind. Vadik ground his teeth. He would avenge their murders. By God, he would.

"What the fuck?" Vadik could not hide his surprise.

Truffle Pig peeled back his upper lip in a tooth-glistening smile. It made him look insufferable. So damn smug.

"I've seen this before. It's a safety feature in case of a power cut and the backup generator packs in. Owners don't want to be locked inside their houses in an emergency."

Vadik nodded.

Perhaps Truffle Pig had his uses after all.

"Yes, of course. I knew that," Vadik said, unwilling to throw the big black Englishman a bone. "This is going to be easier than expected. Follow me."

Vadik sidestepped through the part-open gate and, crouching low, raced for the bushes lining the wall. He found a spot with a good view of the front door and waited for Farzin and Truffle Pig to reach him. The tree he hid behind had a thick, gnarled trunk. It would afford him excellent protection.

He waved Truffle Pig away, pointing him towards a less dense covering of bushes and shrubs. Until the attack, Truffle Pig would be hidden from the house, but when they advanced he would draw fire. Farzin, he kept close.

What next? Had he missed anything?

Think, Vadik.

Prentiss House was quiet. Doors shut, windows and shutters closed. What, or rather who, lay inside? Who and how many? The place could be empty, or teeming with people. Not knowing was the worst thing. Normally, Vadik knew everything. Normally, he planned for every conceivable eventuality. But this situation was alien. Facing the unknown intimidated him. It was ... scary.

Fuck.

Was he scared?

No, certainly not. In his line of business one could not show fear. Any display of fear would be the end of him as a leader.

In an instant, Vadik found breathing difficult. It was as though a rock pressed against his chest. He tried to swallow but could not generate the spit. It was one thing to stomp on a cowering lowlife when you had control of the situation and good men at your command. But this time, they were on foreign soil, and half his men were no more than hired thugs. He had no idea of their capabilities. No idea whether they would even obey him. This made things different. He had no idea what to expect. Vadik did not like the situation one little bit.

He took a huge breath.

Bassza meg! Fuck it!

He was Vadik Pataki! The Lion of Győr. First born son of the Giant of Győr. He would tear apart Pansy and all his miserable people. He would rip out their throats and gorge on their carcasses.

Vadik stepped out from behind the protection of the tree and filled his lungs with cool English air.

"Englishman!" he bellowed. "Are you ready to die?"

CHAPTER FIFTEEN

Wednesday 3rd May – Danny Pinkerton
Amber Valley, Derbyshire, UK

"Sergeant!" the captain called from the entrance hall. "We have company!"

Danny shot a reassuring smile at Marian. At least, he hoped it was it reassuring.

"Wasn't expecting them so quickly," he said, keeping the tension from his voice although his heartrate had risen a little as his old fighting buddy, adrenaline, coursed through his system.

It was the same at the outset of every fight. A friend prepping him for battle: increased breathing, blood pumping hard through pliant arteries, muscles warming, senses tingling. Hearing, vision, sense of smell, all heightened. Everything working towards protecting him from death. The joint thrill and fear of battle. Addictive and terrifying in equal measure.

Danny approached Marian and stood close enough to see her shaking.

"Don't worry," he said, reaching for her upper arm, "Griffin and I have got this sorted. It's what we do."

While the captain locked and bolted the front doors, Danny led Marian to her den and covered her with the cushions and the mattresses.

"Stay down, and don't move until the captain or I come for you."

"The captain?"

She stared up at him through the darkness, eyes shining with tears and terror.

"Griffin, I meant Griffin."

Fuck's sake, Danny. Get a grip!

"All these military terms, guns, traps. Who are you?"

"This isn't the time for our life story. We'll tell you later. I promise."

Assuming there is a later.

Her arm snaked out from under the mattress, and her hand took his.

"Save me, and save my baby, please."

Baby?

"Jesus! You're pregnant?"

Duh, stupid question.

"Thirteen weeks," she said, voice trembling. "Robbie didn't even know. I was planning to tell him this weekend, but ... but ...."

Fresh tears spilled from the bruised eyes.

"Congratulat—Shit, I mean, we'll get you both out of this, Marian. I promise."

"Thanks, Danny. Thanks for ... everything."

"My pleasure," he said, meaning it.

He hurried out of the salon and into the hallway. The captain, on one knee and peering through the gap between curtain and wall as Danny had done hours earlier, signalled him keep low.

"What do we have?" Danny asked, whispering for some unknown reason. No one outside could have heard them through the double-glazed windows.

"A few seconds ago, three cars parked up the other side of the gates. Three men just wandered into the grounds. They're hiding in the bushes to the right, there. See them?"

Danny scoped out an area, fifty, maybe sixty metres distant. A little outside the maximum effective range of their handguns, but not by much.

With a Sig P226, Ryan Kaine was better than ninety-nine-point-nine percent of the shooting population, but even he was limited by the weapon at his disposal. Danny's marksmanship wasn't bad—in military terms, he was first class—but compared with Ryan Kaine, he was barely adequate.

A rifle would have been handy, but no one expected to be involved in a pitched battle in the middle of the Derbyshire country-side. With an SA80, Kaine could have shot the eye out of a potato at more than four hundred metres—even further with the right sights. Give him a sniper's rifle, a British made Accuracy AS50 for instance, his effective range would be well over a mile. Once, on a still day, Danny'd seen him hit the centre of a target at over eighteen hundred metres. The captain had an uncanny ability to steady himself for a shot. He also had a deadly eye.

However, since they didn't have access to an Accuracy, they'd have to wait for the opposition to draw closer.

"Yep, I can see them, sir. Not making much of a job of hiding."

"They can't be certain we're in here. See the one in the suit cowering behind the tree?"

"Just about."

"That's Vadik Pataki."

"You reckon?"

"I recognised him from the video, and he's the one doing all the talking. The other two are minions. Spot the one hiding behind the yellow bushes further over to the right?"

Danny slid his gaze across.

"Nope."

"He's the only one in camo gear. The way he moved, he's had military training. Probably a mercenary. The other two are in business suits, easily spotted. They've been bumbling around like amateurs. I'll keep a close eye on the merc."

Danny pitied the man in camouflage gear. At the first sign of aggression, there would be one less merc on the Pataki payroll.

"I'm surprised there are only three," Danny said, more out of hope than expectation.

"Three cars out there, Danny. There'll be others. Vadik probably let them out earlier. I imagine they're trying to outflank us."

Danny couldn't find any reason to argue with the assumption.

"How come he's so well supplied. How's he managed to raise a bloody army so quickly?"

The captain cocked an eyebrow in a shrug.

"No idea. Perhaps we'll get the chance to ask him sometime."

Danny tilted his head.

"Perhaps."

They watched the activity outside in silence for a few moments. Nothing much happening.

"Better get ready, I suppose."

"You want to take upstairs or down?" the captain asked.

They should have discussed their preferred positions earlier, but there hadn't been a whole lot of time.

"You're the better shot, sir. Maybe you should take the first floor?"

Kaine held up one of his borrowed Sigs and shook his head. "These popguns have a limited range and you don't know how I've setup the kitchen. You also know the upstairs and the grounds better than me. If you don't mind going upstairs, I'll be happy here."

Danny nodded. "Makes sense. Have you tried to contact Corky? My earpiece is dead."

"Mine, too. And the mobiles are out. The Magyars must have a signal jammer."

"That's not supposed to happen. Corky said these comms units are failsafe."

"Nothing's failsafe, Danny. Not totally. You know that."

Too true.

"If we can't use comms, maybe the Magyars can't either."

"Hopefully. We'll have to do this old school. Battlefield hand signals wherever possible. I trust you haven't forgotten them?"

Ouch!

"Captain, you cut me, sir. How many are we facing do you think? Did Blondie tell you anything about their UK strength?"

"Claims there are dozens of them on hand, but he was lying. Can't be that many. Either way, we should be able to hold out until Cough and Stinko arrive. Won't be long now."

"Couple of hours at the most," Danny said, although he didn't really have a clue.

They were both looking on the bright side—the only side to look on if you didn't have any other information to go by. Ryan Kaine and his men were nothing if not optimists. Famed for it the world over.

"Draw them in close, Danny. Good hunting."

"Yes, sir. Good luck."

Danny turned and headed for the staircase.

"Oh, Danny?"

He'd only taken two steps. He stopped and glanced behind him.

"Sir?"

"Don't forget the tripwires," he said, a big wide grin splitting his bearded face.

"Funny, sir. Very funny."

"I try."

His smile fell and he held up a hand. "Hold on, Danny. Movement."

Danny returned to the observation point and stared over the captain's shoulder. Vadik Pataki had stepped out from behind the oak tree. He stood, feet shoulder-width apart, left fist planted on his hip as though he owned the place, which he probably did—at least technically. His right fist held a semi-automatic handgun, but Danny couldn't see enough of it to make out the manufacturer.

"Englishman!" Vadik bellowed. "Are you ready to die?"

"Cocky beggar, eh?" the captain mumbled. "I'll take him out the moment he comes a few steps closer."

"Should I answer?"

The captain shot him a lightning quick glance, but immediately returned to eyes-front. "Not for me to say, Danny. This is your party. Keep it short, though. No telling how long the rest of them will take to surround us."

Thank you, Captain. Very helpful.

"If our roles were reversed, what would you do?"

The smile returned. "Someone once said, 'jaw, jaw, not war, war', but in this situation, I'd be inclined to keep schtum. The longer we can keep them guessing the better. Vadik might start getting cocky and come a little closer."

"Englishman!" Vadik screamed again. "Are you in there?"

"Nope," Danny whispered, "no one here but us chickens."

"Speak for yourself, Danny."

"Kidding, Captain. It's an expression."

"I know, lad. I know."

Vadik ducked back behind the oak.

"Guess I'll head upstairs then?" Danny said, his mouth suddenly very dry.

The captain nodded.

"Good luck, Sergeant."

Danny stood and headed for the stairs.

"Oh, Danny?"

"No, sir. I won't forget the bloody trip wires."

A repeated joke was never funny. Danny ignored the summons and climbed the stairs, two treads at a time. He stepped over the fishing line and, once safely on the landing, he stopped and turned to face his subordinate for the day.

"Sergeant," the captain said, more forcefully, "remember that propane tank?"

"Yes, sir," Danny answered.

The captain's focus remained fully on the view through the window.

"It's fifteen hundred litres, stored in the wooden shed on the other side of the rear courtyard. About thirty metres away."

"Yes, sir?"

Where's he going with this?

"It's plastered in yellow warning stickers. Apparently propane is highly explosive. Rather dangerous."

"I know that, sir. I'll be careful where I'm shooting."

"Thought you might like to know I loosened the outlet regulator."

Ah, I see.

"You did?" Danny asked, smiling.

"I did. Thirty metres is probably a safe distance from the house, wouldn't you say?"

"Probably."

"The shed's likely full of gas by now."

"I imagine so. And even if it isn't, propane's heavier than air, right?"

Yep, he and the captain were on the same wavelength.

"Indeed it is, Danny. If you find it necessary, remember to aim low."

"I will, sir."

Danny headed for the second bedroom, which overlooked the back of the house and gave him the perfect view of the shed with the propane cylinder. Explosive, heavier-than-air gas meets red-hot bullets. A match made in hell?

Time would tell. He crouched next to the window and settled down to wait.

Won't be long now.

CHAPTER SIXTEEN

With Danny in charge upstairs and Kaine's back protected by an expert, one he trusted, he was able to concentrate fully on the frontal attack.

Prentiss House was as good a place as any to make a defensive stand. Solidly built from stone and with an open aspect—they had a good field of view through most of the three-sixty degrees—the two of them ought to be able to hold off an infantry attack. Even though the opposition had superior numbers, of the three he'd seen thus far, only one had demonstrated anything like a decent knowledge of fieldcraft. Unless the attackers had some form of heavy artillery, he and Danny ought to be able to hold them off for a while.

All other things being equal.

From the first time they'd met, in a downmarket bar in Germany, Ryan Kaine always knew Danny Pinkerton would make a good leader. In a fairer world he'd have been an officer, but a lack of academic qualifications had held him back, kept him in the ranks. This operation had shown Danny's true worth. He'd listened to all the advice on offer, weighed up the options, and made the correct decisions. At least, he'd made the same decisions Kaine would have done, had their roles been reversed.

Yep, Danny had Kaine's back, and Kaine had Danny's. The best either could hope for in the current situation.

Marian Prentiss' quiet whimpering underscored the reason for the battle. The poor woman was terrified, and understandably so.

Although she'd been beaten and had learned of her husband's death in the worst possible way, she'd coped remarkably well. The inevitable heartbreak would arrive soon enough but, so far, she'd handled the situation better than anyone could have hoped.

She would survive. No matter the odds against them, he and Danny would protect her.

Vadik stepped out from behind the tree once more. He raised his gun and shot in the air three times.

"A signal!" Kaine shouted for Danny's benefit, probably unnecessarily.

The two men to Vadik's right jumped out of their concealment, and raced towards the house, yelling and screaming, guns in hand. Aiming for "shock and awe".

Good luck with that, guys.

Vadik Pataki stayed put, behind the tree. Safe and sound.

A true coward leading from the rear.

Shouts from the back garden and from each flank added to the noise and told of more attackers. Danny would handle them.

Kaine licked his lips and regulated his breathing. Maintaining control was key to their survival. He knew how things worked in battle. He had plenty of first-hand experience.

The two men closed the gap between front gates and house at different rates.

The one in the business suit, long dark hair flowing, zig-zagged, darting from tree to shrub to bush. In an attempt to minimise his exposure and put off a defender's aim, he was taking much longer to cross the open ground. This one held his gun in his right hand, swinging it wildly with the finger on the trigger. The fool was more likely to shoot himself than anyone he actually targeted. An amateur's mistake.

Kaine dropped him to the bottom of his list and focused on the one in the military fatigues—the dark-skinned mercenary.

Carrying the top-heavy bulk of a big man wearing a ballistic vest, Merc ran tall and fast. He held his Sig two-handed, tucked close, pointing down and to the side. For safety, Merc's trigger finger ran along the trigger guard.

He headed for the window, Kaine's window, not the heavy front doors, pounding the gravel pathway with long, loping strides.

Fifteen metres ... ten.

Still, Kaine waited.

At five metres and without changing his stride, Merc aimed and fired two rounds at the window. Kaine turned and crouched as the windowpane exploded. Glass fragments speckled his back, his hair, and clattered on the tiles at his feet.

Still roaring, Merc dived headlong through the shattered window and through the billowing curtains. He twisted in mid-flight, executed a perfect barrel roll, and righted into a crouched shooting stance, gun raised, raking the room.

Three metres away.

A sitting duck.

Kaine, his back pressed into the wall, shot him in the thigh, a couple of centimetres above the bent knee. An automatic reaction shot, he barely needed to aim. The Sig's report echoed throughout the entrance hall.

Merc screamed and rolled onto his side, pulling his gun around, searching for a target.

Kaine's second round entered Merc's right upper arm, tearing through the bicep where it joined the deltoid. The third shattered his gun hand. The Sig dropped, clattered to the floor. Kaine's fourth round hit the Sig, and it skittered across the tiles and into the foot of the staircase, out of Merc's reach and useless, its handle destroyed.

The howling, cursing mercenary crawled awkwardly away—

using one arm, one leg—heading for the apparent area of safety behind the staircase. Kaine let him go and turned towards the window.

Longhair had finally reached the open space of the driveway. He slowed, stood tall, and lowered his weapon. He cocked an ear. The screaming from the back garden stopped. Only Merc's howling curses broke the silence.

Longhair turned and called to Vadik, whose head popped out from behind the tree. The leader smiled and raised his fist. Longhair responded in kind. Did they assume Merc had won, and the house had already fallen?

Really? That naïve?

Vadik waved Longhair away, barking his orders in Hungarian. Longhair called a response, turned to face the house, and headed straight for the destroyed window. He wore the confident smile of a winner and strolled along with a swagger.

Upstairs, a window smashed and five rapid gunshots destroyed the silence—the multiple sharp cracks of Danny's Beretta. Muffled shots answered, fired from the back garden.

Kaine edged sideways, out of hiding, but he stayed protected by the stonework. He exposed little of himself, but one eye, his gun arm, and the whole of his Sig.

Longhair's smile dropped, along with his jaw. He stopped dead.

Kaine took careful aim. At this range, another certain kill shot.

"Don't do it, son," Kaine said, quiet as a prayer.

For a silent microsecond that stretched out into infinity, Longhair hesitated. He blinked, and his gun arm twitched. Slow. Much too slow.

Kaine's Sig coughed, and the 9mm bullet punched a neat hole in Longhair's forehead. His face had no time to register the shock of impact.

Slowly, the longhaired man in the dark blue suit toppled backwards, dead before he'd made another scuffmark in the gravel path.

Out back, a battle raged. Men shouted, screaming instructions in Hungarian and English.

Gunshots exploded upstairs from Danny, and outside from the men in the garden. Small arms fire, no rifles. A blessing.

Windows smashed, shattered glass tumbled.

Kaine checked the front. Longhair lay on his back in the gravel drive, arms spread wide, staring up at the cloud-filled sky though unseeing eyes. Vadik stayed hidden behind the tree, out of harm's way, at least for the moment. In hiding. A true armchair general. Damned coward. Kaine had no immediate worries from that front.

He turned to face the entrance hall. To his right, on the kitchen side, Merc's smeared blood trail led behind the staircase where Danny had hidden the first body, Nemeth. A useful place away from prying eyes. A good place for a sniper's nest.

He crouched, arcing away from the blood, moving towards the front room where Marian Prentiss lay hidden. His full attention targeted the staircase. He reached the corner where front and side walls met. His view of the darkened space behind the staircase increased. A booted foot, heel on floor, toe pointing up. A lower leg dressed in camouflaged trousers, stretched out straight, bleeding from the bullet he'd taken in the thigh, unmoving. An empty left hand, covered in blood, also unmoving.

Dead?

Still crouching, still hyper-cautious, Kaine raced to the side of the staircase, dropped to one knee. Leading with the Sig, he leaned forwards. Merc's face, pale from severe blood loss, turned towards him. His mangled right arm draped across his chest, the crippled hand still, useless.

Kaine raised the Sig, took aim at the man's left eye.

Brown eyes blinked. Merc lifted his good hand a few centimetres from the floor, all he could manage in the form of surrender.

"No, please," he whispered, pain clear in his low voice and written deep on his face. "No!"

Kaine lowered the Sig. He patted Merc down, but found no more weapons. "Stay right here until this is over. Move, and I'll kill you. Understand?"

"Understood. I'm done."

Merc's hand dropped back to the floor. He closed his eyes, and his chin fell to his chest. Kaine stood and made his way back to his lookout point at the window.

"Captain!" Danny called from the first floor landing above him. "Two flankers coming your way! They've split up."

Kaine stood. He leaned out and craned his neck to look up. Danny smiled down at him. He looked cool, unflustered.

"Thanks, Danny. You okay?"

"Yes thanks. This is fun."

"How many others your side?"

"Apart from the flankers, three for definite. There could be others. Don't know for sure. Bloody propane didn't ignite."

"Didn't think it would. Worth a try though, eh?" he said, winking.

Danny shook his head and sighed. "Now he tells me!"

Kaine was about to say something inane like, "Good luck", or "Take care", but Danny pulled back from the banisters and moved out of sight.

Take care in a gunfight? Yeah, right.

He turned towards the kitchen.

Time to get serious.

CHAPTER SEVENTEEN

WEDNESDAY 3RD MAY – Danny Pinkerton
Amber Valley, Derbyshire, UK

Danny had found the ideal vantage point—bedroom two, overlooking the back garden. It held perfect views of the sprawling lawns and well-maintained borders, and took in most of the outbuildings, including the triple garage, the potting sheds, and the hut plastered in yellow warning triangles.

Unfortunately, that was as far as the "ideal" part of the equation extended.

The original glazing in the Victorian sash windows might have added character, but the flawed manufacturing process and the ripples in the glass it produced made them useless as a sniper's optical aid.

Opening a window wasn't an option at this point, either. If he opened them too early he'd give away his position. He needed to wait.

Danny hated the wait.

Breathe easy, Danny. Take your time.

Three gunshots rang out in rapid succession.

"A signal!" the captain called out.

At the front, men screamed. At the back, more men howled and yelped. Loads more.

Four men, no, five. Maybe more out of sight.

The five broke clear of the trees and bushes planted to hide the perimeter wall. Three wore incongruous business suits and shiny leather shoes. Two others, the ones on the extreme flanks, wore camouflaged military fatigues and armoured vests. One of the soldiers, a huge man with ebony skin, wore the green beret of a Commando. The other was bareheaded, hair cropped short—a squaddie. All five men carried handguns.

No rifles. No grenades. No heavy artillery.

Some good news, at least.

Danny pulled in a long, slow breath and released it, puffing out his cheeks.

Five attackers at the rear, maybe more, and who knew how many the captain faced at the front.

The odds weren't brilliant, but at least they held the high ground and had the protection of thick stone walls. To access the house the enemy would have to cross open ground.

Danny twisted open the lock securing the windows and heaved on the lower casement. Stuck. He tried the upper one. Also stuck.

Thick layers of paint had sealed them both shut.

Shit a brick.

He should have tested the bloody thing earlier. The antique glass would have to go. A shame, but he had no alternative. No time to move positions, and none of the other bedrooms gave such a commanding view.

Danny cast his eyes around the room and chose the only thing movable. A lampstand. He removed the fancy tasselled shade, found the balance point, and held it like a javelin—heavy base end first.

He lined up the makeshift spear, checked his aim for the first shots, and waited, breathing deep and slow.

Still yelling, screaming, the three suited attackers raced towards the rear of the house, bounding over tufts of long grass. They funnelled towards the path leading to the outbuildings that formed the small courtyard.

Still some distance away, the two flankers disappeared behind the walls of the house. Commando would find the kitchen and the shattered bifold door. Squaddie would find nothing but boarded windows until he reached the front of the house and the captain.

Together, Danny and the captain would deal with any others as they showed themselves.

Danny could do nothing about the flankers. He ignored them and drew his attention to the three in the middle as they slowed and gathered closer to the smallest shed.

Two shots shattered a downstairs window. A man yelped—not the captain.

The three suited men in the garden stopped shouting, slowed their approach. They exchanged glances but kept moving, pointed their guns towards the house, aiming low. None looked up to the first floor.

The narrow cement path forced them into single file. A man with close-cropped dark hair and bright blue eyes took the lead. The others followed in tight formation and they drew closer to the propane shed.

Three paces. No more.

Danny pulled back his arm, taking the spear with it.

Blue Eyes drew level with the shed, passed it. Middle man's head turned. He frowned.

Danny punched the base of the lampstand through the glass, dropped it through the opening, and squeezed the Beretta's trigger again and again.

Five shots, five hits.

Holes peppered the shed's lower panels. Nothing happened. No expected explosion.

"Fuck!"

The suits scattered, started firing. Bullets flew through the broken sash, one tugged at Danny's hair. He snapped his head back and pulled into the protection of the room.

He reached up to his hairline. The fingers came away clean.

Jesus. That was close.

Keep your bloody head down, Danny. Don't be so fucking cocky, you idiot.

The three-man barrage continued. The window's upper pane disintegrated, shards dropped to the carpet. Bullets tore holes in the ceiling. Plaster fell in clumps and powder. The light fitting broke and the small chandelier crashed to the floor.

Danny leaned out, emptied the Beretta into the propane shed. Still nothing happened. So much for a fucking gas explosion. Ordinary bullets didn't work. He needed incendiary ammo—or flares.

Downstairs the captain's Sig fired once more. Fell silent.

Firing from the three-man assault team continued, shooting from cover, but shooting wild and wide. Time to move. Rather than crawl through slivers of broken glass, Danny hugged the wall, skirted the room, and slid through the open doorway. Out in the hall, he dropped full-length to the carpeted floor and crawled towards the next bedroom. He slithered closer to the balcony and stole a glance down at the entrance hall.

The captain stood by an open window, Sig pointing through the smashed glass. On the chessboard tiles behind him, a blood smear trailed towards the side staircase, leading to where Danny had hidden Nemeth from Marian. So long ago.

"Captain!" Danny called. "Two flankers coming your way! They've split up."

He glanced up. "Thanks, Danny. You okay?"

"Yes thanks. This is fun."

"How many others your side?"

"Apart from the flankers, three for definite. There could be others, I don't know. Bloody propane didn't ignite."

"Didn't think it would. Worth a try though, eh?" he said, winking.

Danny shook his head and sighed. "Now he tells me!"

The captain ducked below the windowsill and scrambled towards the kitchen. By now, Commando would have reached the back of the house. Danny left the captain to his business.

A momentary pause in the shooting gave Danny time to enter the third bedroom and shimmy to the window. Another sash, but these had replacement double-glazed panels. Modern.

From his new position, he could make out the arm and shoulders of Blue Eyes as he crouched beside the propane shed, taking pot-shots through the window of the bedroom Danny had recently abandoned. He stopped shooting to reload. The others kept firing, but none of the shots came anywhere near Danny in bedroom three.

With his back pressed firmly into the wall, he stood, stretched out an arm to release the window catch, and dropped into a crouch once again. This time, the lower casement slid up easily, but the movement drew Blue Eyes' attention. He screamed a warning and started shooting, firing rapid, wild shots.

While the bullets thumped into the plasterwork around him, Danny took careful aim, and fired twice. The first shot fell short, kicking gravel and dust into Blue Eyes' face. He jerked back and away, gun hand raised.

Danny fired again. Missed again.

Shit. Come on, Danny.

The Beretta's slide shot back, locked into place. Gun empty.

He released the spent magazine, reloaded a fresh one and fired again, three shots. Blue Eyes bucked, took a slug in the shoulder. Screaming, he dived to his side and crashed through the shed door. He scrambled though the opening and slithered into the darkness, still screaming what Danny imagined were either orders to his buddies, or Hungarian expletives.

The other two kept shooting. Danny pulled away from the window as the bullets screamed into the room and destroyed Marian Prentiss' careful renovation job.

Still, that was the least of her problems.

During another lull in the shooting, and with the door to the propane shed standing invitingly open, Danny rolled out from his hiding spot and tried again. He aimed and unloaded four shots into the blackness. Bullets thumped into the shed's concrete base, ricocheted up and away.

Sparks flew, but once again, nothing happened. Danny scrambled back into the room and away from the window.

Breathing hard, he cursed.

Fucking propane wouldn't take the hint.

From the darkness below, Blue Eyes shrieked in clear terror. He must have finally realised where he'd taken cover. The smell of escaping gas would have cut through the acrid tang of spent gunshot. In a blind panic, Blue Eyes raced through the door and smack into one of Danny's bullets. It hit him in the chest, centre mass. No ballistic vest. No protection.

With his momentum halted, Blue Eyes lunged to his side, and collided with the doorjamb. His gun popped, sparks flared, a bullet flew, and the percussive fireball arrived straight from hell.

Blue Eyes exploded through the open door on a cushion of gas and smoke as though shot from a cannon. He flew three metres though the air before he hit the ground and the flames engulfed him.

The heavy boom rattled Danny's teeth and thumped through the stonework. The whole house trembled.

For a moment, Danny stopped breathing. His ears rang, high-pitched and painful.

Black smoked billowed through the shattered windows, filling the bedroom, sulphurous and bitter. He blinked stinging tears from his eyes and pulled up his jacket to cover his nose and mouth.

Still his ears rang, momentarily deafened.

"Well, that was fun," he said aloud, but it sounded muffled over the pounding, high-pitched tinnitus.

He risked a quick glance through the window. In a fraction of a second, the courtyard had turned from a quaint and charming rest area into an active warzone. Almost as quickly as it started, the raging fireball died, leaving behind it gentle flames licking at the remains of the shed and a blown-out propane cylinder that looked like a part-exploded bomb from the last world war.

The brick walls of the triple garage remained intact, but two of the blackened wooden doors would need a new paint job at the very least. To an inexperienced eye, the two smouldering husks lying on

either side of the shed might have been firebombed garden orna-
ments, but were the remains of two suited attackers. Of Blue Eyes,
there was no sign. He might well have been vaporised by the
explosion.

As battlefield deaths go, at least it had been quick.

Danny tore himself away from viewing the carnage and ducked
back into the bedroom. The flankers would have been protected by
the house's granite walls. They, and anyone else, would still be
dangerous. The captain might need a hand.

With the tinnitus still dinging away strongly, Danny opened his
mouth wide and waggled his jaw. Someone once told him it would
help overcome the effects of compression. He was game to try
anything.

His ears popped and creaked. The tinnitus receded a little.

Well, that worked.

The creaking continued.

Danny waggled his jaw again. More creaking. Metallic creaking.

Fuck.

The loft ladder in bedroom four!

The crunching, splintering of a closet door being shouldered
open and the tumbling crash of an upset chest of drawers spurred
Danny into action.

Danny barged himself away from the wall and raced through the
room. He reached the open doorway as a shaggy-haired man dressed
in a crumpled business suit burst from bedroom four and out into the
landing. He caught sight of Danny, yelled, and snapped off the light-
ning-fast whip shot of an old-school gunslinger. The doorjamb
exploded centimetres from Danny's head.

He dived backwards into the bedroom, rolled sideways and came
up on one knee, his shoulder pressed into the safety of the solid wall.

Stupid move, Danny.

Shaggy fired again. Four more shots. Two hit the open door, splitting the upper panel. The third careened though the opening and
punched a neat hole in the opposite wall. The fourth slammed into
an upholstered chair. A throw cushion on the chair exploded.

Feathers flew into the air and fluttered down like gentle snowfall on a still day.

Keeping low, Danny pushed his gun arm through the doorway and fired blind. Five rapid shots aimed in a cross. Shaggy grunted. Stopped firing. Something solid thumped onto the carpeted floor.

Yeah, right!

Sneaky sod was playing dead.

I'm not falling for it, dickwad.

The chances of hitting a moving target when firing blind weren't worth trying to calculate. Danny ground his teeth. What to do?

Think, man.

Danny held the advantage over the smartarse Shaggy. He knew the layout of the upstairs. Shaggy didn't.

The bedroom layout.

Of course.

Danny smiled. He'd been such a bloody idiot. If he hadn't needed his free hand to push himself up off the floor, he'd have used it to slap his forehead for being such a dingbat.

Time to use some smarts for a change.

Crouching low and keeping tight to the bedroom wall, Danny made his way to the door of the Jack and Jill bathroom that separated bedrooms three and four. He held his breath. Slowly, he turned the handle and pulled. The door opened silently. Inside, no sound, no movement.

He risked a quick glance.

Bathroom empty. White tiles, white ceramics, chrome fittings. Same as he'd seen earlier that morning.

Danny stepped inside, padded across the floor, reached the second door and stopped. He pressed his ear to the panel. More silence.

Beretta raised and ready, he leaned aside, yanked open the door, and burst into bedroom four. Shaggy stood with his back to Danny, hiding behind the outer door, waiting for Danny to show himself in the hallway.

"Freeze, dickwad!"

Danny didn't expect it to work, but had always wanted to play the US lawman taking down the bad guy.

Shaggy stiffened. He actually froze!

That's a surprise.

"Drop the gun!"

Shaggy held out his gun hand making sure it was in full view, his finger still hooked around the trigger of a Sig 17 with its extended, twenty-one round mag.

"Drop it, I said!"

Slowly, Shaggy bent at the knees and waist. At the same time, he rotated his wrist and lowered his arm towards the bedroom carpet.

"No shoot! I drop. No shoot."

Shaggy's voice—the rasping, wheezing voice of an asthmatic or a heavy smoker—showed confidence and aggression rather than fear. He'd been in similar situations before.

Danny ran his eyes around the room, searching for other interlopers, Shaggy's backup. He came up empty.

The closet door stood ajar, slammed against the rear wall. One of its upper panels had shattered under the force of Shaggy's shoulder charge. The chest of drawers Danny'd used as a barrier lay on its back. Next time, he'd use a chair hooked under the handle.

Shaggy lowered the gun further, it was within ten centimetres of the fawn carpet. If he was going to make a move it would be soon. Danny lined up his shot between the man's shoulder blades. He couldn't miss. He wouldn't miss.

The gunman opened his fingers and the Sig fell harmlessly to the floor.

"No shoot," Shaggy said, calm and cool. "I stand now. Yes?"

"Slowly."

"Okay, okay. I slow. You no shoot unarmed man in back."

"Don't bank on it, Shaggy. Not after what you bastards have—"

Shaggy took off at a speed Danny didn't expect from such a sinewy man with a rasping chest. He dived through the doorway and darted right, heading for the stairs.

Danny took off in pursuit.

By the time he'd reached the door, Shaggy had made it to the head of the stairs. Danny took aim. Four metres away, a running duck.

"Stop!"

Shaggy's head snapped up and around. Fearless, he sneered, certain Danny wouldn't fire at an unarmed man running away. Two steps down, his lead foot caught the tripwire. The sneer turned to wide-eyed shock, and the running duck took off in flight.

He tumbled through the air, twisting, screaming, arms whirling in a desperate scramble for a handhold. His hands missed the banister and its spindles. His head didn't. It hit the metalwork with a resounding, sickening thwack. Neck bones snapped. Skull shattered. Blood splattered. The body slumped to the lower treads, slid down to the floor tiles, and lay in a crumpled, unmoving mess.

"Should have stopped when I told you to, dullard!"

Downstairs, muted by distance and masked by Danny's receding tinnitus, a man howled in agony.

"Captain!"

Danny took off. He hit the landing at full sprint, stepped over the tripwire, and vaulted beyond the dead Shaggy.

CHAPTER EIGHTEEN

WEDNESDAY 3RD MAY – Midday
Amber Valley, Derbyshire, UK

Kaine headed for the kitchen. With the smashed glass door leading to the garden, it was an obvious easy point of ingress. Conversely, he'd already set up its defences.

He hurried across the open hallway and slammed to a stop against the wall leading to the kitchen, using his shoulder to break his momentum. Sig raised, Kaine dropped to one knee and peered through the opening.

From his new position, the glass oven door acted as a perfect mirror, reflecting the skewed rectangle of sunlight flooding through the bifold doors and showing the green of the garden beyond.

Water bubbled merrily and thin clouds of steam rose from the two large saucepans he'd set on the hob. Their handles crossed each other, and overhung the front of the cooker. Earlier, Kaine had tied the handles together with string he'd taken from a ball he'd found in a kitchen drawer. The string dangled down from the handles, trailed across the floor to the door, and ran straight into Kaine's fist.

He waited.

Upstairs, floorboards creaked, a door slammed open, and Danny's Beretta barked. Rapid gunfire from multiple weapons in the garden peppered the shutters and smashed windows.

For all the world, Kaine wanted to rush to Danny's aid, but he had his own ground to defend. Marian Prentiss' life depended on him and Danny working as a team, separate but together.

Seconds ticked slowly, turning into minutes.

Dark flecks appeared in the reflection. Raindrops on the glass of the unbroken door. Only a few, but they interrupted the reflection's clean lines.

A dark shape broke the vertical line of the sunlit rectangle—the oval of a man's head. It wore a green beret.

A Commando!

Cautiously, the Commando leaned further around the edge of the bifold door, revealing a broad shoulder and the triangle of his upper body. He extended his right arm and the Beretta in his hand entered the kitchen first, probing forwards into the empty space. He stepped fully into the kitchen, head turning, swivelling left then right. The guy was on his guard, tensed for danger.

The concussive punch of a huge explosion hit them hard. Loud enough to shatter eardrums and punch air from unprepared lungs. Protected by the thick stone of the kitchen wall, Kaine did nothing but blink.

The Commando spun towards the noise and his feet flew out from under him. He fell backwards and struck the floor hard. A fraction of a second later, the elbow of his gun arm hit the tiles. The Beretta erupted and the oven door shattered, the shot barely audible after the huge blast.

Kaine grinned. Danny must have finally found a way to ignite the propane.

The Commando flipped over onto his front. He tried to stand, but his boots slipped and slid, unable to find traction on the oil Kaine had poured over the floor when he set the water to boil.

With the explosion still ringing in his ears, Kaine stood, string in one hand, Sig in the other.

"Don't move!"

On Kaine's barked order, Commando froze. His gun pointed at the shattered oven door, well away from Kaine.

Commando's head dropped, forehead rested on tiles. He sniffed.

"Cooking oil?" he said, half to himself, half to Kaine. "Fucking cooking oil?"

"Sometimes, the old ones work the best."

"Wouldn't have worked without that fucking bomb distracting me. No one said you had explosives."

"We didn't. Where's the other one? Your mate."

Slowly, the Commando turned his head. "Can I get up? It's uncomfortable down here and this oil stinks."

"Nah, you're okay as you are. I'm a nervy sort of bloke."

"Bastard."

"Yep, I'm one of them, too."

Kaine glanced over his shoulder into the entrance hall. Where was the other flanker?

"You got a gun on me?" Commando asked, face down, nose grazing the oily floor.

"Yep."

"Really?"

"Want to find out? Move your head, but keep your movements slow and easy."

Slowly, the Commando turned onto his side, keeping his gun pointing well away. His gaze alighted on the muzzle of Kaine's Sig. His lips stretched into a thin smile.

"Okay, you got me. What next?"

"Put your gun on the floor and slide it over to me."

The Commando's eyes flicked up to a point over Kaine's shoulder. He screamed, "Behind you!" twisted, and jerked his gun arm up and around. The Beretta's muzzle caught on the string dangling from the saucepan handles. He tugged. The gun fired, and the bullet smashed into the door of a base unit.

Saucepans tumbled. Scalding water showered down.

Commando screamed. Hands flew to his face. He writhed on the floor, howling, thrashing.

Keeping as clear of the oil and water mix as he could, Kaine entered the kitchen. He ripped both teacloths from the handle of the oven and spread them over the floor for added traction. Then, kneeling, he ripped the Beretta from the Commando's red-raw and already blistering hand and patted him down. One full magazine and a throwing dagger. Nothing else to concern him.

Kaine stood. Keeping his ears open, Kaine stared down at the thrashing man. He winced and sucked air between his teeth.

"Should have stayed down. The old tricks don't always work."

"Bastard!" the Commando screamed from behind his par-boiled hands, squirming, rolling. "You fucking bastard! I can't see! Help me."

Picking his way around the mess, Kaine turned off the gas and made his way past the cooker to the sink. He opened the mixer tap full. Cold water flowed, splashed into the sink. He returned to the doorway.

"Follow the sound of the water. It's cold. Douse your face and hands. It might help."

The Commando stopped writhing.

"Thanks," he said through his hands. "Thanks ... mate."

More floorboards creaked on the first floor, directly above Kaine's head. A door crashed open. Furniture toppled. Gunfire. A Sig, not Danny's Beretta.

Damn. A breach!

CHAPTER NINETEEN

Kaine called to Commando. "If you try to leave the kitchen, I will kill you."

"I-I won't," he mumbled, crawling towards the running water. "I promise."

Kaine believed him.

Footsteps. Running footsteps. A scream followed by thumping and tumbling on the staircase.

Danny!

Kaine checked the Sig's load and raced towards the entrance hall, alert for anything. He met Danny at the foot of the staircase and lowered his weapon.

Thank God.

"Everything okay, sir?" Danny asked, panting from his exertions and reeking of woodsmoke. Behind him, towards the foot of the stairs lay a body, its neck twisted and its head leaking blood. It didn't move.

"I'm fine, Danny. You?" he asked, nodding at the mess on the stairs.

"No problem here, sir."

"The fishing line held, I see."

"Certainly did." Danny nodded. "I heard some clattering in the kitchen. Any issues?"

"One poached flanker."

"The boiling water trick actually worked?"

"Told you it would." Kaine wiped his chin with the back of his hand. "Eyes open, Danny. There's still at least one man unaccounted for. The second flanker."

Two gunshots exploded. Fired from the front garden. Men yelled at each other in guttural Hungarian. A third shot rang out.

Seconds later, a man screamed, more gunshots erupted, and the intact window on the near side of the double doors blew in. Bullets flew, hitting the far wall.

Kaine and Danny turned together and fired in unison. Four shots each. No target. Blanket fire at the window.

A man wearing a black beret tumbled through the shattered glass, bleeding from the shoulder, arm, and hip. In reflex, he squeezed off a shot on the way down. The bullet struck one of the chess pieces, a knight. It removed one of the horse's ears and buried itself into the wall.

The man hit the floor, tried to roll to his feet, but the leg with the damaged hip collapsed beneath him.

Danny and Kaine fired together. The man in the black beret spun and fell onto his back. This time, he stayed down. One of the bullets had torn through his cheek, another blew out his throat. Blood spurted through the ugly holes. Hands grasped at his throat, trying to stem the flow. His right knee bent upwards, the foot twitched, trying to help him stand. It faltered and the leg straightened as the foot slid along the floor. Seconds later, the man's fight for life ended and his arms dropped to his sides. Blood pooled around his head.

"Jesus," Danny said, scanning the hallway and landing, leading with his Beretta, "what a bloody mess."

153

"I'll give you this, lad," Kaine said, sliding a fresh mag into his Sig. "You do know how to throw a party. Loved the fireworks show."

"Thanks, sir," Danny said, throwing Kaine a pained smile.

"How'd you manage to ignite the propane?"

"I didn't. One of the attackers ended up inside the shed. The gas ignited when he shot at me."

"How ironic. Same thing happened with the boiling water. Self-inflicted injuries."

Danny's smile widened. "Who the hell are we facing here, sir? A platoon of the Kamikaze Highlanders?"

"Seems that way."

Danny's grin widened. "Are we done here now, do you think?"

Kaine grimaced and shook his head. "There's at least one more by the gates. Vadik Pataki. Could be others in the cars."

Out front, an engine fired up, wheels spun, and gravel rattled on metal and brickwork. Kaine and Danny raced each other to the shattered windows next to the front doors, and reached them in time to see the bonnet of the right hand BMW reverse into the road and scream off.

"Fuck," Danny shouted, "he's getting away."

He turned towards the front door and reached for one of the upper bolts.

"Leave him, Danny. Let's see to Mrs Prentiss."

Danny threw the upper bolt and turned the key in the lock. "Vadik Pataki set all this up and murdered Robert Prentiss. While he's alive this isn't over. Marian Prentiss will never be safe."

He turned the lionhead handle and tugged on the door. It didn't budge. He looked down, shook his head. He'd forgotten the lower bolt.

"No, Danny," Kaine said, dropping a hand on Danny's shoulder as he bent to work the bolt. "I meant leave him for now. We'll catch up with Vadik Pataki later, on our terms. We'll know where he's heading. Corky's going to be on it the minute the comms are back online."

Almost as though he'd been listening, Kaine's earpiece clicked active.

"*...you there, Mr K? Come back.*"

Kaine tapped the earpiece. "Alpha Two to Control, receiving you. Over."

"*'Bout bloody time you answered. Some armpit's been blocking your signal, but it's just freed up. Corky ain't a happy bunny.*"

"*You're* not happy? I thought this system was bulletproof? Over."

Danny was having trouble with the bottom bolt. He rattled the arm, but it obstinately refused to release. He leaned a shoulder against the door and tried again. This time, the bolt slid free and snapped open, catching Danny's thumb as it slammed against the retaining block.

"Shit!"

He stood, stuck his thumb in his mouth, and sucked.

Kaine coughed out a laugh.

After such an intense firefight where neither of them had received as much as a scratch, for Danny to cut himself opening a door was a hoot.

After a momentary frown, Danny saw the humour in it and smiled, too.

"Yeah, yeah. Very funny."

Danny tugged on the handle again and the door popped open. Kaine followed him out into a much gloomier morning than it had been when he'd arrived. The rain had increased in intensity, sucking warmth from the day. It hammered down, forming puddles on the gravel drive.

Danny's head snapped to the left.

A man, clothes smouldering, manic blue eyes shining through scorched skin, staggered around the side of the house, a gun in each hand, both raised. He started shooting. Bullets flew.

"Look out!" Danny screamed.

He dived across Kaine and fell hard against him. They collapsed in a tangled mix of legs and arms. On the way down, Kaine fired three times. Reflexive, instinctive. Three shots, two hits.

The man's head jerked back. He fell in a heap.

Kaine struggled to stand, restricted by Danny's unmoving weight.

"Stop messing about, Danny. Get off, will you."

Danny coughed, a weak, wet, bubbling hack.

Oh Christ. No!

"Mr K, are you alright?"

"Danny?"

Another bubbling cough.

Jesus. No. Please, no.

Kaine heaved.

Danny's weight shifted, and he groaned as Kaine gently eased him aside and onto his back. He cradled Danny's head, made sure it didn't thump onto the black and white tiles.

"Mr K?"

"Not now, Corky!" Kaine screamed. "Not now!"

He laid Danny flat, kneeled alongside, and checked him for injuries. His head and face looked clear, unhurt. Arms and legs, too. He pulled down the zip on Danny's dark jacket. Nothing. No bullet holes.

Thank fuck.

Probably hit his head and knocked himself out. Kaine blew out a sigh.

Danny coughed again. Bloody bubbles frothed out of his mouth.

Christ!

Kaine ran a hand over Danny's chest, along each side in turn. Found a warm, wet patch under the left armpit. He pulled the arm away. A tiny hole punched through the dark blue polo shirt. Blood spurted through the hole, spread quickly, saturating the cloth.

Danny struggled for breath. Each time his chest expanded and contracted, frothy blood oozed out through the hole. Kaine clamped a hand over the wound and pressed hard.

"Danny! Oh Jesus. Danny!"

"Mr K. Want Corky to call an ambulance?"

Kaine tapped the earpiece into silence and squeezed his eyes tight shut. He'd seen similar chest wounds before. A punctured lung. A nicked pulmonary blood vessel. Danny was drowning in his own blood. He had minutes only. Maybe less. This far out in the country, no ambulance could reach them in time. Not that paramedics could help, anyway. Danny needed a fully equipped and fully prepped operating theatre, and the nearest was over an hour away. Even if Kaine dragged him into a car and broke all the speed records, they wouldn't even make it halfway.

Danny's eyes flicked open. Again, he coughed, this one weaker than the last. Wetter. Even more horrible.

Oh Danny!

On his knees and with his hand still clamped over the seeping wound, Kaine worked his way around to Danny's head. He slid his arm under Danny's limp shoulders, pulled him into his lap and hugged him tight, compressing the wound. Together, they leaned against the stone wall of Prentiss House.

A groan escaped Danny's blood-soaked lips. More blood frothed out. He winced, clenched his teeth.

"Easy, lad. I've got you." Kaine spoke quietly, trying to ease his own pain as well as Danny's.

Danny smiled. "No worries, Captain. Doesn't hurt. Not really."

"Bloody hell, Danny."

An engine roared along the road on the far side of the wall. Tyres squealed as the driver locked out the brakes. A white Ford Focus shuddered to a stop alongside the parked BMW.

Jesus, what now?

Kaine raised his Sig, but lowered it when the Ford's front doors flew open and Cough and Stefan jumped out. They slid through the part-open gates and raced along the driveway, weapons drawn, scoping the area for bogeys. On spotting Kaine and Danny, the blood, and the carnage, they skidded to a stop. Gravel crunched and scattered beneath their military boots.

"Oh shit. No!" Cough gasped, breathing hard, his rebuilt left shoulder hitched characteristically higher than the right.

Beside him, Stefan stood silent, eyes wide, defensive. He searched, checking the sightlines, always on guard. A good, solid soldier.

Danny tilted his head to face them.

"Hi ... guys," he said, "'bout time you got ... here." He paused long enough to spit blood. "This isn't ... what it looks like. The Captain and ... I ... we're just good friends."

Stefan resorted to his default expression—a confused frown—but said nothing.

Cough forced a thin smile. "Yeah, yeah. Pull the other one, Danny-boy. You two go get a room, would ya?" He dragged his eyes from the blood patch on Danny's chest and stared through the smashed window into one part of the kill zone.

"Stefan, check the grounds," Kaine said, pointing towards the kitchen and refusing to use the man's unfortunate nickname. "Danny and I are the only friendlies outside. Take care, some might still be alive. No second chances, understand? Cough, secure the house. Mrs Prentiss is in the front room. She's in the far corner under a couple of mattresses, unarmed. Announce yourself as Danny's friend. She'll be terrified."

Stefan headed off, hugging close to the side of the house and pausing to glance around the corner before continuing. Cough climbed the steps to the portico. He stopped and bent to touch Danny's shoulder.

"Good luck, Danny," he said, choking on the words before entering the house.

They all knew the only outcome, Danny included.

Kaine hugged his dying friend closer and made sure he had a good view of the attractive front garden. It would be his last. He fell silent, listening to the lad struggling over every gurgled breath.

"Captain ... I'm ..."

Kaine squeezed Danny's hand.

"Don't talk, Danny. I'm here with you. We're good."

"Will ... will you do me a ... favour, sir?"

"Of course. Name it."

"Tell Bobbie I ... tell her ... Well, you know."

"Yes, Danny. I know."

"And look after ... Marian Prentiss. She's ... she's pregnant."

Kaine tried to swallow past the restriction in his throat. Couldn't manage it. Tears blurred his vision. He wiped his eyes with the heel of a bloodied hand, the one still holding his de-cocked Sig. He tried not to sniffle. Danny wouldn't appreciate tears from his commanding officer.

"Pregnant, is she? I didn't know."

"Even though ... she's ... not one of *The 83* ... she needed our help."

The skin on his face became more and more translucent as the blood drained away. A pale blue tinge to his lips showed how close he was to the end.

"One ... one more ... thing, sir."

"Yes, Danny?"

"Lajos Pataki ... will you ... will you ..."

Really?

"You want me to kill him?"

Danny turned his head, locked drooping eyes with Kaine and smiled. It must have taken most of what he had left.

"No ... sir. Flush that ... fucking toilet for me."

Kaine held Danny close and tight, and he laughed. He laughed until the tears took over—until the life left Danny's eyes and he grew still in Kaine's arms.

CHAPTER TWENTY

W EDNESDAY 3RD M AY – Vadik Pataki
Amber Valley, Derbyshire, UK

"*Kibaszott pokolba!*" Vadik cursed aloud.

The attack had started so well. A concerted and bull-roaring all-out assault designed to instil terror in the hearts of the occupants. Shock and awe. The cowards in the house, Pansy and his cronies, would have been shitting themselves.

Truffle Pig reached the house first. He broke through the pitiful defences, brave in his actions, bold even. A man worth his wages even if he was black. He crashed through the broken windows, firing his weapon as he entered. Three shots from inside the house followed by screams of pain suggested the black mercenary had been successful.

Farzin, a short way behind, stopped his darting, serpentine rush and turned to Vadik, his long hair flapping around his head.

"That was easy, *fönök*. So very easy," he called.

Together, they punched the air as brothers.

"Go help him find Lajos," Vadik ordered, waving Farzin towards the house. "And keep the woman alive. I have plans for her."

Dark plans.

He would take her back to Hungary and use her as one of the family's whores. After being strung out on horse for long enough, she would beg to please any man, just for one more fix. A fitting life for a woman who had caused Vadik Pataki so much inconvenience.

As Farzin marched towards the front, rapid shots exploded from the rear garden. Obasi, Eliasz, and the others had reached the house and found their targets. Vadik whooped. He had plotted the encounter with the precision of a military genius. The mission was back on course. They would clean up the mess here at the house and take over the business as planned. Papa could not fail to be pleased and proud of his firstborn son. No longer would Vadik suffer the ignominy of being called the Bastard.

Only then did things turn to shit.

Something moved behind the smashed front window. A leather-clad arm pushed through the opening, its hand holding a black semi-automatic. Farzin froze to the spot.

One second later, maybe two, Farzin flinched. Then came the shot that ended his existence.

A single shot, fired through the window by the man in black leather.

The hair at the back of Farzin's head billowed as though ruffled by a puff of air. Blood and other stuff sprayed out in a red halo. Slowly, Vadik's oldest friend fell backwards to the drive. He lay still. Dead.

Szar!

"No!" Vadik screamed. "Farzin. No!"

He punched and kicked the tree behind which he had orchestrated the assault.

The one who shot Farzin from inside the safety of the house was a fucking coward. He would die!

Die! Slowly. Painfully.

As the gunfight raged at the back and sides of the house, Vadik edged further behind the tree, peeking out with only one eye. Multiple cracks and pops broke the stillness. Bullets whizzed, ricocheted. Glass smashed. Men shouted, shrieked, and screamed. Some were dying. Vadik did not recognise the voices.

He turned towards the gates. From his seat in the BMW, Wilfred stared at him, through a face with skin as pale as Lajos on a normal day. His blue eyes, normally wide and awestruck, were filled with shock and terror. What did he think of Vadik, hiding behind a tree? Where once he looked on in awe, what did he think now? Pity? Disgust?

Well, fuck the geek. Fuck him to hell.

What did Vadik care? Vadik was the Lion of Győr! He planned and calculated and schemed. He instructed people what to do. He drove while others obeyed.

More gunshots and screams echoed through the English country-side. Then the rain started. Splodges of wetness sprinkled the leaves and flowers, dripping down the back of his neck.

Fucking English weather.

What was he going to do now? How was he going to fix the hideous shitstorm?

Then, the thunder of a massive explosion vibrated up through the earth. Orange flames shrouded in black smoke climbed into the air from behind the house.

What the fuck? They have bombs?

In the car behind Vadik, Wilfred squealed. Vadik spun. Wilfred, eyes wide, mouth open, squealed again and applauded. The terror on his face had turned to delight.

Why?

He must have thought Eliasz responsible for the explosion, but that was not possible. Eliasz had used his only charge to destroy the electricity sub-station and cut the power to the house. Such was the naïvety of the boy. He had no understanding of what was happening. Once again, the boy's reaction showed his ignorance and inability to grasp the wider picture. Wilfred laughed and clapped again. Vadik could not understand the mentality of the child who showed genius in some things, yet idiocy in others. If the family had not needed his technological skills, Vadik would end him. Those

Vadik could not understand, he could not control, and they had to die.

More shooting drew Vadik's attention back to the battle.

The flames died almost as quickly as they had been birthed, no doubt doused by the increasingly heavy rain. Screams of dying men, men Vadik knew and others, struck his ears. More gunshots followed. More agonised howls.

Still, Vadik waited. Maybe the battle was not lost. After all, how many men could Pansy have amassed in so short a time? Maybe he was alone after all. Perhaps the explosion had been the final, desperate act of the defender. An act of suicide.

Movement at the side of the house. A shadow emerging.

One of the men Obasi had led into battle appeared on the path, the one who always wore a black beret, a beret from his military days that made him look so ridiculous. Rohan. He skidded to a stop, looked from Vadik to the house and back to Vadik. He started running, not *towards* the house but *away*, heading for Vadik and the gates.

Fucking coward.

Vadik raised his gun and fired twice, aiming low. The bullets thudded into the ground ahead of Rohan. He skidded to a halt once again, holding his arms away from his sides.

"You fucking coward," Vadik screamed in Hungarian, raising his Glock, aiming at the ugly face of a filthy weakling.

Rohan shook his head and waved his hands.

"But it is over, *főnök*," he shouted. "Our men are dead."

"Go. Kill them all!" Vadik yelled. "Kill them or die now!"

Vadik lowered his Glock a fraction and pulled the trigger again. He missed again, but only by a centimetre or two. The bullet hit a rock at the side of the path and screamed off into the air, but the miserable coward got the message.

"*Te rohadék*," Rohan screamed.

Yes, I am a bastard! And proud of it.

Vadik waved his gun towards the house again and the beret-wearing chickenshit finally took the hint.

Rohan turned towards the house and started running. He fired at the intact window. Glass smashed. Shards fell into the house. The coward continued screaming. Continued running. Closer, closer. Nearly there.

More shots, these from inside.

Rohan buckled, twisted, and fell through the shattered window and disappeared into the darkness. More gunshots marked his end.

Fasz!

Vadik moved into the protection of the tree once more. The bark was rough under his hand and against his cheek, but from its coarse texture and bulk came strength. The strength to stop bullets. The strength to save his life.

Fasz, who is in there? How many?

These were not questions Vadik could answer. Not today, if ever. The battle had not gone well. It was time to leave. Regroup. Protect himself. To hell with Lajos and the woman. To hell with the soldiers in the house. To hell with his men, who even now must all be dead or dying.

He would go home, recover. Live to fight again. Only the next time, the next fight, he would be better prepared with more men and more complete information. Better intelligence would have saved the day. Wilfred should have warned him about the strength and disposition of the defenders inside the house—Pansy and his fucking men.

Yes. That is it.

Wilfred was to blame for the disaster, not Vadik.

Damn the witless boy to Hell.

Wilfred was paid to gather information. So why did he not provide it? He would pay dearly for his mistake, but not right away. Vadik needed the fucker to book flights and get them through customs. Only when Vadik had reached the safety of home, would it be the time to extract his revenge. Yes. Only when they were safely on home ground would he punish Wilfred, the one ultimately responsible for the failure of the mission.

Vadik pushed away from the protection of the life-giving tree and, crouching low, raced to the car.

Screaming at the useless Wilfred, he dived behind the wheel, and smashed the kid in the face for the pleasure it gave. Blood spurted from a split lower lip.

Bassza meg! Fuck you!

Vadik fired up the engine, turned the dial to *Sport Mode*, and selected reverse. The SUV's rear wheels spun and bit into the gravel before finally gaining traction. The car shot backwards into the empty road. Vadik spun the wheel and expertly faced the car to the east, heading back along the way they had arrived. The leather-clad steering wheel felt good in his hands. Natural. He had always been a superb driver. Driving came naturally to him. All cars, fast or slow. Tractors, even.

He mashed the pedal into the floor pan, the tyres spun on wet tarmac before catching. The SUV leapt forwards, gaining speed rapidly on the wet roads. Rain slammed down, cutting visibility to nothing. The sensors picked up the downpour and the wipers started up automatically, clearing the screen in a few swipes.

In an instant, the first corner was upon them. He hit the apex at breakneck speed, twitched at the wheel, fighting a slight oversteer. They struck the grass verge on the road's outer edge, but the stiffened shocks under *Sport Mode* took the strain, and the SUV stayed on the road. Vadik ground the pedal harder into the mat.

In the front passenger seat, Wilfred whimpered. One hand held tight to his computer tablet. The other trembled and struggled to fasten his seatbelt securely.

Tears ran down the cheeks of the weakling boy, mixing with the blood from his cut lip. Let him cry. What did Vadik care? The moment they reached safety, Wilfred would have every reason to blub.

Vadik smiled even as he gritted his teeth. Speed was power and an aphrodisiac. He loved speed, but they needed more than the SUV was currently providing.

Another a sharp right-hand curve approached. Vadik eased the car over, took the racing line, and they careened around the corner at speed.

A perfect turn.

As expected, it had not taken him long to learn the SUV's new setup. Its points of balance. Its strengths and weaknesses.

Go, Vadik. Go!

"*Főnök!*" Wilfred screamed. "Too fast, you go to fast!"

Wilfred held tighter to his unfastened seatbelt, his ashen face standing out white against the blood. Vadik laughed out loud.

"Never fear, little man," he shouted over the scream of the racing turbocharged engine. "Vadik Pataki knows how to handle a car such as this."

If Wilfred had bigger balls, he would find a roadmap on his tablet and navigate for them, but not a chance. The way the idiot's hands shook when he tried and failed to fasten his seatbelt, and the way his chin crumpled in fear, told Vadik it was pointless to ask.

Ahead, in the distance, the dipped headlights of an oncoming car bobbed and swerved around an upcoming corner—the first vehicle to pass since their arrival at Prentiss House. Vadik grinned. He had left the battle zone at exactly the correct time. Once more, his senses and superior intellect had saved him. Even better, the onrushing headlights were showing him the position of the next corner through the rain-washed gloom.

Headlights glared through the spray, and a flash of white shot by on their right. The two cars passed at a combined speed in excess of one hundred and seventy kph. Vadik whooped his pleasure. He loved the dominance that power gave him. This was better than sex.

The next corner, another right-hander, closed upon them. Vadik mashed his foot to the throttle. No need to slow for such a gentle bend.

So what if the assault on the house had been a disaster? Nobody at home would know what had happened. So what if Lajos and the takeover bid on *Prentiss Haulage* was dead? Papa might rage, but Vadik would shift the blame to Wilfred, Lajos, Farzin, Obasi, and the others. Not even Eliasz would escape the culpability. He glanced at the still-bleating Wilfred. Apart from Vadik, only Wilfred knew what had happened at the Prentiss house. But Wilfred would not live to tell the tale. His time was already measured. Vadik smiled inwardly, but showed nothing on his lips.

I apologise in advance, my young friend. But I do promise you one thing. Your death will be quick and painless.

Yes, Vadik would make it quick and painless. After all, Wilfred had served the family well for so long, and Vadik was not a monster.

Quick and painless.

The least he could do.

He returned his attention to the road. By the merest fraction, he relaxed the tension in his right foot, eased the pressure on the accelerator, and tweaked the steering wheel into the turn.

The corner arrived faster than expected. Much faster. A massive puddle covered the outside lane, but it mattered not. Vadik Pataki had the skills to cope. If the family business had not pulled him in other directions, he would have made his name on the Grand Prix circuit. Maybe one day, he still would. He allowed a smile to spread on his face—a face many women had described as ruggedly handsome.

Beside him, Wilfred screamed.

CHAPTER TWENTY-ONE

WEDNESDAY 3RD MAY – Afternoon
Amber Valley, Derbyshire, UK

With extreme care, Kaine lowered Danny's body to the chessboard tiles. Biting back the tears, he stepped out from under the cover of the portico, raised his head to the weeping sky, and released a silent scream.

Danny's dead!

He'd taken a bullet to save Kaine.

The driving rain cooled his face. He held out his hands, washed off Danny's blood as best he could, and wiped them on the grass running around the path.

Danny's dead!

Kaine blinked the rain and tears from his eyes and turned back to face the house, trying not to look at Danny.

Cough appeared in the open doorway. He glanced down at Danny and closed his eyes for a moment before focusing his attention on Kaine.

"Report." Kaine's voice cracked. He cleared his throat.

Cough pushed his way through the door, keeping a respectful distance from Danny. "It's carnage out back, sir. Two bodies burned to a crisp. Two dead in the hall, and two more out front here"—he pointed to the carcasses of Longhair and the arsehole who'd killed Danny. "There's one par-boiled in the kitchen but alive, and another survivor behind the stairs. Neither of them will cause us any trouble."

"What about Marian ... I mean, Mrs Prentiss?"

"Unharmed but terrified. Stinko's looking after her. Better with women than I am, sir. Gentle, you know?"

"Thanks, Cough. I ... Christ, what a bloody mess."

Cough dipped his head. "In the middle of the English country-side, too. Never thought I'd see the day ..." He let the thought trail off and allowed sadness to cloud his face. "What do you want me to do with the other one?"

"Sorry. What other one?"

"There's a blond geezer tied to the downstairs bog. Looks in a bad way. He's mumbling shit in foreign, too. Can't understand a bleeding word he's spouting. I take it you or Danny put that bullet through his arm and leg and stuck him there for a reason?"

"We did. He's Lajos Pataki, Vadik's brother."

Understanding dawned and Cough lifted his chin. "Ah, I see. Corky briefed us on the situation during the drive here."

"You didn't release him, did you?"

"What, the blond one tied to the bog?"

Kaine spun away to wipe his eyes and take a deep, cleansing breath. He'd make time enough to mourn Danny's loss later. Work needed taking care of first. He turned back to Cough and nodded. "Yes, him."

"'Course not. I figured you'd want to deal with him yourself."

"Is he going to live?"

Cough shrugged. "No idea. Maybe. If he gets medical treatment soon. Gonna lose the arm, though. Already turning black and started to pong something terrible."

"Good. Hope he suffers, but keep him alive. I might yet have a use for the murdering scumbag."

169

"The doc's on her way. Should be here inside the hour."

Lara's on her way? Here?

"No, tell her to stay away. It's too dangerous. I don't want her anywhere near this place. You hear me!"

"We tried stopping her. Corky did, too. But you know the doc."

"Corky?"

Damn it. He'd almost forgotten about him. How was that possible?

Cough nodded again. "He told me you'd powered off your earwig. Didn't want to disturb you, so he's been keeping me in the loop instead. You'll be off after Vadik, I suppose?"

"No point. He's long gone by now. But we'll catch up with him soon enough. We know where he's heading."

"No, sir. That's where you're wrong."

"Sorry?"

"Vadik didn't get far. Only a couple of miles."

Kaine's heart leapt as he read the excitement in Cough's eyes.

"Explain yourself, Sergeant," he asked, getting down to business.

"He's the useless arsehole that was driving the fuck-off big BMW that nearly sideswiped us on the way in here. Driving like a madman, he was. All over the fucking road. I asked Corky to see if he could find him. There's only one road out of here for five miles. Like I said, sir. He didn't get far. Couple of miles away he took a corner too fast in the rain. Totalled his BMW."

"Corky has eyes on the car? There's a surveillance camera this far out in the sticks?"

Cough's thin smile carried no mirth. "No sir. He's monitoring the emergency services radio channels. Five minutes ago, Vadik called for an ambulance. Poor man's screaming for help. Says he's trapped in his car. The paramedics aren't likely to reach him for another thirty minutes, though. Off you go, sir. Stinko and I've got this place covered."

Kaine suppressed a whoop. He clapped Cough's good shoulder and took off, sprinting around the side of the house to the burned-out fire pit the rear courtyard had become. The blackened, scorched woodwork made the place look as though a bushfire had roared through the area. Fortunately, the rain had doused the flames and prevented another flare-up.

He found the Triumph lying on its side, but otherwise undamaged. It had been protected from the propane explosion by the garage's brick wall. The helmet still hung from the handlebar where he'd left it.

Kaine heaved the bike upright, confirmed his Sig was de-cocked and tucked safely into the inner pocket of his leather jacket, and straddled the seat. He grabbed the skid lid, turned it the right way up to allow the gathered rainwater to dribble out, and pulled it over his head, letting the strap dangle. He keyed the ignition and waited for the electronics to scroll through the start-up sequence. The bike caught first time, and Kaine raced around to the front, counteracting the rear wheel skid as the big bike fought the gravel for traction.

Demonstrating his usual forethought, Cough had made it to the gates and yanked one fully open, allowing Kaine a straight run through.

Kaine slowed the bike enough to yell, "Back soon," and check for traffic before pulling onto the empty road. He opened the throttle and the powerful Triumph sprang forwards.

The rain stopped as quickly as it had started—as though someone upstairs wanted to make Kaine's job easier—and the bike handled the waterlogged road and its weather-damaged surface well. The powerful beast had been designed with such conditions in mind.

Kaine didn't push the bike beyond its limits, didn't need to. He still had plenty of time before the first responders were due.

Less than two miles into the ride, he eased back on the throttle to negotiate a sharp right-hander with a flooded outside lane. He slowed further as he passed the apex and found the expected break in the hedgerow where a wide-bodied vehicle had left the road and ploughed through the dense bushes. It had probably aquaplaned on the deep puddle.

Kaine worked the hand and foot brakes together, rolled the Triumph to a gentle stop, and kicked out the prop stand. He leaned the bike over and dismounted. After tugging off the helmet and hanging it on the handlebars, he combed his gloved fingers through his sopping hair and took a leisurely stroll to the verge.

In the field three metres below the road, the dark blue BMW X5 rested on its passenger side, the motor still purring on fast idle. For the German engine to keep working after such a heavy shunt stood as proof of the manufacturer's impressive build quality.

Raindrops fell from overhanging leaves and burst into steam as they hit the vehicle's piping hot exhaust.

Apart from the cracked windscreen, which had popped out of its housing and lay beside the bonnet, the SUV didn't show that much damage. In fact, it seemed pretty much intact from where Kaine stood, looking down. He wouldn't have been surprised to find the vehicle still driveable once it had been set back on all four wheels.

Inside the cab, driver's side, a man coughed.

"Hello?" Vadik called. "Is anyone there?"

Kaine grabbed hold of branches to prevent himself pitching headlong into the mess, and sideslipped down the muddy, damaged bank.

"Hello?" Vadik yelled again. "I am trapped. Help me!"

Kaine reached the flat part of the field, removed his right glove, and tucked it into a pocket. He pulled out the Sig, racked the slide, and worked his way through the boggy ground to the front of the SUV. Finally, the Beemer's engine coughed and died. Kaine paused and took a moment to absorb the tranquillity.

Birds twittered in the treetops, welcoming the sun's return. Rain glistened on foliage and turned cobwebs into decorated chandeliers. Some forty-odd metres away, in the bottom corner of the field, cows grazed on lush grass, oblivious to the nearby destruction. England could be such a strikingly beautiful place. Danny would have enjoyed the scene.

Danny!

Temporarily, Kaine shook his mind free of the dreadful loss of a close friend and stood back to examine the SUV. A buckled grill and a crumpled front nearside wing showed what happened when a tonne of careering metalwork met a hedge and destroyed at least one sapling.

"Why are you just standing there? Help me, damn you!"

Kaine ignored Vadik's demand and continued his scan. Vadik hadn't been the only one in the BMW when it crashed through the hedgerow. Unfortunately, the man in the passenger seat wouldn't be taxing the skills of the approaching paramedics. In fact, he wouldn't be taking up the time of anyone but the Coroner's people.

The remains of the front passenger demonstrated the dangers of not wearing a seatbelt, and explained the reason for the windscreen's dislocation. Photos of the crash might prove useful as aversion therapy. The car's impact with the hedge and the instant reduction in forward momentum had thrown the fair-haired man through the windscreen. The passenger's airbag hadn't deployed in time to save him.

When human skull meets toughened and laminated glass at any significant velocity, neither material is likely to survive unscathed, but the skull will always suffer the greater damage. The passenger's torso and arms dangled through the opening. The top of his head had been crushed on impact. Blood seeped and dripped from the wound, forming a wide pool on the mud and grass below. Bits of white brain matter floated in the puddle like the solid parts of a cauliflower soup. Pieces of skull, still attached to the dome by scalp which acted as hinges, flapped in the gentlest of breezes.

Kaine sneered. With Danny lying dead at the farm, he didn't give a rat's arse for the passenger, or the bellyaching driver.

"Help me, fuck you!"

The driver's airbag had done its job, saving Vadik from serious injury. His seatbelt held him in place and he dangled sideways, leaning towards his dead associate. Although evidently unharmed, he didn't look particularly comfortable. He struggled, wriggled, slammed his fists into the steering wheel, but couldn't free himself from his restraint.

"Hi there, Vadik. Thanks for hanging around." Kaine smiled—at least Danny would have appreciated the humour. "You've just saved me no end of time."

"You know me?"

"Yes, Vadik Pataki. How'd you guess?"

"I-I ...."

"I recognised you as the coward hiding behind the tree at Prentiss House."

Pataki's eyes bugged. He stopped struggling and grabbed the steering wheel so tight with both hands, the skin around his knuckles bleached white and the steering column screeched.

"Who ... who are you?"

Kaine smiled, raised his weapon, and strode towards one of the men ultimately responsible for Danny's death. He leaned over the partially decapitated corpse and jammed the Sig's muzzle into Vadik's forehead so hard, his head jerked back against the seat's headrest.

Kaine pressed even harder. Vadik winced.

"We've never met," Kaine said, surprised at how calm he sounded, "but I'm the man who's going to end your days."

Vadik whimpered. "No! Please!" He peeled one hand from the steering wheel and held it up in surrender. "Please don't!"

"Begging? You're begging for your life? Robbie Prentiss didn't beg for his life. He didn't have time. You sneaked up behind him and blew his brains out."

Pataki's eyes widened even further.

Slowly, Kaine slid his index finger through the Sig's guard and curled it around the trigger. A gram or two of added pressure and it would be over.

"Money? Y-You want money?" Pataki screamed. "How much? One million euros?"

Kaine didn't respond, didn't react.

"Two! Two million euros. Cash money. You will be rich."

"I don't need your money."

"How much can I give you? How much do you want!" Tears bled from the dark eyes.

"You killed Robert Prentiss and Danny."

Droplets of sweat popped out on Vadik's forehead. They formed rivulets that ran down his face and dripped from the tip of his nose and the point of his chin. Heat radiated from him and he trembled. Here was a man with a fever who knew that death stood close by.

"Danny? Who is Danny?"

Kaine peeled back his upper lip. "You never knew Danny," he snarled. "But Danny was my friend, and you killed him. No amount of money's going to bring him back."

He rammed the Sig harder against Vadik's forehead. The condemned man whimpered.

"Y-You killed my half-brother, Lajos. We are even. Please, please do not kill me."

Kaine eased some weight off the Sig.

"Lajos is still alive, Vadik. At least for now. He says you planned it all. He claims he tried to talk you out of killing Robbie Prentiss and his wife."

"N-No, no! That is not true." Pataki shook his head, grimacing under the pressure of the Sig's muzzle. "That is a lie. Lajos and Papa planned the whole thing. I was forced into it. Papa runs the family with a rod of ... rod of ..." The light in Pataki's eyes changed. Fear turned to cunning. "Kill me and my papa, Viktor Pataki, will never rest. He will hunt you down and kill you and all your family and all your friends."

"In that case," Kaine said, tilting his head to one side as though considering his options, "I'd better go talk to him, eh? See if we can't come to some sort of an understanding."

Kaine smiled. He pulled the Sig away, de-cocked it, and slid it into his jacket pocket. Almost as an afterthought, he took the glove from the other pocket and tugged it over his sweating hand.

"That is right, Englishman," Pataki crowed, rubbing the mark of the muzzle from his forehead, which suited Kaine well enough. "You go to see Papa. Negotiate for your life, *gyáva*. If you spare me, he will let you live. That is his way."

"Who said anything about sparing you?"

"What? What did you say?"

175

"No, Vadik. I never said you were going to live. With Lajos alive, I already have a half-decent bargaining chip. A half-brother bargaining ship, if you like. Truth is, Vadik Pataki, I don't need you at all, and neither does the world."

Vadik released his hold on the steering wheel and pushed his hands through the hole where the windscreen used to be, waving them in surrender.

"What? No, no! Papa is the *Giant of Győr*. He will kill you!"

Kaine confirmed his footing, and gave Vadik Pataki a grim smile.

"He can try, Vadik. Plenty of others have."

Kaine batted aside Vadik's arms and reached both hands through the opening. He grabbed Vadik by the chin and the back of the head and wrenched, hard and fast.

The wet squelch of snapping vertebrae—the sound of a drumstick being torn from a roast chicken—ended Vadik Pataki's screams as instantly as it ended his life.

When the police finally arrived, a bullet in Vadik's head would hardly encourage them to write the scene off as an unfortunate and tragic accident. On top of everything else, the piece of filth wasn't worth the price of a bullet.

The cops would probably wonder how a man with a broken neck had managed to phone for an ambulance, but it wasn't Kaine's responsibility to answer the police's questions or help them clear up their investigations.

He stepped back to give the crash scene a final once over.

A metallic glint at the side of the passenger caught his attention. He drew closer and pulled the flap of a jacket aside and discovered a rectangular box of electronics the size of a 1980s mobile phone. He had no idea what it was, but knew a little man who'd be able to determine its function. The unmarked box of tricks might have been responsible for the breakdown in their comms system. Kaine made sure the device was powered down and set it to one side while he searched the BMW's cabin and the pockets of both corpses as best he could. Not the easiest of tasks while wearing leather bike gloves.

In the end, he found a tablet computer with a cracked screen and two top-of-the-range smartphones. Added to the 1980s mobile, they made a nice little haul and might well come in handy for the next phase of Kaine's rapidly developing plan for vengeance.

He stood back from the SUV, raised his mobile, and took a picture of the scene. Something told him it might come in handy with future negotiations. He turned away and began the short climb to the waiting Triumph, making no attempt to obscure his footprints—it wasn't necessary. A light rain had started up again and a fast-running micro-stream had formed where he'd trampled the undergrowth. By the time the first responders arrived, the water would have wiped away all trace of him.

Astride the Triumph once again he looked down at the wreckage. One third of the Pataki clan lay dead. Two more remained alive, but how long would he allow that to remain the status quo?

CHAPTER TWENTY-TWO

Danny's dead. Oh Jesus, he's dead.

The ride back to the Prentiss House gave Kaine time to think, and the enormity of the loss slowly sank in. Danny, the smiling, eager kid he'd first met in a Munich bar nearly eight years earlier—the kid who'd turned into a thoroughly decent and reliable friend—was gone.

Again, Kaine had to fight back the tears. Blurred vision did nothing to help him keep the bike on the road, and he cracked open the visor to allow fresh, clean air to cool his cheeks and dry his eyes.

Danny's dead!

Kaine took his time. If he'd had his way, he would have turned the bike around and headed anywhere but Prentiss House. Anywhere but the place Danny died, the place where his body cooled in death. But the living needed him. Kaine had to bury the loss and fight the pain, at least for a while.

Marian Prentiss had lost someone that day, too. She'd lost her husband, the father of her unborn child. She'd spent much of the previous hour hiding under a mattress in fear for her life. She'd been listening to a gunfight and an explosion that, to her, would have meant the loss of her farm, too. Her home.

What must she be feeling with her home a battleground, the blood of half a dozen corpses staining her land and her house, and with no one but two total strangers dressed in military uniform for company?

And three survivors.

Kaine couldn't forget the three surviving combatants. The one-handed Merc, the poached Commando, and the remaining half-brother, Lajos Pataki. The half-brother ... yes, the half-brother.

The broken bones of a plan, which had started to form when he'd first arrived at Prentiss House started knitting together. A plan that satisfied his desire to avenge both Danny's death and the cold-blooded murder of Robert Prentiss. A plan that relied on Lajos Pataki's continued survival and his eventual return, alive, to his Papa—assuming he survived the journey home.

Kaine plotted vengeance. Hot vengeance! Sod that nonsense about retribution being a dish best served cold.

Damn them. Damn them all to Hell!

He ground his teeth and opened the Tiger's throttle.

Concerns for keeping Lajos alive drew his thoughts to Lara. The medically trained Lara, who, despite everyone's concerns, was racing towards a battlefield in the heart of rural England. Racing towards death and destruction.

Jesus, what a Godawful mess.

He'd lost men before. Good men who'd died in battle, fighting for Queen and Country—whatever that meant. But this was different. Danny had placed himself in danger to protect a woman and her unborn child, and he'd done so voluntarily. As Kaine raced the growling Triumph through the quiet, leafy lanes of the English countryside, everything seemed so bloody unreal. This wasn't some dust-blown, fly-encrusted Middle Eastern desert, or a mountain range in the Hindu Kush, but a rain-washed rural valley in the East Midlands, for Christ's sake.

Such a terrible, Goddamned waste.

And Bobbie. How the hell was he going to tell Bobbie? Hadn't she suffered enough after the treatment Pony Tedesco dished out to her mother? Poor Bobbie. Lara would want to accompany him to deliver the news, but it was his job, not hers. Danny was one of his men. Delivering the news was Kaine's responsibility.

Later, Ryan. Later.

He negotiated the sharp left-hander and reached the straight outside Prentiss House. Someone, probably Cough, had opened both gates and moved his Ford and both BMW X5s from the entrance.

From Kaine's angle of approach on Chequer Way, the area looked normal, tranquil, untouched. But as he pulled off the narrow road onto the gravel drive and passed through the gates, the farm became the obvious site of a recent gun battle. The smashed front windows, the bloodstained and rain-soaked gravel, and the puddles of blood covering the black and white portico tiles, gave the place the surreal air of a film set.

One thing in their favour, the large house hid the damage caused by the propane explosion, which was just as well. The bodies were missing, too.

With another heavy downpour to wash blood from the driveway, a swabbed portico deck, and a pair of replacement windows, the front of the farm would probably look as good as new. Damn near pristine.

Cough had reversed the Ford and the BMWs to one side and parked them facing the gates. One of the BMWs' tailgates stood open.

Kaine parked the Triumph alongside the Ford and dismounted. He tugged off the skid lid, hung it on the bars by its strap, and marched towards the front doors. Cough and Stefan appeared around the far corner, coming from the back garden. They each had the hand of a blackened corpse and were dragging it behind them. Stefan's expression hadn't changed much since earlier, but Cough looked decidedly uncomfortable. Green about the gills. Death affected people in different ways, even veteran soldiers like Ashley Coughlin.

Straight-faced, Cough nodded to Kaine and he and Stefan dragged the toasted body to the BMW and tossed it unceremoniously into the back.

"Wouldn't it be easier to reverse the SUV around to the rear courtyard and load it from there?" Kaine asked.

"Yeah, it would be, but there's no room, what with all the rubble and the other BMW, which is already full of dead people, by the way."

"Oh," Kaine said, up-nodding. "I see."

His eyes drifted from barbecued bad guy in the boot to the front of the house and the gated entrance.

"Anything wrong, sir?" Stefan asked, dusting some of the ash from his gloved hands.

"With all the gunfire and that explosion, I'm surprised we've not been inundated with neighbours."

"We were, sir," he said, raising his eyebrows in a double-hitch. "Well, not exactly inundated, like. But this red-faced farmer drove up on his Massey Ferguson, wondering what was going on. Only he weren't that polite about it. Turns out we've been upsetting his cows. Bloke was worried about his milk yield, or summat. Quite aggressive about it, he was."

Kaine hadn't heard Stefan say so much in one go before and managed to hide his surprise.

"What did you tell him?"

"Weren't me, Captain. Cough talked to the geezer." Although totally out of place given the circumstances, Stefan's conspiratorial smile was quiet refreshing. It brought some humanity to the scene.

Cough stepped alongside to answer. "I told him we were filming for the new series of *Our Girl*, sir. Said he should have received a letter about it last month."

"*Our Girl?*"

"A TV show about an army medic, sir," Stefan answered, using extravagant hand signals to show the army medic in question was female—and a looker.

"Never heard of it," Kaine said, ignoring Stefan's lurid non-verbal description. He turned to Cough. "The farmer. He fell for it?"

Cough shrugged. "Seemed to, sir. At least he calmed down when I told him the producers would be contacting him next week to discuss any necessary compensation."

Kaine nodded. "Nice one, Cough. Thinking on your feet like that."

"Thank you, sir. I um, ... also gave him a hundred quid and asked him to act as our local consultant for the afternoon."

"Really?"

Cough's smile matched the one Stefan gave. "Right now, he's parked up the road, redirecting traffic and explaining what's happening. Hopefully, he'll keep any rubberneckers at bay."

"You're kidding. It worked?"

"Yes, sir. Well, I think so. A mean, we haven't had any other visitors since he buggered off, counting his cash."

"Amazing what a few quid will buy you these days."

"Not so much the money, sir. You'd be surprised what some people would do on the promise of getting a mention in the credits of a TV show."

Kaine sighed. "Yes. I probably would. Remind me about the money, though. I don't want you out of pocket."

Cough waved the issue away. "I imagine you've been doing some tidying up of your own, sir?" he asked, nodding in the direction of Derby.

"You could say that."

"So, we won't have to worry about Vadik Pataki turning up with another attack team, spitting nails?"

"No, we won't. No chance of that at all."

"Yep, I thought so. There were two men in the car that passed us. What happened to the passenger?"

"Lost his head, I'm afraid." Kaine winced, but didn't explain the joke. There would be plenty of time for a full debrief. "He did leave me with a trail of breadcrumbs though."

"Yeah? That's good."

Kaine glanced at the bloodstain near the front door, where he'd last seen Danny.

"We placed him in the back of our Ford, sir," Cough said, reading Kaine's mind. "Figured you'd want to send him back to his family for a decent ... well, send off. Don't worry, sir. We treated him with respect."

"I know you did, Cough." He paused for breath. "But Danny didn't have any family. To begin with, we'll take him to Mike's place. Danny loved the farm and it'll be fitting. Afterwards, the sea. Bobbie, his girlfriend, knows the farm and can visit, but ... not just yet, eh?"

"Understood, sir. I imagine a visit to Hungary is on the cards?"

"For me, Cough. And maybe a few of the others, but not for you or Stefan. If you're willing, I have other plans for you two."

"Your call, sir. Whatever you want, I'm up for it. Can't speak for Stinko, though." He turned to the younger man. "What do you reckon, mate?"

"You can count me in, Captain. Danny were a mate o' mine. Whatever you need me to do, I'm game."

Kaine nodded his thanks and moved on. "How's Mrs Prentiss?" he asked Cough, but Stefan answered.

"Crying her eyes out, Captain. But she ain't hurt or nothing. Reckon it's down to shock mainly."

"Can you look after her while Cough and I have a quiet word with Lajos Pataki?"

"The man in the crapper?"

Kaine nodded. "The very one."

"Yeah, no bother."

"Thanks, Stefan."

The youngster turned and hurried back the way they'd come, heading towards the kitchen, but halfway to the corner of the house he stopped and turned.

"Don't suppose we've got time for a cuppa, sir?"

Kaine grinned. The soldiers' need for a refreshing, recuperative brew spanned the generations.

"Sorry Stefan, I'd love one, but we can't hang around too long. Despite your arrangement with Farmer Giles, someone else might have called the cops. Besides, we don't have time to boil water without power and, funnily enough, there's no gas left. Refreshments will have to wait until we reach the farm."

Stefan broke out his second grin of the day.

"No probs, Captain. I'll go see how Mrs Prentiss is getting on," he said and hurried away.

"A happy soul," Kaine said to Cough as they headed towards the closed front doors.

"Not much of a conversationalist, sir. But he is reliable, and Mrs Prentiss seems to have taken to him."

They reached the front doors. Kaine stopped and lowered his voice. "Good, I'll want you and Stefan to protect her until this is over. Will you do that for me?"

Cough's expression turned serious. "Yes, sir. How long's this likely to last, though? Situation seems a little complicated to me. And fluid."

"Let's go find out, shall we?"

"Time for a visit to the loo, is it?"

"Yes, Sergeant. I'm feeling a little flushed."

Cough winced. "Oh dear, sir. That's beneath you."

"Sorry, Cough. I'm a little off my game right now."

Time to shape up.

CHAPTER TWENTY-THREE

Contrary to Kaine's original expectations, but much to his relief, Lajos Pataki still breathed. In fact, he seemed to have rallied a little, although he did babble happily into the toilet bowl as though he'd lost his grip on reality. He spoke in a strange singsong Hungarian with a smattering of English swear words mixed in. His head flopped over the bowl and his speech sounded hollow.

The man's injured arm was in a bad way, its colour dark, the wound already festering. Kaine had seen crush injuries before and understood the process. The loss of blood to the limb caused by the injury and aggravated by the life-saving tourniquet had produced an early onset of putrefaction. Already the arm smelled of old blood and rotting meat. Kaine doubted anyone could save the arm, and he couldn't generate one ounce of pity for the sorry specimen of humanity.

Kaine stood over the miserable creature.

"Lajos Pataki," he said, but the small man with the white hair ignored his name and kept up the mumbling.

Kaine leaned forwards and pulled the chain attached to an old-fashioned, high-level cistern. The flush echoed loudly in the close confines of the washroom.

Lajos Pataki choked and squealed, and turned his head as much as the noose would allow. He coughed and spluttered until the water finished running, but it had the desired effect. The little man stopped babbling and started shouting—in fluent Hungarian.

Although Kaine didn't understand the words, he caught their meaning easily enough.

"That woke the bugger up," Cough said, through a chuckle. "A little harsh, though, mind. I thought you were joking about feeling flushed."

Kaine glanced at Cough unable to hide a scowl. "This bastard ordered Marian Prentiss' death and was deeply involved in her husband's murder. There's no need to waste your sympathy on him, Sergeant. Besides, I was carrying out Danny's dying wish."

The words, "Danny's dying wish", tore out his throat even as he spoke them. How the hell was he going to keep it together in front of the men ... and Lara.

Cough scoffed. "No sympathy here, Captain. Just didn't want you drowning the fucker before he's puked up all the intel we want."

"Good point, but there's no need for the kid gloves any more, Sergeant." Kaine pointed outside, towards his bike. "In the bike's top box, I've got two mobile phones, a computer tablet, and another gizmo that might have been used to block the mobile phone signals. I'm betting they're full of the information we require. This piece of filth probably won't add more than background colour, but he might just help me get over Danny's loss. I need a punching bag."

Kaine kicked Lajos Pataki in the ribs with the inside of his boot, more to underline his intention than to cause real damage. Again, Lajos Pataki squealed.

Normally, Kaine wasn't one to beat up a helpless captive, but this day was anything but normal. Not that he had any real intentions of unloading his fury on the injured man, he just wanted Lajos Pataki to *think* he would. And since the miniature Hungarian thug understood English, Kaine wasn't going to explain his real intentions to Cough.

"If you say so, Captain." Cough winced at the blow and his confused frown matched Stefan's default expression.

Kaine winked and rubbed his hands together. "I do, Sergeant. I do indeed."

The comms unit clicked in Kaine's ear.

"Cough," he said before tapping the earpiece into life, "untie this piece of filth and drag him into the kitchen. And there's no need to be to be too gentle about it, either."

"Foxtrot One to Alpha One, are you receiving me? Over."

Lara.

The breath caught in Kaine's throat. He swallowed hard before answering.

"Alpha One here. Reading you strength five. What's your ETA? Over."

"Should be there in ten minutes. How are you? Over."

Kaine gritted his teeth and waited for Cough to drag the squealing man away before answering. "I've had better days. Who's with you? Over."

"No one. I'm alone. Over."

"Damn it, Foxtrot One. Turn back. There's nothing for you to do here. Over."

The last thing Kaine wanted was for Lara to witness the way he intended to deal with Papa Pataki's only surviving son. He'd never performed an amputation before, but he'd seen plenty done in the field. Anyway, how difficult could it be to saw off a man's arm if you didn't really care about the outcome or the pain inflicted during the process?

"I understand there are surviving casualties. Over."

Kaine gulped.

"None that matter. Over."

"I'll be the best judge of that!" she snapped. *"Foxtrot One, out."*

Damn it, Lara!

The earpiece clicked into silence. He tapped it once.

"*Whatcha, Mr K. How you doing?*" Corky answered Kaine's summons, his manner significantly less surly than usual.

"How'd you think I'm doing, Control?" Kaine barked, but he didn't mean it to sound so hostile or to forget radio protocol.

"*Yeah, Mr K. I get it. Stupid question. Corky's gonna miss Danny, too. Lovely bloke, he were. Really decent.*"

Kaine took a breath. "No. No. My fault. Shouldn't have snapped. I'm sorry. Over."

"*What can Corky do for you. Mr K?*"

"Force open a line between Foxtrot One and me. She's gone silent and I want her to turn back. Over."

"*Foxtrot One? Oh, you mean the doc. Nah, not worth it, Mr K. Corky's been trying to get her to change her mind since she learned what happened. She ain't listening.*"

"But she's alone, damn it. Over."

"'*Course she is. Ain't no one around to back her up. There's only Connor and Mike at the farm. And Mrs A, of course, but she's on a video conference with the DCI. He don't know nothing about what's going on over there with you and … Danny. Me an' the doc thought it best to keep him out of it. Him being the fuzz an' all.*"

For once, Corky was making perfect sense. It would be best for everyone concerned if Jones could be kept well out of the Prentiss mess.

"Okay, Control. Are you going to be available for a while? Over."

"*Yeah, Mr K. Corky's sticking around for as long as you need him to. You got anything particular in mind?*"

"I've recently acquired some mobile phones and a tablet. I'm going to need the information they contain asap. How can I get them to you? Over."

"*There ain't no need. Corky can access the information remotely. Easy-peasy. Want your hand held through the process?*"

"Sorry, I'm about to become a little busy. Can you walk Cough through it? Over."

"*Yeah, no worries. Prob'ly be easier doing it with Mr C, seeing as how*"

you're so useless with techie stuff unless it's used for blowing stuff to pieces."
He delivered the insult with a chuckle, sounding more like the old
Corky.

Kaine ignored the unjustified dig at his lack of knowledge of the
intricacies of IT. "I also found a piece of electronic equipment that
might have been used to block our comms signal. Thought you might
be interested in dissecting it. Maybe you can work out a fix. Over."

*"Yeah, sounds like a good idea. Corky'll tell Cough where to post it.
Someplace Corky can arrange a collection."*

Kaine didn't ask for details. Corky had never revealed his location
and Kaine had no intention of prying. Partitioning of sensitive information was a mainstay of keeping his people safe.

"I assume you're monitoring police radio traffic? Over."

*"Yep. Sure. Ain't no one's called the fuzz about the gunfight. Not yet,
anyhow. Corky's guessing there weren't no neighbours close enough to hear
the explosion, neither."*

Only Farmer Giles, but Cough had dealt with him well enough.

"Okay Control. Let me know the minute anyone takes an interest.
We'll need as much warning as you can give us. Over."

"Will do, Mr K."

"Alpha One, out."

Kaine tapped the earpiece into silence and headed for the
kitchen.

Someone, probably Stefan, had found a couple of large table
cloths and thrown them over the oil and water mix to make the floor
less slippery. They covered the blood, too.

Commando, his face red and blotchy and painful-looking, sat on
the floor in the corner, knees bent, hands tied behind his back. His
eyes were closed and he shivered, probably fighting the shock. No
matter how well-trained or prepared, serious injuries stimulated the
body's natural reaction to pain, and Commando clearly wasn't any
more immune than the rest of the human population. The bullet-
riddled Merc lay beside him on the floor, bleeding slowly onto the
tiles.

Neither man presented an immediate danger and, being

English hired hands, neither would have much useful information to offer. To begin with, Kaine turned towards the primary object of interest.

Cough had dumped Lajos on a dining chair. The pint-sized thug leaned forwards, arms still tied behind his back, the bonds secured above the smashed elbow. His head rested on the table, keeping his injured arm clear of the chair's back. Sodden white hair fell into his eyes.

The second he spotted Kaine, he sat up straight, jogged his arm, and screamed in Hungarian.

Kaine shouted over the tirade. "Speak English, moron. Or we'll get nowhere!"

Lajos bared his teeth. "Do you know who I am, *szar az agy számára?*"

Kaine's earpiece clicked. *"He's just called you 'shit for brains', Mr K. That there is one nasty little man."*

Kaine sighed. "Thanks, Control. But I have this. Alpha One, out."

For the moment, he ignored the insult and signalled for Cough to join him in the doorway.

"Yes, Captain?"

"Can you go fetch that stuff from my top box. Corky's going to tell you how to help him access the intel."

Cough's frown deepened. "You going to be okay here, Captain?"

"I will, but he won't." Kaine nodded to the man with the soggy white hair and the soon-to-be-missing arm.

Cough hiked his shoulder. "Fair enough, sir."

While Cough slid past Kaine, heading towards the front door and the Triumph, Kaine pulled out his Sig. He bypassed Lajos, whose gaze followed him all the way across the kitchen to the trembling captives in the corner. He squatted in front of them, but made sure he could still see Lajos at the table. Although the man was grievously injured and apparently toothless, Kaine would never willingly turn his back on a potential threat.

"Listen carefully." He waited for the two injured Englishmen to look up and meet his eye.

Commando managed the feat before Merc, who looked in significantly worse condition.

"You two are lucky to still be alive, agreed?"

They both nodded. Neither spoke.

"Want to stay that way?" he asked unnecessarily.

Again, they nodded.

"My friend, Danny, died today and I'm barely keeping my shit together. Nothing would suit me better than to bludgeon you money-grubbing bastards to death with the leg of a chair. But Danny was a good man, and he wouldn't have appreciated that. He'd say there's been enough death, today. Me? I'm not so sure. You can either live or die. I don't give a crap. Understand?"

"Yes," Commando answered, managing to force the word past his damaged lips.

Merc didn't seem to have enough strength to speak.

"There's a medic on the way. She'll be here in a few minutes. I can either let her treat you or not. My decision, not hers. Answer my colleague's questions, you live. Keep schtum, you die. What's it to be?"

"Ask us, please. We'll tell you anything we can," Commando said, answering for them both.

Kaine tapped his earpiece. "Alpha One to Control, are you receiving me? Over."

"*Corky here, Mr K. What's cooking?*"

"Sorry to disturb you, Control. Are you finished with the techie stuff? Over."

"*Not quite, but Corky can multi task if necessary.*"

"Excellent." Kaine dug into his jacket pocket for a spare comms unit and stuck it into Commando's ear—the undamaged one. The man winced, but otherwise accepted the offering without complaint. "I have a couple of men here desperate to tell you everything they know. *One of them has the backup earpiece.* Over."

He emphasised the information, hoping Corky would take the hint.

"*Understood, Alpha One. Over.*"

Kaine grinned to himself. No one could ever accuse Corky of being slow on the uptake.

"Thank you, Control. I want names, addresses, how they were contracted by the Patakis. Basically, pump them dry. If you can't verify any of their answers, please let me know. I'll be awfully keen to hear about it. Over."

"*That's an affirmative, Alpha One. Control, out.*"

The only thing surprising about the response was Corky's adherence to correct radio protocol. It showed how seriously he took the situation. Danny's death cut deep.

Lajos Pataki groaned and shifted in his chair. Kaine wagged the Sig at him and he froze, eyes locked on its muzzle.

Kaine stood. Commando lifted his head to follow, wincing at the movement.

"Don't look at me, son. Concentrate on the questions. Your lives depend on it."

Commando lowered his head.

Kaine returned to the dining table, grabbed Lajos by the scruff of his neck, and yanked him to his feet. He dragged him through the smashed bifold door and around the back of the house. Lajos screamed and howled the whole way to the fire-damaged courtyard.

Kaine threw the man to the paving slabs and stood over him. He levelled the Sig at his captive's right eye. Lajos squirmed onto his side, leaning away from the damaged arm.

"Stop, please," he pleaded. "Do not kill me!"

"Is this the part where you offer me money?"

Lajos nodded, desperately latching onto any hope on offer. "Yes, yes. Money. We have money. Name your price. Five hundred thousand euros? Cash. I can get cash. It is yours if you let me go."

Kaine tilted his head and added a dramatic sigh. "A little more than the two hundred thousand you offered us earlier, but still pitiful."

"Half a million euros is a lot of money." Lajos panted, struggled to speak.

"Vadik offered me two million, and he's dead."

"Dead? Vadik is dead?"

Lajos blinked, but Kaine could tell by the expression the man was anything but upset by the news. No love lost between the half-brothers, or so it seemed.

"Yep. Two million euros didn't buy Vadik's life, but at least he valued himself at more than half a million." Kaine stretched his lips into a thin smile. "You're Papa Pataki's only remaining son. What's your life worth to him?"

"Five!" he shouted. "Papa will give you five million euros."

Lajos used his good elbow to push himself upright, his face contorting with the effort. He saw a potential way out of his hole and was frantic to grab it with the only working hand he had left.

"Five million euros for Papa Pataki's only living son? Nope, not enough."

The soles of Lajos' once highly polished but now badly scuffed hand-made Italian loafers, slipped on the paving slabs beneath him as he tried to work his way to his feet. Halfway to standing, the shoes lost traction, and Lajos fell, landing arse-first on the deck. His pained groan was music and Kaine let loose a cruel laugh.

He levelled the Sig, lining the sights up with Lajos' groin and scratched at his beard. God, he would really enjoy a shave.

"Not worth my while keeping you alive for loose change."

"Ten million euros!" Lajos screamed, panting even harder after his abortive efforts to stand.

"Papa Pataki will pay ten million euros for you?"

"Yes! Yes he will."

"Does Papa have that much cash lying around?"

Lajos stopped panting and shot Kaine a quizzical look. "What do you know of Papa?"

"Only the little Vadik told me before I snuffed out his life. Papa's a hard man, I suppose?"

"Yes. Very hard. Papa is the *Giant of Győr*," he announced as though it would instil some sort of terror into Kaine. "If you kill me, he will hunt you down and destroy you, your family, and anyone you ever called a friend."

Kaine sighed. "You and Vadik seem to have been reading from the same script."

"Huh?"

"Never mind. So, if I kill you, the terrible 'Giant of Győr' will hunt me to the ends of the earth and kill me slowly. Is that what you're saying?"

"Yes. You will die in great pain."

"Okay." Kaine shrugged. "In that case, there's no point in sparing your life, is there? I've already killed Vadik, so there's absolutely no hope for me, right?"

Lajos shook his head violently, the damp white hair flopping about his face. "No, no. Vadik was the bastard son. He meant little to Papa. I am the favoured one. Spare me, and you will live. Ten million euros. I promise."

Kaine scratched his chin again, apparently trying to make a decision. "Getting closer. Make it fifteen and we have a deal. I'll even let our medic treat you ahead of the other two."

"Yes. Yes! Fifteen million euros in cash. Please, please let me live!"

"And you'll negotiate the handover with Papa?"

"Yes. I will make the arrangements. He will pay. I swear it."

"Okay, Lajos, old friend. You and I have ourselves a deal."

Lajos Pataki, the man who ordered Marian Prentiss' death, broke down. He sobbed. Tears rolled down his colourless cheeks. He kept repeating the word "*Köszönöm*", and looked like a lost child bawling for his mummy.

In the distance, a car's horn blared three times—one long, two short—and the increasing whine of a racing engine drowned out Lajos' pitiful snivelling.

Good timing.

The horn repeated the signal, Morse Code for the letter "D". Seconds later, the engine note changed as the driver dropped down three gears in rapid succession. Tyres squealed on drying tarmac and crunched on gravel.

Kaine allowed himself a grim smile.

Although he'd rather not have exposed Lara to danger, her

medical expertise would come in handy. Keeping Lajos Pataki alive had suddenly taken on a great deal more importance.

"This is your lucky day!" he said, grabbing Lajos' shirt collar once again and dragging him to his feet.

He screamed and hopped on one leg, keeping his right foot off the ground. Kaine looked down. The right ankle was a bloody mess. It gave him another idea. A minor modification to his rapidly developing plan.

He called out, "Cough!", and the man himself emerged from the kitchen.

"Doc's here," he said.

"Yes, I heard the signal."

Kaine pushed Lajos away. He stumbled, but Cough caught him and held him upright.

"Take this cretin into the kitchen and keep your eye on him. All of a sudden, he's become rather valuable to the team."

"Will do, sir."

Cough hooked a hand under Lajos' good arm and dragged the hobbling, bawling man towards the shattered glass door.

"Wh-Who are you people?" Lajos demanded.

Cough jabbed the butt of his gun into the Hungarian's temple hard enough to stun, but not to cause real damage. "Shut the fuck up, moron. You might be valuable, but that doesn't give you leave to ask questions. Just be glad you're still breathing."

Kaine left Cough to his babysitting detail and hurried around the side of the house, heading for the front and Lara.

CHAPTER TWENTY-FOUR

By the time Kaine reached the front, Lara had already climbed out of her car—a rented Ford Kuga—and was burrowing in the back for something.

"Doc," he called, using her title to give her the heads-up.

She straightened and shrugged a heavy medical pack onto her shoulder. He wouldn't insult her by offering to carry it, at least not while they were in the field and with company.

"Captain," she said, waiting by the car for him.

He stopped a pace away from her, wanting nothing more than to pull her into a hug and break down. Damn the stiff upper lip nonsense, Danny was dead.

Lara had left the Ford's tailgate up. It offered them some privacy, but not enough.

"Oh my God, Ryan," she whispered, eyes filling, "Danny's ... Danny's really gone?"

Kaine shot a sideways glance at Cough and Stefan's white Ford, and the covered body draped across the back seat.

"He took a bullet that was meant for me," he said, voice catching. "Lara, he saved my life."

Lower lip trembling, she nodded. "And the man who killed him?"

"Dead."

She nodded again. "Good."

Given her abhorrence of violence, the response surprised Kaine, but Danny was like a younger brother and Lara was only human. She took a deep, centring breath before speaking again.

"Corky said the comms broke down. What exactly happened?"

"Later." Kaine shook his head. "Now's not the time."

He stepped back and gave her the once-over. Dressed in military camouflage gear, desert boots, a peaked cap, and a dark green bandana, she'd come prepared for action.

"Where are the casualties?"

"In the kitchen." He led her around the side of the house, following the gravel path, and gave her an outline of what to expect. As they approached the destroyed bifold doors, he turned and held out his arm to stop her. "Cover your nose and mouth with the bandana. I don't want the casualties to see your face."

Without question, she did as he instructed. They stepped over the threshold and entered a place that looked closer to a military field hospital than a kitchen.

"I said you'd treat this one first," Kaine said, pointing to Lajos, "but ... you're in charge here."

A tear-stained Lajos Pataki started to say something, but thought better of it when Cough raised his gun and waggled the butt in his face.

"Quite right," Lara said, her hazel eyes scanning her patients' wounds. "When did you ever qualify to run triage?" She spoke with the authority of a professional medic.

Kaine raised his hands.

"Sorry, Doc. Point taken. I'll leave you to it."

He nodded to Cough, and although he said, "Sergeant, give the doc any help she needs," he actually meant, "You're in charge of security. Take care of her for me."

Sergeant Ashley Coughlin knew his job, and he knew how important Lara was to Kaine. He'd protect her with his life, as would everyone on Kaine's extended team.

Kaine left them to it and headed for another person in need of protection. Their numbers were increasing, but he didn't mind taking on the responsibility of yet another endangered soul. No matter how many he protected, it still wouldn't wipe his slate clean. The eighty-three deaths would remain on his conscience forever.

Miraculously, the front room had survived the firefight totally unscathed. Marian sat in the corner of the sofa, a cardigan draped over her shoulders, a cushion hugged to her belly, and a tissue in hand. Stefan stood guard over her.

When Kaine arrived, she jumped to her feet. "Where's your friend? Where's Danny? Stefan won't tell me anything."

Kaine hesitated for a moment, trying to find the right words, but there was no easy way to say it.

"Mrs Prentiss," he said, "Danny didn't make it."

After a fractional delay, her eyes opened wide in shock.

"Oh my God, I-I'm so ..."

She threw a hand to her mouth, collapsed back into her seat, and folded over. Her shoulders quaked. Kaine sat alongside her but kept a slight gap between them.

"Danny was my friend," he said, "but you didn't really know him, did you?"

She straightened, wiped her nose on the tissue, and shook her head.

"No, I-I didn't know him at all. But he was a good man. I could tell that the moment I caught sight of him outside the hospital yesterday."

Kaine nodded and turned towards her. "He told me what he saw. Suspected you were being beaten by your husband. Wanted to help you."

"He ... Danny made a mistake. Robbie would never hit me. Not ever." She glanced up at the blank TV screen attached to the wall. Her brown eyes filling up at the memory of what she'd seen earlier. The horror of her husband's death returning afresh. "Robbie may have made mistakes when it came to running a business, but he loved me, and ... I loved him so much."

"Mrs Prentiss—"

"Marian. Please call me Marian." She dabbed tears from her puffy eyes.

Kaine nodded. "Marian it is."

Stefan shuffled, and a pained expression crossed his face.

"Yes, Private?"

"Erm, excuse me, Captain. Is it safe to stay here so long?"

"Good question. The doc's just arrived. We have a few minutes while she makes her assessment. Control is monitoring the airwaves for relevant traffic."

"He can do that, sir? I mean, in real time?" Under different circumstances, Stefan's confused frown would have been amusing.

The question surprised Kaine until he remembered how little interaction Stefan had had with Corky. He'd never really witnessed the miracle that was Corky in action.

"Yes, Stefan. He certainly can."

"What about Vadik Pataki?" Marian asked. "The piece of filth who murdered Robbie. The man is pure evil. He's the one who drove me to hospital. The one Danny mistook for Robbie. He'll be back, I know he will. He ... they will never leave us alone." A hand dropped to her slightly rounded belly. "The baby and I will never be safe."

"Marian," Kaine said, placing a gentle hand on her shoulder. "Vadik Pataki's dead. He'll never hurt anyone again."

She shook off his hand. "No, you don't understand. This is about more than one man. Vadik's brother and their father, the whole evil clan—"

"Lajos is in the kitchen. Badly hurt. To be honest, I'll be surprised if he survives the day. As for the father, the so-called Giant of Győr, well"—Kaine paused for a moment to give Marian an encouraging smile—"I have plans for him and his people."

"You know about the Patakis?"

"Not really. At least not yet. As I said, I have plans. First though, we need to find somewhere safe for you and the baby."

He smiled again but it didn't have the encouraging effect he wanted. Marian Prentiss burst into tears again.

"We're never going to be safe. No matter where we go, they'll find us."

"Not with a new identity," Kaine said. "New papers, a new location."

Kaine couldn't ignore the sense of déjà vu. He'd offered Melanie Archer the same package. Although she'd refused his offer of a new life in a new location, she had her reasons, illogical though they'd seemed at the time. As far as Kaine understood, Marian Prentiss would have no such objections. With an unborn child to protect, she should jump at the opportunity of a new life away from danger.

"No," she said. "That's not possible. How can I go anywhere? I don't have any money. It's all gone. All of it."

"Money's not an issue, Marian. The Giant of Győr, Viktor Pataki, is going to fund your new life. Not that he knows it yet."

"What? How?"

"I'm still fleshing out the details in my head. But I can assure you, money will not be an issue. Will you trust me on this?"

Marian blinked, shook her head. "I-I ... don't—"

"Danny was one of my closest friends." Kaine hesitated long enough to gain her undivided attention. "Viktor Pataki is directly responsible for his death. Trust me, Marian. He *will* pay. He'll pay in blood as well as in cash."

"Who are you? The police?"

"No," Kaine said, "not the police. My men and I have slightly more latitude than the police."

She crushed the sodden tissue into a tight ball and frowned.

"Danny and Stefan call you Captain. Are you soldiers?"

Kaine tilted his head to one side. "Something like that. Although we're mostly self-employed these days."

"Self-employed. You mean, mercenaries?"

"No, Marian. Not at all. That term has rather negative associations. Those people in your kitchen—and the ones who worked for the Patakis—they are mercenaries. Hired hands. My men and I are different."

"What are you, then?"

Good question.

How could he describe himself and his men? If not mercs then ... what?

"We're volunteers, Marian. The good guys who can do what the police can't. We take on cases like yours and deliver proper justice."

"Volunteers?"

"Yes, that's right. And we're volunteering to sort out this mess for you and your baby."

"Why? Why are you doing this?"

Kaine paused and swallowed, almost unable to speak.

"It's what ... Danny would have wanted."

"But there are so few of you. What can you do against a mob like the Patakis?"

"You'd be surprised at what a few good people can achieve, Marian. And, trust me, we are very, very good at what we do."

Stefan stiffened and jerked his head up. His gaze focused on a spot beyond Kaine's shoulder, but he relaxed when Lara emerged from the kitchen and hurried towards them.

Kaine patted Marian's hand and jumped to his feet. "Don't worry. It's the medic."

"A woman?"

"She was, last time I looked." On this occasion, Marian did return his smile. "Stefan, would you mind taking Marian upstairs to gather some belongings? We'll be away as soon as we can."

"I packed earlier, remember?"

"Yes, I know. But you have a little more time now. Don't bother with too many clothes, just pack the ones you're most comfortable wearing. Take the most important, sentimental stuff. Photos and the like. You won't be able to return here. Never. No need for passports or wedding certificates, either. We'll organise some new ones for you later."

The blow showed on her pale and bruised face as her changed situation struck home.

Kaine was sick of seeing women who carried bruises and suffered broken bones at the hands of angry and entitled men. Melanie Archer had been beaten both recently and throughout her marriage, and now Marian Prentiss stood before him, damaged by the fists of a thug. Would it ever end?

He turned to Lara, whose own facial bruising—the legacy of her meeting with a South African bigot—had only recently faded.

So much pain, so much brutality.

And now Danny.

Christ, what a world.

After Stefan had escorted Marian from the room and they'd reached the stairs, Lara lowered her bandana to reveal a concerned expression.

"You were right," she said.

"Really? Makes a change. What about?"

She tutted and shook her head. "The two minor casualties will need hospitalisation, but Lajos Pataki is the most serious case. He'll need more treatment than I can offer him, especially if we want to try and save that arm."

"Who said anything about saving his arm? If it keeps him alive long enough to get him home, you can chop the bloody thing off for all I care."

"Ryan!" she snapped, and shot a glance over his shoulder for fear of having shouted his name too loudly.

He stared her down hard. "You've never heard of a battlefield amputation?"

"No, darn it! That's out of the question!" she said, lowering her voice to a whisper. "He needs an operating theatre and an experienced orthopaedic surgeon."

"Not a chance. If you don't operate, I'll do it myself. Either that, or I'll release the tourniquet and you know what happens then."

They both knew.

Earlier, in the kitchen, Kaine checked Lajos' wrist below the tourniquet. He'd found no pulse. No pulse meant tissue death and a build-up of both toxins and blood pressure. Releasing the tourniquet would allow those same toxins to flood through Lajos' circulatory system and cause all sorts of damage. Damage including acute renal failure along with a load of other medical conditions, none of which would end well for the patient.

"Really? You'd do that?"

For the first time since they'd met, Kaine scowled at the only woman he'd ever really loved. A reluctance to demonstrate exactly what he was prepared to do to exact vengeance had been one of the reasons he didn't want Lara around.

"In a heartbeat. You know who these people are and what they're capable of doing, right? They killed Danny and Robert Prentiss, for God's sake!"

"I know that, but he's my patient and I have a responsibility to do my best for him—for them all."

Kaine took gentle hold of her upper arm. "Do whatever you can for him. Either amputate, or not, I don't care. But whatever you do, we're out of here within the next half hour."

She tore her arm away. "For pity's sake, Ryan. I'd need more time than that."

"You have all you need in your bag, right? And you know what's entailed?"

Lara blanched as the implications of what he was forcing upon her hit home.

"Yes, I ... removed a dog's shattered leg once, but that was in my clinic, under sterile conditions. Not in a farmhouse kitchen. And it was a dog, Ryan, not a man. I mean, we don't even have access to hot water, for God's sake!"

"Lajos Pataki's not a man! He's a murdering monster. Remember that, and remember what happened to Danny! Do it, Lara. Keep him alive if you can. Now, what about the other two?"

She shook her head as though finding it difficult to concentrate.

"I-I made them comfortable and patched them up as best I could. Sterilised their wounds. They're in no immediate danger. One will probably lose his hand. There's too much damage. And no, I won't be amputating it, no matter what you say!"

He smiled in relief as Lara showed her mettle.

"As for the other one," she continued, "the one with the scalds. He'll probably need skin grafts for his hands, but his face isn't too serious. Boiling water, Ryan? Really?"

Kaine held up his hands. "Don't waste your sympathy on him. He did that to himself while trying to kill me. Right"—he stood up straighter—"better get on and treat Lajos. The minute you're done, we're out of here—whether he's ready to move or not. You can call an ambulance for the other two when we're on the road."

"Ryan," she said, tears forming, "I don't know if I can do this. It's all too ... awful."

"Think of him as an animal in pain. You'll be easing his suffering. Does that help?"

"No. Not one little bit."

Kaine shrugged. "Apparently, back in the American Civil War, a decent surgeon could remove a limb in less than ninety seconds." He raised an eyebrow, but decided not to add a cheeky grin. "I'm giving you a full thirty minutes. What are you complaining about?"

"Ryan, this isn't funny."

"That bastard had a hand in Danny's death. No single part of this is funny, Lara." He took a breath. "Need any help with the operation?"

"Yes please. Someone should hold him down. I've given him ketamine for the pain, but it will be a while before the full effects kick in."

"Ask Cough to lend a hand."

"Cough? I thought you might ..."

Kaine looked aghast. "Me? Hell no. I'm far too squeamish to take part in a medical operation. I'd probably faint away on you."

"Ryan, don't be ridiculous."

"Do your best, Lara. And hurry."

"And while I'm hacking a man's arm off, what are you going to be doing?"

"Me?" he said, glancing at one of the bloodstains decorating the floor in the hall. "I'll be planning a little road trip. After all this mayhem, I reckon the gang needs a holiday."

Lara gulped. "I'm really going to do this, aren't I?"

He cupped her cheek. "Sorry, love. If there was another way, I'd take it. You know that, right?"

She closed her eyes and leaned her face into his hand.

"I know, but it's too horrible."

"You're using ketamine, you say?"

"I am."

"Isn't one of the side-effects possible memory loss?"

"Yes. One of the reason it's sometimes used as a date-rape drug. Why?"

"Maybe Lajos will forget some of what happened here. We might be able to use that." Kaine remembered the idea that had struck him earlier and dropped his hand from her cheek. "By the way, how's his ankle? He was limping and there was blood."

She shook her head, her expression dismissive.

"Looks much worse than it is. Plenty of blood but it's little more than a scratch. All he needs are a few stitches."

"Hmm."

"Why?"

"Do me a favour, will you?"

Her eyes narrowed in suspicion.

"Another one?"

"Yes please."

"What did you have in mind?"

"After you're done lopping off his arm, can you bandage the ankle heavily. Make it look like it's broken?"

"Ryan, what on earth for?"

"We might need it as a convincer."

"You're not making any sense."

"And you're wasting time." He checked his watch. "You now have less than twenty-seven minutes."

"Darn you, Ryan Liam Kaine. The second we're out of here, you're going to tell me what you have in mind, okay?"

"Yes, I promise. Now, go. Do your stuff, Doctor."

Frowning, she turned and hurried away.

Kaine watched her go, silently wishing her well and hoping she'd learn to forgive him. When she disappeared into the kitchen, he stepped deeper into the front room and tapped the earpiece. "Alpha One to Control, come in. Over."

"*Corky here, Mr K. And don't worry, the comms unit you gave the Commando is offline. You and dear old Corky are alone in hyperspace. Whatcha need next?*"

"Everything check out with Commando and Merc? Over."

"*So far, yeah. They ain't nothing but hired guns. Don't have a Scooby 'bout the big picture, but they did give Corky a line on the Pataki family's operation in the UK. Pretty small potatoes, by the way. More or less one cousin and 'is dog. Want me to shut him down?*"

"Might well do. After the dust settles a little, I was going to take a bunch of the lads and pay a house call. When news gets out about Danny, there won't be any shortage of volunteers baying for Hungarian blood. Over."

"*You can do it like that, of course. But Corky has a cleaner way in mind. More clinical, you know?*"

"Care to explain? Over."

"*Yeah. Although Cousin Pataki's here legally, he's selling drugs and women in Hull. Only small scale right now, but it's a growing business. Corky can set him up for a police raid any time you fancy it. And since he's part of an organised crime gang, the National Crime Agency will want to be involved.*"

"Sounds like a good idea to me, but hold off for a while. We don't want to tip our hand to Papa Pataki. Over."

"*You mean the 'Giant of Győr'?*" Cork asked, his voice bubbling with sarcasm.

"Yes, the very man. I'll let you know when you can drop Cousin Pataki in the mire. Meanwhile, do you mind running one of your world famous deep dives on the Pataki family's operations in Győr, please? Over."

"*Already on it, Mr K. You'll have the first level rundown by the time you reach the farm.*"

"Excellent. Thanks, Control. Did you find anything interesting on the phones or on the tablet I liberated from the deceased in the BMW? Over."

"*Yeah. Quite a bit, actually. Corky will include the important stuff in the report. That gizmo, though. Brilliant. Really clever bit of kit.*"

"Was it responsible for blocking our comms earlier? Over."

"*Sure was. Corky can't wait to get his hands on it. Might help develop a work-around to stop something similar happening to our comms system again. Wouldn't mind having a chat with the inventor if you can arrange it.*"

"Doubt that'll happen anytime soon. I suspect he was the second fatality in the BMW. Over."

"*Shame. The guy was one clever dude.*"

"Do you have Viktor Pataki's phone number to hand? Over."

"*Sure do, Mr K.*"

"Just a sec"—Kaine pulled out his mobile and navigated to the contacts screen—"ready. Fire away. Over."

Corky dictated the number and Kaine tapped it in for later use.

"Okay Control. Here's the final request for the moment. Can you start building a legend for Marian Prentiss. We can hide her away in a hotel for a few days with Cough and Stefan for protection, but that's only ever going to be a stop-gap. Over."

"*Whoa. This helping you lark is becoming a full-time job, Mr K.*"

"Sorry, Control. Am I asking too much of you? Over."

"*Nah. If that ever happens, Corky's gonna let you know sharpish.*" Corky laughed. "*Or maybe he'll just stop answering your calls. Laters, Mr K.*"

"See you, Control. And thanks again. No idea where we'd be without you. Alpha One, out."

Kaine tapped the earpiece into silence and took a breath. He looked down. His hands were still stained with Danny's blood. They shook with the adrenaline washout and he formed fists.

Oh Jesus. Danny. I am so sorry.

A gut-churning scream from the kitchen echoed through the whole house. Clearly, Lara had started the operation. Kaine shuddered and swallowed the bile bubbling up from his gut.

Confessing to being squeamish about medical procedures hadn't exactly been a total lie.

CHAPTER TWENTY-FIVE

WEDNESDAY 3RD MAY – Viktor Pataki
Pataki Compound, Outside Győr, Hungary

Viktor Pataki, the all-powerful Giant of Győr, stood with his hands clasped behind his broad back, staring through the open window and breathing deeply of the cool evening air. The wide valley, his valley, stretched out below him to the west, the shadows thrown long by the setting sun. He had built the compound to protect his legacy. His powerful legacy, and it was being threatened on all sides.

Born in poverty, Viktor had ripped the awful power he wielded from the very core of the land by the pure driving force of his will. He protected that power with the fury of a jealous God. No one would take it from him. No one!

Men with rifles patrolled the grounds, a testament to his strength and influence. They would repel any attack. They would willingly give up their lives to protect their leader, their Giant. He inhaled another deep breath of the sweet, pure air of his Hungarian homeland, but it felt wrong. A bitterness fouled his nose hairs, the bitterness of anger, frustration, and curiosity.

Where are they?

From England, he had heard nothing since early that morning. Something bad had happened. He sensed it deep within his bones.

Viktor turned to face the room. The men cowered beneath his baleful glare. As well they might. With one simple dismissive wave of his mighty hand, he could have any one of them gutted, skinned, and eradicated from the Earth, and no one would lift a finger to protect them. Police would enter the compound at their peril. If necessary, his brave men would defend their Giant from an army division. He was impregnable. Unstoppable. All-powerful.

So, what had happened in England?

"Not one word from either of them?" he growled at Peder Torok, who shuddered under the onslaught, as was the way of such a creature.

"I-I am afraid not, *főnök*," Torok answered. He swallowed deeply, wrung his hands, and gave that sickening, fawning half-bow, half-smile of his.

Hateful insect.

A sycophant of the worst order, but as the chosen man of Lajos, Viktor let him live. Without Lajos, the insect would have been "disappeared" long, long ago.

"And Cousin Ido?"

"He has heard nothing, *főnök*. I spoke to him one hour ago, when both Vadik and Lajos failed to make contact."

Things were turning to dirt. What was the point of having the terrifying reputation of the Giant of Győr when nobody trembled and no one replied to his calls?

Viktor had planned the operation with the precision of a military strike. A little intimidation, minimal bloodletting, nothing serious. Money had even changed hands. Every section of the plan should have been accomplished by now. The money transfer had completed on time and without challenge. Even now, the Pataki family should be in legal possession of a new business operation, but something had gone wrong.

"I paid good money to that little blond geek for his fancy toys!" he howled and thumped his chest. "I even let him tag along as he begged. Now, I cannot even talk to my sons. What the fuck is happening in that vile backwater of a country? What of Robert Prentiss?"

Again, Torok wrung his hands. Much more of that, and he would lose them, finger by finger.

"Has it not made the BBC news?"

"No, *fönök*. I have been watching the local and national reports via the internet, but there has been nothing related to the ... operation."

Viktor's angry roar rolled around the room like thunder.

"By now, the body of Robert Prentiss should have been found, apparently dead by his own hands. Do so many prominent people commit suicide in England that it is no longer newsworthy?"

"Perhaps the body has yet to be discovered, *fönök*. As you know, part of the plan was to have the workforce sent home for the afternoon."

"*Idióta!*"

Viktor picked up a nearby tumbler and threw it at the useless fuck. The coward ducked, showing surprisingly good reflexes. The glass smashed against the wall, and the pieces fell to the carpet.

"Do not tell me what I *know*. Tell me what I *do not* know."

"Forgive me, *fönök*, but ..."

He squatted to collect the broken pieces. Another of the men, the one with no name who wore square glasses, assisted him.

"...but?" Viktor demanded.

Torok straightened, leaving the other man to continue the clean-up.

"If you like, *fönök*, I will contact the British police and tell them there is a body. I will do it anonymously."

Viktor reached for another tumbler, but only one of the six remained. When had he broken so many? He left it intact rather than have to drink his night-time *pálinka* direct from the bottle.

"Do not be stupid. That would raise suspicions and ruin my plans. No. If not before, the body will be found in the morning when the administration staff arrive for work. We must be patient."

Viktor ran his fingers through his hair, raking the long strands back from his forehead and away from his eyes. So many women complimented him on his thick, wavy hair. Although now greying in parts, he was proud of his mane. At sixty-eight, he had the strength and energy of a man half his age. And the women, whores and fillies alike, still trembled under his potency. He was not known as the Giant of Győr without good reason.

"You have tried telephoning the Prentiss home?"

"Yes, *főnök*, but there is no answer. And all the portable phones have been powered down. It is a mystery."

"Contact Cousin Ido. Instruct him to send people to investigate."

Torok lowered his head, but kept his eyes fixed on Viktor and the remaining tumbler. The miserable creep showed a laudable sense of self-preservation. Perhaps he was not so stupid after all.

"Yes, *főnök*. But Hull is a long way from Derby. It will take Ido's men more than two hours to—"

The ornate telephone on Viktor's desk jangled, cutting off Torok mid-sentence. All eyes in the room turned to the device that rarely spoke. Viktor signalled for Torok to answer. He never responded to telephones himself. What other use did servants have?

Torok rushed to the desk, nearly tripping over the rug in the process, and plucked the handset from its cradle. He turned his back towards Viktor. In deference rather than insolence, Viktor assumed.

"*Helló? ... Helló? Ki van ott?* ... Yes, I speak English."

The man chosen by Lajos fell silent while he listened. A few seconds later, his shoulders sagged. He spun to face Viktor, eyes staring wide, his dark face many shades paler than before.

"It is for you, *főnök*," he croaked, holding out the phone. One hand covered the trumpet mouthpiece, both hands shook.

"Take a message, *idióta*."

"No, *főnök*, the Englishman insists on speaking to you."

"Insists?" Viktor bellowed. "He insists? Tell him to go fu—wait, an Englishman, did you say?"

"Yes, *főnök*," Torok said, his voice stronger, but still quaking. "And the man says he has Lajos!"

Viktor snatched the telephone from the quivering minion and pressed it to his ear. It was warm and damp from sweat and the shiny oil Torok insisted on plastering all over his hair. Viktor wiped the earpiece on his sleeve and held it slightly away from his head.

"Who this?" he demanded in excellent English.

Viktor prided himself on his fluent mastery of the English tongue.

"Is that Viktor Pataki, the so-called 'Giant of Győr'?" The English accent always made them appear aloof and superior, but the way the man used his honorary title stank of sarcasm.

Viktor bristled.

"It is. Who the fuck you are?"

"Are you the father of Vadik and Lajos Pataki?"

Viktor ground his teeth. Hot anger flared in his belly, threatening to boil into a rage. Who was this soft-spoken man who risked death in such a way?

"Yes. Answer question, dolt! What you know of my sons? What you want?"

"I know a great deal about your sons. They happen to be ignorant, murdering savages. Rather like their father, I imagine. As for what I want. Well, I want to deliver a message."

What is this? A joke?

"You have message?"

To speak to the Giant of Győr in such a way, the Englishman had to be insane. A madman. An *őrült.*

"Well, I have good news and bad news. Which would you prefer first?"

"What!"

In an instant, his boiling rage cooled, turning his blood to ice. The Englishman was taunting him. Viktor had to keep control. Concentration was needed or he would miss something important. He signalled for Torok to pick up the extension. His old telephone did not have a loudspeaker facility.

"No preference?" the Englishman said, almost conversationally.

The man was clearly a lunatic. For two *filler*, Viktor would have slammed the telephone down on him but, inside madness, there often hid some grains of sanity. Perhaps the Englishman *did* have news of his sons.

"Okay," the English lunatic, the *őrült*, continued, "I'll start with the good news. Lajos survived the operation."

Operation?

Viktor stood taller, stretching his commanding frame.

"Survived operation? What operation? What you tell me?"

"Not too fluent in the old English, eh Viktor? Okay, I'll speak slowly, and try to be crystal clear. Unfortunately, Lajos was shot a couple of times. One bullet shattered his elbow. The other ruined his ankle. We had to operate or he would have died."

"Doctor? You are doctor?"

"No, Viktor. Not a doctor. I'm a killer."

A killer?

Viktor *was* talking to an *őrült*.

"In fact, I killed the snivelling ingrate Vadik. That happens to be the bad news, by the way—"

"Vadik? Vadik dead?"

Viktor slumped onto the top of his solidly built desk. It stood up well to the weight of his muscular frame.

Vomit.

He wanted to vomit, but could not show weakness in front of the men. As vultures, they would circle the carcass of anyone they saw as weak and failing, and they would try to rip the power from him. Viktor stiffened his back and expanded his massive chest.

"Yes, Viktor. Vadik is dead. Deceased. No longer breathing. And I'm the one who snuffed out his life. In fact, I snapped his scrawny neck like a dry twig. *Are you listening to me now, Giant of Győr?*" *Őrült* shouted the final sentence. Anger and insult clear in his words.

On the other side of the desk, Torok allowed his jaw to drop. He shook his head in disbelief.

"You kill my son? You kill Vadik?"

"Yes. I did. And I enjoyed it, too. The bastard deserved it."

"No! It is lie!"

"You don't believe me?"

"No. Vadik not dead. Vadik is lion. He not dead!"

"Check your printer Viktor, old man."

"What? What you say!"

"You heard. I'll call you back in two minutes."

The telephone line died. *Őrült* had hung the phone up on him. How dare he!

Torok replaced the handset and stood. "May I leave the room, *főnök*?"

"What? What did you say?"

"I need to leave the room, *főnök*. To check the printer in the office."

Viktor waved him off.

"Of course. Go, go!"

The insect hurried from the room and returned a few moments later, looking even more pale than before, as if that were possible. In his trembling hand, he held a sheet of paper. He approached Viktor, but kept a safe distance and stretched out his arm.

Viktor snatched the still-damp photograph from the trembling hand and stared at it in horror. He howled in anguish. In the picture, Vadik and Wilfred hung side-by-side in a destroyed car. Wilfred was clearly dead—no one could survive with so much of his head missing. Vadik, though, appeared intact, without a scratch. He might even have survived the crash unscathed, but his head hung from his shoulders at a strange angle. Unnatural. His neck was broken. Vadik, his elder son, stared at the camera lens through dead eyes.

Vadik was dead. Of that, there was no doubt. Dead at the hands of an English *őrült*.

The telephone on his desk jangled again. This time, Viktor snatched it from its cradle and roared in Hungarian. He ranted, and he called on the Old Gods to bring down their wrath ... The line clicked into silence. *Őrült* had hung up on him again.

Again!

Viktor slammed the handset into its cradle and stood over it, his hands balled into fists. He fumed. The men around him remained still and silent. They knew what was good for them.

215

The heavy clock on the mantlepiece ticked away the minutes.

Three minutes passed and stretched into four.

Still, Viktor waited. He fumed.

Őrült would ring back. If he did not want something from Viktor, he would not have called in the first place. Next time, Viktor would listen. Only by listening would he learn enough to …

The telephone burst into life. Slowly, under great control, Viktor opened his fingers and picked up the handset.

"Englishman?" he asked, his voice little more than a whisper.

"Yep, it's me. Are you calm enough to listen?"

"You kill Vadik?"

"I most certainly did, Viktor old man. Told you I was a killer. And you know what?" *Őrült* paused, clearly waiting for a response.

Viktor finally obliged him with a, "What?"

"Before I snapped his neck, your bastard son cried like a little girl. He begged for his life. Offered me two million euros to spare him. He said you, Viktor, would pay me in cash. Pitiful it was. Pitiful. Such a coward. And you know what else?"

Viktor filled the next pause more quickly.

"What else?"

"I enjoyed ending his life, but I would have preferred taking more time over it. At least the body's recognisable. More or less in one piece. Fingerprints clear as day. No doubt the UK police will contact you in due course. They'll want to know where to ship your son's rotting corpse. But, as I said, it's not all bad news. Lajos is still alive. Minus an arm and with a broken leg, but alive."

Viktor jumped to his feet. It had taken all his strength not to scream at the Englishman, but he could take no more.

"What you want, Englishman?" he roared. "Money? You want money?"

"Tut, tut, Viktor. What part of 'shut up and listen' didn't you understand?" *Őrült* asked, quiet and calm once more.

"You want money?" Viktor repeated.

"Maybe. I haven't decided yet. Let me think about it."

"If Lajos die, you die! I hunt you down and castrate—"

"Okay, I can understand you're upset. No father should outlive his children, but one more word, and I'll end this call and reconsider my plans."

"Fuck you, Englishman. I castrate you and make you eat own testicles!"

"Okay, I've had enough of your macho posturing. I'll call back in a few days, when you've had time to calm down a little. You never know, I might even let you talk to Lajos—assuming he's still alive. So long Viktor, 'Giant of Győr'."

The line clicked and, once again, the dialling tone burred into his ear, along with the pounding of his own blood.

Viktor stood. The room shook to his roars. The whole house trembled to his anger. He turned to face Peder Torok, who stood across the desk from him, the extension receiver still in his hand.

"Do not just stand there, you snivelling piece of shit. Do something!"

"I-I … What do you want me to do, *főnök*?" he asked, finally dropping the handset to the great desk.

Szar!

A good question. What could the moron do? What could anyone do?

"Can you trace that call?"

Torok blinked. Shook his head. "I-I don't know how, *főnök*. That sort of thing was Wilfred's responsibility."

"So? Go get the geek. Tell him to—"

His eyes fell to the photograph on the desk and reminded him of another death. The death of the geek.

Szar!

Again, Viktor roared, and again he threw a tumbler to smash against the wall. What did it matter if it was the last one. With Vadik gone and Lajos held by an English *őrült* what did it matter if he drank from the bottle?

He turned to the other men in the room. Andris and Balint had been with him since the beginning. Strong and reliable, they now had grey hair from age and experience, but were not blessed with brains and had no initiative. They would follow, but never lead, which is why they had survived so long as his employees. Viktor could turn to them for their strength of arms, but not for their advice.

The five others stood and stared at him with their fingers stuck up their useless assholes. They were newcomers, brought into the family firm by Vadik or Lajos, or both. Viktor did not even know all their names. Could they be trusted?

No. He could trust no one whose names he did not know.

"Andris, Balint, stay. And you, Torok. Everyone else, go. Go!"

He waved them towards the door. They looked from one to the other and then turned towards Torok. None made a move to leave.

"Why are you looking at him? I said *go*!"

He tore the Makarov 9mm from its holster under his arm and jerked back the slide. Bulgarian-built from an original Russian design, with an eight round magazine, the Makarov never left his side, and had never let him down. Viktor slept with it under his pillow. He aimed at the one in the middle, the tallest one with the shaved head.

"Fuck off!" Viktor yelled. "All of you!"

Finally, they understood the message and raced from the room. He turned the gun on Torok. His finger reached for the trigger.

"Why the fuck did they look to you?"

Torok's eyes bulged even wider. His arms shot up, hands waving in front of his face as though they could appease Viktor or stop a bullet.

"I don't know, *főnök*! Please."

"Why did they look to you!" he repeated, screaming. "Are you plotting against me?"

"No, *főnök*. Oh God no! I would never—"

"Now that Vadik is dead and Lajos gone, do you dare to make a move on the *Giant of Győr*?"

Viktor lifted the Makarov higher, lining up the sights with Torok's sweating, crinkled forehead. He added more pressure to the trigger.

"Please, *főnök*. *Please, no!*"

Sweat poured from Torok's face. His raised hands shook and his chin twitched. He dropped to his knees on the carpet. Much longer and the young traitor would soil himself.

Viktor held his pose for a count of five, then lowered the Makarov and laughed. He laughed long and hard, and angry.

"You nearly pissed your pants!"

Torok swallowed. He lowered his hands and hung his head in shame.

"*Főnök*, I would never act against you. Please believe—"

Viktor aimed, pulled the trigger. The Makarov spewed fire. The bullet smashed through the top of Torok's head and exploded out the back. He slumped, lifeless to the floor. Blood and brains soaked into the rug.

No matter. The room was long overdue redecoration.

Viktor turned to his trusted men.

"Never could stand that snivelling coward." He sniffed and turned his back to the corpse. "Balint, go outside and tell those men what happened here. Remind them who is in command. Any more hesitation will see more death."

Balint dipped his huge head and hurried from the room like the good soldier he was. He closed the door quietly as he left.

"Andris, get someone to take away the rubbish. Remove the rug and replace it with one from another room."

Andris reached for the desk telephone.

"No, use your portable," Viktor barked. "The English lunatic, *Őrült*, will call back."

"You think so, *főnök*?"

"Of course he will. Why would else he contact me? It was not just to gloat. He keeps Lajos alive to trade him for money."

"Assuming Lajos *is* still alive, *főnök*," Andris said, head lowered and speaking with his usual humility.

"Lajos lives," Viktor murmured, punching his chest with the side of his fist. "He lives. I feel it here."

"Yes, *főnök*. Forgive me," Andris said and dug into his pocket for a portable phone.

He turned away to make the call, speaking quickly and quietly.

Moments later, Balint knocked before entering and closing the door again.

Under the protection of two trusted men, maybe his only remaining trusted men, Viktor relaxed a little. He made safe the Makarov and returned it to its holster.

"Do the men understand who is in charge here?" he asked.

The huge Balint, who stood half a metre taller than Viktor, fixed him with his good eye. He had lost the use of the left in a hunting accident when they were still young men, but it did not seem to affect his aim with a rifle. As for his accuracy with a pistol? Well, Viktor had that covered, as Andris usually hit anything he aimed at if it did not stand more than twenty metres away.

"Yes, *főnök*. They understand. There will be no more hesitation."

"Good, good."

"And now, *főnök*? What do we do?" Andris asked, always the more talkative of the two.

"Now, Andris, we wait. And while we wait, we toast the life of Vadik. He may not have been the most gifted of men, but he was my son, and he will be missed."

"And avenged?" Balint asked.

Viktor nodded. "And avenged. Most definitely, he will be avenged."

Viktor wandered to the small table beside the empty fireplace, picked up the bottle of *pálinka*, and unscrewed the top. Before he could raise the bottle to his lips, two quiet raps on the door stopped him.

"Come!" he bellowed.

Three of the men he dismissed earlier, entered. The tall one with a shaved head brought a black tarpaulin, the others carried a rug furled up into a sausage.

While they scraped up the mess that used to be Peder Torok, Viktor raised the bottle of *pálinka*, called, "To Vadik!" and drank deep. The fiery liquid scorched his throat on the way down. He handed the bottle to Andris who took a pull and passed it to Balint who did the same. Neither man wiped the neck of the bottle first, as was their way. A good way. It showed all three men were brothers.

While Viktor, Andris, and Balint continued drinking, the other men completed their gory task. Once they had rolled up the body, first in the blood-saturated rug and then in the tarpaulin, they carried it away. None said a word, and none looked up from his task. They had learned their lesson.

Viktor smirked.

A lesson they will never forget while they live.

He retrieved the bottle from Balint and they took it in turns until they had drunk it dry, making a different toast to Vadik before each round.

Once it was empty, they stood by the window overlooking the grounds and the wide, sprawling valley and fell silent. On other such sombre occasions, Viktor would have called for more bottles and for food, but a funeral feast would have to wait. It would wait until they had the body of Vadik home, and Lajos, too. Hopefully, Lajos would still be alive.

The sun touched the rolling hills on the horizon, turning from orange to red, and bleeding across the cloudy sky. It reminded Viktor of the blood seeping from Torok and soaking into the rug. Perhaps he should not have killed the friend of Lajos. Perhaps Viktor should have reined in his temper. If Lajos returned ... when Lajos returned ... he would miss his friend, especially if he really was a cripple. If he really was a short man with one arm, Lajos would need all his friends around him.

Viktor shook himself awake.

No, killing Torok had been necessary. It served as a reminder to anyone who needed one. The five men in suits would spread the word that age had not weakened the resolve of the Giant of Győr. No, the Giant of Győr would not be insulted. He would not be ignored.

But what of Lajos? What would happen to him when Viktor was no longer around to protect him? Viktor would not live forever. Twenty years, maybe twenty-five. How would Lajos the One Arm survive without the protection of his father? How would he grow the family business? After all, expansion had been the whole point of the English adventure. It was the reason they chose the cretin, Robert Prentiss, in the first place. And talking of Prentiss, had Vadik completed that part of his mission before the mad Englishman ended his life? Did Robert Prentiss still live, and what of his pretty young wife?

"Andris," he said, surprised the *pálinka* had not yet affected his speech.

Andris stiffened, stood as tall as he could. His grey eyes shone bright, but from the *pálinka*, not with grief for the loss of Vadik. In truth, Vadik would not really be missed. Vadik had not been a likeable man. He had no grace or skill. Were he not the illegitimate son of the Giant of Győr, Vadik would never have lived as long as he had. But he *was* who he was and, as such, he would be mourned.

"Yes, *főnök?*"

"Contact Cousin Ido. Tell him to send someone to Prentiss House. I want to know exactly what happened today."

"As you command, *főnök*," Andris said, and picked up his portable.

He turned away to make the call.

The desk telephone rang for a third time. Once more, its bell cut through the silence of the large room.

"The Englishman!" Viktor growled and hurried to answer the call.

This time, he would listen.

This time, he would remain calm.

This time, Viktor Pataki, the Giant of Győr, would keep cool and calm. Viktor would be a man of ice. The time for fire would come, and it would come soon.

CHAPTER TWENTY-SIX

WEDNESDAY 3RD MAY – Viktor Pataki
Pataki Compound, Outside Győr, Hungary

Viktor picked up the ringing telephone and held it away from his ear. He beckoned Andris and Balint closer so they could hear. Although both men's breath held the sweet smell of the *pálinka*, they were rock steady. Neither man swayed.

"This Viktor Pataki," he said, quietly, "Is that you, Englishman?"

"P-Papa?" Lajos spoke. His voice weak, trembling. "They took my arm, Papa." He cried and repeated the words. "They took my arm!"

Viktor bit down hard on the inside of his cheek to fight back the rising anger. He had promised to keep himself in check. Now was not the time to explode. Anger would come later.

 In the background of the call, the dull roar of heavy traffic rumbled, partially drowning out the words of Lajos. And he sounded hollow, as though he was speaking in a small metal box. The Englishman might be moving Lajos in the back of a van.

"Lajos, my boy, at least you are alive. The Englishman murdered Vadik, your brother."

"*Half*-brother," Lajos spat, showing signs of the fire that might yet help keep him alive. "He was my half-brother, Papa. I-I am your real son."

In spite of the situation, Viktor showed Andris and Balint a grim smile, proud of his remaining boy.

"Where are you?"

"I-I do not know. They put a blindfold on me and I have been unconscious. The ... the Englishman is holding the portable phone to my ear. He gave me a message for you, Papa ...."

Viktor waited for his boy to speak but the silence dragged on, broken only by the whistling roar of fast-moving traffic.

"Tell me, Lajos," Viktor said, encouraging his boy. "Why is the Englishman keeping you alive?"

"Fifteen million, Papa. H-He wants fifteen million for my safe return."

What!

"Fifteen million euros?" Viktor roared, all pretence of control leaving him.

"Y-Yes, Papa."

The swish of cloth against the microphone of a portable telephone followed a weak whimper. Immediately afterwards, the quiet, taunting voice of the *őrült* said, "Yes, Viktor. Fifteen million euros in cash for Lajos' life. Sounds a lot more than he's worth to me, but then again, he isn't my son."

"Fifteen million, in cash?" Viktor gasped.

"Yes, but don't worry, I'll give you until noon, the day after tomorrow to gather it. That's midday Saturday. I want used bills, no larger than hundreds. Got that?"

Viktor read the time on his watch—a little after seven in the evening. The Englishman had given him over forty hours to collect the money. Not a problem. Not in terms of the money. Viktor always kept large deposits of cash available with which to run the business. After all, no one with sense would trust banks after the crash. But paying ransom for Lajos would set a dangerous precedent. Pay once, and it would be the end of the family and the end of the Giant of Győr.

"I need more time."

"Midday Saturday. One second late, and I put a bullet in your son's brain. Assuming I can find it."

In the background, Lajos gasped. The Englishman chuckled.

A joke. *Őrült* made a joke at the expense of his boy! The filthy pig!

"And one more thing, Viktor ..." the Englishman paused for, what? Emphasis? An insult?

"What?"

"You must deliver the money yourself."

Ha! As though that will ever happen.

"Of course, Englishman. Of course. Where I bring money for Lajos?"

"I'll give you directions closer to the time. Wouldn't want to give you time to set up an ambush, now would I?"

"Keep Lajos safe. I bring money. You have word of Viktor Pataki, the Giant of Győr."

Viktor paused, expecting to hear the Englishman say something, even if only to laugh again, but he heard nothing.

"Hello? Englishman?"

Nothing but the dial tone.

"He has gone," Viktor snarled and passed the handset for Balint to replace.

"You cannot deliver the money yourself, *főnök*," Andris said. "It will certainly be a trap."

Viktor scowled up the taller man. "Of course it will be a trap. And of course I will not go. This is a job for Wendt. Tell him to make himself ready."

Both Balint and Andris grinned. They had not forgotten Wendt and his uncanny similarity in size and shape to Viktor. Add a long wig and he would pass for Viktor, at a distance.

The Giant of Győr held as much power and controlled as much wealth as many a head of state. If those people could use *doppelgängers*, so too could Viktor.

The moment the English lunatic showed himself to kill Wendt, he would die, along with anyone who stood beside him. Even if Lajos was not safe from the withering crossfire.

After all, a cripple could never command the loyalty of the men after Viktor was gone. No. A new successor must be found. Plenty of cousins would make better leaders than Lajos. In any event, who wanted a cripple for a son? A one-armed man who cried over the telephone and begged for his life?

How could such a snivelling creature come from the seed of Viktor Pataki? He had been right all along. Lajos' whore of a mother, Viktor's first wife, *had* been unfaithful. One only had to look at them, the difference in their height and their colouring to tell that Lajos was no son of his. Viktor had dark hair and stood a full six centimetres taller than the weakling.

No, the family's expansion into the UK was over, at least for the time being. They would turn elsewhere for their future growth. A new outlook. A new successor groomed. A new chapter.

But first, *Őrült* would die. The murder of Vadik would be avenged, and the lost honour of the Giant of Győr would be restored.

CHAPTER TWENTY-SEVEN

Saturday 6th May – Evening
Hungary

Kaine yawned wide, sucking in the oxygen of life. Fighting the growing fatigue.

The van's headlights funnelled out, cutting cones of white through the blackness. A blue sign flashing past on an overhead gantry announced their route took them towards Budapest via Győr. Hungary's capital lay some one hundred and twenty kilometres to the far side of their destination.

Kaine yawned again, struggling to keep his eyes open. Nearly twenty-four hours behind the wheel with only two stops for fuel would do that to a driver. He wound down the passenger window, hoping the blast of cold evening air would wake him enough to continue, but he could barely focus on the road ahead. The GPS screen turned into little more than a blur.

"Cold back here, Ryan," Lara called out.

It had taken some persuasion, but she'd allowed Lajos to regain consciousness long enough to speak to "Papa" before sedating him again. According to Lara, keeping Lajos in a drug-induced coma gave his body the best chance of fighting off the infection and the shock of losing an arm. The man had taken a great deal of punishment and the medic in Lara wanted to keep her patient as comfortable as possible. Kaine, on the other hand, didn't give a damn how much the little creep suffered.

Try as hard as he could, Kaine was unable to drive the image of Danny dying in his arms, or of his covered body in the back of Cough and Stefan's white Ford, from his mind. The memories would burn inside him forever. And so they should.

Lara felt Danny's loss as much as Kaine. That was clear, but a lifetime of tending to the sick and the injured had bred in her a caring heart. She wanted the best for all the creatures under her protection, no matter what atrocities they'd committed.

Lara Orchard was a better person than Ryan Kaine, and no one who knew her could deny it.

A truck blew past them in the opposite direction, driving a cushion of cold, wet air into the cab. Kaine shuddered. Fully awake at least for the moment, he wound up the window and wiped the moisture from his face.

"Better?"

"Yes, thanks. Are we nearly there yet?"

Her question, delivered in the singsong voice of a child made him smile.

They'd breezed through Vienna over an hour earlier and the bright lights of Hegyeshalom shone in the van's wing mirrors. The E75, a dual carriageway the Hungarians called their M1, stretched out long and straight ahead of them. Dark and flat. Interminable. One of the most boring lengths of road he'd driven on in many a year. Still, after the days they'd suffered recently, "boring" wasn't the worst thing ever. He needed "boring" to recover his sense of self. Even though the drive from Derby to the Channel Tunnel, and the thirteen-hour trip from Calais drew out into infinity, "boring" was good, and the long drive gave him time to plan.

"Another forty minutes ought to do it," he said.

"Want me to take over the driving?"

"No thanks," he said, "I've seen you behind the wheel." He added a cheeky smile.

"Ouch. What's wrong with my driving?"

He glanced in the rear-view and winked.

"Nothing, love. Absolutely nothing. Honest!"

Her hazel eyes looked as tired and gritty as his felt. At least he didn't need the tinted contact lenses for his current identity as Bill Griffin, retired Royal Marine, who was currently on holiday with his wife of twenty-odd years, Beth. For all the border crossings, they'd taken the slight risk of smuggling a heavily anaesthetised Lajos Pataki in a trunk bolted in the back of the van. As expected, they'd not been searched a single time at any border post.

The benefits of free movement within the EU. How long would that last?

A slip road, Junction 142, Lébény-Mecsér, split off to the right, arced sharply away, and disappeared. The motorway arrowed ahead into the black. The tail lights of a few cars picked red dots into the night. Dipped headlights of oncoming vehicles occasionally made him blink but, in the main, the road was surprisingly deserted.

Minutes past in relative silence. Lara checked her patient's vitals, while Kaine contemplated the upcoming showdown with the so-called Giant of Győr. Pitiful. Viktor Pataki happened to stand at a mere one hundred and seventy centimetres, or five foot seven inches in old money. Significantly taller than his surviving son, but three inches shorter than Kaine. The Giant of Győr? Did Viktor Pataki understand irony when he heard it?

Who cared? It didn't matter. Nothing mattered other than extracting payback for Danny. Although Lara didn't hold with vengeance, she knew better than to try to talk him out of it more than the one time at Prentiss House.

Another sign flashed by—*Győr 19 km*. One thing about driving on the continent, kilometres counted down a damn sight faster than the mile markers they still used in the UK. The van's speedo showed seventy miles per hour. He ran the calculation. Fatigue made it take longer.

"Less than fifteen minutes."

The GPS narrator announced a turn onto the M85 in one kilometre. Kaine eased his foot off the accelerator and slowed to sixty. With his reaction times compromised, the last thing they needed was a shunt.

After negotiating a couple of roundabouts, they filtered onto a two-lane tarmac road. He slowed even further to allow for the new conditions and the increased traffic as they closed on their destination—northwest Hungary's most important city.

"How's our patient doing?" Kaine asked, more to break the quiet and hear her voice than because he gave a toss.

"Temperature's slightly elevated, but given what he's been through, he's holding up remarkably well. The wound looks clean. It's early days, but I can't see too many signs of infection. Physically, he'll probably recover. Psychologically, though? Who knows?"

And who cares?

"PTSD might be an issue," she added, "but that's beyond my remit."

"At least he's alive," Kaine muttered. "Danny isn't."

"Sorry?"

"Nothing."

She slipped through the gap between the seats, slid into the passenger seat, and fastened her safety belt. Traffic slowed them even further.

"Ryan, are you really going through with this?"

Kaine fired a glance through the rear-view mirror to make sure their patient was in no condition to eavesdrop.

"Lara," he whispered, "let's not go through this again. You're here to keep him alive. I'm running the handover. End of discussion."

"Remind me again why we're over twelve hours late. The transfer was supposed to take place midday yesterday."

"We've been through this already."

"Humour me. I've been a little busy with him"—she jerked her head towards the back—"and I haven't had much sleep lately. My memory's a little fuzzy."

"No it isn't. You're trying to pick holes."

"No, I'm not. I'm trying to keep you awake."

He took a breath and cracked the window again, but only by a couple of centimetres.

"Too cold?"

"No, I'm fine. And stop prevaricating. Why are we arriving a day late?"

Kaine tried rubbing the tiredness from his eyes. It only succeeded in spreading the grit.

"Okay. Bear with me."

A break in traffic on the westbound lane gave him the opportunity to overtake a slow-moving convoy that included a huge truck and trailer and a petrol tanker. He indicated left, dropped two gears, and mashed the throttle into the floor mat. The Ford Transit sprang forwards with all the youthful energy of a sloth on tranquilisers.

"Ryan!"

The headlights of an oncoming vehicle flashed at them in the far distance. He cancelled the indicator and aborted the manoeuvre, tucking back in behind the trailer.

"Sorry. Must be more tired than I thought. Anyway, where was I?"

"Trying to avoid telling me the plan."

"Tenacious, aren't we?"

"Ryan Liam Kaine, get on with it."

"Okay, here goes. Delaying the handover has two benefits. First, it's given us time to organise. It's taken far longer than I imagined to put all our ducks in a row."

"Ducks? We have ducks?"

"One or two."

"Which are?"

"You'll find out when we reach Győr."

"You're deliberately keeping me in the dark?" Her eyebrows knitted into a frown. "I really don't like that, Ryan."

"No, it's a surprise. I know how much you like surprises."

"I like nice surprises, not shocks."

He grinned. "This is a nice one. I promise."

The tension in Lara's forehead eased a little. "Okay, what's the second benefit?"

"We haven't contacted Papa Pataki since Thursday. He has no idea where we are or what we're doing. By now, he'll be climbing the walls, and anything that puts him off his stride works in our favour."

"It'll make him angry, unreliable."

"Men like Viktor Pataki are always angry and unreliable. I wouldn't trust him as far as I could throw Lajos."

"You're not really going to arrange a ransom exchange, are you?"

"Yep. Most definitely." He winked and added what he hoped was a confident smile. "Why not?"

"You can't be that naïve. No crime lord going by the ridiculously overblown title of 'The Giant of Győr' is going to merrily hand over fifteen million euros to ransom his son. The loss of face would ruin him."

"Of course he won't, not merrily or any other way. He's going to try and screw us over. But we're smarter than he is."

"We are?" Doubt and worry showed on her lovely face.

"We've done this sort of thing before."

"When?"

"Back in better times, DefTech negotiated with dozens of kidnappers. Most of the time, we were successful, too. This time, we're taking that experience, but reversing the roles."

"Oh, right. I see."

She didn't look convinced.

"Trust me, Lara. I do know what I'm doing."

"But we're in the middle of Hungary, Viktor's back garden. He has the local knowledge and access to men."

"Which is why I needed him off balance. And ..."

Lara sighed. "And?"

"The delay's given us time for a full recon. We needed time to pick an ideal spot for the transfer. We've identified a few likely looking places. It's amazing how clear satellite imagery can be these days. Especially when you have someone like Corky to help."

Corky and others.

"Ryan."

"Yes?"

"Will you answer one question?"

"Of course. Shoot."

"Is this really all about the money?"

"And revenge, why?"

"We don't need the money. There's plenty in the Trust to give Marian Prentiss a new life."

"No there isn't." Kaine shook his head firmly. "The Trust's money is for *The 83*. Marian Prentiss doesn't qualify."

"A few million pounds would barely put a dent in the capital. The cumulative interest alone would more than cover the costs."

"No, you're wrong. There's a principle involved here. I took those millions to help the victims' families. I can't go dipping into it, willy-nilly—"

"Willy-nilly? What sort of an expression is—"

"What's wrong with 'willy-nilly'? Under the circumstances, the expression is pretty apt. Better than swearing, which is what I'd rather be doing right now."

She sighed, expansively.

"Yes, okay. So, the fifteen million euros, which is close to thirteen million pounds, is to cover Marian Prentiss' new life?"

Kaine shook his head again. "Not all of it. Even with a kiddie on the way, that's far more than we need to set her up for life. Some of the cash will be for the lads. They'll probably have to earn it."

The GPS indicated a right turn off the main drag in eight hundred metres. Kaine slowed the van further. "Ah, here we go. Don't know about you, but I'm in real need of some refreshments. I hope our host has the kettle on."

"Our host?"

"Yep."

"I thought you'd never been to Hungary before?"

"I haven't. But our host has."

"You going to give me any clues?"

Kaine glanced at her and winked. "Nope. That's the surprise I was talking about just now. Won't be long."

"Ryan Kaine, you can be an exasperating man."

"Now tell me something I don't know."

He indicated right and made the turn, and they drove down a long, quiet suburban street on the outskirts of Győr. Not quite the middle of enemy territory, but close enough to give Kaine goosebumps.

Five more turns and fifteen minutes later, the British-accented voice on the GPS told them they'd arrived at their destination—a villa at the end of a cul-de-sac surrounded by a white-painted wall.

Kaine pulled into the entrance, flashed the headlights three times —one long, one short, one long. The heavy metal gate slid open on near-silent runners. Floodlights powered up, instantly illuminating a well-kept front garden mainly laid to lush green lawn but edged by flower borders. Kaine nosed the van through the opening and into the property. He pulled alongside a double garage whose up-and-over doors had levered open at the same time as the gate as though carefully choreographed.

The garage was plenty tall enough to accommodate the van—one of the prime reasons for renting the place—and Kaine reversed alongside the garage's other occupant, a shiny new, silver-grey Range Rover. He killed the engine and took a moment to revel in the silence and the calm. Lara did the same, closing her eyes to do so.

A few short moments later, he breathed in deeply and exhaled in a long sigh.

"Ready?" he asked.

"As always." She smiled and squeezed his knee.

"Thanks, but don't do that in front of the men or they'll all expect the same medical support."

Lara shook her head and raised her eyes to the van's roof.

"Idiot."

"Yep, that's me. Shall we go?"

"I'll just check the patient."

While Lara made her way into the back, Kaine pushed open his door and stepped outside into the floodlit brightness. It was balmier than he expected. He still needed his jacket, but didn't need to pull the zip all the way up.

Before he could take another step, the house's front door opened and the bulk of a very large man filled the open doorway, backlit by the light streaming out from an inner hallway.

"Good evening," Kaine called. "Fancy meeting you here."

They closed the distance between them quickly and clasped hands, reinforcing the shake with a forearm grip. Both men smiled grimly, each knowing the reason for their unscheduled meeting.

"Evening, Captain. Expected you a little earlier. Any trouble?"

"Nope. We took the scenic route."

"There is no scenic route through western Hungary. Where's the doc?"

"Tending to her patient."

"Should have left the bastard to rot."

The rear doors of the camper van burst open and Lara stepped down onto the paved driveway. She turned towards the sound of their voices. Her classic double-take and shocked expression made Kaine smile.

"Rollo!"

She raced along the driveway and dived into the Quartermaster's powerful and open arms.

CHAPTER TWENTY-EIGHT

SUNDAY 7TH MAY – Before Dawn
Győr, Hungary

After Rollo had extricated himself from Lara's clutches, he helped Kaine carry the comatose Lajos Pataki into the smallest of the bungalow's four bedrooms—and the one easiest to secure.

In case he was feigning, they didn't say much in front of the patient, and cuffed his remaining hand to the metal bedstead, much to Lara's distaste.

"He's just lost an arm and is heavily sedated. The cuffs are unnecessary," she said, glaring at Kaine.

"This isn't up for discussion, Doc," he said, following Rollo into a well-appointed kitchen diner.

After settling her patient, Lara joined them for supper.

Rollo provided an almost-acceptable meat stew. Kaine couldn't identify the meat in question, nor any of the vegetables apart from a couple of roughly chopped carrots. In his day, Rollo might have been one of the Special Boat Service's best instructors, but his skills in the kitchen were almost non-existent. His new wife, Marie-Odile, never let him near her cooker unless it was to make coffee. At least Rollo could produce a decent coffee.

Kaine and Lara ate for fuel rather than pleasure, and the three of them held a muted conversation around the dining table.

Kaine gave Rollo a more detailed overview of the battle of Prentiss House and Danny's death, than he'd given Lara, and she listened intently. Saying little, Lara dabbed her eyes with a tissue the whole time and had turned in as soon as she'd finished half a bowl of the stew. Kaine nearly applauded her for eating that much, but Rollo had done his best and wouldn't have appreciated the sarcasm. Before she left, she kissed them both—Rollo on the forehead, Kaine on the cheek.

Rollo had given him and Lara the room next to the patient. It had an ensuite and Kaine held off the inquisition until he heard Lara running a shower. He opened with the gentlest of salvos.

"How's Marie-Odile?"

"Brilliant, sir. She sends you both her love."

"She doesn't mind you disappearing without notice?"

"No, Captain. My new wife"—he reddened at the novelty of his status as a married man—"understands the nature of my ... occupation. She knows I'll have to leave at a moment's notice from time to time. Thanks for including me on this operation, by the way."

"Did you doubt it? Why wouldn't I?"

"Well, now I'm an old married man, I was worried you might think I'd gone soft. Lost my edge."

Kaine leaned back, made a great show of giving the hulking Quartermaster the once over. "Apart from that slight thickening around the waist—"

"You cheeky young pup."

Rollo straightened in his chair and tensed his washboard stomach. Like Kaine, Rollo kept himself supremely fit. Irrespective of their advancing age, with Kaine in his early forties, and Rollo knocking on the doors of the half century, neither carried a single gram of unnecessary fat.

Kaine raised his glass in defence and refused to give ground.

"Not that I can blame you, Colour Sergeant. Marie-Odile puts together a mean spread. All those rich Bordelaise sauces, bound to make you pile on the blubber."

"If you say so, sir." He knocked back the rest of his rum and set the glass on the table, pushing it away, its job done for the night. "Shall we get on with business?"

Kaine cast an eye around the living area. Modern, clean, utilitarian. A good place to set up shop.

"How'd you find the place?" he asked instead of the more insulting, "How secure are we here?"

"I booked it through an intermediary. We're safe, sir."

"The owners?"

"A couple of young thrusters. Live in Budapest. This is their second home."

"Good. You brought the equipment I asked for?"

"Of course."

"All of it? The Accuracy?"

"Yes, sir. Chambered for the 7.62x51mm NATO cartridges. I popped into the villa on the way here. I don't imagine you'll have the chance to test fire, but that can't be helped. The existing setup should hold for your purposes."

"Depending on the distance to target and the weather conditions. You've identified the best site?"

"Yes, Captain. I've not exactly been idle for the past two days. The best one on the list is the abandoned warehouse facility forty clicks from the Pataki compound. Good sight lines to the target area, and multiple access roads for a quick getaway. A few hills, too."

"Hills, in this part of Hungary?"

"Like I said, Captain, it took a while to scout all the locations you and Corky identified on the satellite."

"Good. Any decent pictures?"

"Better than that. I flew a drone over the site this evening just before dusk. Marvellous things, drones. The film's on my laptop."

"Excellent. I'll view it in the morning after I've had some shuteye. I'm seeing double right now."

"Right you are, sir. Anything else?"

"The payload?"

Rollo's neatly trimmed beard—a recent innovation courtesy of Marie-Odile—bristled as he stretched out a broad smile. "As always, I saved the best part 'til last. You're going to love Paddy's latest toy. It may be small, but it packs one heck of a wallop."

Kaine hadn't seen Michael Patrick O'Hara, the team's walking talking cliché of an Irishman, and their explosives guru, since the Southampton mission, and hoped the man still held up to his reputation. His whole plan depended on it.

"PETN?"

"Nope. Something Paddy cooked up in his garden shed. Looks a little like peanut butter. God knows what the stuff's made of, but Paddy claims it's more stable than PETN and thirty percent more powerful. He gave me a small supply to play with before I left on the honeymoon, but I've not had the chance to test it before now. Been a little ... busy."

Kaine had seldom seen Rollo blush before and held off making any comment.

"However," Rollo added, hurrying along, "you know Paddy."

Kaine dipped his head and gave up a grim smile. "If he claims it's more stable and more powerful than PETN, it is. Where'd you put it?"

"I heated it up and poured it into an empty can of cola."

"You heated it up?"

Rollo shrugged. "In a saucepan on a camping cooker. Followed Paddy's instructions to the letter."

Kaine imagined Rollo cooking a blob of peanut butter while hiding behind a tree somewhere. The image would have been hilarious had the circumstances been different.

"Rather you than me, Colour Sergeant."

"Yes, sir. I lit the blue touch paper and retired to a safe distance."

"So, the stuff solidifies when cool?"

"Yep. I poured it into the can and left it to stand."

"Will one can be enough?"

Rollo scrunched up his face. "Only needed half a can, sir. I called

Paddy before leaving Bordeaux and gave him your specifications. He told me the weight I needed and Bob's your auntie's husband. If it doesn't do the job ...." He scratched the back of his neck.

Marie-Odile had even forced him to let his hair grow. Gone was the military buzz cut. Rollo now sported a number four on top and a number two on the back and sides. The new, softer look suited him, but Kaine would never tell Rollo. Old school military men like Kaine and Rollo didn't go in for that sort of thing.

"Paddy's never let us down yet," Kaine said.

"There's always a first time." And there was the gloomy Quartermaster Kaine knew and loved.

"But the explosive is only a little 'appetiser'. Nothing to do with the main course."

"If you say so, sir."

"I do, Rollo. How do I detonate the can?"

Rollo's grin returned. "That's the really clever part. The copper core of the standard NATO cartridge projectile combined with the aluminium in the can and the heat from the friction turns the actual can into the detonator. Basically, shoot the can and 'boom'!" He threw open his fingers to mime an explosion.

"And without the copper?"

"The can is perfectly safe."

"You're certain? I don't want some passer-by to drop another can into the bin and blow themselves to pieces."

"You haven't seen the drop site yet, sir. Completely deserted. Not even the homeless use the place. Besides," he added, "I tested the can's stability against shock."

"How?"

"Last night, I dropped it from a footbridge onto a concrete cycle path. Nothing happened."

"A bit dangerous. What if it had gone off?"

Rollo shrugged and scratched his neck again. "There are loads of bloody cyclists rolling around the place in their spandex gear. Losing one or two won't make much of a dent."

"Rollo, Lara and I ride mountain bikes when we get the chance."

"Exactly my point, sir. But I'm only kidding. I made sure the park was deserted before I dropped the can."

"Good. The only casualties I want on this mission are Patakis and the people who work for them."

"I know, sir. So, when are we off?"

"Not 'we', Rollo. This is a solo operation. Your job is to protect Lara. She'll want to tag along and take care of her patient. I don't care what it takes. Even if you have to cuff her to her bed, Lara's not leaving this house until the handover's complete. Understand?"

"I'll do my best, sir."

"Consider that a direct order, Colour Sergeant Rollason. Protect Lara from herself. Is that clear?"

Rollo stiffened to a seated attention. "As crystal, sir."

"Good." Kaine yawned. "And now, Rollo, I need my rest. Big day ahead tomorrow."

CHAPTER TWENTY-NINE

Sᴜɴᴅᴀʏ 7ᴛʜ Mᴀʏ – Viktor Pataki
Pataki Compound, Outside Győr, Hungary

"You late! Where you were?" Viktor screamed down the telephone line.

Three days he had been waiting and not one single word from *Őrült* until now. Viktor slammed his fist into the table.

"Tut, tut, Viktor. Is that any way to talk to the man who's taking such good care of your son? Don't you want Lajos back?"

Again, he sounded so reasonable. The soft voice of an English moron. If things worked out as he planned, Viktor would take *Őrült* by the balls and squeeze until they popped like plums in his fists.

"Where you were?" Viktor repeated, this time with less volume and slightly less anger. "Why you no call before?"

"Do you have my money?"

His money? *His* money! The money belonged to Viktor, not the Englishman. Viktor peeled back his upper lip. *Őrült* would not live long to enjoy any money.

"Yes. I have money. Fifteen million euros. It ready yesterday as instructed. Why you no call? Why you no give delivery location?"

"I told you to have the cash ready and bundled by noon on Saturday. Didn't say anything about the actual time of the delivery or the location."

"You play games, *te egy kurva fiam?*"

The Englishman delayed his response. Keeping Viktor waiting. This time, it would not anger him. Viktor could cope with any mind games *Őrült* chose to play.

"Viktor, Viktor," *Őrült* said, almost sadly. "Calling me a 'son of a bitch' is hardly in keeping with the spirit of our burgeoning relationship."

He understood? *Őrült* understood the curse? Viktor needed to hold his Hungarian tongue, at least until he had Lajos back and the Englishman in chains at his feet.

"I am sorry. It not happen again," Viktor mumbled, almost choking on the words.

"Okay, I'll let it pass *this time.*" Steel edged *Őrült's* voice.

"Where you want money?"

"Down to business are we? That's better. Are you familiar with the abandoned Gorski Warehouse near *Dunaszeg*?"

Viktor paused for a moment to think.

"*Igen*, yes."

"Good. You know what a dumpster is? A rubbish skip?"

Viktor ground his teeth. *Őrült* spoke to him as though he were a simpleton. Of course he knew the word "dumpster".

"It is metal *szemeteskukák!*"

"Yes, that's right. Rubbish bins. Be there in ninety minutes. Midnight. Bring my money, in person. Drop the bags by the middle one of three yellow skips on the western side of the car park where I'll place a sign. Open both bags and hold up some of the money so I can see it. Come alone."

No. That would not work. Wendt would be in no condition to drive after drinking in his courage.

"Not possible," Viktor said, thinking fast. "I not drive. Need driver. Okay?"

Viktor held his breath. Everything depended on *Őrült* agreeing to this one little change in his plan.

Another pause.

"Okay, just you and your driver. I see anyone else, I disappear and Lajos dies."

"I give you money. You give me Lajos right away. That is deal, yes?"

"No, not quite. I'll collect the cash and count it. Make sure it's all there. Then, I'll phone to let you know where to collect your boy."

"You not trust Viktor?"

Őrült laughed. "Trust you? Don't be stupid. I trust no one."

"Lajos for cash, you said. Why I believe you?"

The mocking laugh died away and became a sigh. "What alternative do you have? Now you only have eighty-eight minutes. See you soon, Viktor."

The telephone line clicked and the dialling tone burred. Viktor turned to Andris, who had replaced his handset. A frown wrinkled his dark face.

"You know what to do Andris, my friend?"

"Yes, *főnök*. Wendt is waiting in the kitchen, fortifying himself with wine."

"Is he drunk?"

"Not so much that he cannot walk, *főnök*. I thought it best to allow him a glass or two to find his courage, as usual. The warehouse is less than twenty minutes away. I have plenty of time to get him ready."

"Good. Even though it may be his final appearance, he must play his role well." Viktor nodded and turned to his other favoured man. "Balint, you will go now. Take three of your best men. That whole area is deserted most of the time. Deploy your men around the perimeter. They are good with rifles, yes?"

"The very best, *főnök*."

"Good. Kill anything that moves."

"Anything, *főnök*? You do not want us to identify the target first?"

"No, kill anyone you find in the warehouse complex."

"But Lajos might be—"

"You did not hear the *őrült*, Balint? He is keeping Lajos in another place. The Englishman will not have Lajos close for fear of him being taken and of losing his ace in the hole. And if Lajos does fall into the firing line, so be it. The English *őrült* killed Vadik, and he has insulted the family honour. He must *die*."

Balint dipped his head in acceptance of the instructions. He would obey. Balint always obeyed. It was how he had survived so long in the family although they shared no blood.

"Go now. Move swiftly and silently. And keep me fully informed."

The two trusted men hurried from the room.

Slowly, thoughtfully, Viktor crossed to his favourite window. The double row of floodlights illuminated the grounds, *his* grounds, and dispelled the black of the night.

How had it come to this? Vadik had been despatched to the afterlife, and Lajos, crippled and held hostage for money, would likely follow him soon.

Viktor should never have listened to the madcap proposal Vadik developed. He made it sound so simple, so profitable. Yet, the English adventure had ended as a total disaster for the family. He personally, the Giant of Győr, had lost so much face, it might take years to recover.

Fifteen million euros! A mere drop in the ocean for the family finances, but what the ransom represented—weakness—meant so much more.

Damn the English *őrült*. Damn him to the fires of Hell.

For half a *forint*, he would lead the assault personally. Yes, he would take *Őrült* and drive him into the fiery pits of Hell.

Oh how Viktor would love to have *Őrült* before him, begging for mercy. It would restore his credibility. It would restore the majesty of the Giant of Győr. But gone were the days when Viktor could leave the compound with impunity. Too many people knew what he looked like. The family members of too many victims wished him harm, and his delicately balanced arrangement with the authorities

—paid for in euros and in violent coercion—would not stand if the police saw him walking the land. It was for that very reason he had allowed his sons to take the lead in England. And the result had been catastrophic.

Viktor reached for the *pálinka* bottle and a glass and poured a full measure. One of the servants had replaced all the smashed tumblers without hi noticing. He glanced down at the plush new carpet. A replacement for the bloodied rug. The room had been restored to its former glory. Now, he needed to restore the balance of power.

Guards patrolling the grounds cut dark holes in the floodlights. A show of strength, demonstrating the impregnability of his compound. Viktor drew strength from his lofty position, the master of all he surveyed.

He knocked back half the glass of *pálinka* and allowed himself a satisfied smile.

A wind blew through the trees running along the high walls and casting their shadows over the lawns. It bent branches and made the leaves dance. It would be cold at the Gorski Warehouse. Cold and dark. The perfect place for Balint to set up his ambush. The cold would not matter long to *Őrült*. He would find plenty of warmth awaiting him in Hell.

CHAPTER THIRTY

SUNDAY 7TH MAY – Overnight
Gorski Warehouse, Near Dunaszeg, Hungary

Kaine peeled back his sleeve and pressed the button to illuminate the dial of his wristwatch. 22:47.

Any time now.

He'd been lying in the same prone position for seven hours straight. Long enough to memorise the terrain, and to confirm the sightlines and the distances to all the potential targets—especially the prime one.

Kaine's chosen spot couldn't have suited his requirements any better. He held the highest ground in the area—the flat roof of a six-storey warehouse—with a commanding, three-sixty-degree view of the surrounding terrain. He could see anyone approaching for kilometres around without having to stand or crane his neck too much.

Plastic bags tied at irregular intervals to the rusted and broken chain link fence surrounding the disused industrial zone—tied by Rollo during his original scouting mission—had been fluttering all day. The bags showed him the strength and direction of the wind and allowed him to adjust the sights on his 'scope accordingly.

After the sun had set fully, a largely clear sky provided enough starlight to make the view through his night vision binoculars almost as clear as day.

Since sunset, the intermittent wind speed had increased to an average of around fifteen kph, occasionally gusting to twenty. It made the six-hundred-and-twenty-metre shot slightly more difficult than it would have been on a dead calm day, but well within his operating parameters. To hit the cola can under these conditions might take more than one shot, but the sound and flash suppressor on his AXMC would make it difficult for the opposition to locate his sniper's nest quickly. It would give him enough time for two or three shots. Probably more than he needed.

He peered through the rifle's night 'scope and confirmed his target for the thousandth time that evening. The cola can showed monochrome at the foot of a yellow skip that hadn't been emptied since the warehouse closed down. Black bin liners, stuffed and torn, spewed their rubbish in piles to be picked over by the local wildlife—dogs, cats, and rats. The perfect place for the Pataki family to drop the money to ransom a piece of filth like Lajos.

Much earlier that day, Kaine had taped a white sign with a black, downward-pointing arrow to the side of the middle skip. The arrow pointed to a cleared area of concrete at the base of the skip, some three feet to the right of the carefully positioned cola can.

Whoever placed the bag of cash at the foot of the skip would have a foul-smelling surprise in store. According to Kaine's intel, it wouldn't be Viktor, the Giant of Győr. Lajos Pataki's Papa hadn't left the safety of the Pataki Compound for over five years. Not since a particularly brutal run-in with a rival family who'd tried to muscle in on one of the Pataki family's smuggling businesses.

Blood had flowed through the streets of a village to the east of Győr, and many lives had been lost—some of them innocent civilians. Shortly thereafter, Viktor Pataki had reached an unofficial and highly illegal "accommodation" with the local police and the regional authorities. The accommodation had the tacit approval of the Hungarian Government, a notoriously corrupt institution that made the Russians look highly ethical and honest in comparison. The prime reasons the Magyars hadn't reached the same notoriety on the international stage as the Russians, resulted from the size of the population—less than ten million—and the inherent weakness of the Hungarian economy.

The deal required Viktor to remain inside the Pataki compound at all times. If he were to set foot outside, he would be liable to face imprisonment for the rest of his days. Lajos said his Papa considered the house arrest an insult and beneath him, but he adhered to the rules just as long as it suited his purposes.

The conditions of Papa's velvet incarceration were far from the only information Kaine had garnered from Lajos, who had been ever so forthcoming under Kaine's gentle persuasion. It hadn't taken much to prise the injured man's tongue from the roof of his mouth. A threat to remove his remaining hand with a rusty hacksaw had done the trick.

Kaine had found the hacksaw hanging in the garage and had ordered Lara from the bedroom. He didn't want her to see him in his role as torturer, but needn't have worried. Simply resting the blade on Lajos' remaining wrist made the wretch dissolve into a babbling, screaming, pleading mess. A mess desperate to tell him everything he wanted to know—and more.

Lajos took Kaine through the Pataki Compound's layout and its fortifications. He almost boasted about the near-impregnable fortress in the middle of a valley so wide and open it would take an army to approach with all the equipment necessary to storm the place.

Yes. Lajos Pataki had been ever so helpful, and his information had come in rather handy. With it, Kaine had developed a comprehensive two-part plan. The first part of which—the initial drop and sting—was currently in play. Kaine would launch part two a little later.

A distant white light flickered on his retina.

To the northeast, the direction of Győr, car headlights flared, dipped, and bobbed on an uneven surface. At less than two kilometres away and with the car closing fast, the lights snapped off, plunging the area into darkness once again. The driver had extinguished the headlights on a stretch of open road in the middle of nowhere.

Kaine exhaled.

Here they come.

Showing lights in the gloom was a stupid move almost calculated to draw his attention. He trained the night glasses on the area. The driver had parked a big SUV—which stood out grey under the high-resolution night optics—on a grass verge at the side of the service road leading to the industrial estate. All four doors opened and the SUV disgorged four men, their silhouettes bulked out by full military body armour. Three wore helmets, and all carried weapons. He couldn't be certain, but their outlines looked like AK-15 assault rifles. Russian made and, in the right hands, lethal.

Kaine bared his teeth in a vicious smile.

Bring it on!

Viktor Pataki was playing dirty. A four-man assault team was hardly a "keeping to the rules" approach to ransom negotiations. Maybe Lajos was as expendable as he'd claimed, as far as Papa was concerned.

Kaine adjusted the focus on his night glasses and studied the interlopers.

A huge, gorilla of a man led the four-man team along the service road. At the main gates, some two hundred metres distant, they stopped, and Gorilla spoke briefly and quietly. Seconds later, the column crept through the open gates and split into two teams of two.

The first pair turned north, hugged the inside of the fence, and made their way to the rear of the loading bay and the car park. Eventually, the two split up. One man dropped into hiding behind a bush, lying prone, facing the courtyard. He shouldered his weapon, taking careful aim at Kaine's primary target—the central skip. The man's AK-15 sported a bipod stand and a night vision 'scope as large as the one on Kaine's Accuracy. A sniper.

The second man crawled a further forty metres and took up a similar position at the side of a single-storey building, directly opposite Kaine's position. Both men lay within one hundred and fifty metres of their target and had easy kill shots at anyone collecting the ransom money.

Sneaky little ratbags.

Kaine marked their positions on the internal map in his head and turned his attention on the other pair.

Led by Gorilla, the second team waited at the gates until their mates were in position before heading straight for the main building, where Kaine hid.

Kaine wriggled back and away from the Accuracy. He left it on its bipod stand, hidden under the camo tarp, primed and ready for action, and crawled to the far side of the roof.

A waxing gibbous moon peeked out from behind a bar of dark clouds, making the night vision glasses redundant. Kaine popped his head over the roof's edge.

On the ground below, Gorilla and his much smaller buddy reached the metal fire escape bolted to the outside of the wall, the one Kaine had used to scale the building that afternoon.

While Gorilla and his AK-15 shuffled around to the corner of the building, presumably to find a good vantage point for the ambush, Buddy started climbing. The fire escape creaked and groaned under his weight. It hadn't complained anywhere near as loudly when Kaine used it. Buddy must have weighed more than Kaine, much more. He couldn't have been that small, but standing next to Gorilla, he'd looked closer in size to Lajos.

With little time to consider his options, Kaine squirmed away from the roof's edge and crawled closer to the head of the fire escape. One thing in his favour, the four interlopers didn't seem to be wearing night vision glasses or comms gear. None had spoken since forming a group at the gates. Such a weakness, he could exploit.

As Buddy approached the halfway point, breathing hard, the metalwork pinged and scraped against the brickwork. The up and over handrails trembled and shuddered under the heavy load.

Kaine pulled the hunting knife from the sheath strapped to his calf. Once Buddy's eyes broke the line of the roof, he'd be able to spot Kaine's sniper's nest. Despite the grey tarp covering the Accuracy, Buddy had to recognise it for what it was and call a warning down to Gorilla.

To take out all four men clean and fast, Kaine needed surprise and more than a little luck. Although slicing Buddy's throat would keep him from screaming out, Kaine's timing had to be perfect. He couldn't strike until, in death, Buddy's bodyweight pulled him forwards onto the roof, rather than throw him backwards into the air to land in a bloody mess at Gorilla's feet.

Knife drawn, Kaine waited.

Buddy's heavy breathing grew louder, his battle gear and the rifle strapped to his back taking its toll on a man unused to climbing ladders while wearing such a load—around thirty kilos, including the weapon. The task looked easy enough in the movies, but climbing in full body armour took training—continuous training—and lots of it. Two-thirds of the way up the climb, at the middle of the fifth floor, Buddy stopped for a much needed breather. A deep voice hissing up from below and Buddy's breathless response confirmed a number of things. Gorilla was in command, impatient, and under the impression that he and his men were alone. He probably suspected that they'd beaten the kidnappers to the draw. Finally, and much more importantly, the shouted call and response confirmed they weren't in radio contact.

Amateurs.

Not the time to relax, though. Under the correct circumstances, even amateurs could get lucky.

Kaine almost felt pity for ending the life of such an underprepared man, but the memory of Danny's final breaths drove the sympathy away. All that remained was cold, hard anger.

Under Gorilla's "gentle" encouragement, Buddy started climbing again. Twenty-three rungs later, his shaggy hair broke the roofline, head lowered, mouth open, sucking in great gasps of the chill night air. He continued climbing, hands sliding up the curved rails, paying no attention to his surroundings, concentrating on his footing on the slippery treads.

Kaine needn't have worried about Buddy spotting the Accuracy under its camouflage tarp. The man wouldn't have noticed a troop of scantily clad cheerleaders dancing to *The Star-Spangled Banner*. He was plainly terrified of heights.

Buddy placed one foot on the creosote-covered roof and levered himself between the handrails, grunting heavily from the effort. Once his second foot planted onto the flat surface, he took two paces forwards, clapped his hands to his knees, and drew in some more ragged breaths.

Kaine crouched in the deep shadows, awaiting his moment.

Gorilla called again from below. Buddy turned and grabbed the handrail before leaning over the edge, his face deathly pale in the moonlight.

Kaine smirked. Gorilla had sent a man with vertigo up a corroded ladder to the rooftop of a six-storey building. These fools deserved everything coming to them.

Gorilla shouted again, this time with more force and anger.

Keeping his eyes tight shut, Buddy nodded and called out, "*Igen, igen. Jó vagyok!*" before jerking his head away from what, to him, must have appeared like the precipice into Hell itself.

Buddy puffed out his cheeks and turned away from Kaine to face the centre of the roof. His head jerked to his left, towards the Accuracy and Kaine's nest. He stiffened, unshipped his rifle, and brought it up. He sucked in a breath in preparation for shouting.

Knife raised, Kaine leapt up from his hiding spot. He clamped his left hand over Buddy's mouth and jerked up and back, exposing his throat to the razor-sharp edge of Kaine's blade.

One cut, left to right, ear to ear. He sliced through tendons, blood vessels, and cartilage.

Blood spurted, steaming in the cold air. It warmed Kaine's gloved hand and painted his knife dark.

Buddy gurgled, fighting for breath. He dropped the AK-15, and it clattered to the bitumen-covered surface.

Kaine took Buddy's full weight, holding him tight while the gurgling, kicking, and arm-flailing slowed and weakened. Finally, it stopped.

"That's for Danny," he whispered into the dead man's ear.

Slowly, quietly, Kaine lowered the corpse to the surface and left it lying face-down in the pool of its own steaming blood.

He checked his watch. 23:28. Time was flying. Who next, Gorilla or the snipers?

Gorilla's insistent call from below made Kaine's decision for him. He picked up Buddy's rifle, checked the load, and flipped the selector to "semi". Time for a calculated gamble. The snipers hiding on the far side of the carpark were more than three hundred metres upwind. He doubted they would hear a single rifle shot.

With the AK-15's sound suppressor secured and the rifle raised, Kaine strode to the edge of the roof and coughed.

Below, at the corner of the building, the pale oval of a bearded face looked up. It scowled and the mouth opened in preparation to shout.

Kaine aimed and squeezed the trigger once. As usual for an AK-15, it pulled slightly to the left. Gorilla's right eye doubled in size, and the back of his head exploded. His huge body crumpled and fell in slow motion.

No more Gorilla.

Kaine removed the mag and the bolt, cleared the chamber, and dropped the AK-15 over the edge. It landed, tail-end first, and the wooden butt shattered. No way to treat a decent weapon, but no one else would be able to use it against him—or against anyone else for that matter.

Keeping low, Kaine scurried back to his nest, peeled away the tarp, and dropped into position. He chose his first target—the sniper from the first pair—and slowed his breathing and his heartrate.

Sniper One's nest stood some one hundred and fifty metres closer than the cola can. Rather than adjust the sights, Kaine used dead reckoning and lined up the four-hundred-metre shot to allow for the wind direction and speed and the slightly reduced elevation.

The first man had set up his shot but, rather than maintain his firing position as any half-decent sniper would have done, he lay stretched out with his head lowered, chin resting on his folded arms. The man was relaxing, maybe even trying to sleep.

Pathetic.

Kaine centred the mil-dot reticle on Sniper One's ring finger, six centimetres below the crown of his head, to allow for the reduced distance to the target. On the fence above and behind the sniper, one of Rollo's plastic bags danced and fluttered.

Kaine waited.

The bag's billowing movements slackened.

Kaine filled and then emptied his lungs to slow his heartrate even further. He took up the trigger's half-centimetre slack.

The plastic bag stilled.

Smoothly and gently, Kaine squeezed the trigger. The AXMC bucked and cracked as the NATO cartridge exploded into deadly life. The bullet punched a hole through the top of Sniper One's peaked cap and the muffled retort echoed throughout the courtyard.

Kaine worked the bolt, ejected the empty shell, reloaded a fresh round, and prepared his next shot.

Sniper Two's head jerked up and turned towards his friend, confusion written clearly on his grizzled face. He shouted something in a stage whisper. Did he think Sniper One had prematurely discharged his weapon?

No matter.

Kaine's second shot smashed though Sniper Two's jaw and erupted out the side of his neck. His body slumped and fell still. The man wouldn't have felt a thing.

Kaine breathed again. The other four men in the abandoned warehouse complex didn't.

He took no joy in ending their lives, but wouldn't mourn their deaths either. If the Giant of Győr's advance team hadn't been so inept, they might have killed Kaine instead, as was their clear intention. They were in the wrong game and their ending would cause him no lost sleep.

His watch read 23:41.

The cloud bar rolled in front of the moon. Darkness descended once again. Kaine returned the AXMC to its active position and lined up the sights on the primary target. He released the locking nut on the adjustable footrest to drop the muzzle by a couple of degrees. Information from the Sniper Two kill shot made the adjustment necessary. The cola can centred in the reticle once more, and he was good to go.

Breathing slowly and easily, Kaine loosened the stiffness from his neck and shoulders and counted down the minutes.

CHAPTER THIRTY-ONE

Another pair of headlights brightened the darkness behind him. Kaine turned onto his side. He followed the brilliant white cones as they drew closer, slowed, and turned onto the access road.

23:54.

Six minutes early.

The Drop Team was keen to spring the trap.

Good luck with that, guys.

Their vehicle passed the first car without slowing and smashed through the part-open gates. An oversized set of bull bars protected the grill and bonnet of a dark Mitsubishi Shogun. The driver pulled to a sideways stop in the middle of the car park. Dust billowed, and the roar of the Shogun's powerful engine dropped to idle.

Before the SUV's suspension had stopped bouncing, the front passenger door flew open, and a shortish man with a barrel for a chest and long, dark hair stepped down. The wind whipped strands of hair around his head, partially covering his bearded face. The

Shogun's tailgate rose and the long-haired man turned towards it, stumbling slightly as though infirm—or drunk.

The driver jumped out and joined the first man at the back. Together they heaved a large canvas bag from the rear and carried it towards the drop point, leaving it in exactly the right position, close to the foot of the middle skip.

They repeated the process with two more bags. Fifteen million euros in notes no larger than hundreds would weigh around one hundred and sixty kilos, not easy for one staggering old man to carry. Whoever the man with the long hair was—definitely not Viktor Pataki—needed the driver's help.

"Viktor" knelt in front of the first bag, and took his time doing it. Either he had bad knees and a dodgy back, or he was feigning the infirmities.

He pulled back the zip, rummaged around, and pulled out a couple of bundles of what certainly *looked* like banknotes. He raised the bundles over his head, replaced them, and did the same thing with bags two and three. The third time, he split one of the bundles and fanned them out to show whoever was watching that the money was real, not simply stacks of paper.

That's a surprise.

"Viktor" zipped up the moneybags, said something, and held out his hand for the driver to help him up. When standing, the two men glanced around before hurrying back to the Shogun.

Kaine gave them enough time to reach the car but not enough to climb in. Since their arrival, the wind had dropped to the lightest of zephyrs.

He took his shot.

The first bullet missed—low, two centimetres to the right—and ricocheted into the night.

"Viktor" and his driver yelped. Panicked, they scrambled for the safety of the Shogun. Doors opened.

Kaine adjusted the aim, fired again.

The second bullet hit the can dead centre. It exploded into a fireball of orange and yellow. Black binbags erupted, throwing foetid rubbish high and wide, covering the Shogun and its fleeing passengers in kilos of indescribable, well-rotted filth. The explosion ignited the jerrycans of petrol Kaine had buried in the rubbish to act as the accelerant, and the canvas money bags disappeared behind the flames. Along with the rubbish, the cash burned fierce and bright. At least, it appeared to.

Kaine would have loved to sit and watch the slapstick fun, but he had other things to do. He pocketed the four empty but still warm NATO shells, jumped up, and hefted the Accuracy. After a quick visual search to confirm he'd left nothing to assist a police investigation, he turned and headed towards the fire escape. He sidestepped around Buddy's cooling corpse, hung the Accuracy across his back by its strap, and descended.

By the time he reached firm ground, the filth-covered Shogun had screamed through the gates, and was bouncing along the access road, paying scant attention to the niceties of safe driving. It sideswiped the parked car but continued without stopping.

The driver and the false Viktor probably couldn't understand why Gorilla's team hadn't opened up on the sniper who'd covered them in grime and had apparently destroyed all that lovely cash.

For the first time since losing Danny, Kaine laughed.

CHAPTER THIRTY-TWO

During the four-kilometre yomp from the warehouse complex to where he'd hidden his car—off the road and behind a low hedge—Kaine stopped once to watch the flames that lit the sky slowly die. He allowed a grim smile to form and tapped his earpiece.

"Alpha One to Alpha Two. Are you receiving? Over."

Rollo's response was instant. *"Alpha Two here. Receiving you, strength five. Foxtrot One has ears, too. Sitrep, please. Over."*

Kaine didn't need Rollo to tell him Lara would also be listening. He'd have been shocked to learn she wasn't.

"Situation green, Alpha Two. Repeat, situation green. Four interlopers neutralised at scene. Two others left to report home to Papa. Please tell Foxtrot One to relax. Over."

"Did the can work as expected? Over."

"That's an affirmative, Alpha Two. Couldn't have gone better. Over."

"Really? It actually worked? Over."

"It did, Alpha Two. The paperwork will be ready for collection in about an hour or so. You'll need to wait for the temperature to drop a little first. Over."

"*Will do, Alpha One. Is the other package ready for delivery? Over.*"

"Hope so, Alpha Two. On my way to check it's still warm. Over."

"*Any additional instructions? Over.*"

"Just make sure the area is secure before you collect the paperwork. Although the 'picnic area' was deserted when I left it, there's no telling who the firework display might have attracted. Wouldn't want you to run into a reception committee just to pick up a few sheets of paper. Over."

Kaine allowed his wry smile to grow. If Rollo could deliver unnecessary information, so could he.

"*Thank you, Alpha One.*" Rollo snapped. "*I do know how to suck eggs. Foxtrot One says 'take care'. I don't. Alpha Two, out!*"

Kaine tapped the earpiece inactive and resumed his easy yomp, using the inbuilt compass in his diver's watch to guide him. No rush. The money would be safe behind the hinged lid of the skip, which the explosion had dislodged and now covered the delivery bags. Rollo and Lara would retrieve it in an hour or so, once the area had cooled enough to raise the lid.

The money would come in handy. No way would he willingly destroy the wherewithal to deliver Marian Prentiss and her baby a safe future.

———

Thirty minutes later, after he'd watched his hidden Range Rover from a safe distance for ten of them, Kaine pulled open its tailgate and took in the sorry sight of his trussed and gagged prisoner. Lajos Pataki's purple face and blue lips showed early signs of asphyxia. When the courtesy lights popped on, Lajos' eyes bulged in fear.

"Hello Lajos, old friend. Surprised but happy to see you're still in the land of the living."

The bound man whimpered and struggled weakly at his bonds.

261

"Take it easy, son. I'll set you free in a minute. Just need to tidy up first."

After breaking down the Accuracy and stowing it carefully in its rugged carrycase—watched the whole time by his captive—Kaine removed his knife and polished the blade on Lajos' jacket, whistling as he did so. He held up the knife and allowed its honed edge to catch the limited light source. Lajos' whimpering started up again and he shook his head.

"Easy, son. Now isn't the time to panic. You'll do yourself a mischief."

Kaine leaned further into the luggage area and pushed out the knife. Lajos squealed and tried to back away but, lashed as he was to the anchor points in the floor by his wrist and ankle, he had nowhere to go. Kaine grabbed him by the hair and pulled his head forwards. The blade cut through the knot holding the gag in place, and Kaine yanked away the sodden band. Lajos spat out the cloth wadding and gulped in air as though he'd been starved of it for hours—which happened to be the case.

"Did you catch sight of the firework show?" Kaine asked as soon as Lajos' breathing quietened enough for him to take notice.

Kaine giggled to maintain the show of madness.

"What ... what was it?" Lajos asked, still gasping. Tears filled his eyes and rolled down his cheeks.

His skin colour had returned to normal for him—a pale, almost translucent white—but his remaining hand still showed red beneath the restrictive zip tie.

"That, dear Lajos, was the sight and sound of fifteen million euros going up in flames."

Lajos gasped again, this time in shock rather than for air.

"You burned it?"

"I did."

"On purpose?"

Kaine slapped Lajos' cheek hard enough to sting, but not enough to damage.

"Everything I do is intentional, son."

The stunned man shook his head.

"But why?"

"I did it to make a point. Money means nothing to me. You people killed my friend and Robert Prentiss. In exchange, I killed Vadik and burned the cash, but I also spared your life. In my book, Papa and I are now even."

"Even?"

Kaine nodded.

"You will not kill me?"

"Nope. I promised to send you back after receiving the ransom, and I always honour my commitments. Even though Papa tried to double-cross me, I'm happy to return you to him."

"Double-cross? How?"

Kaine scuttled out of the luggage area and leaned against the side column. He described Gorilla and Buddy and explained what he did to them and the would-be snipers. He also described what happened to the money—after a fashion. Lajos listened in slack-jawed and silent horror.

"They are dead? All dead?"

"You recognised the men?" Kaine asked.

"Y-Yes, some of them. The one you call Gorilla sounds like Balint ... Balint Sarkozy, one of Papa's men from the old days. The days when he started out. Papa will not be happy. Neither will Andris, who was a cousin to Balint."

"Andris?"

"The man who drove Wendt and the money."

Kaine sniffed. "Wendt is Papa's body double?"

"Yes. He is older than Papa, but the same size and build. The stumbling showed he was drunk. Wendt no longer has the stomach for danger."

"Standing in for the Giant of Győr can't be an easy gig."

"No," Lajos said, lowering his tearful eyes. "Wendt is the third, and the longest serving. The other two died in service to Papa."

Kaine rubbed his hands together and reached up to the tailgate's handhold. "I'd love to stay and chat, but it's time to go home, Lajos."

"R-Really? You *are* taking me home?"

"Man of my word, remember," he said, adding a wink.

Kaine lowered the tailgate and made his way to the driver's seat.

Yep, a man of my word.

———

Kaine drove the twenty-seven kilometres to the Pataki compound slowly and in silence. Andris and Wendt needed plenty of time to reach Viktor and tell the Giant of Győr what had happened. Who knew, they might even have wanted to wash down the Shogun, and shower and change their clothes first. Arriving in front of the Giant of Győr covered in rotting filth might not have been the best way to ensure their longevity.

A low, wide valley opened up around them, dark, but lit by stars, the moon, and the Range Rover's headlights. The road they took, a two-lane badly metalled blacktop, ran parallel to the *Rába*, a lazy and minor tributary of the Danube.

Five kilometres from Pataki land, their quiet road turned sharply to cross the river. Kaine stopped on the near side of the bridge. He pressed the button to raise the tailgate and pushed open his door.

"Please!" Lajos wailed.

Kaine stepped out of the cab and headed around to the back. "Please what?"

"Please, don't kill me."

Kaine sighed. "What part of 'I honour my commitments' don't you understand?"

"I-I ..."

Kaine cut Lajos free of the zip ties and drag-carried him, screaming in pain, from the back compartment and deposited him in the dust and gravel at the side of the road.

"You are leaving me here?"

"Why not?"

Lajos held up his trembling hand, reddened from being so tightly bound for hours. He pointed to the calf-length plaster cast covering his injured ankle. "My leg is broken. I cannot walk. Out here, I will freeze to death before morning."

Kaine sneered. "Don't be so damned pitiful. It's not that cold and you have that lovely, expensive jacket to keep you warm."

"But, I ... I cannot stay—"

Kaine raised his finger to his lips for silence. He returned to the Range Rover, pulled the collapsed wheelchair from the back, and snapped it open. He rolled the chair closer to Lajos, activated the brake, and unceremoniously dumped the limp and helpless man into it. If Lara had included a blanket to wrap around her patient's knees, Kaine wouldn't have used it. He stood to one side and waved an arm at the distance.

"Recognise this place?"

Lajos twisted and turned his head, peering into the darkness.

"Yes," he said, eventually. "This is *Rábatona* Bridge."

Kaine pointed northwest. "The compound's that way, right? About five kilometres?"

Lajos nodded. "Four ... four and a half, maybe."

"Good. I'll be off now. As soon as I'm far enough away from here, I'll telephone Papa and tell him where to collect you. Won't take your friends too long to get here. Of course, you can always try wheeling yourself home. Although, with only one arm, I can't see you getting very far. You'll be going round in circles."

To keep in character, Kaine chuckled and let it build into the uncontrolled maniacal laughter of a madman.

"You really *are* letting me go?"

"As I said, son. Your family killed my friend and Robert Prentiss. I've taken one of its sons, some money, and a number of its soldiers, but I have returned you alive. I have no wish to extend this war. Tell your father, this ends here. Tell him if he makes one move against Marian Prentiss or her family, I will destroy him and the rest of the Pataki clan. Marian Prentiss is now and will always be under my protection. Do you understand?"

"Y-Yes, I do. I do."

Kaine patted Lajos' reddened cheek.

"Good, Lajos. Very good."

Lajos swallowed hard and looked up, making direct eye contact for almost the first time that night. "M-May I ask you a question?"

"But of course, we're the best of friends. Feel free to ask anything you like."

"Who ... Who are you?"

"Not that it matters, but my name is Ryan Kaine."

Lajos frowned. "I don't ... Wait! Ryan Kaine? The terrorist who murdered all those people on that plane?"

"Yep, that's me." Kaine grinned and double-hitched his eyebrows.

It didn't suit his plans to argue the details or put Lajos straight.

"My God! Ryan Kaine? And you let me go?"

For the moment.

"Yes, indeed."

"Why? Why are you setting me free?"

"I've already told you. I keep my promises, and besides, you are my messenger boy."

Kaine grasped the wheelchair's handles, released the brake, pointed Lajos in the right direction, and gave him a healthy shove. The wheelchair rolled into the centre of the bridge and ground to a halt, sideways at the apex of the arch. Lajos turned to stare at him, dumbfounded.

"Remember what I said, Lajos. If Papa doesn't let the matter drop, *I'll be back.*"

Kaine winced at the bad Arnie impression, hurried back to the Range Rover, and took off at warp speed. The rear-view mirror showed him a red-lit and rapidly diminishing image of Lajos Pataki's stunned face.

CHAPTER THIRTY-THREE

SUNDAY 7TH MAY – Viktor Pataki

Pataki Compound, Outside Győr, Hungary

"*Idióta, kretén!*" Viktor roared.

He kicked out. Hard.

The pointed toe of his shoe connected with Wendt's fat ass, driving him to the floor. Viktor followed it with a kick to the belly and ground the heel of his shoe into the miserable old man's hand. Wendt screamed and the bones crunched. Viktor pulled back his foot for a head shot.

"*Főnök, no!*"

Andris stepped between Viktor and Wendt. He held up his hands.

"Wendt is not to blame, *főnök*. He did exactly what was required of him."

Viktor growled and lowered his foot. As usual, Andris had a good point, and he made it well. He turned to the men lined up against the wall, and pointed to a fat one with the blotchy skin who always reeked of sauerkraut. "You, take him away. Have the housekeeper treat his injuries."

No one could say the Giant of Győr did not show pity or forgiveness.

Fatso bumbled into action and dragged the screaming ignoramus from the room. Viktor turned his back to them and stared at his long-time advisor.

"Where is Balint?"

"I've no idea, *főnök*. As planned, we separated before reaching the warehouse and I gave him and his men plenty of time to set up the ambush before we were due to arrive at the site to drop the money. Balint telephoned me to say they were about to leave their car and get into position. Since then I have heard nothing from him."

"He does not answer his portable?"

"No, *főnök*."

"And after the explosion, what happened?"

Andris shrugged and held his hands open once again. "Wendt and I took the car and made a rapid escape, covered in filth. We stopped along the route, expecting to hear gunfire from Balint and his team, but all was silent and dark—apart from the raging fire."

Viktor ground his teeth and made fists with his powerful hands, when he really wanted to use them to throttle the person responsible for the loss of his son and his money—*Őrült*.

"My money, burning? So much cash. Is it all gone? Are you certain?"

"The bags were right next to the bomb, *főnök*. I do not see how they could have survived the inferno."

"Why would *Őrült* burn my money?"

Viktor paused. The cogs in his head whirred, spun, interlocked, tumbled. Evil thoughts arrived. He tried to ignore them, cast them away, but could not do so. Was it treachery? A double-cross? He dug a hand inside his jacket, found the handle of the holstered Makarov, and closed on Andris.

Andris stood his ground, but kept his hands raised and open.

"Did Balint double-cross me?" Viktor growled, leaning closer to his man. "Did he take my money?"

"No, *főn*—"

"Are you in on this with him? Are you trying to deceive me?"

"*Főnök!* No, I swear."

"Because if you are—"

The desk telephone's insistent ring interrupted Viktor, mid-threat. These days, the fucking thing never stopped ringing. He pushed past his longest-serving employee and snatched up the handset, while maintaining his grip on the Makarov.

"*Helló?*"

"Hello, Viktor. How are you doing, old chap?"

"*Őrült?*"

"Don't call me a lunatic again!" the Englishman shrieked.

Viktor signalled for Andris to pick up the extension and waited until he was in position before replying. "You have money. Where Lajos?"

"It wasn't very nice of you to have Balint and his men set up that ambush. Not at all what we agreed."

Viktor took a moment to breathe. The Englishman knew so much. He knew everything. How was that possible?

"You know the name Balint?"

"Yep, Lajos told me. As it turns out, your only surviving son is a rather chatty fellow. Not the most sparkling of wits, mind you. I won't be inviting him to any future dinner parties, but he is rather informative."

"Where Lajos is?"

"I left him alive and well at *Rábatona* Bridge. You might want to send someone to collect him. He's not too sprightly, I'm afraid. Can't wheel himself all that far with only one arm. Actually, he's spinning himself around in tight circles. A pitiful sight, really." *Őrült* laughed long and hard. "Oh dear, I crease myself up sometimes."

Őrült was enjoying himself. The English had a phrase for it. What was it? Barking mad. Yes, that was it. The man was barking mad. There was no reason to him. To burn all that money. Illogical. Out of his mind. The fact that he could not be reasoned with and was completely unpredictable made the man doubly dangerous.

Viktor turned to Andris and urgently waved him on his way.

Andris replaced the extension telephone, signalled to one of the men, and they rushed from the room.

"You hurt Lajos again?"

"Not at all, but being tied up in the back of a car for hours on end isn't the most beneficial post-operative treatment protocol. Not according to my medic, that is. But he's young and should recover, given time. Might even walk again if the bone sets properly. Mind you, he will have difficulties tying his shoelaces."

Another cruel laugh spewed down the telephone line. *Őrült* was enjoying taunting Viktor. He enjoyed toying with the Giant of Győr. Somehow, someday soon, he would learn the error of his ways.

"Where Balint is? I not pay you again for his safe return."

Őrült sighed. "Haven't I already demonstrated what I think of your money? Fuck your goddamned money."

"What you do with Balint!"

"I killed him, Viktor. I killed him and his three friends. They are all dead."

Isten a mennyben! God in Heaven.

Viktor dropped into the chair next to the desk.

"Dead?" he gasped. "You kill them all?"

"Yep. Couldn't avoid it, I'm afraid. They would have done the same to me, right?"

"I-I ..."

"Viktor, oh mighty 'Giant of Győr', listen to me," he said, again taunting. "I've returned Lajos to you as a sign of my good faith. He has a message for you. Listen to what he says and listen carefully."

"Why wait? You give me message now."

Silence.

"*Helló?* Englishman? *Helló? Helló!*"

The line clicked dead and the intermittent dial tone burped into his ear. Viktor screamed. He called down an ancient curse on the heritage of the lunatic Englishman and slammed the handset onto the desk. He turned to the remaining guards. Five stupid-looking men about the same age as Vadik stared back at him, their expressions vacant. What use were these fools?

Balint was dead. Murdered by the Englishman. The old ally of Viktor had not betrayed him, and Andris had not sided with Balint against him. *Szar*, Andris was his last remaining friend from the early days, and Viktor had insulted him in front of the others. Would he forgive Viktor his anger, the affront? Should Viktor ask the pardon of his friend?

Szar nem! Shit no!

He was Viktor Pataki, the Giant of Győr. Viktor would never beg. Viktor would plead with no one.

No one!

Andris would be upset over the death of Balint, of course he would, but he would remain loyal to his *főnök*. Andris would bring Lajos back home, and Lajos would identify the English *őrült*. Lajos would also help Viktor find Marian Prentiss so they could send the bitch and the whole of her pitiful family to Hell, alongside her husband.

No one toyed with Viktor Pataki and lived. No one! The world would tremble in his wake. *Őrült* would die along with the whole Prentiss tribe. History books would chronicle the deeds of the Giant of Győr. They would tell of his wrath and his terrible vengeance.

Viktor looked up to find himself in the middle of the room. When had he stood up and started pacing? He stopped mumbling to himself, stopped his wandering, and pointed to the man on the far end of the line, a man who appeared to have more spark about him than the others. Perhaps the square glasses made him seem more intelligent.

"You!"

The man stiffened.

"Yes, *főnök*?"

"Your name. What is your name?"

"Jael, *főnök*."

Viktor wiped his mouth with the back of his hand and nodded.

"Come here."

The man crossed the room and stood before Viktor. Did he tremble? Did he wilt under the dominant gaze of his *főnök*?

Yes, he did. Good. Very good.

The men *should* tremble. They should all quake before him. It was right for underlings to pay such a tribute. This one, Jael, could not meet the eye of his boss, his *főnök*, but he focused his attention on Viktor's barrel chest.

Viktor looked down. His right hand still dipped inside his jacket and rested on the butt of his Makarov. Another oversight, but this one was a powerful way to keep the men under his control.

"Yes, *főnök*?" Jael asked, his voice low, subservient.

"You have the number for the portable telephone Andris uses?"

The young man nodded. He pulled out his own portable and showed the screen to Viktor.

"Call him. Find out what is happening with Lajos."

"*Igen, főnök*," Jael said. Without hesitation, he dialled.

Viktor turned away from the man. He headed for the drinks table and the bottle of *pálinka*. He picked it up. Empty!

What?

Why was the bottle empty?

Did no one do their jobs correctly anymore?

He pointed at the next man in line. "You! Go fetch me a fresh bottle. Do it now!"

"Yes, *főnök*," he said and all but raced from the room.

That was more like it. Viktor needed the people around him to obey. Obedience was good. Essential for an individual's survival.

"*Főnök*?" Jael said.

Viktor spun to face him. "What?"

"I have Andris," he said, holding out his portable.

Viktor ripped it from his hand. "Andris? You have Lajos?"

"Yes, *főnök*," he replied, but something in his tone made Viktor uneasy.

Was Andris still upset by his ill-judged accusation and by the demise of Balint? Maybe Viktor should try to placate him. Should he offer Andris solace? Perhaps. Perhaps not. In either event, Andris would have to be watched—and watched carefully.

Since the death of Vadik, things had begun to fall apart. Viktor growled. He should never have agreed to the English adventure, but Vadik had made it all appear so easy.

"The English are weak and flabby," Vadik had announced. "They will fold like wet tissues."

Lajos had agreed and look what had happened to him. To them both.

Vadik dead. Balint dead. Lajos crippled, and now, there were doubts as to the loyalty of the once-trusted Andris.

Things were turning to shit in his hands. No! Viktor could not allow things to continue in this manner. He would think on it. Plan his next move carefully.

"How is he? How is my son?"

"Alive, *fŏnök*."

"Bring him home to me."

"*Fŏnök*, I think it would be better to take him to the hospital. He is seriously injured and in great pain."

What is this?

Andris arguing with his *fŏnök*? Did the turncoat want to keep Lajos from his Papa and his home. Why?

Viktor paused. He knew why. Yes, yes.

The intentions of Andris were obvious. He wanted revenge on Viktor for the perceived slight. He wanted money. Andris wanted to use Lajos as a lever, as had *Ŏrült*.

"No! Bring him home. He needs to be here, with his family and his friends. I will send for a doctor. Once here, under my protection, he will receive the best care possible."

And he will be able to answer all my questions.

"Yes, *fŏnök* ... as you command."

The whole world might try to stand against Viktor Pataki, but the Giant of Győr would endure. He and Lajos would rebuild. The family would prosper.

It was time to clean house and resume control.

CHAPTER THIRTY-FOUR

Sᴜɴᴅᴀʏ 7ᴛʜ Mᴀʏ – Viktor Pataki
Pataki Compound, Outside Győr, Hungary

Twenty-three minutes had passed. Seventeen minutes since the telephone call from Andris. Where were they?

Viktor stood at the open front doors, waiting, and as each second dragged by, he became more and more certain of the betrayal.

Andris, the evil, snivelling traitor had abducted Lajos. The swine had kidnapped his only son to use for ransom. Andris had stolen Lajos to take his revenge for the insult and for the death of Balint.

Damn his black heart.

The pressure built. Viktor paced and tried to fight off the headache growing behind his eyes. The cold night air should have chilled him to the bone, but the burning anger kept him warm.

Twenty-four minutes.

How long did it take to drive less than five kilometres? Five minutes? Ten? Why was it taking so long?

Andris and Lajos should have returned long ago.

From his lofty position at the top of the steps leading down to the

274

front courtyard, he could see all the way to the entrance gates and the two armed guards who patrolled them. Beyond the gates, the land dipped away into the darkness of the night and to the confines of the woods. If he re-entered the house and climbed upstairs to the master bedroom, he would have an even better view, but that would make it seem as though he was hiding, running scared.

Where are you, Andris?

The bespectacled Jael guarded the left side of the opening. Another man took the right. Strong and silent, former soldiers hired by Vadik, they stood tall and stiff. They held their semi-automatic rifles at the ready and their sidearms holstered. Viktor rarely stepped beyond the safety of the house, but tonight of all nights, he soaked in the chill air.

Twenty-six minutes.

How long should he wait before ordering a countrywide manhunt for the traitor? Too quickly and he would appear like a panicked child. Too slowly and Andris would have time to escape. Half an hour. Thirty minutes. Any longer would be foolish.

Twenty-eight minutes.

Lights! In the distance, along the only road into the valley, headlights cut through the darkness. Moving at the pace of a snail.

The portable in Jael's pocket buzzed. He answered.

"*Fōnók*," he called, smiling. "It is the guard on the front gate. Andris is coming. Driving very slowly."

At last.

"Good. Tell them to open up."

Viktor, hands clasped behind his back, watched the main gates open and the headlights draw ever closer. Eventually, they broached the opening in the wall and added to the floodlights that turned night into day.

Slowly, the white Shogun rolled to a stop at the front of the house, and out climbed Andris. He nodded to Viktor, his expression grave, and opened the rear passenger door. His driver jumped out and raced around the back to raise the tailgate. He grunted under the load of a wheelchair.

A wheelchair for Lajos!

The reality hit Viktor hard. *Őrült* had turned Lajos, his only living son, into a cripple. Feeble and infirm. How could he lead an army from a wheelchair?

Viktor waved a hand at one of the men.

"Help them."

It took two men forever to pull a limp Lajos from the SUV and settle his near-lifeless form into the wheelchair, and even longer to carry him and the chariot up the steps and onto the flat entranceway.

Viktor would have to order the building of a ramp. A ramp. The compound needed wheelchair access for his crippled son! The embarrassment of it made his skin crawl. No, he would have them build the ramp around the back, out of sight. It would become the entrance for the servants and the infirm. The underlings.

The driver wheeled Lajos forwards and stopped in front of Viktor. Andris looked down on him, sorrow filled his eyes. Andris had been with Viktor since long before the birth of both Vadik and Lajos. He had warm feelings for Viktor's son.

Another reality sank in.

Viktor had been too quick to think badly of Andris, his one true friend. He had been far too quick to apportion blame. The grief of losing Vadik had worn Viktor down. It had made him suspicious, irrational. Such unwarranted suspicions would eat away at his sanity. On the other hand, being wary had kept him alive for so many years. He sixth sense for danger had given him the edge over so many of his fallen rivals.

Yes, Viktor would keep his eyes and ears open. The potential for treachery lay all around.

"What took you so long?" he demanded of Andris.

"My apologies, *főnök*, but Lajos cried out in agony at each bump in the road and at each turn. It seems the painkillers they gave him have worn off. I ordered the driver to slow down to walking pace."

"Okay," Viktor grunted, nodding, "but you should have telephoned."

"Once again, I am sorry, *főnök*. But Lajos fell asleep and I didn't want to wake him."

In his shabby wheelchair, Lajos stirred. His head lolled, lifted, and turned to face Viktor. Pale blue eyes, the same eyes as his harlot of a mother, met his.

"Papa?"

Viktor stood tall. He would not bend the knee to his son in front of the men. Such actions would show humanity—and weakness.

"Yes, Lajos?"

"Papa, they hurt me. They cut off my arm and shot me in the leg. My ankle is broken. They hurt me, Papa."

Viktor hid the sneer that started to form and turned it into a cough. Pataki men did not bawl in public. In the face of pain and danger, Pataki men were strong and brave. They suffered though discomfort in stoic silence. Even though Vadik was a bastard son, a half blood, when he met his end Vadik would not have been such a pitiable coward.

"I can see that, Lajos. Be strong, boy. I have sent for a doctor. He will arrive soon. As for painkillers, there are drugs aplenty in the house. You will be pain free very soon."

Lajos sniffled. Tears fell from his pale blue eyes and his chin trembled.

So feeble. So pathetic.

This coward was no longer a son of Viktor Pataki.

"Thank you, Papa. Thank you."

Viktor turned to the driver. "Take him to his room. I will visit soon."

Andris held out his arm to stop the man wheeling away the cripple.

"*Főnök*," he said, speaking quietly, "shall I ask one of the house-keepers to make up a bedroom on the ground floor? It will be some time before Lajos can manage the stairs."

Viktor sniffed and considered the suggestion. Although a good idea, Andris should not have countermanded the orders of his *főnök* in front of the men. It was unacceptable!

"Very well, Andris. Have them use one of the rooms in the back. One overlooking the garden."

Andris dipped his head and said, "Immediately, *főnök*." Only then did he lower his arm and allow the driver to wheel Lajos through.

Viktor waited for the driver and another man to disappear into the bowels of the house before striding towards the main room. Andris followed close behind like a good hunting dog walking to heel.

A hunting dog, yes. But what or who was his prey?

Viktor headed towards the small table. The dolt Viktor had sent earlier had followed instructions and replaced the empty *pálinka* bottle with a fresh one. Viktor broke the seal and poured himself a full measure.

"Andris," he said, "a drink?"

"Please, *főnök*," he said, nodding. "It has been a long day."

Viktor poured a stiff measure and held up his glass.

"To Vadik," he said.

Andris took his glass from the table and clicked it against Viktor's. "And Balint," he added.

"Vadik and Balint," Viktor announced. He downed his drink in one swallow, as did Andris.

Viktor refilled both glasses, and this time, they sipped. He crossed to his favourite window. Once again, the hunting dog followed close. The servants had left the floodlights burning, as they always did while Viktor was awake. The lawn, cut to stripes in the English fashion, stretched out before him as though nothing had changed.

"What happened out there, Andris?"

"At the warehouse?"

Viktor sipped again and nodded.

"They must have been waiting for us."

"They? More than one man, you think?"

Andris stared deep into the golden liquid before answering. "It had to be many. Balint knew what he was doing, *főnök*. As did his men. They were all skilled hunters. Experienced. It would have needed many men to take them out so swiftly and so efficiently." He drank deep of his *pálinka*, emptied the glass, and offered it up for another refill.

Before Viktor could tell him to pour for himself, someone knocked on the door.

"Come!"

It opened and one of the maids entered. The girl was one of the not-so-pretty ones. She curtsied and waited by the door, expectantly.

"Well? What is it?" he bellowed.

The ugly girl clasped her hands together and held them tight against her stomach.

"E-Excuse me, *főnök*," she stuttered, "the sickroom is ready and Master Lajos has asked to see you."

"Did he?" Viktor asked, trying to make it seem as though he cared.

"Y-Yes, *főnök*. He told me to tell you he had a message from the one who killed Vadik." She curtsied again. Her French maid's outfit shimmered as she trembled under his gaze.

A message, szar!

The Englishman mentioned a message. It had slipped his mind. With so much going on, how could Viktor be expected to remember it all?

Viktor slammed his glass down next to the bottle on the table and marched across the room. He brushed the terrified girl aside and asked, "Where is he?"

"The blue room, *főnök*. I will take you."

"I know where it is, girl!"

He hurried past the staircase, heading for the small room favoured by the whore who birthed Lajos. She used it as a breakfast room. However, it did overlook the garden as Viktor had instructed, and it made an appropriate sickroom.

Footsteps behind him confirmed that Andris still followed. Ordinarily he would have told his right hand man to stay outside, but Viktor wanted to keep him close. He needed to gauge the reaction Andris had to whatever Lajos said.

Andris was one of the worst poker players Viktor had ever faced.

He could never hide his emotions. If he had something planned that would upset Viktor, Andris would show it in his dark eyes and on his mobile face, and Viktor would have his proof. What he did with that proof, however, Viktor would decide at an appropriate time.

As Viktor burst into the room, the housekeeper jumped up from her chair in the far corner, but remained silent. She had been with the family for many years, and she knew her place.

In rapid time, the servants had removed the dining table and chairs and replaced them with a single bed, the head of which had been pushed against the wall opposite the French doors that granted access to the gardens. In the bed, a pitiful-looking Lajos lay, propped up on three fat pillows. His face was even paler than usual. It appeared drained of blood as though he had suffered the attack of a vampire. His right arm ended above where the elbow joint used to be, the stump swathed in fresh, clean bandages. A cage beneath the bedclothes lifted them from his damaged leg, taking away their weight. The wheelchair in which Lajos arrived stood to one side, an ugly thing made of chrome, its plastic cushions cracked and torn. It was all Lajos deserved.

The boy looked up, his tear-filled eyes alight with the arrival of his papa. He tried to sit up, but whimpered and grimaced in pain. Viktor raised his hand, and Lajos settled back into the pillows.

The housekeeper remained silent until Andris closed the door behind them and Viktor nodded his permission for her to speak.

"*Főnök*," she said with all the reverence he deserved, "I have made him as comfortable as possible."

As though I care.

"Good, good." Viktor nodded, but maintained his distance from the sickbed. "And the doctor?"

"On his way, *főnök*. We expect him within two hours."

"Two hours? Why so long?"

"He travels from <u>Tatabánya</u>, *főnök*. The doctor in Győr refused to make the journey."

"Dr Paiva rejected my summons and my money?"

The housekeeper lowered her gaze. "Yes, *főnök*."

"After all the business I have given him over the years, he dare refuse me now?"

Viktor roared. It made the woman tremble and Lajos wince once again. He took a moment to calm himself.

Viktor glanced behind him. "Andris," he said with exaggerated calmness, "when we are finished here, send someone to Dr Paiva. Demonstrate what happens to people who reject the invitations of the Giant of Győr. Make an example of him."

"Certainly, *főnök*. I will go myself."

"No, Andris. Send one of the others. Depending upon what Lajos has to say, I may have something else for you to deal with."

Andris nodded and clasped his hands in front of his belt. He edged away and stood with his back to the wall, defending the room.

Viktor waved a hand to dismiss the housekeeper. She scurried away and would only return after he had gone. He approached the side of the bed but kept his distance from the taint of weakness.

"What message do you have for me?"

Lajos swallowed, and his, "I am thirsty, Papa," sounded dry and raspy.

Viktor stiffened. He snapped his fingers at Andris, who rushed forwards and helped Lajos take a sip of water from a glass someone had placed on a side table. He then returned to his position by the wall and resumed his role as guardian.

"Better now?" Viktor asked.

"Yes, Papa. Thank you."

"Okay, speak. What did the Englishman say?"

Lajos blinked twice and then raised his head from the pillows to speak.

"The man wants no war with you, Papa. He returned me as a sign of his good faith. He says he has taken Mrs Prentiss to a place of safety and she is under his personal protection. He also says this ends here."

"He said that?"

"As near as I can recall, Papa. He says if you take no further reprisals, he will leave us alone."

"You hear that, Andris?" Viktor asked, turning sideways and stepping back so he could see both bodyguard and cripple without having to strain. "The Englishman kills Vadik and Balint and all the others, and he expects no reprisals! He is a coward, running in fear, with his tail tucked tight between his legs. No reprisals, he begs. No reprisals in exchange for returning Lajos alive, but in this condition? What answer should I give to him, Andris?"

Andris opened his mouth to speak, but closed it again, saying nothing.

"Yes, Andris. You are right. There is no answer. There is only action. No reprisals he says? Ha! We shall see."

"Papa?"

"Yes, Lajos. What is it now?"

"The Englishman," Lajos said and paused to take a breath. "He said one more thing."

"Yes?"

"He ... told me his name."

"His name?"

"Y-Yes, Papa." Lajos glanced from Viktor to Andris and back again. He swallowed deeply, but said nothing further, as though too scared to say the name of the man who had murdered his brother.

Such a coward.

"Well, boy? Tell me his name!"

Lajos lowered his eyes. "Ryan Kaine, Papa. He is Ryan Kaine."

CHAPTER THIRTY-FIVE

SUNDAY 7TH MAY – Viktor Pataki
Pataki Compound, Outside Győr, Hungary

"Who?"

Viktor turned to Andris for the answer.

"You know, *főnök*. The plane crash last year, in the North Sea. Dozens died at the hands of the terrorist, Ryan Kaine. He is ex-military. A man of pure evil."

The news images returned as Viktor recalled the story. Ryan Kaine was an enigma. A fugitive. A vicious killer. Police forces throughout Europe were searching for the man, but none had found him. Not one sign of the man in so many months. Ryan Kaine was a ghost.

"Ryan Kaine, the terrorist? Do not be ridiculous. Why would a man such as he offer his protection to a nobody like Marian Prentiss?"

"I-I don't know, Papa."

"Describe him. What did he look like?"

Lajos closed his eyes. "A-Average height. Wavy hair, flecked with grey at the temples. Full beard, also greying. He has around forty years of age."

"His build? Is he big, like me, or slim, like Andris?"

"Not so tall as Andris, but just as wiry. And his eyes, Papa. Brown and lifeless. There is cold death in his eyes."

"As there is in mine, Lajos?"

"Yes, Papa."

"Shorter than Andris, you say? And thin? No, that is not possible. Ryan Kaine is a Royal Marine Commando, yes? A member of the SBS?" Viktor aimed the question at Andris, who nodded. "Commandos are powerful men the size of poor Balint. The man who held you is lying. He is using the name Ryan Kaine the same way as parents use tales of the *Mumus* or of *Zsákos Ember* to scare their children into obedience. He is trying to scare the Giant of Győr! As if that were possible. It is pitiful. Yes, Andris?"

"Yes, *főnök*," Andris agreed. "It is as you say. I doubt the real Ryan Kaine would ever risk his freedom or his life for the Prentiss family. The English *őrült* has decent military skills, but he is not Ryan Kaine. And even if he were, it would not matter."

The dead-eyed stare Andris gave Viktor, along with his bunching jaw muscles and his white-knuckled fists, said everything. Andris would spend the rest of his life seeking vengeance for the man who killed Balint and Vadik, be that man Ryan Kaine or the Devil himself.

"Papa. What ... what will you do?"

Viktor ignored the question and spoke instead to his man, Andris. His good, loyal man.

"We will call the man *Őrült*, not Ryan Kaine. For that is what he is —a crazy man. Agreed?"

"Yes, *főnök*."

"Lajos?" Viktor glowered at Lajos and waited for the cripple to nod his agreement before continuing. "Good. *Őrült* has hidden Marian Prentiss from us for the time being. He has taken her under his protection and has destroyed my money. We will find a way to punish her and, perhaps, draw him into the open."

"What do you propose, *főnök*?"

Viktor paused to let his mind race through the various options. The plan came quickly. He was born for such moments.

"If we cannot hurt her directly, we will do it indirectly."

"How, Papa?"

"With the help of the dead Wilfred, Cousin Ido created a dossier on the extended Prentiss family. He has the names and addresses of both sides of the family of Robert Prentiss and Marian Turvey. Mothers, fathers, aunts and uncles, cousins, and their children. I understand there are thirty-seven in total. I want them all dead before the end of this month, Andris, you will go to England and supervise the *pogrom*. Wipe these people from the face of the earth. Will you do that for me, Andris?"

Andris stiffened. "Happily, *főnök*. I will leave straight away."

"Take with you any man you require."

Andris sneered and shook his head. "There is no need, my *főnök*. With your permission, I will act alone. Vadik was a son to me. I will avenge his death, and the death of Balint, too."

"Good, good. Your targets are unsuspecting civilians. None will present a challenge to your particular skills. Make their deaths as painful as you see fit. And bring me photographs of each kill for my album."

"Of course, *főnök*. It will be my pleasure."

Andris bowed to Viktor, nodded briefly to Lajos, and left the room grinning wide. Light had returned to his eyes, the light of excitement, the light of retribution. He would take great delight in completing his new task.

Viktor rubbed his hands together—something his crippled son would never again manage—and breathed in deeply. He had been too quick to doubt Andris, who loved Viktor and looked upon his sons with the kindly eyes of an uncle. Andris loved his role as the Pataki family enforcer, and was almost as highly skilled and efficient as Viktor himself.

Yes.

Andris could be trusted and was now totally restored into the favour of his *főnök*. All was right with the world.

"Papa?"

Viktor glanced at his son, almost unable to look at the invalid in his pitiful sickbed. "What?"

"I-I would never question your orders in company, but ...."

Viktor waited for him to continue, but the cripple remained silent, his head turned away, chin on his chest.

"But what?"

Still, the cripple refused to speak.

"Speak, boy!"

Lajos lifted his pale blue eyes and found those of Viktor. "M-May I speak openly, Papa?"

"Of course, my boy."

For the moment.

"What did you want to say to your Papa?"

"The Prentiss family ..."

"What about them?"

"Are you sure killing them all is the right thing to do?"

"What!" Viktor drew closer to the bed and clenched his fist. "You dare to question my orders? You challenge me—"

Lajos flinched and held up his hand.

"Papa, I ... Please, let me speak."

Viktor relented. He would not beat the cripple. At least not yet. He opened his hand, flexed his fingers, and stepped away from the bed.

"Continue."

"Ryan Kai—*Őrült* said he would do nothing further if we did the same."

"So, Lajos One Arm," Viktor said, jeering at the infirmity of his weakling son, "what would you do in my position?"

"Papa, in your position," he said in a near whisper, "I would let the matter drop. We have suffered significant losses and have gained nothing in return."

His true colours shone through. The colours of a weakling with a huge yellow stripe running down his back.

"You snivelling coward!" Viktor snarled. "This is exactly what I would expect from the son of a whore."

"Papa!"

"You expect me to do nothing? You expect me to sit here and lick my wounds while *Őrült* laughs at me? While the *whole world* laughs at me?"

"Papa, I—"

"If I did nothing to avenge Vadik and the loss of my money, what do you think would happen next?" he roared.

Lajos One Arm fell silent.

"Well?"

"I-I ..."

"The world would see me as weak, incompetent. The families we have been fighting for years, the Kordas and the Horváths, those filthy vultures"—he made fists again and leaned forwards to threaten the squirming cripple—"they would gather together. They would drive us into the Danube and we would be finished. Finished!"

The chin of Lajos One Arm trembled, but he found the courage to say more. "W-We have our compound and our wealth, Papa. We are safe here. Why risk everything?"

"Enough!" Viktor screamed.

He leapt forwards and swung. His open-handed slap rang out around the sickroom.

Lajos squealed and cowered in his bed.

"Do not speak of this again. Andris is on his way to England. He will obey my orders. Do you hear me?"

Apart from his snivelling, Lajos One Arm fell silent, covering his slapped cheek with his hand.

"I asked, 'Do you hear me', boy!"

"Y-Yes, Papa. I-I hear you. Please don't hit me again."

"Hit you? Hit you? Do not be ridiculous. I did not hit you, my boy. The Giant of Győr would never hit a cripple. That was merely a love tap."

Viktor sneered, turned on his three-inch heel, and left the sickroom. If he had his way, Viktor would never enter it again. Illness and infirmity made him uncomfortable and he refused to be uncomfortable in his own home.

Outside, the housekeeper stood before him.

"Any news from the doctor?"

"No, *fönök.*"

Damn his soul. If the man did not arrive on time and as expected, he would answer to Viktor. He would answer in blood.

"See to the cripp—See to Lajos. I think he has hurt himself."

"Certainly, *fönök.* And you, sir? Is there anything you need?"

"Send one of the girls to my chamber. I am in need of company."

"Which one, *fönök?*"

"The youngest and the freshest, of course. It has been a trying day and I need some ... relief."

The housekeeper, who had many girls under her care that met such a description, bowed. Once, many years ago, she had warmed his bed. Now, with her ugly, old-woman wrinkles and the white scar on her cheek—given to her by Viktor the one and only time she failed to please him—she now sent others in her stead. Delighted she no longer filled his requirements or his bed.

"Certainly, *fönök,*" she said and reached for the handle of the sickroom.

"Send the girl before you see to Lajos, woman. My needs take precedence over those of everyone else in this household."

Viktor left her to grovel in his wake and headed for the staircase. As he climbed, he undressed, dropping each item of clothing as he removed it. What was the point in maintaining a houseful of servants if they had nothing with which to occupy them?

By the time he reached the landing at the top of the staircase, he was naked and proud to show the world his raw animal power.

CHAPTER THIRTY-SIX

Seventy-two hours.

Three whole days without news, without contact from either Andris or Cousin Ido. Seventy-two hours without receipt of the first photographic memento.

What was happening?

The first day had passed without undue concern. Andris needed time to travel to England and make contact with Cousin Ido. He would need time to plan the first hits. When the evening of the second day arrived and there was still no news, Viktor reached out, but his telephone calls remained unanswered and his messages ignored. He could reach neither Andris nor Cousin Ido. Where were they? What had happened to them?

Andris should have completed the first kills by now. Something had gone wrong.

All through the third day, Viktor raged through the mansion, berating all within to answer his questions. None could. He ordered one of the new men—another of the nameless creatures hired by Vadik—to travel to the UK and investigate. The man, a cretin who could barely speak Hungarian let alone English, begged to be released from such a duty. When the fool claimed to have no passport, Viktor drew the Makarov and aimed it at the man's privates. He would have shot the creature then and there, but one of the others volunteered to travel in his place.

During that day, Wednesday, he had even relented and allowed the wheelchair-bound cripple into the main room, and they talked. Lajos One Arm had tried to calm Viktor, to reason with him. Once again, he tried to change the mind of the Giant of Győr and encourage him to cancel the *pogrom*. Their discussions ended when Viktor threatened to shoot the miserable cripple through the head.

The one positive feature of the whole mess was Lajos One Arm finding his voice and his balls. In the past, he would never once have questioned the plans of his papa, let alone for a second time. Perhaps the boy did have balls, did have a future, after all.

By late evening on the third day, with his frustration building, Viktor summoned the housekeeper.

She arrived without delay and stood in the open doorway, as instructed.

"You called, *főnök*?"

"Send the girl to my room. I am in need of entertainment."

"Which one, *főnök*?"

"The one from the other night. She pleased me."

"I am sorry, *főnök*, but she no longer available."

"Where the *fasz* is she?"

"The doctor took her away to hospital, *főnök*. Her injuries were very severe. She may not survive."

Szar.

Slim, with blonde hair and big blue eyes, the child had been a real beauty, at least to begin with. She would be missed. Still, he had plenty more to choose from.

"Send another. Make sure this one has not been defiled."

Viktor dismissed the disfigured woman with a wave of his mighty hand and retired to his chamber to await his entertainment for the evening. If he did not find release that night, he would surely explode.

———

Viktor sneered at the naked child who gasped and struggled to pry his hand from her throat. Tears fell from a face of youthful beauty, a face that carried the bruises and the split lip he had given her when she hesitated to undress before him.

Beating her made him hard.

Her struggles made him harder.

He would plough her, pummel her, and she would scream with each thrust. Her screams would make him harder still. Viktor relaxed his grip so she could breathe, and he pushed her away. She flew backwards and landed in a naked heap at the foot of his four-poster bed.

He stood over the child, admiring her unmarked, hairless body. Unmarked, at least for the moment.

"To my bed, child. Get on your hands and knees before your master. You will see and feel the reason I am known as the Giant of Győr!"

She cowered, unmoving beneath his gaze. Viktor bent, grabbed her long hair, and dragged her to her feet.

The bedroom lights shut off. As did the floodlights. The room fell to total blackness.

Bassza meg! Fuck it!

Yet another fucking power cut? There had been so many in recent months. At any moment the generators would kick in and deliver enough power to feed the whole compound. Viktor yanked the hair of the child and flung her onto the bed. Again, she squealed.

She would keep until the power returned. Without being able to see the terror on her face or the pain in her eyes, Viktor would not enjoy the ride half so much.

"We will wait for the lights, child. Prepare yourself for ecstasy!"

Outside, in the garden, a voice blared out over a loudspeaker, the words muffled by the thick stone walls of the house. One of the guards shouted and another replied. From the house came more shouts, these of annoyance and confusion.

Gunshots cracked. Multiple gunshots.

What the fuck?

Close by, in the hall beyond, a glass smashed. Seconds later, the handle on the bedroom door creaked. The noise made him shudder.

Viktor held his breath.

A sound. The swish of a door sliding over carpet. Movement in the near total darkness. A dull grey light appeared and then vanished as the door closed again.

"*Helló*, Viktor," a man said. "You just wouldn't listen, would you?"

A man. English accent. *Őrült!*

Mary, Mother of God!

CHAPTER THIRTY-SEVEN

Darkness stretched out for kilometres around, ending at the aura spilling over from the city of Győr, some ten kilometres to the west. The compound, lit as it was by dozens of floodlights producing brilliant white light that turned the blackness of night into a defined halo of day, couldn't have been easier to approach. Whoever designed the setup as a system of defence didn't have a clue.

Cool, dead calm, cloudless sky, full moon. Perfect conditions for a night-time assault. Colour Sergeant William "Rollo" Rollason couldn't have wished for better.

From his position, half way up an oak tree some seventy-five metres from the south face of the compound, Rollo counted six guards armed with military assault rifles, mostly AK-15s, but two carried AK-47s slung over their shoulders. Two men—one standing on either side of the front gates—smoked and chatted the night shift away. The others patrolled the grounds in pairs. Like the overconfident amateurs they most certainly were, each pair kept to the same

293

route and maintained more or less the same pace—easy meat for snipers during a surprise attack.

Rollo's earpiece clicked.

"Bravo One to Alpha Two. All set here, over," Paddy O'Hara's announcement came as something of a relief.

Team Bravo's role in the operation, especially Paddy's expertise in demolition and PeeWee's knowledge of household electrics, was pivotal.

"Took you long enough, Bravo One. Any trouble? Over."

"Not at all, Alpha Two. Not at all. On such a lovely evening, a couple of our wee friends needed a little lie down, so they did. Ready to cut the external power just as soon as you give the word. Over."

Rollo grinned. Paddy's "our friends needed a little lie down", meant that he and PeeWee Ricardo had run into—and neutralised—one of the patrols at the rear of the compound while making their way to the single-storey outbuilding that housed the generators. Whether the "neutralisation" had been permanent or temporary was entirely at their discretion. Although, after what had happened to Danny, Rollo didn't expect any of his men to offer much in the way of quarter to Viktor Pataki's hired thugs.

"Thank you, Bravo One. Hold fire for now. I'm still awaiting contact from Alpha One. How many bogeys your side? Over."

"There were four, but two are out of commission. If me ol' maths stands up to scrutiny, that leaves two alive, for now. We have eyes on both and can take them out at will. Over."

"Alpha Three and I have another six out front under observation. Same conditions apply. Alpha Two, out."

Rollo descended the tree and stood in its shadow waiting for Alpha Three's return. He'd only worked with Connor Blake a few times, but had never found the athletic Londoner wanting.

He checked his watch. 23:48. Time marched on.

Movement in the darkness three metres to his left betrayed the arrival of his partner for the night. In terms of a covert approach, it wasn't bad, but Rollo and the captain wouldn't have announced their arrival so early or made it so obvious.

"Alpha Two," Blake whispered, "permission to approach?"

"Granted."

Blake stood and advanced, one hand raised, the other holding a L22 Carbine, his weapon of choice. "Didn't want you taking no pot-shots at me, Colour Sergeant. Hence all the noise."

"Any louder and I'd have shot you anyway. Just for waking me up."

"You wasn't dozing, Colour. You was up that there tree. I saw you, clear as day. It's a wonder them buggers in the compound didn't clock you and start shooting. Tut, tut."

Cheeky bugger.

"Have you delivered the presents?"

Blake flashed a set of brilliant white teeth. "Sure have, Colour. As instructed. One outside the front gates, two more on top of the wall at each corner. When they go off, the buggers are gonna wet themselves."

"That's the plan, Alpha Three."

Blake turned to face the floodlights.

"The captain's taking his time," he whispered, without tearing his eyes from the compound. "I expected his call before now."

"He'll take as long as he needs, Sergeant. The captain's played this bang on. Viktor Pataki's going to be all over the place. Right now, the 'Giant of Győr' doesn't know whether to shit, shave, or sing soprano."

"Understood, Colour. No idea why the captain don't just get Paddy to nuke the fucking compound and be done with the lot of them. This way's a lot more sticky."

"Nuke the place?"

Blake nodded.

"Only a small one, like. I ain't talkin' intercontinental ballistic missile or nothin'," he said, adding another wide smile. "Be a lot easier and cleaner."

"Didn't you listen to the briefing, Sergeant?" Rollo pointed to the mansion. "There are innocent civilians in the house."

"Yeah, I heard. Don't mind me, Colour Sergeant. Just like flapping me gums while waiting for the director to shout, 'Action'."

"Anyway, the captain doesn't work that way. He prefers to use a scalpel rather than a mallet."

"And his way's more hands-on, right?"

"Exactly." Rollo checked his watch again. The time hadn't moved on much. "Okay, down to business." He tapped his earpiece into action. "Alpha Two to Charlie One, are you in position? Over."

"*Charlie One to Alpha Two, that's an affirmative. Two more bogeys on the eastern flank. Both are in the open and lit up. One wrong move and they're toast. Over.*"

Team Charlie consisted of "Fat Larry" Kovaks and "Slim" Simms. Both had known Danny since Boot Camp and neither would offer the bogeys any more sympathy than Paddy or PeeWee.

"Did you deliver your present, Charlie One? Over."

"*Affirmative, Alpha Two. Delivered, primed, and ready for broadcast. Over.*"

"Alpha Two to Delta One, report. Over."

"*Three more bogeys on our side, Alpha Two. One down, two others in plain sight. The gift is in place and live. Over.*"

Nate Montero and Jeff Baines, Team Delta, hadn't known Danny for as long as the others, but that didn't matter. Danny had been a teammate and they'd volunteered for the mission the moment Rollo had sent out the call.

"Alpha Two to all, listen up," Rollo spoke slowly so none of the men would misunderstand. "Line up your targets now. When Alpha One's in position, the floodlights will go dark and I'll play the audio. Give them one chance to drop their weapons. One chance only. Alpha Two, out."

Rollo kept the earpiece active and settled down to wait.

―――――

"*Alpha One to Alpha Two. Are you receiving me? Over.*"

At his side, Blake jerked upright. Rollo puffed out his cheeks. *About time.*

"Alpha Two to Alpha one. Reading you strength five. Over."

"I'm in position, Alpha Two. Light them up. Alpha One, out."

Rollo tapped Blake on the shoulder. "Here we go, son, get ready."

"I were born ready, Colour."

Rollo clicked the selector on his SA80 from safety to single shot and lined up his target—the guard manning the left side of the main gates. Blake would deal with the one on the right.

"Alpha Two to Bravo One, you are green for go. I repeat, you are green for go. Over."

Rollo counted seven seconds before the floodlights blinked out, along with the house lights. No muffled explosion, no flickering, just pitch black where there was once bright light. As usual, Paddy O'Hara had met his brief to perfection.

Rollo's target stood out brilliant white against the grey, lit up by the thermal imager built into the night 'scope on his SA80 semi-automatic rifle. The man barely reacted. His head—sporting a mop of curly hair—turned towards his buddy and his jaw moved in speech.

Not happening, boys.

"My target's chilled. He ain't hardly moved," Blake whispered. "Bugger don't 'ave a Scooby about what's happenin'."

"They're used to power outages. Expecting the generators to kick into action at any moment."

"Gonna give them that wakeup call?"

"Yep. Sure am."

Rollo released his hold on the SA80's handgrip and pressed the button on the device clipped to his jacket. Seconds later, a powerful voice boomed out from the loudspeakers dotted along the compound's defensive walls—the "presents" they'd delivered. It boomed out in Hungarian, the speech powerful and authoritative.

The captain had written the script, and a local had translated it into perfect Hungarian, thinking she was being tested for work with a UK broadcaster. An actor had recorded the speech under the same impression. PeeWee built the hardware specially for the occasion, and Corky designed the software. A truly collaborative process designed with one aim in mind—to wreak havoc, spread fear, and minimise unnecessary loss of life.

Rollo doubted it would work, but he admired the captain's efforts. Even in his grief over Danny's passing, he still wanted to offer Viktor Pataki's hired men the chance to reach tomorrow. Rollo wouldn't have bothered, and most of the men felt the same way.

The amplified voice boomed out: "*You are surrounded by elite members of the Hungarian Defence Force under the Command of Brigade General István Orbán. If you drop your weapons and assemble at the front gates, you will not be harmed. You have sixty seconds to comply.*"

Rollo's target, Curly, reacted as expected. He shouted to his friend, and raised his weapon, but couldn't find a target. Paddy's system had been set up not only to amplify the volume, but to focus the sound to a point in the centre of the compound. No one inside would have a clue where the noise actually originated from.

Connor Blake's quiet laugh bubbled up at Rollo's side. "My bloke's wetting hisself. I reckon he's about ready to fold."

The loudspeaker voice returned with the countdown, again in Hungarian.

"*Huszon ... tizenkilenc ... tizennyolc ...*"

"*Twenty ... nineteen ... eighteen ...*"

Either Curly was made of sterner stuff, or he'd completely lost the plot. He raised his AK-15 and pulled the trigger. The rifle's reports echoed into the night.

Rollo squeezed his trigger once. Curly stopped firing. The AK-15 fell from his hands, and his body crumpled to the dust.

You asked for it, son.

As the countdown continued, Blake's weapon coughed.

"There goes another bad guy," he said, and lined up his sights on a different target. "Shit."

"What's wrong?" Rollo asked, trying to locate Blake's second target.

"The two fuckers over by them rose bushes just dropped their guns and threw up their hands."

"Too bad. Keep your eye on them. Make sure they head towards the RV point. Where's the other two?"

"Over by the fountain, last I saw them."

Rollo swung his weapon to his right and picked up the final pair. They were standing in front of the fountain as Blake said. They'd also dropped their weapons and had their hands raised high above their heads. One looked at the other and said something. A moment later, with the countdown two seconds from zero, they stepped over their abandoned rifles and hurried towards the main gates.

"That were bloody easy," Blake said, sounding disappointed.

Rollo sniffed. "Either the Giant of Győr doesn't pay enough to inspire loyalty, or he recruits from the weakest part of the gene pool. Keep your eye on them all."

The front door to the house opened inwards and two men stepped out, arms raised, hands empty.

"Eyes up, Sergeant."

"I see them, Colour."

A bald man appeared behind the first two, his arms held low, keeping his hands hidden by the men in front. Rollo turned his rifle on the man, who seemed to be pressing the others forwards.

Without warning, Baldy's right arm hitched up, the hand full of Sig 17. He darted to his right and raced for the cover of the garage attached to the side of the house.

"Where the fuck's he think he's going?" Blake asked.

Rollo took the shot.

Baldy twisted at the waist and slammed into the granite wall. He left a smear of blood on the stonework as his body slid to the ground.

"Don't know, don't care," Rollo said, and meant it.

"Either he's the worst gambler in the world, or he don't want the army getting hold of him. Bet he's sorry now."

The two remaining men at the front door stretched their arms up higher and showed empty hands, their eyes on the fallen Baldy.

Rollo let go of the handgrip and took hold of the handheld unit. "Time to see if this thing really works."

He raised the device to his lips, spoke slowly, and let the Corky-generated app translate his words directly into perfect Hungarian. At least that's what Corky claimed it would do.

"You two by the front door! Keep your hands raised and make

your way towards the rendezvous point at the front gates. Walk slowly."

Without hesitation, the two men started walking.

Rollo lowered the translator.

"Well bugger me," Blake said. "Bloody thing actually works."

"Always knew it would, Alpha Three. Corky hasn't let us down yet."

"We really gonna to let them go, Colour?"

Rollo nodded. "After taking their mugshots and their fingerprints and making sure they're unarmed. Yes, we are."

"Seems a real shame to let them walk."

"Won't be for long, Sergeant. We'll bring Interpol into the loop the moment we're done here. None of these bozos will be free for long." Rollo held out the translator. "Here, take this thing. Drive them all to the gates and hold them there until we're ready to tag and bag them. I'll check in with the others."

Blake took the black box and showed great restraint in not using it although his cheeky grin showed just how much he wanted to.

Rollo stepped away, but kept one eye on the movement in the compound. "Alpha Two to all, report please. Over."

"*Delta One here, Alpha Two. All clear our end. Two bogeys down. Sending one survivor your way. Over.*"

"*Bravo One here, Alpha Two. Another two on their way to you, Alpha Two. Over.*"

Ten seconds passed without a further response. Ten seconds that dragged out into minutes.

C'mon Larry. Where the hell are you?

"Charlie One, this is Alpha Two. Report please. Over."

"*Charlie Two here,*" Slim responded, breaking protocol. "*Over.*"

Damn it.

Rollo cast his eyes towards the eastern edge of the compound, wondering whether it would be safe to leave Blake in sole charge of so many captives.

"Report in, Charlie Two. What's wrong? Over."

"*One bogey down permanently. Sending the survivor your way. Over.*"

"Where's Charlie One? Over."

"Flat on his arse, Alpha Two. Over." Slim spoke through a chuckle.

His happy response turned Rollo's growing worry into instant relief. Fat Larry and Slim Simms had a decades-old friendship that had been forged in war. For Slim to be so relaxed meant that Fat Larry was okay. The only thing hurt would be his pride.

"Care to explain, Charlie Two? Over."

"He, er ... took a little tumble and lost his earpiece. Idiot's looking for it now, Alpha Two. Over."

"That's valuable proprietary equipment, Charlie Two. It can't fall into enemy hands. Don't come home until you've found it. Over."

"Understood, Alpha Two. I'll get Control to ping it for us in a minute, but wanted Charlie One to try finding it on his own first. You should see him on his hands and knees scrabbling in the dirt. A real hoot. Over."

"Behave yourself, Charlie Two. This is an active operation. Alpha One is still inside the hot zone. Keep your wits about you. Over."

"Roger that, Alpha Two. Over."

Rollo smiled at the imagined picture of Fat Larry and Slim in action. "The instant translation app seems to be working a treat, Charlie Two. Use Charlie One's unit to instruct the survivor. Assuming he hasn't lost that, too. Make your way to the RV point when you have the earpiece and not before. Alpha Two, out."

Connor Blake chuckled. "Fat Larry ain't gonna be living that down in a hurry, eh?"

"Keep your eyes on those men, Sergeant."

No time for any more banter. The captain was still inside and might call for assistance at any moment.

CHAPTER THIRTY-EIGHT

THURSDAY IITH MAY – Viktor Pataki
Pataki Compound, Outside Győr, Hungary

Viktor quivered. His bowels loosened, as did his bladder. It took all his massive willpower not to soil the carpet.

The Makarov.

Oh God!

Where did he put his Makarov?

Light, brilliant white light, exploded into his eyes—the light from a powerful flashlight. Momentarily blinded, Viktor squeezed his lids tight shut. Afterimages burned into his retina—the orange outline of a man carrying a handgun and a flashlight. Unable to stop himself, Viktor opened his eyes. The afterimages faded slowly, but *Őrült* remained.

Blessed Mother, save me!

"Move, and I end you right now, Giant of Győr!" *Őrült* said, his words confident and mocking, his voice quiet.

The child on the bed whimpered. Useless little bitch.

The light lowered. Viktor blinked and his eyes cleared enough to let him see the green dot of a laser target drilled into his chest. It held steady. Impossibly so. As though clamped to a tripod stand. A single trigger squeeze would deliver a bullet into his heart. Instant death.

"Englishman?"

"Yep," he said, still calm and strong—fearless. "I'm the one you called a lunatic."

Again, the child on the bed whimpered.

An instant later, the bedroom lights flicked back on, blinding. Power had returned to the house, but the outside compound stayed dark, the floodlights remained extinguished. Őrült switched off his torch and slid it into a jacket pocket. The hand rose again, this time to reinforce his hold on the weapon. He stood before Viktor, legs apart, gun held in a two-handed grip, rock-steady.

Squealing, the girl crawled to the head of the bed and pulled up a sheet to cover her nakedness.

"Tell her to leave," Őrült said quietly. "Tell her she is safe. Unlike you, I don't make war on children."

"Tell her yourself."

The gun Őrült held so steadily fired. Viktor screamed. Pain, indescribable pain, mind-numbing agony, hammered into his left knee. He collapsed to the carpet, writhing. The woollen fibres burned his bare arse.

"*A térdem!* My knee!"

"You have another," Őrült said, as cold and heartless as any killer Viktor had ever seen. "Tell her what I said!"

Viktor flinched, breathed deep. His left leg twitched. Bone ground against bone. The bullet had shattered his kneecap, smashed through sinew and cartilage, doing untold damage. Blood flowed onto the carpet. He grabbed his knee with both hands, squeezed tight, trying to hold it together. Agony. Tears flowed. Blinding, stinging tears.

"Go!" he screamed to the girl in Hungarian. "Tell the men to save me. Save their *Óriás*. Five hundred thousand *forints* to every man who comes to my aid."

Again, the gun barked. This time the bullet grazed his right wrist and drilled a hole into the carpet between his legs. It missed his balls by no more than a centimetre. The flesh wound burning his wrist was nothing in comparison to the fire raging in his destroyed knee, but it bled like a stuck pig. Sweat poured out of him. Cold sweat. The sweat of fear.

"Half a million *forints*?" *Őrült* scoffed. "Is that all you think you're worth? That's not even fifteen hundred euros. Pathetic!"

"Y-You understand Hungarian?"

Őrült, dressed head-to-toe in black, face hidden behind a black ski mask, removed one hand from his pistol, a semi-automatic of some kind with smoke rising from its barrel. He tapped his ear through the mask.

"Universal translator, courtesy of a friend of mine. There's a slight delay, but it's pretty damned good. Like something out of *Star Trek*."

The eyes of the girl stood out like onions, but she did not move.

"Tell her to go. She can tell anyone anything she likes. It won't do you any good."

Viktor released a bloody hand from his shattered knee and wiped his eyes with his knuckles.

"Go, girl. The man wants you to leave. He will not shoot. Tell the men what I said! Tell them to come to me."

Viktor braced himself ahead of the next shot, but the weapon stayed silent.

Őrült turned his head towards her and nodded. He also waved her to the door. Still crying, she bounced from the bed and ran across the room, her feet barely touching the carpet. At the door, the bitch stopped long enough to say, "Thank you", in faltering English before opening it and stumbling away. *Őrült* kicked the door closed behind her. The lock clicked and Viktor was alone again. Alone with an *őrült* intent on his destruction.

Would the child tell the men? Would she act to save the life of her *főnök*?

His knee pounded. Fresh pain throbbed through it with every beat of his speeding heart. The agony made his head swim and his vision grey. He needed to vomit, but could not allow that to happen.

While keeping his gun steady and aimed at the heart of its target,

Őrült moved to the side of the room and lowered himself into the chair that stood against the wall. The chair usually held the fresh meat as they awaited the attention of their *főnök*, but this time, it held what? Death?

His mouth dried. Viktor could not swallow.

Had *Őrült* risked his own life just to kill him? Surely it could not be that simple? One thing in his favour was the ski mask. Why hide his identity if his intention was simply to assassinate Viktor?

What did the madman want? Money perhaps. Money to replace the ransom he burned at the warehouse. Yes, there might yet be a way out of this horror.

Őrült leaned forwards in the chair and rested his elbows on his knees, the weapon still held in both hands, and still pointed at its target. The dark, lifeless eyes behind the mask stared at Viktor. They carried no emotion, not even hate.

Do not remove the mask! Please, do not remove the mask!

As long as the ski mask kept his face hidden, Viktor had hopes of survival. He could negotiate.

Money. How much will it take?

"Well now," *Őrült* said, "we finally meet in person. Can't say I'm impressed. I expected a big man, huge like one of those incompetent fools I killed at the warehouse. What was his name? Balint, right?"

Viktor blinked, trying to clear the tears and the stinging sweat from his eyes. The agony dulled his senses, made thinking difficult.

How much money will it take?

"Yes ... yes, Balint. What you want?"

Where were the men? They should have arrived already. He forced himself not to look at the door. He needed to keep *Őrült* occupied. He needed to buy time.

"You want money, yes?"

Do not look at the door!

He glanced to his right, unable to do otherwise.

Őrült removed a gloved left hand from the gun and moved it up to his chin.

Not the mask. No, not the mask.

He hooked his thumb under the hem of the ski mask and yanked it up and off his head. He revealed his face! Hope died. Viktor was a dead man. As though he could read the thoughts, *Őrült* nodded. His lips stretched into a humourless smile.

"Yes, Giant of Győr," he said, speaking quietly in that soft and arrogant English voice of his, "you *are* going to die tonight, but not before I tell you why."

Strangely, the pain in his knee faded. Viktor released his hand-hold and used his good leg to help him squirm backwards, towards the nearest wall. All the time, he expected the final shot, the one to end him, but it did not come.

Once at the wall, he leaned back and allowed his powerful shoulders to slump.

"Kill me, *Őrült*. I not play your games. End this now."

The gun in the steady hand of the Englishman lowered, its aim now levelled at Viktor's belly. Was his intention to shoot Viktor in the guts? Allow him to die slowly with the torment of blood poisoning?

Briefly, the multiple pops of semi-automatic rifles raised his spirits. The men were coming! But no, the shots came from far away. Outside in the grounds and beyond. Inside the house, it remained quiet. Quiet and ominous.

Where are they? Where are my men?

"Don't get your hopes up, Viktor. That's just my people mopping up the ones who refuse to lay down their arms."

"Your people?

Again, *Őrült* smiled. Again it contained all the humour of death.

"Didn't think I'd come alone, did you? Me, facing fifteen heavily armed thugs, alone? And that doesn't include the seven guards *inside* the house. Not likely, old chap. Too much of a risk even against your bungling fools." He breathed in deeply and released the breath as a sigh.

Fifteen men outside, he said. How could he know how many guarded the compound? *Őrült* must have had help. Briefly, anger overtook the pain pulsing through his knee.

"No," *Őrült* continued in his taunting manner, "I needed help. My friends are dealing with the riffraff. By now, the ones outside who didn't surrender are dead. And don't expect help from the ones on this floor—your Praetorian Guard. They're dead, too." Őrült sighed again. "Didn't put up much of a fight, I'm afraid. Good help is so hard to find when you're a tinpot little dictator. Don't you think?"

"My men, dead? H-How?"

Őrült reached down to his right calf and pulled a dagger from its sheath. Although the double-edged blade shone under the lights, dark stains near the hilt told of its recent use.

"Giving men weapons and assuming they know what they're doing is a mistake, Viktor. Poorly trained men don't put up much of a fight. I killed all four before entering this room."

"Dead?" Viktor gasped. "All four?"

Őrült nodded slowly. "The non-combatants, the unarmed servants will be okay, though. The girls and women in the cellars, too."

"You ... you know of the girls?"

"We know everything, you piece of filth," he snapped, showing the first signs of emotion. Again, he breathed deeply, slowly, fighting to control his anger, or so it appeared.

"All you had to do was let the matter drop. But no, you had to take it to the next level. The men on this floor and the ones outside, they didn't have to die tonight. They could have lived. I would have left you alone. No point trying to destroy all the evil in the world. I have others to protect. No, Viktor. I would have sent evidence of your role in Robert Prentiss' murder to a friend I have in the UK police, and he would have passed it to Europol. Eventually, they would have moved against you. It might have taken a while and given you a few more weeks of freedom. A few more weeks of life. But ... it's too late now. Much too late for that."

The Englishman was starting to ramble.

"Ordering the deaths of the extended Prentiss family was a big mistake. Your final mistake."

"What?"

How did he know?

The Englishman continued, ignoring the interruption.

"As I told you, Marian Prentiss is under my protection and, by default, that includes her whole family. I couldn't let your man hurt them."

He knows everything. How?

"What you mean?"

The dead eyes of *Őrült* narrowed. They locked on his. Death grew even closer.

"I imagine you wondered why Andris hasn't been in touch since you sent him on his merry way?"

"Andris?" Viktor gulped. "What you know of him?"

Őrült shook his head slowly, pretending to be saddened. "I'm afraid you won't be hearing from poor Andris, at least not in this life. Truth is, he didn't even make it to the main road into Győr. I killed him before he left the valley. He's still there. His carcass is feeding the local wildlife."

"Andris dead?"

"Yes. You see, he wouldn't listen to reason. He insisted on joining his friend, Balint. I was happy to oblige."

Andris and Balint, both dead at the hands of this skinny English-man? His longest serving men, his loyal friends dead. How was it possible? An informer inside the house. The only explanation.

"How you know I send Andris to kill Prentiss family? Lajos? Did Lajos betray me? Is that why you return him?"

Őrült smiled and shook his head again. "No, Viktor, old sport. Lajos gave me the layout of this mausoleum. He told me where your bedroom is and the disposition of your guards, pitiful though they were. But no, he isn't a spy, Viktor."

"How you get information? Answer me, damn you!"

"You told me!"

"What?"

Another smile stretched out on the bearded face. This time, it appeared genuine. "Or, to be more accurate, the wheelchair told me."

"*What?*"

"Before sending Lajos home, we planted a bug in his wheelchair. Whenever you spoke to him directly, we heard it all. Everything."

"No!"

"'Fraid so, old man. In fact, Lajos' leg isn't broken," he said. "All your son has is a badly gashed ankle. I had my medic encase his leg in plaster to give a reason for the wheelchair."

"*Te rohadék!*"

Őrült pressed a finger to his ear. "No, Viktor, I'm not a bastard, but I am a killer. And when the mood takes me, I'm not averse to a little thievery."

"Thievery?" Viktor frowned. "What is 'thievery'?"

"Theft, Viktor. Stealing. Robbery. Larceny. In short, when the opportunity presents itself and the victim is a piece of filth such as yourself, I take whatever I see fit. In your case, I took all your money. A friend of mine"—he tapped his ear once again—"the same chap who developed the translation app, emptied your account in the Magyar Bank of West—"

"*No!*"

"Yes."

The way *Őrült* spoke, with confidence and certainty, left Viktor in no doubt of the truth of his words.

"Thirty billion *forints* left your account this afternoon, headed to" —he waved his free hand in the air—"who knows where." *Őrült* paused.

Viktor could not speak. He flinched and another blast of torture exploded from his knee.

"Thirty billion *forints* sounds a lot, but it's only ninety million euros, or eighty million pounds. Not too bad a haul, especially when added to the fifteen million from the ransom—"

"Ransom? But you burn the money! You burn it!"

"Nope. I only made it *look* like it went up in flames."

Madness!

"How?" Viktor asked, shaking his head. "Why?"

"The 'how' is easy. The explosion was a precisely shaped charge, designed to blow the rubbish out and away from the skip. It also ignited two jerrycans of petrol while the money bags remained safe behind the lid of the skip.

"As for 'why'. That's simple really. I wanted to keep you off-balance and confused. If money wasn't a driver for me, I wanted you to wonder what was. I even thought it might make you back off. My mistake was to imagine you were rational, but you turned out to be a total fruitcake."

"Money? You do this for my money? Simple greed?"

"No. Some of the money's going to Marian Prentiss, to help set her up in a new life, and some will pay for my men's time. The rest will go to your victims. The women and girls we are about to release from your cellars. After what they've suffered, they'll need counselling and long-term support. And that's all the time I'm wasting on you, Viktor Pataki, Giant of Győr!"

He slapped his free hand to his knee and used it to push himself to his feet, grunting as he did so.

"And now, I die?" Viktor demanded.

"Yes, Viktor." *Őrült* nodded. "And now you die."

He raised the gun and took careful aim at the right eye of the Giant of Győr.

This is the end?

"What of my son, Lajos?" Viktor forced out the words through a parched mouth.

Őrült shook his head.

"More than once he tried to convince you to change your mind about killing the Prentiss family. It made me think there may be hope for Lajos. I'm prepared to give him the benefit of the doubt. I'll be keeping a close eye on him for a while, but Lajos is going to live. At least for the moment. Goodbye, Viktor. Goodbye, *Giant of Győr*."

Viktor raised his hands. "No! Please, no! I beg of you."

CHAPTER THIRTY-NINE

Bristol Channel, Off the North Coast of Devon, UK

The leased fishing boat bobbed and weaved in the high-running swell. A stiff south-westerly breeze cut the caps off the waves and a cold sun cast long shadows over the roiling water, shooting sparkles of light into Kaine's eyes. He blinked as the stinging salt spray hit his eyes, making them water. At least, that's what he'd tell anyone who asked.

Salt spray.

Yeah, that's right. The salt.

Danny loved the sea, as did the others—Rollo and Mike. They'd lived on the sea, trained and fought on the sea. Some of their friends had died on the sea. The sea was where they all felt most at home.

He wasn't so sure about Lara, they'd never really discussed her association with salt water. She swam well enough, but preferred riding her horses. She held tight to the boat's rail as though in fear of falling over the side and into the grey foaming swell. The auto-inflate life jacket would have kept her afloat, but who would want a dip in that water without a full drysuit?

Kaine released an involuntary shiver at the thought.

Cough and Stefan looked green and seemed one more corkscrewing lurch away from hanging over the side and hurling their breakfasts into the murky deep. Back on dry land, in Ilfracombe Harbour, he'd offered them both an out. As landlubbers, they didn't have to brave the dangerous waters and the bucking little trawler. They could stay safe and dry. Neither had wavered. Danny, their friend, their crewmate, needed a good send off, and they wanted to be there to say goodbye.

That was then, back on the firm safety of dry land. If he asked them the same question now, in the heart of an angry and highly agitated Bristol Channel, would they change their minds?

Probably.

Paddy, PeeWee, and the other members of *Task Force Győr* waited back at the harbour—the boat could only hold so many mourners. They'd done their part. They'd all risked death to avenge Danny, but they would be around to send him into the next life at the wake. Yes, Ilfracombe Harbour would see one hell of a party that night, but for now, the men waited. Cough and Stefan had won the draw. They even appeared to appreciate the honour ... at least they had at the time.

Connor Blake had asked to attend. Like so many others, he wanted to pay his respects, but Kaine asked him to stay on the farm with Melanie Archer. Blake was her bodyguard and, despite the eleven-year difference in their ages and their highly disparate back-grounds, the two seemed to enjoy each other's company. Blake had agreed to be a permanent member of her protection team for the duration of her time as a fugitive, however long that might be, and was duty-bound to stay with her. After the wake, Cough and Stefan would assume their duties alongside Blake. As for *where* they'd be hiding Melanie, that remained to be decided. She certainly couldn't stay with Mike much longer. At some stage, his neighbours would surely notice all the extra activity on the farm, especially if it were in the shape of an escaped convict and her three-man escort.

As the wind blew and the waves slammed into the boat, Kaine's mind shifted back to the second worst thing about the whole sorry mess—second only to watching Danny's life drain away in his arms. The day after returning from Győr, he and Lara made the trip to Bobbie's university.

———

Lara offered to break the sorry news alone, but Kaine couldn't allow that to happen. Although he dearly wanted to, he refused to hand over that particular task. As team leader, delivering such information was his responsibility.

At first, Bobbie took the news in stunned disbelief. Then, the tears started flowing.

Kaine expected anger and recriminations. He expected her to blame him for Danny's death, but she just fell into his arms and cried her broken heart out. He hugged her, patted her back, and allowed his own silent tears to fall. Lara stood back and left them to their shared grief.

As it turned out, Bobbie and Danny had discussed the possibility of him dying on a mission. A military man—and a damned good one —the quiet, nine-to-five life was not for Danny. He chose danger over safety. The battlefield over the office. After all, Bobbie and Danny only met because she and her mother were members of *The 83*, and Danny had been part of Kaine's team who'd risked their lives to save her and her mother from butchers.

Danny knew the dangers, as did Bobbie. But it didn't make his loss any easier to carry.

"Danny loved you," Kaine had said, when she'd cried herself out, at least for the moment. "He wanted me to tell you that."

Kaine didn't add that Danny said it with pretty much his final breath. Some details were best left hidden.

"I know," she said, wiping her eyes on a tissue. "He loved you too, Captain. Would have done anything for you."

"He saved my life, Bobbie." He hadn't intended to tell her, but she deserved to know at least that. "He took a bullet that was meant for me. I'm so sorry."

She sniffled and wiped her nose.

"You'd have done the same for him."

"In a heartbeat."

They moved to a sofa under the only window in the small room, and Kaine helped her sit.

"The mission," she asked, looking up at him through the tears, "was another one of *The 83* in trouble?"

"No, not this time," he said, unable to lie, but unwilling to elaborate.

"What happened? Why was he in Derbyshire?"

Kaine's control left him as the emotion took over. He turned away, unable to speak.

Lara answered for him. "Danny was doing what he did, Bobbie. Helping people. Saving lives."

With Kaine's silent, nodded permission, Lara gave Bobbie the details, leaving out only the names and locations. They stayed with Bobbie until her mother, Angela, arrived to offer comfort and take her daughter home.

Before Kaine and Lara left, he told them of his plans for Danny's body. They wanted to attend, but Kaine forbade it. He couldn't allow either to be part of an illegal burial at sea. Instead, they'd be able to visit the headstone he'd erect on Mike's farm any time they wanted to.

Danny had loved the farm almost as much as he loved the sea. Reluctantly, Bobbie and her mother agreed.

———

Kaine tore his eyes from the grey water and stared up at the cloud-filled sky, fighting the tears. He couldn't show his emotions to the men. Not the thing to do. Not at all. Stiff upper lip needed, *damn it.*

Where's the rain? It should be raining.

Beside him on the bucking boat, Lara allowed the tears to fall unchecked—a much healthier way to grieve. While Kaine gripped the rail and stopped them falling overboard, she hugged tight to his free arm, needing his support. He needed hers, too. She propped him up as much as he did her.

God, what a bloody mess.

Danny's attempt to save Marian Prentiss from an abusive marriage had ended in violence and multiple deaths. Only now, with time on his hands, might Kaine give vent to his true feelings. Yet, still he refused.

Overhead, herring gulls screamed and jeered at him, reminding Kaine of another time he'd been on a fishing boat at sea. That time, the mission changed his life forever. This time was different. Just as traumatic, but different.

Kaine lowered his eyes to the heavily weighted body wrapped in the Union Flag, and lying on the wooden board. Then, he turned towards the living.

The men waited, expecting him to say something over Danny's body before sending him to the deep.

Danny's body. Jesus!

During his time as an officer in the Royal Navy, he'd sent so many letters of condolence home to families but, until now, he'd never spoken over a grave.

What the hell could he say?

"Tell the truth," Lara had said that morning. "Speak from the heart."

Sounded easy enough at the time, but how could he say anything with a rock rammed down his throat? Lara released her tight hold on his arm long enough to squeeze his hand.

Time.

They couldn't stay out there all day. Someone on a passing boat might notify the coastguard.

He nodded to Mike in the wheelhouse. The CPO eased back on the twin throttles and cut the engine revs. The prop slowed, giving them only enough forwards motion to give the boat steerage and keep it facing into the swell, which minimised the rolling and reduced the potential for the waves to swamp them.

No need for a Bible. Danny wasn't a believer. He wouldn't have wanted Holy words spouted at his burial. Kaine stepped away from Lara. The next part, he had to do alone.

"Danny was a good man," Kaine said, pushing the words past the restriction in his throat, desperate for his voice not to break. "One of the best I've ever known."

Crap.

The words were so damned weak. Pitiful.

Speak from the heart.

"Danny was a quiet man. A man of few words, he didn't talk about himself much. But, over the years, I learned a few things about the man I called a friend. Danny ... never really knew his father. The man buggered off when he was still a kid. His mother died from cancer when he was a teenager and he spent a couple of years in care. He joined the navy at sixteen and discovered his first real family. Danny found friendship and a life he loved."

A huge black wave broke over the side of the boat, soaking them through and washing away in the scuppers. Kaine ignored the ice-cold water and carried on.

"First time I met Danny was in a bar in Germany. If I had any sort of an imagination, I might be able to embellish the story, make it more interesting. I'd say something like, Danny saved my life, but he didn't ... not that time. Back in Germany in '09, he actually saved my best leather jacket ..."

Kaine spoke for a few more minutes, raising the odd sad smile of remembrance. Danny had been loved.

In turn, Rollo, Mike, Cough, Stefan, and Lara spoke a few words over the body and touched the hem of the flag. When they were done, Kaine and Rollo raised the foot of the board, and Danny slid into the welcoming water.

They stood in silence for a moment while the sea claimed the body of their friend. Kaine had no idea what to do next. How to end the tribute.

"Ah the hell with this," Rollo roared, slapping Mike on the shoulder. "Let's get back to dry land. Bloody freezing out here. Danny wouldn't want us catching our deaths. He needs to be sent on his way with a drink or three, and I need some rum to warm my belly."

Cough and Stefan forced out a bawdy laugh. Rollo's words even made Lara smile.

Mike clambered back into the wheelhouse and opened the throttles, full bore. He spun the wheel to port and they ploughed through the heavy seas.

Kaine held Lara tighter and they stared into the rumbling grey waters.

Danny was gone.

He was gone, but he'd be remembered by so many good friends.

His family.

The END

ABOUT KERRY J DONOVAN

#1 Amazon bestselling author with the US-based Lucky Shores thriller series and the Ryan Kaine action thrillers, and creator of the popular DCI Jones Casebook series of crime novels, Kerry J Donovan was born in Dublin.

A citizen of the world, he currently lives in a stone cottage in the heart of rural Brittany, which he took five years to renovate with his own gnarled and calloused hands. The cottage is a pet-free zone (apart from the field mice, moles, and a family of red squirrels).

He has three children and four grandchildren, all of whom live in England. An absentee granddad, Kerry is hugely thankful for the modern miracle of video calling.

As a mature student, Kerry earned a first-class honours degree in Human Biology and a PhD in Sport and Exercise Sciences. A former scientific advisor to The Office of the Deputy Prime Minister, he helped UK emergency first-responders prepare for chemical and biological attacks in the wake of the 9/11 atrocities. This background adds a keen scientific edge to his writing. In a previous life, Kerry was a furniture designer/maker, and he holds swimming and triathlon coaching qualifications.

As the owner of a pristine Honda NC750X, you'll often find him touring the less well-known regions of Europe in search of interesting locations for his novels.

A life-long sports enthusiast and open-water swimmer, the moment Kerry catches a glimpse of the ocean, it's off with the bike leathers and on with his trunks and goggles.

Kerry's life experiences help him add an extra layer of realism to his stories and his characters. For example, you'll find the water-borne adventures of his action hero, Ryan Kaine, a former member of the Royal Navy's Special Boat Services, as authentic and exciting as a night-time dip in the Bay of Biscay.

kerryjdonovan.com

Printed in Great Britain
by Amazon

44990547R00189